GIFTED

BOOK ONE OF
THE PERSPECTIVE TRILOGY

MATT SALMON

For my Father.

He taught me to love,
He allowed my dreams to become reality,
And he cared for our family above everything else.

Without you, this book would not exist.

CONTENTS

ILLUSTRATIONS

*"It was only a dream. It'll go away in time.
All bad things do, right?"*

Dr. William Hart

Prologue – Vision

"Do you want me to tell you the truth, William?"

The questioning voice disturbed my soothing sleep. I shifted away from the warm slumber of my bed and fell into the unknown depths of my mind. I left my life, floated away into my subconscious and was carried into a light that erased my existence. I stared blindly into the vast blank canvas in anticipation of the dream.

"The world is waiting to change. It's underneath your skin. It's emanating within everyone around you. It is emitting impatiently throughout the world. You and the other billions live under a fragile web of lies that has been created to keep you all safe from the uncontrollable change..."

The light pulsed once and transformed into a series of images. They filled my mind and intensified my senses. I had been blind, unable to see, but now I was finally receiving a glimpse of the truth.

"What you are about to see is the truth. It is a path that you do not have to follow, but it is the truth, William. Seeing the truth will not only change your life, but also all those you know. This path will change your world forever."

I focused on a familiar image that reacted to my senses.

I saw myself crouched over my holo-phone and my palm stretched over the small thin object. My skin strained, until the screen suddenly flashed, twitched and cracked. The body of the casing began to shake and a burst of electricity poured out from the battery, wrapping itself around the phone. The glass splintered and the rupture ripped the device apart, sending the pieces flying across the room.

"Simply fascinating. Would you not agree, William? Would you like to see some more? Please, I insist."

The dream twisted in a blur of colour, throwing me away from the crackling image, across the metropolitan neon sky of Prima,

1

and slammed down into a grim alley. The filthy underbelly of my home swayed in response to my presence.

I listened intently to the melodic voice that continued the hum through my senses.

"Your path is entwined with two other people. Together, you will decide the future."

I watched a feral girl running down a ruined street in the rain, her feet splashing unsteadily, the water sizzling from her bare arms, as she entered the disgusting alley. The girl staggered past several dumpsters and a broken window, as she was drawn to a flickering light ahead. It emerged from a barrel on fire that streamed liquid flame out its mouth and let small embers slip out the holes in its side. It was surrounded by a group of homeless people that seemed battered by life. She approached the group by the fire and they spoke briefly. My perception shifted closer so that I could see her face. The girl was crying under a curtain of raven black hair. Soft liquid streams flowed from her eyes, scorching through the filth that covered her face and left trails of sorrow running down her cheeks.

Her skin and clothes were covered in dirty ash and specks of blood…

The fire in the barrel shifted suddenly, flaring with swift intensity. The girl's face became contorted with anger, her eyebrows narrowing and her eyes becoming wild. Her mouth opened and her palms splayed outwards towards the barrel of flame. The fire screamed out and erupted upwards into the night sky. It lit up the grim alley in a fury of fire and rage.

Around the fierce fire, I saw blue and red lights slowly growing closer to the alley. The homeless scattered as armed forces arrested them, led by a man with slick blonde hair and gun-metal eyes. I was ripped away from scene as the girl's screams found my eardrums.

"You must find this girl if you want to survive. Together… you might have a chance of saving each other."

The dream shifted again, ripping itself away from the girl and flowed out of the alley. It soared up and over my home, Prima, the first great city. The glittering modern metropolis whirled past, mighty skyscrapers and ancient places of worship fluttering by my senses. The setting sun blasted off the snow coated mountains on the horizon and the gentle cascade of the river that flowed around the city glimmered with artificial light. My focus slipped around the monuments and the spectacles of Prima as my eyes flicked between them.

"Are you still paying attention, William? We have lots to see and not much…"

Time flickered backwards, allowing the moon to fall through the vast sky until it was replaced by the setting sun. I stopped above the Priman prison in Old Street at the heart of the great city.

My gut sank and my mind itched viciously.

I slipped through the roof, crashing past cells and prisoners, until my focus found a solitary prisoner in shackles being led by armed guard. They seemed wary of this white-haired man, who seemed broken and devoid of purpose that walked himself to incarceration. The prison guards kept their distance, their hands tightening around their weapons, as quiet fear gripped them. The prisoner's head shifted sharply, as his attention was snatched by a violent event occurring beyond the prison, and I saw a glint of his piercing green eyes.

The ethereal voice hummed into my senses again.

"No matter what path you choose, this man will find you. That is inevitable. Whilst the girl is your beginning… this man is your ending."

The prison suddenly imploded around the broken man, the walls caving in around him. The guards fell to the floor. Earth, burning metal and glass sliced through the air, as though they were leaves in an infernal autumn hurricane. The prisoner stared ahead, looking straight towards where I should be with those fierce green eyes; a circle of green light with a bullet of black at the centre.

My focus flipped out of the prison, sending me over Old Street, as a brutal flash of fire ripped into the heart of Prima. It pulsed savagely and bled outwards. It started as a small dot of crimson, illuminating the surrounding buildings. It grew violently, blasting outward and destroying everything in its path. Buildings were broken and thrown outwards like old toys. The wave of fire spread out viciously and killed everything it touched. It turned men to ash and splintered the earth with ease.

The moment flickered with white noise as it tried to correct itself. The incident burned falsely in my mind. It seared painfully as though I was forgetting something vital…

"I hope you were paying attention. I'll see you soon, William…"

The voice drifted away as the explosion burnt me out of existence. The fire destroyed Old Street, erased my dream and threw me out into reality.

I awoke with a yell, cold sweat dripping down my head. The room swam and I staggered out of my damp bed. The floor swayed and I balanced against a nearby wall, breathing deeply as I made my way to the bathroom. I turned the light on with a wave of my hand and plunged my face into the sink. The cold water stunned my skin and slowly brought back my focus. I continued to press the icy water into my eyes and the fog of my nightmare began to lift at last.

"William? Are you alright…?" My wife asked from our bed.

I breathed out heavily as my weary eyed partner met me at the bathroom door. I must have woken her up again.

"Sorry, Adele," I whispered, worried I'd wake our children. "It was just a dream…"

"The same thing?" Adele asked.

"It'll go away in time," I smiled roughly. "All bad things do, right?"

Our eyes met in the mirror. Adele's eyes were bagged and weary. I looked back at my own. They were scared.

"It was just a bad dream, Will," she said firmly and pressed her hand into my shoulder. "It didn't happen to you. You weren't at Old Street, okay?"

"I know…" I murmured. "You're right, as always, I just wish the dreams would go away."

"They will…" she yawned. "I don't know about you, but I need my beauty sleep. Don't take too long. You've got a busy week ahead."

"Night," I said quietly after her, as I recalled the dream again.

"It just felt so real…"

I turned to my wife, but she'd already tucked herself into our bed.

I looked at myself in the mirror and dried my face with a towel. The fear in my eyes had become replaced by lines of confusion. My reflected dark skin was wrinkled and stressed. I rubbed my face with my spare hand, feeling the coarse stubble of my beard. It would go away in time. All weird sleep patterns do eventually. I checked my watch. It was far too late. I had to wake up to drop the kids off to school in a couple hours.

I tried desperately to remember the details of my dream, but they were already fading from my memory. The images rattled through my mind, disjointed and disturbed, without any chronological cohesion. The moments dissipated like a candle being blown out at night. The strange vision distressed my mind as it always had done for as long as I could remember.

It didn't matter. It was just another bad dream…

MONDAY

Mark Bolton

1 – A New Day

The journey to work always sent a creeping chill down my spine. It started at the pit of my neck and trembled uncomfortably down my back. Twice every day, as I went to and from work, I'd see the same devastating sight and I couldn't help feeling cold and empty.

It felt like something was missing.

My car hummed under my feet as I moved towards the next set of traffic lights. I imagined the engine working under the hood as the car came to a halt. The machine calming, the gears clicking down, the pistons stopping, the electricity rippling gently until the engine finally came to a total stop. I reached down and ran my finger across the pale blue button that triggered the handbrake.

I sighed as the devastating view of Old Street touched the corner of my eye again and I restrained myself from looking out of the window.

I glanced up at the mirror as a truck braked just in time to see the traffic lights. It stopped mere inches from the rear of my car. I shook my head and raised an arm at his ignorance. He flicked his middle finger up casually and smirked nastily into my mirror. My teeth gritted as I ignored the impolite Priman.

Looking up, I saw that the lights were still red and I turned the radio on with my voice.

"…forecast of torrential smog rain this week, so make sure you pack those hydrophobic umbrellas!" The radio host chattered. "Also a reminder of the minute silence at two-thirty in memory of the fallen…"

I took off my glasses and rubbed my temples. There was definitely no chance of getting away from the horrific view today.

A new voice replaced the radio host and grabbed my attention.

"It has been exactly three years since disaster struck the great city of Prima," the clear voice tolled, which I immediately recognised to be Vincent Cain, leader of the Cain Corporation. "Today, on the first year of the twenty-second century, we shall

7

honour their memory as a community in defiance to the terrorist attack that took so many loved ones away from us."

The back of my neck shivered as the radio host returned to the broadcast. The mere mention of the attack scratched my mind and made my skin crawl in repulsion.

"…Vincent Cain's privately-funded corporation rose to power in the aftermath of the Global War to become a figurehead of Prima society. Cain Corporation saved hundreds of injured Primans from the ruins of Old Street…" the radio host announced, before I silenced them with a swipe of my hand.

I couldn't hear anymore. Not today.

The lights turned green. I flicked the handbrake off, revving the automatic engine into action and ignored the lines of stress that had started to form on my head already. The road opened up and I drove into the far lane, allowing the abrupt truck to overtake me. Out of the corner of my eye, I saw him show two fingers this time. I could never get away from the Pruckers, a name I'd amalgamated for the Priman truckers, which constantly rattled my patience. I felt it was a suitable portmanteau. They were always rude and always in a rush, despite the consistently halted traffic.

The morning rays of the sun curled into my eyes, flashing to seize my attention. They pierced my vision and I winced with irritation. The light blinded me repeatedly as it flickered through the shattered remains of Old Street. I commanded the car to shade the side window and the violent sun was blocked from view.

The next set of traffic lights hit me and I had to brake again. I passed my hand over the blue touch button and came to another halt. There were far too many lights down Circuit Road.

I felt the guilt building in my shoulders, so I re-commanded the car to un-shade the window. The dead deserved my respect, so I reluctantly allowed my gaze to fall outside. The cold crawl shivered along my spine and into my mind, as I looked at the remains of Old Street.

A stained glass window from an ancient temple broke the light and made it translucent. I marvelled how the explosion hadn't shattered the window all those years ago. I looked beyond it towards the broken network of metal that represented the remnants of the central district. Ahead was a deep black crater that was the epicentre of the explosion. Surrounding the hundred metre wide crater were the cracked remains of the old highway that spiked upwards towards the glaring sun. The remains of buildings grew taller and less broken the further away they were from the epicentre. The whole area was a couple miles wide. The broken heart of Prima had been left raw for the great city to see ever since the incident three years ago.

I often wondered why they didn't fix up Old Street, bulldoze all of it and start afresh, build over the rotten past, but I told myself once again that it served as a memorial to our dead. It was important to many people to leave it untouched.

Besides... everything beyond the explosion had been reconstructed. The very tarmac that I was driving on was a reinvention. Circuit Road had been built around the site to allow the population to view Old Street on a daily basis, improve traffic significantly and also barrier the entire dead district.

My wedding ring hugged my finger as the traffic light remained red. I had been on holiday at the time. Just me. It was my deserved break away from everything. I smiled as the hot sun, crystalline ocean and open sky cleared my stressed imagination. The peaceful memory made the tension begin to drift from my body. It was a world away from this great city of sadness and destruction.

The memory crumpled as I scratched the back of my head. Adele and the kids had remained here, whilst I'd been away on holiday. I stroked the ring with my thumb and sighed gratefully that we lived on the other side of Prima. I remembered the seemingly endless flight home when I heard the news...

The sky over Old Street was hugged with ominous clouds. The morning sun spiked through some of the clouds in the far distance. The sky rumbled and I observed that the far horizon was a lighter shade of grey. The radio was right, heavy rain was coming.

I caught my distant reflection in the mirror and focused on my

9

face through the polished glass. My brown skin shone dully in the dawnlight and my eyes dilated as the orange rays glittered over my glasses and over my brown iris. I scratched at my unshaven cheeks and full black goatee. I needed to get up earlier in the morning. It was getting tough taking the kids to school before work and I wished Adele would take them every now and then. I knew that she started earlier than me, but to sleep in, just for once, would be so refreshing.

Especially with these dreams that kept haunting my…

A vicious horn sounded from behind, as another Prucker raised both his arms furiously and pointed at the green light ahead.

I swore once, and in a flurried panic, I slapped my hand down to find the handbrake. I slammed my foot to the pedal and the car reacted to my motion. It shot forwards too quickly. My vision blurred from the Prucker in the mirror, across the chilling view of Old Street and finally settled on the hooded girl rushing across the road.

Her body hit my car with a sickening thud. She bounced off the bonnet and landed with a clunk as she rolled to the pavement and fell across the road into a neon-lamp. My mind stung with a sudden sense of repetition. I shook the stray thought aside and braked sharply, pulling rapidly to the pavement beside her. She yelled out once and I spotted the white of her teeth scream out. Her thick dark hair flew up and covered her face. She swayed slightly, before her head fell down towards her chest.

Another vicious horn sounded as a third damn Prucker overtook my parked car. I raised my arms in response and signalled towards the injured girl, who was silent at the side of the road.

My hands shook violently as I took out my phone that was no bigger than my little finger. The holographic telecommunication device was made out of two thin bars that connected either end of the phone. They slid open, separating and extending in my hand, and formed a hollow rectangle of metal that hummed once as it awoke. The projectors lit up all along the edges as the holo-phone turned itself on. The screen ignited with a flash of blue light and lit up my hand. Using my finger, I quickly traced the shape of a circle in the hologram. The tiny machine responded as it recognised my bio-signature and the emergency numbers illuminated the air.

Realising how useless I was being, I finally went over to the injured girl and called out to her. No response. I closed my phone to lock it and cursed myself for not going straight over. With my right hand, I gently pushed her thick hair out of the way and pressed my fingers against her neck to search for a pulse. I waited a moment, until her vein pushed up against my fingers. Sighing in relief, I checked her breath and found it easily. I just had to make sure she was conscious now.

"Hart," I said gently to her. "Can you hear me? My name is Dr William Hart. Can you repeat that for me?"

She stirred under her mass of hair, mumbling incoherently and I shook my head.

"Hart," I repeated. "I need to know if you've been knocked unconscious. Say Hart."

"H…Hart," she mumbled.

"Don't move," I said and felt my shoulders drop in relief. "You may have cracked your skull."

I slowly touched her arm, which was cradled against her chest and she flinched in pain.

"Get off me! I'm fine," she yelled whilst rising to her feet, clutching desperately at the neon-lamp behind her. She pulled her thick hair aside and I saw her hungry face. Her dark eyes glared at me for a moment, before fading as she swooned over. I reached out and caught her just before she hit the ground.

"Calm down. Just relax. I'm not going to hurt you, I mean, again. I'm not going to…" I cleared my voice uncomfortably. "Just come here and sit down, okay?"

I helped her towards my car and pressed my thumb against the pad that unlocked the door. It slid open with a soft fizz and I helped the stranger into the passenger seat. Her feet hung outside as she fell against the pristine cushioning.

"Breathe slowly and drink this," I said offering her a bottle of water that I always prepared in the morning.

11

Our eyes met again. Her fading pupils narrowed with confusion, a strong sign of clarity that also revealed her judgement.

She wore a tailored coat, which was certainly not the fashion that teenagers wore at the moment. It was hooded and black, lined with old leather that stretched down the sleeves and around the front, circling her body in protective segments. Some parts of her jacket were made of another material that stretched and allowed the clothing to be flexible. The coat was strong, but malleable.

Her hair was heavy and dark; some parts formed into dreadlocks and were braided with strange wooden shapes. I smiled lightly as I recognised the designs from the African great city of Kubra, which made me recall my own heritage. I smiled lightly. My father might have understood the meaning behind the designs in this girl's hair. Meanwhile, her face was gaunt and looked like she hadn't seen a full meal in a long time. Her facial features were European and Asian, possibly inherited from Prima and Mengxiang, the great city that had been destroyed in the Global War.

I'd never met anyone like this girl before.

In the tense silence, I felt the thin phone in my hand and opened it. I traced a circle and found the emergency numbers.

"I don't want an ambulance," she said at last, but I continued to raise the phone to my ear. She closed my holo-phone with a shaking hand. "I can't go to the hospital. You have to understand that I just can't go."

I looked back to check if she was still confused. Her pupils were no longer faded. They were clear and concentrated.

"Wait…" she continued. "You said you were a doctor?"

I smirked, marvelling at her level of awareness after I'd hit her with my car. I sat next to her and gently started to examine the back of her head. "I currently specialise in researching the potential innovation of the central nervous system. I'm not a general practice doctor."

"So you can't help me," she said preparing to move. "What's the point in having a doctorate if you can't help someone?"

"I know enough to help, so please stay. I owe you for hitting you in the first place."

She chuckled darkly and settled back down. I began separating her hair to view her scalp.

"You have a lot of hair," I commented. "Doesn't it get in the way?"

"I like it," the stranger shrugged. "So… care to explain the point of having your useless doctorate?"

"It is not useless. Doctorates represent profound certified knowledge in their appropriate field of study. Not all doctors know how to look at head injuries, so you're lucky to have bumped into me."

"Excuse me! I bumped into you?"

"That's not what I meant."

"So, do you deliberately crash into people to actually put this apparent doctorate to use?"

"Look, I didn't mean to…"

"I'm joking. Don't worry. I'm not exactly in a position to sue. You can keep your doctorate… for now."

I paused to think of an appropriate response and then I moved on to look at her head. "I don't know how much longer I'll be working anyway. I've hit a bit of a wall recently." The girl moved her head to nod, but I held it still with my hand. "Don't move. I'm trying to see if you've fractured your skull." She tensed slightly, but slowly relaxed and allowed me to continue to look at the wound.

"So you're a head doctor?" She asked slowly.

"Not quite" I replied. "The central nervous system is all over the body. Thousands of nerves everywhere that send signals through your spine and up into your brain." Her raw scalp became visible as I parted her thick hair, it was red and swollen, but luckily it wasn't bleeding. I gently placed a finger on the wound. "Tell me when you feel any pain."

She waited for a moment and grunted as I drew closer to the centre of the bruise.

"There you see? You had a reaction. I touched you here…" I said whilst placing my finger on the spot again to cause her a

13

small shock of pain. "It starts at your skin as a small electrical signal, that then shoots off to tell your brain that you are in pain, then shoots back to tell your skin that it hurts."

"Okay, I get it," she said rubbing the spot at the back of the head and shrugging me off. "What's so different about what you do? People have known all about the..."

"Central nervous system?" I corrected.

"That's what I was going to say," she mumbled.

"Are you genuinely interested in my work?"

"Would I even ask if I wasn't?"

"I hit you with my car!"

"You could have driven away, but you didn't," she shifted her weight. "Would you mind looking at my arm? I think it's sprained."

"I'm more of a head expert," I explained.

"You are literally the worst doctor I have ever..."

"I'm just going to cool down the swelling on your head," I interrupted her jokingly and then lightly added, "I'll give your arm a quick look after, okay?"

"That would be good," she smiled lightly.

I grabbed the water and a packet of tissues I kept in a side compartment of the car. I wet the tissue then placed it gently against her head. She didn't wince.

The dead view lingered in my peripheral vision and I rolled the tension from my shoulders. My head itched as I imagined the girl's pain at the back of her cranium.

"They've told me if I don't start practically applying my research, then they're going to shut me down. I have equipment that completely maps out the thousands of nerves in the body, but my employers want an expansion of my work. They want something physical that they can use. "

"Well that sucks," she scoffed. "If I were you, I'd just quit the job and do things my way."

"If only," I smiled wryly. "I'm afraid that I have a family to feed."

"Family only ties you down," she said solemnly. I looked at her, but her face remained neutral. "At least your work will end up actually doing something beyond a holo-screen."

"That might not be a good thing. Let me put it in perspective. My employers are the Cain Corporation, perhaps you've heard of them?"

The girl's body froze and tensed for a moment. It would seem she had definitely heard of Vincent Cain.

"Not really," she lied. "You work for Cain?"

"He pays the bills, but you can probably understand how demanding he can be to work for," I replied and she calmed down, slowly offering her arm for inspection. "I have something to pitch for Cain, but it's currently more theory than anything else. I believe I can find a way to create nerves for inanimate objects. I'm going pitch it as 'metal skin'. My device is going to be called the Nerve-Plug. It will be a new way to feel technology that is connected to your body."

"I don't get it. How can that even work?"

"You plug it in," I said smiling lightly. It was rare I got the chance to explain my work. "I've developed two components to the Nerve-Plug. One plug can sense all the nerves in your body and another that can connect to a piece of machinery, like a prosthetic limb, and sense all of its components and when it is being touched…"

"Wait, slow down, info overload…" she interrupted as she put the pieces together in her head. "You're going to help people feel their lost limbs again. That's what this is all about?"

"I want to help people feel complete again," I smiled lightly and she seemed to like that idea too. "So far, I can't connect the two components together. The signals don't match. The body won't accept an alien signal. It's similar to how our blood won't accept a virus. It fights against the foreign body."

"That's heavy on the head…" she sighed, rubbing her bruised head.

"Ah yes, your concussion. Sorry, I didn't mean to overload your brain."

"It's fine," she mumbled. "So you need to find out how people felt?"

"No. I find out how people feel, not felt, that's the wrong

tense."

"Yes, I know, I'm not stupid, but don't you need to find out how the person felt before they lost their limbs? You know, like phantom pain, when their memories of feeling are coming back to them?"

"I don't think you understand the nature of my work, you see…"

"No, I think you're looking at this from the wrong angle," she interrupted again. "You're working with a bunch of machines and chattering away like one to try and explain it. Machines can't feel. You're trying to play Frankenstein on a bunch of robots and that's never going to happen. You should find out how people used to feel before they lost a part of themselves. Get that in writing and then you can do all your fancy techno-nonsense to solve your problem."

I was speechless. This stranger was talking about a level of work that had never been done before. Yet, the more I thought about it, the more it was possible. The embers of possibility grew into a blazing inferno of reality. I had the equipment. I could observe how a person's nerves reacted as they remembered when they had their limb. Was it even possible to put a memory on a computer and turn an emotional connection into a physical one?

I couldn't think straight. This stranger had ignited my mind with the concept she had presented.

"It's Hart, right? I've got to go," she mumbled. "I can't stay here long."

She was looking down Circuit Road and through the roaring traffic at something I couldn't spot. From my point of view, it looked like she was staring at the green traffic lights glimmering between the mass of rushing metal and plastic vehicles. The girl left my car and picked up her fallen rucksack.

"Wait! I didn't catch your name," I called and she hesitated in response.

"My name is Raven," she answered bluntly.

"Raven?" I asked curiously.

"You got a problem with that?"

"It's just a strange name. Sure you don't want that

16

ambulance?"

"You think I'm concussed?"

"I think you need a re-evaluation in a couple days time, especially as you are so un-keen to have an ambulance. Here's my number," I reached down and found my contact card from my wallet. "Call me and I'll give you a decent lunch. I'll take a look at your head again and we'll see how your arm is doing."

She still looked unsure, so I decided to be honest with her.

"I'd like to talk to you again about my work," I explained. "I think you're onto something, and in case I don't get anywhere, I'd really like to see what you think."

"You're not meant to care about people on the side of the road…" she smiled slightly.

The jagged buildings across Circuit Road caught my eye, as they always did, and filled me with a deep dread and sadness. I scratched my head before looking back at the stranger.

"It's a special day," I replied. "It's the least I can do."

"I'll think about it," Raven replied and took the card from my hand.

"Your name's Raven?" I asked again.

"You haven't been watching the news much, have you?" Raven's eyes flicked again down the road and she pulled her hood up to cover her face.

"I usually come home late from work," I said confused. "Why?"

"I've got to go," she said and began to walk away. "Drive safe, Doc."

I laughed and climbed back into my car. Raven vanished down a grim alley full of rubbish and out of sight, leaving me alone in my car, my brain on fire with possibilities.

Before my inspiration extinguished, I pulled out my phone and drew a diagonal line across the screen to cancel the ambulance. I drew a gentle capital "M" through the light and the name of one of my closest friends floated into air above my shaking palm.

2 – How to Grow a Leg

The translucent human brain floated in the hologram above my head. To this day it was still the most complicated and beautiful thing in known science. How it worked, responded and how it retained memory was still a on-going mystery to the scientists of the twenty-second century.

I watched the hologram with wonder as it rotated above me. With a swipe of my hand I removed the outer layer of the brain. Stretching through the light, I selected the option to show the nerves of the brain and highlighted them blue. The nerves glistened and pulsed like a network of spider webs. They interlocked and separated from one another, filling every last gap of the brain. The electrical impulses were moving too fast for my human eye to pick up, so I reached through the light and pulled a small bar down to its lowest level. The pulses slowed until they became visible to my eyes. They were glistening rivers of connections. A dark blue impulse flashed in the lower half of the brain. This was where the spine connected with the skull. It glowed once then spread out along the network of webs, jumping from one thread to another. I followed its path until the impulse reached its destination, flashed and then fled, smoothing its way back down the spinal cord.

The electrical impulse I'd just seen could've been anything from pain in an opposable digit, to hunger rising up from the stomach, or simply an epiphany about one's insignificance in the universe.

The brain on display was my own that I had scanned a month ago. I could repeat the scanning process, but I wasn't getting closer to identifying the answer I would need to solve my problem.

I needed a new brain from someone who I knew well enough to understand some of their thought patterns and daily habits, but also had a connection to the nature of work I was doing.

Two knocks sounded against the glass of my laboratory door.

"Is that you, Mark?" I called out.

"How do you open this damn door?" His voice was muffled, his outline was blurred behind the clouded glass. I took off my glasses and smiled as he rattled the door.

"Have you tried pulling it?"

"There isn't even a handle. Open up! I haven't got all day."

"Put your hand on the pad to the left," I said and brought down the door security in the hologram. The pad became visible and so did a list of the names and faces of all the people who could access the door.

"Like this?" Mark shouted inappropriately loud, even though I could hear his voice perfectly well through my nearby speaker, whilst a dull image of his hand appeared in the hologram.

"Perfect. Look straight ahead, I'm just going to take a little photo…"

"A photo?" Mark exclaimed.

"Smile!" I proclaimed. His face appeared next to the image of his hand and I triggered the scan. A blue line scanned Mark's hand and within moments his handprint was floating next to his awkward smiling face. I swiped across my desk and brought up the holographic-keyboard and with a series of quick jabs I typed 'Mark Bolton' into the system.

Mark entered through the double glass doors, limping lightly as his broad build filling the space as he walked in. His hair was thick and brown. His nose and cheeks were slightly red from a considerably copious amount of fluid consumption at his pub. His gut swelled slightly to show off the beer belly that matched his rosy complexion.

He looked bewildered by all the technology in the laboratory as his hand ran over his slightly receding hair-line and into his thick brown locks. That was the one great difference between us. I liked all the gadgets that I knew he couldn't abide. Whilst he would much rather be serving and chatting to customers at his pub, I was quite content sat behind my desk. I preferred to be in control of everything without un-needed interference. It got things done quicker.

"So this is where you've been hiding all this time," he said smiling. "Have you shown Adele this little hideout of yours yet?"

"Not yet, but maybe soon," I answered. Mark's wandering gaze finally met my own and he paused suddenly.

"You alright, Will?" Mark asked. "You seem different."

I shrugged once and tried not to think about the adolescent who I'd knocked over this morning.

"I guess it must be seeing you at work," he continued in awe of my workplace. "It's not quite the same as…"

"Sorry," I interrupted him. "Is this all a bit weird?"

"A little," Mark laughed. "It's just a bit of a surprise." He nodded towards a nearby chair and I signalled that he could sit.

He was right though. It was peculiar seeing each other here. His rough broad bulk stood in stark contrast to the white walls of my lab. I wanted to call security downstairs and ask them if they could rustle up two bottles of beer and a bag of crisps to make it seem a bit more natural.

"Look, I have to be honest with you…" he continued. "You said you wanted my help, but I think you've got the wrong bloke. I can barely even work these new holo-phones."

His heavy hands pinched together like crab claws as he tried to signal that he had absolutely no technological knowledge.

I believed him without a moment's hesitation.

"I pretend to know what you do here, but I honestly I don't. It's to do with the brain and feelings, right? No? See? I'm clueless!"

"Bolt. Listen to me." I used his nickname to get his attention. "There is no-one else I know that is better qualified to help me."

"This meeting is a waste of your time, Hart. Wait a minute… I'm not even vaguely 'qualified'. You haven't got anyone else to call, have you?"

"In a manner of speaking…"

"So I'm here because there is literally no other choice of person?"

"You're the best choice, Bolt!"

"And the worst, because I'm the only choice. You need to get out of this white room and find a few more friends, buddy. I bet you have a friend-finder on your fancy little light-up phone."

"I have plenty of friends, thank you very much, and whilst there is an application for that, I do not personally require it, because you are exactly what I need."

"Look at this lab and look at me. You've got the wrong bloke."

"What if I told you I could give you back your leg?"

Mark's face dropped. His skin became pale and his body seemed to shrink. Hope flickered across his features and I knew there was nothing more he could want in the world. His hope crumpled quickly as several creases formed in his forehead as he leaned forwards.

"Is this a sick joke, Will?" Bolt said sharply. "My leg is gone. I won't be dragged across town to be messed about."

"This isn't a joke. If I'm right, then you could go back to being 'Bolt' again. You used to run for miles every day, Mark. I've seen the pictures on your walls. The trophies and the triumphs. You used to be one of the strongest athletes in Prima…"

"Then Old Street got turned to ash. My home. My family. My leg…" Mark fell back exhausted.

Perhaps this wasn't the best idea. I couldn't ask one of my best friends to relive a life trauma all over again.

I didn't have a choice. Mark was right. I didn't have anyone else to ask.

"Just give me five minutes to explain myself. If you're offended, then I promise to stop coming to your pub. But, if you stay, I promise to do everything in my power to give you back your leg."

Mark was tense. I couldn't tell if he wanted to punch me in the face or hug me. Instead he reached down and twisted. His left leg came away in his hands. I'd never seen it before. Not many people actually knew that he had lost his leg three years ago in the Old Street incident. He always refused to even talk about it.

I'd only seen his ailment affect him once since I'd known him.

Bolt had warned this ginger bearded man to ease up on the drinking. He had downed eight pints and it was only ten o'clock. Adele and I were sat across the pub and I remember joking that I'd have a word with the unpredictable individual. Bolt had

21

laughed at that. As he walked back to the bar, the man suddenly tripped up Bolt, sending him crumpling to the floor. Bolt screamed in agony.

Before I had the chance to stop him, Bolt had kicked the man three times in the gut, cracked his head against the floor, and began pulling the man up by his stupid beard, before I made my way over and pried the pair apart. Bolt shrugged me off before throwing the ginger idiot into the street. Bolt had limped back into his pub. His trouser leg was torn and speckled with blood, but I could see the glimmer of dented metal underneath. He immediately threw everyone out and the pub had shut for the night.

I had called his mobile to check up on him the following morning, but he didn't answer. I was halfway to work when I got the phone call saying that Mark Bolton had been arrested for assault last night and he needed me to pick him up from the cells. I had obliged and Bolt nodded roughly in appreciation when he climbed into my car.

I knew that meant a lot to him. As he climbed out of my car and went back into his pub, he turned and told me that he owed me big time.

Bolt laid his cold metal limb on the table with a heavy thud. For a moment I didn't seem real. However, as I reached over and held it, the reality of Bolt's ailment lay heavily in my hands.

It was a fairly simple design. It bent at the ankle and at the knee, but nowhere else. There were no arches in the foot. There were no muscles either. He had no way of propelling himself forwards like his own leg did. At the top were electrodes that sensed impulses in the thigh of his left leg and put them into movement.

"If I can't do it… then I will at least upgrade your leg," I said quietly.

"How much do you want, Will? This is the best I can afford."

"I want a week of your time. You come here every day this week and we work together. I'll examine you and your leg and try to make a connection."

"A connection?" Bolt asked curiously. I had to try and get him to understand. Just as the strange girl had understood earlier.

"I'm finding a way to connect machines to our bodies. It'll be called the Nerve-Plug. If I succeed, you will be able to feel your prosthetic as though it was your own leg."

Mark nodded several times and then paused for thought. He took his metal leg from the table and held it in his hands. His eyebrows furrowed as he re-attached the limb and I felt obliged to look away. As I looked out the window at the clouded skyline, I spotted the dark smudge of the disaster zone in the distance. My brain crawled briefly at the sight.

"Who is Lucy Quayin?" Mark said suddenly.

"How do you know her?" I said surprised.

"I don't. She's just come up on your light up display thing."

I spotted Lucy Quayin's face and handprint shining next to Mark's in the hologram and swore crudely under my breath.

Behind me, the double doors opened and I recognised the clacking of heels as my employer crossed my laboratory. Lucy Quayin was the Director of Cain Corporation, who only answered to Vincent Cain himself. I turned to face her with the best smile I could muster. Quayin wore a pinstriped suit that flared slightly at the bottom. Her bright blonde hair was ripped back into a ponytail and her glasses lay on her nose. Her finger tapped once against the metal trim of the sophisticated eyewear and they flashed yellow. The clipboard, which she held in her manicured hands, she used to swipe at the hologram. Lucy pushed the translucent blue brain and Mark's file aside, so all that remained was her own amber file. She tapped a brief password into my keyboard and removed the security that withheld her access to the room. Lucy Quayin could now enter my space, unrestricted, in her own time and with as much company as she pleased.

"Doctor Hart. I'm here to talk to you about time, more specifically, about your poor use of it. You were late this morning and I don't care to hear the excuse. Our system also picked up the arrival of a Mr..." she paused and cast a slow eye over my friend, "...Mark Bolton entering your laboratory and I've started to wonder whether any work is being done at all. Perhaps you are spending your remaining hours here socialising? You see, I'm not paying you for that, Doctor."

I remained quiet. Still holding a vague half-smile on my face, but truly boiling with rage. If only she knew how much of my life I had poured into my research.

"You are the future and you don't even know it," she continued in disappointment. "We've given you everything and we've had nothing in return. We are paying you for physical results and so far you have nothing to show but numbers, graphs and theorems. In the last generation, we haven't made any fresh technological advances…"

"Are you kidding?" I exploded in disbelief. She raised an eyebrow and perhaps for her own amusement she allowed me to continue. "In the last century alone we've seen phones reduce from the size of bricks to paper-thin cards and into holo-screens. There's no wired connection anymore. I can reach down into my pocket and take out this tiny phone and call my wife in mere seconds."

Quayin remained silent at my defiance. She was humouring my rant and so I continued to cement my opinion.

"We have just moved from touch technology into no-screen technology, Miss Quayin. Only last year the holo-market opened up for the public. We can move our finger through thin air and connect with a non-physical hologram that can actually create a global physical response. Don't even get me started on transport! The days of the fuel-powered vehicles are considered ancient by modern standards. Fossil fuels are abolished in favour for green electricity. We have rapid flights domestically, internationally and even inter-planetary, before the Global War and the Luna Rupture. We had a great city on the moon, and bases on other planets that I would have been able to call on my holo-phone right now! Communication and travel have become practically instant and almost entirely energy efficient!"

Lucy Quayin paused to absorb the moment.

"All we've achieved is greater connection," she said. "There's nothing new. All that is happening is that we are becoming lazier in our triumphs by simply making a phone smaller or a mobile connection quicker or a rocket-powered tin can more accessible. The universe is shrinking and time is slowing."

Now it was my turn to be silent. She was right.

"The Luna Rupture was the event that ended the great cities fight for dominance," she continued with arrogance. "We were practically gods before the Global War ended when the moon city's weapon fired and the world technologically regressed back to the age of steam power. We had teleportation, magnetised and laser weaponry, cybernetic implants, but the aftermath of the Global War ripped all of that away from us. When we eventually crawled out of the filth, we returned to the exact same place. I'll humour you… we could blast you into the cosmos and, yes, you could contact your wife seven hundred million miles away from Saturn, but we could already achieve such long distance communication long ago with the telegraph. It took much longer and a lot more effort, but it was still communication at its most basic level. There is nothing physically new. We have the opportunity to re-invent, but it's being squandered by scientists with limited imagination. The world has not run dry of potential. We are limited by people like you, Doctor Hart. It is a shame your potential is wasted by your meagre effort. There is nothing in this world that can re-invent it like your work will."

"The world doesn't need changing," I finally replied. "It needs healing."

"The time for change is coming sooner than you think, William. Only you can't see it yet," she said bluntly. Her eyes were sharp and pierced my own.

"The level of possibilities that my technology represents are considerably vast," I said. "We need to be cautious about how we proceed."

"Caution is for the weak-minded. You don't have the guts to see the potential here. You won't do what needs to be done to complete your research. We must explore all avenues that this technology poses and that does logically include military and enhancement application."

"First and foremost, as we have discussed before, all I want to do is help people feel whole again."

"That will be done…" she snapped impatiently.

"But you want more! Once I finish this project, what happens to all my research?"

"If you finish it, William," Quayin snipped. "Our patience has ended. You have a week."

"That's impossible."

"Cain Corporation expects a full presentation of your work presenting all avenues of application. If you can create this Nerve-Plug, then you can stay. Your pay check will improve substantially, your space will increase and we will give you staff to assist you in your work."

"But will I be in control of the application of my research or not?"

Lucy Quayin's eyes suddenly flicked towards the hologram. It was flashing blue, red and green; the citywide sign for an emergency broadcast. We all took out our phones that were receiving the same signal, even Mark's re-activated fifty-year-old touch screen phone was flashing.

I nodded lightly at them both. Mark rose heavily from his chair, his expression unreadable. Lucy was also uncomfortable, leaning against a wall as elegantly as her heels allowed and signalled me to answer the broadcast.

Stretching out, I touched the centre of the flashing broadcast. The colours stopped and sank into my clenched fist. With a sigh I released my hand and the hologram convulsed once, before a series of lights shot out and lined up. They formed a countdown to two-thirty, which was less than five minutes away. The lights in the lab began to dim so that only the countdown was visible. Lucy's voice rose from the darkness behind us.

"This is your last chance," Quayin said slowly. "If you succeed, which on a personal note I highly doubt, then Vincent Cain will decide the application of your project."

"And what happens if I don't meet your deadline?" I asked.

"You will be relieved and your work will become mine to follow as I personally wish. The presentation is Friday at seven. All the board members and shareholders, international correspondents from the other four great cities, and official

26

Priman personnel will be there. Any family and friends are also apparently welcome. The press should also be there to document the event, but that's still undergoing beneath a mountain of paperwork I won't bore your pre-occupied brains with."

"All this attention for me?" I laughed.

"Not quite," she said smugly. "There will be a summary of our endeavours since the Old Street tragedy. Your piece will be part of the Corporation's vision for the future."

"Very well, Miss Quayin. It looks like I have no choice anyway..."

"I look forward to Friday," she finished and remained with us as she decided to watch the broadcast.

The countdown had a minute to go. I breathed out deeply to relax, but all I could think of was Old Street. The cold creeping crawl that accompanied the image of twisted metal and the broken buildings burned into my mind.

I remembered Adele and how she was currently home alone waiting for me. I cursed myself. I had promised my wife that we would be together for the remembrance.

Once I heard the news of Old Street three years ago, I had immediately tried to rush back to make it home with my family. However flights were delayed by almost a week. No one was going in or out of Prima for a long time. They were afraid that further attacks were going to take place. Communications around the city went haywire as the primary broadcast tower had been knocked out in the blast. We had no choice but to sit in the waiting room in that blank airport for an immeasurable amount of time. Constantly in the same waiting room, staring at the pale ceiling, waiting for any news of when I'd be allowed to leave. I was unable to contact home at all. I was unable to find out if they were alive or dead. News reports were pure madness. No one knew what had happened, how many had died or when we were going to be allowed to go home. The simple act of waiting was relentless torture.

That airport waiting room was hell on earth.

When I finally landed there was a man waiting to meet me. He was sleekly dressed in cream and had dull lime eyes. He'd been instructed to drive me through town to help navigate the chaos on the streets. He told me he worked for Vincent Cain. I thanked him for his hospitality. I asked him if he knew what had happened to the Central University of Prima, specifically the unit of Advanced Science, as I worked there lecturing neurology, mechanical engineering and intuitive robotics. He told me swiftly that the entire campus had been destroyed in the fire along with all of its inhabitants. I told him that meant I was now unemployed. He promptly gave me the Cain Corporation details and told me to call them. They would need bright minds for the future.

The man drove me home and that was the first time I saw my family. I walked through my own front door and they looked at me with shock and then with joy. Tears poured from my eyes and their blurred faces filled my vision. I embraced my family, held them tightly, never wanting to let them go, before slowly slumping to the floor with the exhaustion of jet lag…

I scratched the back of my head and shook away the rough memory.

We still didn't find out who had survived for weeks after the incident. It didn't make sense why everything had taken so long, until we realized the truth.

There were no bodies to find.

The timer reached zero and the lights expanded to form a face. The familiarity of the floating visage was comforting, but also made me feel cold.

Vincent Cain was a face that the entire great city knew.

Amongst all that madness, Cain Corporation had been a figure of control, apparently stopping the incident growing out of control. Whilst Priman emergency services were severely occupied, his privatised company captured numerous individuals involved, saved countless lives and helped with the organisation process in the aftermath of the incident.

Cain was given Priman government support in return for his help. Funding and personnel that would've been given to security and healthcare was re-directed and the Cain Corporation grew fully into existence. It evolved from a private army into a fully-fledged business over a single month. Cain wished to manage several projects, most completely unknown to the public eye, so he promoted Lucy Quayin to Director to deal with expansion. Between them both, Cain Corp now dealt with private services across Prima ranging from medical to military applications.

Vincent Cain had saved us from extinction and was leading the memorial broadcast. Seeing him in this significant moment sent a mixture of cold emotions rippling through my head. I cast them out. This wasn't the time for insecurities and doubts. It was a time of remembrance.

"My Priman brothers and sisters, here we exist on the 15th of August 2101 and I am honoured to speak on behalf of all that live within the embrace of our great city, Prima. The first great city, or as my grandfather would have said, 'La Prima Grande Citta'. We have stood together, worked together and believed in one another. Together, we have brought a new bright future into reality."

Vincent seemed content, yet his grey metal eyes were stoic. It was hard to tell with these holograms. The image still felt artificial even with the high quality technology.

"We cannot forget our fallen friends, families and colleagues that died," Cain paused and breathed in lightly, the image flickering slightly to adjust to the live stream. "In 2098, three years ago, an explosion tore Old Street apart. Many were crushed in the initial shockwaves that measured level seven on the Richter scale and the final blast killed everyone in a mile radius instantly. Any survivors we found within five miles of the blast were either burnt, blinded or severely injured by fallen debris."

I felt Mark shuffle awkwardly next to me. It was a small mercy that he wasn't any closer to the centre of the blast.

"The cause of the explosion is still unclear and that is the greatest tragedy. We still cannot find the cause behind all those deaths," Vincent said solemnly and I saw a blur of blonde hair and heard a clack of heels as Lucy Quayin suddenly left the room. "I have the latest figures of how many were taken from us that day. 1,853 people have been confirmed dead. Another estimated 100 people are still missing. Also, as you all well know, within the five-mile radius around the blast zone there were 63 survivors. Beyond the blast, over 2,000 citizens were injured and many more left displaced after the incident. We honour our dead and will pay tribute to them by having every lost name engraved along Circuit Road. Today... we remember them. May we continue to work in beloved memory of those who are no longer with us. We will now have one minute of silence to remember our fallen."

Vincent Cain faded into the hologram and images of the incident began to flow in and out of the light. It showed the old buildings tall and strong. There was a flash of red light and the structures were shown again, this time torn and shredded by the explosion. Another flash of blue light emerged and showed the buildings around the epicentre of the explosion now. They were gleaming pinnacles of our new society. They stretched at twice the height that they used to. They mirrored the success we had found since the incident with the help of Cain. A glimmer of green cascaded over the hologram as it reset to the first image. The hologram began to flow slowly between the three images in sequence whilst a calm music rose up from my desk's in-built speakers.

Old. Death. New. Again and again. Birth. Life. Death.

The symbols of the religion of Fate were dotted around the hologram. The three sisters of Fate were calling out to Prima, echoing their grief for the disaster.

"Nono. Decima. Morta," I whispered the trio deities of Fate in a solemn prayer for the dead.

I sighed deeply and considered how lucky my family were. I saw Mark hunched over slightly. His face was overcast and his eyes burned with a strange anger every time the destroyed Old Street appeared in the hologram. As one of the survivors near the blast, it had changed Mark. Not just physically... but mentally.

The images finally faded away and the hologram returned to normal as the floating blue brain re-appeared above our heads.

Mark was still consumed by his thoughts so I left him to think. I returned to my desk and shrugged the tension out of my shoulders. Reaching up, I grabbed the brain, shrank it into my palm and gently pushed it into a nearby folder. There was no way

I could get the results I needed in one week. It was better to cut my losses, go home and just prepare some sort of written thesis on neuro-robotics to publically publish.

"What are you doing?" Mark asked confused as I packed away more digital files into the folder.

"I can't do what Quayin wants. There is no way I'll be ready in a week. It's time to pack up."

"Stop. If you want my help, then you've got it. You're onto something here and I'm not going to watch you throw that away, Will. Besides... I want to see that bitch's face when we blow everyone's minds on Friday."

"You're serious?"

"I don't think I've been so serious in years. You're stuck and if you genuinely think I can help you do this, that my accident is the key to your research, then I'm here to stay."

"What about the pub and all your customers?"

"I can hire some spotty teenager to fill in a few hours here and there," he laughed. "So what do you say?"

I couldn't believe what I was hearing, but even as his offer entered my head, a dozen ideas and theories started to sprout and grow and fill my body with an energy that I hadn't felt in years.

I grabbed the folder with both hands and tore it open, so all the files were thrown out in a blast of blue light. They spread out into all corners of the room, spinning lightly as they travelled.

"Let's get to work."

3 – Home Comforts

The car slowed down as I reached my home. The engine purred lightly as I turned into my driveway. I paused slightly outside the garage before saying "*open.*" The wide metal door lifted into the roof and I drove into the dark space, the hum of my vehicle echoing off the near stone walls. It growled as it came to a stop. I collected my bag, stepped out the car and as I said "*close*", the garage door fell down behind me in a single fluid motion. The space plunged into a calm darkness. I breathed out once and said "*lights.*"

I was blinded briefly as the neon bulbs sprang into life. I adjusted the dimmer on the wall and turned the blinding whiteness into a pale shade of blue. The light shined gently off my small workshop in the corner. It was a small area made out of three long desks that were covered and cluttered with components and parts, both small and large, odds and ends, all to tinker with in my spare time. There were car batteries, old drills, light bulbs, a box of tools, solar panels, along with many other objects I couldn't fully see in the light. I missed tinkering in that space. It had been such a long time since I'd had any time for myself.

The door behind me sprang open with a sharp clang as metal hit stone. I jumped at the sound and spun round as Theo emerged from the open door. He roared once in an attempt to scare me and leaped into my chest.

"Surprise!" Theo yelled. "I made you jump, didn't I?"

"Yes, Theo. You made me jump…" I groaned.

"I got you, Dad. You actually screamed!"

"I didn't scream."

"You did."

"I did not."

"Where have you been? I'm starving. Mum's not letting us eat yet."

I looked at my watch. I was an hour later than usual. Adele

wouldn't be happy about that.

"Now you know you can't be in here…"

"I know, I might hurt myself, but I wanted to surprise you!"

"Which you did, now go run and tell your mother I'll be there in a second."

The light to the house was obscured slightly and I saw the silhouette of my wife blocking the way into the house.

"You can tell me that yourself," she said firmly.

She looked angry to say the least. Her big frizzy hair seemed wild and untamed in this light.

"Go inside, Theodore," Adele echoed. "You know you shouldn't be in here. Your father and I need to talk."

My son jumped off my body and quickly ran inside, wanting to be as far away as possible from the wrath of his mother. I envied how easily he'd escaped the situation. I sighed and thought that perhaps when Theo was older I could show him a few tricks in the workshop…

"You said you would be back," Adele said grabbing my attention.

"I know I did…"

"I had to sit here on my own through that minute. You promised me, Will."

"I know, but I had a breakthrough. I was with Mark…"

"You were with Mark?" Adele stepped into the garage to look me in the eye. "Decima be damned, why were you at Mark's pub?"

"I wasn't at the pub, Adele. I simply asked Mark to come visit me at work," I tried to explain.

"Like that is any better? I'm not getting any sense out of you today. Can't you tell I'm upset? Okay, fine. You have twenty seconds to explain yourself."

"What, oh, really? And what if I don't?"

"Fifteen seconds and counting…"

I looked at Adele and judged whether it was best to tell her about today. She stared at me impatiently, raised her watch and began counting the final seconds down with her firm eyes. Today wasn't a good day to test her.

"I was driving to work and I hit someone with my car. She made me realise that I could solve my research by accessing the memories of someone who had lost a part of their body. I called Mark, because there really isn't anyone else I could call. My employer, Miss Quayin, came in and tried to fire me, but instead I now have to give her some sort of revelation in science by Friday. If I don't succeed, then she can use my research to do anything she likes! So, yes, Bolt is helping me try to achieve that or else we'll probably witness an upgraded brand of warfare before the New Year. Plus I will be unemployed and I'll have wasted the last few years of my life working for Cain Corporation."

Adele stood, seemingly blown back by my outburst, as waited with breathless anticipation. She took a moment to take all the information in before nodding.

"You were seven seconds over, but yes, it sounds like a tough day."

"You're letting me off the hook? I hit someone with a car!"

"Did you apologise? Will she sue you? Is the car damaged?" Adele asked.

"That was three questions. Yes, no and dented."

"Wait, okay, no. I'm afraid you've lost me."

"You asked the questions! Of course I apologised. No, I think she was homeless and the car is luckily only dented," I answered. "Although I reckon I will be able to pop the dent. If I pour boiling water on the metal, lift the bonnet and use a small wooden tool to invert the concave…"

"I honestly don't care how you fix the dent, Will," she interrupted. "I was just worried about you, but it looks like everything is fine! But don't you *ever* leave me on my own again when you promised you wouldn't!"

"I'm sorry, I promise I won't…" I paused. Adele seemed genuinely hurt. "How are you doing?"

"It's been tough, but I'm alright," she said without looking at me.

"Come here," I said to her with my arms outstretched and she fell into my arms exhausted. Adele had been hiding her pain all day for the kids and now we were alone she could let go. I hugged her and felt her cry into my shoulder. I lifted her face up with my hand and kissed her gently on the lips. "I love you, Adele Hart."

"I love you too, you annoying fool," she said with her smug smile.

"That's my girl. Now let's go eat."

She wiped her face to make it strong for our children and walked back into the house. She almost tripped over Theo eavesdropping on the way. She quickly clipped him lightly around the ear before heaving the flailing boy into the kitchen.

I felt my heart drop in my chest.

Adele's parents had died in the Old Street incident. After a few months of hearing nothing, we were informed that their bodies were found together in a parked car a few miles from the centre of the blast. She didn't talk about it much, but she sometimes commented that we couldn't change the past. Remembering is painful. We should focus on the future.

I couldn't even imagine being in her shoes today. I felt truly guilty that I hadn't been by her side during the incident or during the remembrance.

"Isabella Hart!" Adele screamed from the kitchen. "Come down here. Dinner is ready!"

As usual, there was no answer.

"William. Go get Isabella," Adele told me. "Dinner is going to get cold. If our daughter likes her food frozen, then tell her she is welcome to eat whenever she likes. However I believe the majority of the human population prefer their dinner somewhat warm. But hey! That might just be me!"

"I'm on it, Madame Hart..." I replied enjoying the usual routine of the pre-dinner amble. I was used to fetching child number one. It had become my rather efficient part-time job. I was getting quite good at it. Perhaps I should quit the pursuit of connecting man to machine and take on a full time career of dragging my first child down the stairs. Perhaps I'll just see how this week goes first...

I shrugged off my jacket and put it over the nearby coat hook and dropped my bag before ascending the staircase. My daughter's room was the first on the left and there was a faint echo of music coming from behind the door. I knocked three times before entering. Izzy lay on the bed with a pair of holo-glasses and wireless glowing headphones stuck into her ears. They were a more outdated version than the trim eyewear that Quayin had been wearing earlier. Izzy's gadget shone a pale colour of aqua that pulsated slowly. I touched her on the shoulder and she jumped, pulling the glasses from her face.

"Hi, Dad," she gasped in surprise. "What's up?"

"Dinner is ready," I told her routinely. "You better be quick or your mother might explode. I'm not even joking, she literally might explode with impatience and hunger."

"Okay, got it," she said quickly, her eyes flashing anxiously towards the holo-glasses lying on her bed.

"What were you watching?" I asked.

"Oh… just some whales," she muttered.

"Whales?"

"Yes… whales," she shrugged. "So what?"

"Whales went extinct years ago, Izzy." I coughed lightly with embarrassment as I continued, "They couldn't… reproduce anymore."

Izzy looked back with the same twinkle in her eye that her mother had. Her mouth crinkled upwards as she tried to stop herself from laughing at my discomfort.

"Are you sure it was whales?" I asked.

"I'm not stupid, Dad. It was a pair of whales in the southern ice cap. There are two great cities down in Antarctica and I've always wanted to learn more. This zoo is at Eden, which was specially created for the survival of marine life nearing extinction. It was filmed through live web-feed by a submersible drone they keep in the water tank."

I raised the aqua glasses to my face and I saw the two ethereal creatures spiralling around each other in a vast space of water that was fenced off by sheets of glass and metal in an upside-down dome. The pen looked like it was capable of expansion and could be moved easily under the surface of the ice. I saw the silhouettes of several tourists within the interconnecting network of the dome watching the enclosed wildlife. The whales circled past the drone and made it waver against their current. Their huge fins sent a cascade of bubbles shimmering to the surface of the icy water. I could see more dark silhouettes of people standing above the pool, studying the giant creatures every movement.

"They say they are the last existing whales," Izzy told me. "They found them together trapped under the glacier off Eden's Bald coast. They got them out by recreating some marine sounds, and they swam out and saved them. They live in Eden now with the other creatures they've rescued and preserved. I think they've been attempting to re-create them artificially. Because, like you said, they can't reproduce. It's something about their cells not being able to match up anymore. They were trying to clone their cells so they have a higher success rate in bonding, but nothing seems to be working so far. It sucks."

"That's all very lovely, honey, but where did you get these holo-glasses from?" I asked her.

"Dad. Please. It's fine. Don't worry about it."

"Tell me where you got them."

"It's a learning resource, okay? I booked it out of school."

"How long ago did you book them out?"

"It was like three months ago, but they haven't noticed and no one has asked me for them or anything."

"You have to return those tomorrow. They're very expensive."

"They're so cool though! They teach me loads that the teachers don't at school. I like learning through images and being able to interact with the information. I really like them, Dad. It makes me want to do research outside of Biology."

She stared at me with those chocolate brown eyes that her mother had. She knew how to melt my gullible heart.

"Okay. Here's the deal," I said.

"Yes?" Izzy asked, her face lighting up.

"Return them tomorrow…"

"But Dad! That's not fair."

"Don't interrupt and let me finish my sentence. Return them tomorrow. Get top marks in your Biology exam and I'll try to get you a pair of holo-glasses from work."

"You'll get me some Cain Corp glasses?" Izzy's jaw dropped.

"I'll try. I know someone downstairs from research and development. I hear there might be some state of the art, probably won't even be in retailers for another year, holo-glasses in production."

"Thank you, Dad!"

"I saw my boss wearing some today, so I know that they exist. Now I haven't even done anything yet, but get the work done, then we'll talk."

My daughter's smile beamed as I sat down next to her on the bed and held the holo-glasses lightly in my hands.

"You know... all you had to do was ask nicely and we could've tried to work something out," I told her. "See? Isn't this great when we just take the time to talk like adults?"

"But you're always so busy..." she said quietly.

"I know. Well, that's going to change. I'm working very hard this week with Mark Bolton."

"The guy from the pub?"

"Yes, but that isn't relevant. He's helping me with work. Anyway I think we're onto something..." I said trailing off. It was best not to explain all of this to my daughter, especially the part where I may be out of the job at the end of the week and that I work for people whose intentions have always been somewhat vague.

"Come on, before your mother bursts a blood vessel..."

"William Forest Hart and Isabella Daniela Hart," said my wife from the bottom of the stairs, cutting off my sentence. "Theodore and I have begun eating our food because we are hungry. If you do not want to eat, then you may starve. However we shall not be joining you in poverty tonight. Food shall be consumed. I am not a hotel. You may not jingle a little bell and demand room service. I will not be bringing it up to you. You are fully capable human beings. You have legs. So use those limbs, stand up and walk down the stairs, sit at my table, eat my beautifully prepared food and don't you dare whinge to me when your food is cold!"

"Coming!" We both shouted in unison, as we hurried swiftly

38

down the stairs and dashed into our normal positions at the dinner table. The table was empty other than a mischievous Theo who sat opposite me.

Adele appeared from the kitchen. She was startled at our sudden appearance and then she smiled smugly as she brought in both of our meals. She exited swiftly and returned with two more plates for herself and Theo.

Apparently they hadn't started eating at all.

"Now that was clever, sweetie…" I said in response to her little trick.

"Shut up and give thanks to the Fates, before we all fall asleep from your general lateness," she replied.

"Love you too," I said smugly back.

"Thank the Fates. Now," she snapped lovingly back at me.

I put both my hands together and extended my fingers into a small triangle in routine prayer and felt the sides of my mouth lift into a smile as I looked at my family. The tiny six-year-old Theo sat opposite me; he copied my hands and held them over his head in an exaggerated pyramid shape. Adele sat next to me with her head bowed and eyes closed softly. Her hands lay together in the simple triangular symbol on her lap. The light bounced gently off her brown skin and showed the supple grace her bare neck bore. It was when she was calm like this that she was most beautiful. Finally Izzy sat the furthest away from me diagonally across the table. She too had her eyes closed like her mother. Her frizzy hair dangled precariously over her eyes in some form of fringe.

"Nono, Decima, Morta," I murmured.

"Birth, Life, Death," my family echoed gently.

"Thank you sisters of Fate who weave, measure and cut the thread of our lives. Nono, we wish to thank Adele for this beautiful meal tonight," I said gently. "It smells delicious by the way."

"I'm hungry," Theo cried in ravenous torture.

"Thank you for our horrible children who I dread meeting every day. Theo the master of surprises and constant whinge-bucket."

"The dinner might hibernate at this rate, Dad…" Izzy said.

"And let us not forget Izzy. The newly discovered whale lover who is fuelled by her raging hormones. When you get a boyfriend, I cannot wait to meet him. Blubbery blowhole and all."

"Hey!" Izzy said.

"Wait what?" Adele questioned.

"Cool…" Theo cooed.

I interrupted them all by clearing my throat.

"Sister of life, Decima, I want to say thank you for our lives. We are blessed to be here on this day." The atmosphere of the room dropped slightly, as even Theo knew that today was important. "We are truly blessed to have one another and to be able to eat together. Adele? Do you wish to say something?" I asked her carefully.

"We must remember my parents, nanny and pappy, today of all days. Sister of death, Morta, their lives were cut too short. I know you kids didn't know them that well, but they loved you dearly," she smiled at me. "I wish they could be with us today. Izzy, would you like to say something?"

"But I've never given thanks to the Fates?" Izzy said. "I'm not sure if I believe in them…"

"You're a young woman now," I said to encourage her. "You can believe whatever you like. This simply gives us a moment to thank the things that matter to us. I'm sure you can think of something."

"Well, I want to say that I miss our grandparents too. I wish I could have known them more. I was only twelve when it happened, but I still remember them. And, yes, sister of birth, Nono, bless all the creatures of the world. Help them give birth, especially the ones that are going extinct, as that will stop them being dead. Bless those ones, as they don't have the family that we do."

"That's very good," Adele said hiding a small delicate smile.

"I'm hungry. Can we eat now?" Theo cried out in suffering.

"Fates bless us, and yes to that!" I said and tucked into the meal. It was spaghetti bolognese, which made my stomach rumble in anticipation. I thrust my fork into the pasta and spun it to collect a clump and put it swiftly in my mouth. It was hot, soft

40

and spiced. Perfect. I hummed in enjoyment as I chewed the food. I dived in again and noticed the mess I was making on my shirt.

"Dad?" Theo cried out suddenly.

"What's wrong child number two?" I replied.

"I don't get it…"

"You were born second, and that's why I call you number two."

"I get that!" Theo laughed. "I mean… I don't understand what you said to Mum. You said that you hit someone? Does that mean you punched somebody? Because that's not very nice."

"Theodore!" Adele cried "What have we told you about eavesdropping?"

"That it's naughty…" Theo mumbled.

"Exactly," Adele said. "Although whilst we are on the topic, we might as well talk about it. Did you maim this homeless person? Are they still there at the side of the street?"

My family stared at me, waiting for my answer.

"I personally made sure she was alright. Like I said, I apologized and sent her on her way. That's about it." I explained.

"Wait," said Izzy. "You actually hit a woman?"

"I hit a girl with my car on the way to work. I was distracted by everything. They're fine. Honestly. Okay, everybody?"

"It is very easy to get distracted on Circuit Road. I always hate walking that way. It must be so much worse for you…" Izzy said slowly.

"Isabella," Adele snapped over sharply.

"Sorry Mum," Izzy mumbled quickly, before looking back at me with anxious eyes. "I only wanted to ask if you knew where this girl is now?"

My mouth opened to give an answer, but none came.

"Will?" Adele asked.

"I don't know where she is now. She didn't seem to have anywhere permanent to go. I offered her a free meal sometime this week. She was quite bright actually. She helped me get a few ideas brewing for work."

"How old was she?" Izzy asked.

"Near twenty, I guess. It was hard to tell, but definitely a few years older than you." I replied.

"Okay. Cool…" Izzy said quietly.

"Cool," I echoed and we all continued to eat in silence.

"Did she…" Izzy piped.

"Can we please just drop it and enjoy dinner?" I replied swiftly.

"It's interesting. It's not about your work or about today…" Izzy said, staring absently down, whilst playing with the pasta with her fork. "It's something completely different."

I sighed. Anything was better than talking about today.

"What did you want to ask?" I asked.

"Just wanted to ask if she said what her name was?" Izzy replied.

I paused and remembered how the girl had refused wanting an ambulance and how she had shivered after I told her I worked under Vincent Cain. I wanted to tell my daughter that her name was Raven. Yet it was clear this girl was trouble. It was important that I kept my family out of it entirely.

"No," I lied to my family. "She didn't tell me her name."

I saw the black screen of the television out of the corner of my eye and remembered that Raven had commented that I didn't watch the news.

"*Television. On. Local news*," I said looking at the screen.

It flickered and flashed onto the news channel and I swiftly muted it with my voice.

"What are you looking for?" Adele asked cautiously.

"Nothing in particular. I just feel disconnected to what's going on in the outside world."

"Just don't let your dinner get cold…" she said and pressed a gentle hand on my shoulder. I looked at her with confusion and saw that everyone had finished their food. I needed to talk less and eat more. The kids had already begun clearing away their plates. Everything had happened so quickly without me even noticing...

"Never let food go cold. Good life lesson for the future," I smiled faintly and looked at my children's expectant faces. "Your mother and I will do the washing up tonight. You're both excused."

My attention flowed back to the screen as the kids left and escaped upstairs to their rooms. Within moments I heard a dull hum of oceanic music as Izzy turned her holo-glasses on to watch her marine mammals, whilst Adele walked upstairs to make sure Theo actually got into bed.

"*Un-mute*," I said to the television screen, which instantly began chuntering information into my eardrums.

"…after the message from Vincent Cain this afternoon, we are left wondering what will happen next? Cain Corporation has been hunting these criminals for three years, but they are also commenting that they still have work to do. Can there really still be individuals out there involved…"

A video from the past rose in the background. It was an address by Cain shortly after the incident where his four main associates and many other private soldiers surrounded him. The news continued to talk over the muted video, but I couldn't hear it. My vision was focused on Cain and his colleagues.

"*Pause*." I told the television.

Cain was frozen in a vision of self-confidence. He was giving the speech that would regain control over the chaos and guide the citizens of a ruined great city into the future.

On his left, stood a sharp elderly man who seemed distracted by all the surrounding news reporters. His hair was tied back into a silver ponytail and his stare was dead and cold. His skin was starkly pale.

On Cain's right, was a brooding brute of flesh, possibly Russian, who was wary of the crowd and ready to protect Cain.

Below him was Lucy Quayin. Her face was dirty and her hair blew outward in a mad mess. She was a nervous wreck compared to the tyrant of a woman who had confronted me today.

Finally, there was a man who was the strangest of them all. He wore decimated clothes that looked like a prisoner's uniform. He was bleeding heavily from his side and his white hair hung over his face. He looked like he had walked straight out of the blast zone. His bright green eyes shone out like two emeralds through

43

all the madness on the screen. He sent the same curling shiver down my spine as the ruins of Old Street did.

I didn't know these men, not the pale man with the silver hair or the immense brute, but that broken man with those green eyes… there was something horribly familiar about him.

I heard Adele coming down the stairs and I un-froze the screen. Carrying my plate into the kitchen, I started to pack the dishwasher. I felt her settle in the dining room next door, so I packed the machine alone. I told it to auto-wash and the display told me that it weighed the dirty crockery and applied the appropriate amount of powder. It hummed as it began to wash the dishes. I always thought it was rather sophisticated for a dishwasher.

Adele was crying gently and she sat watching the news. I swore in my head for having left the television on.

"I didn't mean to upset you…" I said quietly, indicating the news.

"It's good to watch it, Will. For both of us," she smiled firmly, eyeing my response with caution. "It's important to learn to adjust. I never asked you. How are you doing today?"

"I am absolutely fine, Adele," I laughed, as I saw how roughly the news affected my wife. "Don't worry about me."

"I always worry about you, Will. I can't help it. Especially…" Adele stopped herself and sighed heavily. She looked away, as more tears began to fall from her eyes.

I crouched next to her, took off my glasses and kissed both her cheeks to take away her tears.

"See? That's better already," I murmured.

"Sorry for arguing with you earlier…" Adele cried softly.

"It's understandable. Being married so long I'm surprised you haven't got rid of me by now."

"Nonsense. I'd have no one to complain to anymore."

"You would have the kids."

"I guess… but you're more fun to argue with."

"I'm glad you find my dismay enjoyable," I kissed her lightly; like it was the first time we kissed all over again.

"I love it when you do that, Mr Hart."

"Hey! I didn't get my doctorate for nothing, so I would appreciate being called my official title."

"Shut up, Will."

"I think you will find that's Doctor Will!" I corrected proudly.

"You only got that bloody doctorate to pretend to be clever."

"No. I got it so everyone would know of my cleverness upon meeting me. Now, Doctor Hart says that you should get yourself upstairs to bed. Sleep deprivation turns you into a grumpy hag."

"I think we both need an early night," she said smiling back and walked out the room. I heard her voice call out from halfway up the stairs. "Oh, Doctor Hart? Don't take too long. I might fall asleep on you otherwise…"

Momentarily oblivious to her insinuation, I suddenly perked up with excitement. I left the room to follow her, before remembering that I'd left the television on.

A girl was on the screen. She was walking down a street with her hood up. Her dreadlocks were hanging low and her eyes stared fiercely at the camera. I recognised her instantly, as the television continued to preach.

"…with knowledge into the terrorist attack, she is known to be dangerous and extremely resourceful. Do not communicate with the young woman known as Raven, as she is known to manipulate citizens into believing she is helpless. If you have any knowledge of her whereabouts, please inform your local authorities…"

"*Television. Off,*" I said whilst walking out the room. Ignoring the broadcast, I grabbed my jacket off the hook, picked up my bag from the floor and ascended the stairs to join my wife.

4 – Message from Beyond

I fell asleep knowing that the same dream would visit and I would wake up sweating as I'd done for so long. It felt like the dreams had been attacking irregularly for as long as I could remember.

It was an inevitable torturous routine.

I rolled away from Adele and breathed out deeply. I focused only on my breath going in and out of my body and eventually began to relax. I gave in to the feeling, forgot myself, and released into the covers of the bed.

"Do you want me to tell you the truth, William?"

My mind stopped whirling and finally came to a gradual halt, allowing my subconscious to rule my prone sleeping body.

"The world is waiting to change. It's underneath your skin…"

Once again, I watched my phone being ripped apart and scattered across the room. It was a routine set of motion now. I knew exactly where the many pieces of my phone landed in the room and how they would bounce off the floor before they stopped sparking.

The dream shifted as it always did and I moved with it in my sleep. My mind stirred in discomfort at the familiarity of the dream.

The girl once more moved down the alley and her anger exploded the barrel of fire, scattering the homeless and leaving her alone.

However this time it was different. I stayed with her longer.

She stared at the shattered remains of metal in horror. She raised her glowed hands as they steamed away the sweat on her skin. She breathed in deeply and the anger faded from her eyes. There were others approaching, a flash of lights and a flood of armed soldiers surging into the alley behind her. They were led by Vincent Cain, his metal eyes burrowing towards the girl. She looked directly up and I recognised her at last.

I was torn away from Raven before I could fully comprehend it was her.

Back at the prison that I knew would be destroyed, I watched the broken man with green eyes being led to his cell. The anticipated cold chill ran down my spine before the explosion even happened. I felt the rumble in the distance as the first shockwave began. The building was ripped apart and the green-eyed man jumped for cover.

He had survived the blast.

I rose above the prison and watched Old Street die another horrific death. The fire ripped apart people and roads as it always did. The fire reached me, but I didn't feel it.

I did not burn and wake up as usual… I remained asleep.

White noise began to flutter against my eardrums. I gazed back at the crippled Old Street. Numb and frozen, my subconscious worked against my busy mind. The dream was changing. Old Street flashed falsely, before it disappeared entirely.

A brief image of the waiting room in the airport scratched across the back of my mind.

I screamed, wretched and roared. Images of Raven and the green-eyed man flashed again. These people who I'd thought were a mad construct of my vivid imagination were actually real. Recognition made my dream swell.

I knew the green-eyed man. I'd seen him earlier.

"This man is your conclusion," the dark voice curled into my ear, as I writhed in my sleep. *"It doesn't matter what I show you. Your meeting is inevitable."*

I was thrown towards Cain's conference after the rescue operation at Old Street. It was the same scene that I'd seen on the television.

Vincent Cain walked through the crowd followed by four others. A bewildered Lucy Quayin stumbled, trying to usher the press. She clawed her dirtied blonde hair back into a vague ponytail and shuffled through distraught people asking after their loved ones. She was saying the same thing over and over again in a growing panic.

"I don't know what happened!" Lucy yelled. "Mr Cain will tell us what to do. Just wait one moment. Please wait! Vincent Cain is about to speak."

The crowd surged violently and Lucy twisted with sudden panic.

"Stranz! Where are you?" Lucy yelled out into the crowd of growing voices. "Anton! Make us a path!"

Anton Stranz emerged and separated the crowd instantly for the entourage, his bulk immediately creating space and dividing a path amidst the chaos. His small eyes peered through his muscled face. Stranz smiled coarsely at Lucy and she nodded her appreciation.

"Clear space!" Stranz roared. "Vincent Cain is coming through!" His voice was grated and he seemed oddly focused, as though crowd control was his profession. He twisted to his contrasting colleague. "Have you got him, Foshe?"

Pierre Foshe's white skin creased with irritation. He was much older than the rest of the group. Deep crevices crossed his pale face and lined his eyes. The old man dragged a bloodied broken man with green eyes to the podium with his gnarled hands. He was disgruntled that he had to perform this kind of manual labour. The blood was already dirtying his clothes and was seeping into his blotched skin.

"The weak get left behind," Foshe snarled and left the ragged prisoner in the filth. "Only the strong survive."

The conference began as Cain addressed the audience, but I was only focused on the destroyed individual lying on the ground. He rose up, leaving a bloodied imprint, shrugging away helping hands and ignored the voices around him. His green eyes shone through bruised lids and set themselves upon Cain's elevated platform. He limped and, slowly but surely, he climbed onto the podium.

Vincent paused mid-speech and then smiled richly.

"The wounded and lost will rise and stand tall once more!" Cain announced proudly and placed a hand on his newest colleagues shoulder. Lucy Quayin head lowered. Stranz ignored the interaction and focused on the sway of the urging crowd. Foshe's lip curled at the sight of the green-eyed man standing beside them. The green-eyed man nodded at Cain who continued with his speech.

"Find the girl and she will show you the truth. She will save you," the dark voice whispered and erased the entire scene. Time flickered forwards and I was pulled away.

Raven was hunched over in the filthy underbelly of Prima. Beside her was the burning, smoking carcass of a previously beautiful motorbike. Its gleaming paintwork and polished metal quickly dissolved under the heat of the fire. She heaved herself up, looking briefly down at the dying vehicle before running through the darkness and down the dimly lit street. It was raining fiercely. Cars shot past her as she sprinted across the street and dodged the blasting traffic, before she dived into another alley. Her head was bleeding profusely and her arm hung out at an awkward angle. It looked broken. She was in a lot of pain. Lightning flashed and illuminated a nearby ladder. She began to climb it with one arm awkwardly and clearly in a lot of pain.

There was another flash. A pair of emerald eyes filled my vision. They pierced my dream. They left me as a powerful blast slammed into my dream. Raven was falling and clutching her chest. She'd been shot. There was another flash of light and I was dragged away from the scene.

"You have found them both in your reality. These are moments in time. Some are past and some are future. Some are fixed and some are not. Now. It is up to you what happens next."

I struggled away from my subconscious and spoke out at last.

"What do you want from me?" I asked out into the ether.

"I want you to see the truth, William," The dream wavered, hesitating slightly before continuing to show more images.

The green-eyed man was lifting an unconscious Raven through Cain Corporation. I saw that he wasn't that much older than her. He wasn't even thirty yet. He pressed his palm against a touch-pad and carried her into a prison cell. He chained her arms over her head. He looked at her for a moment, before leaving the room. I stayed with Raven and watched as her breath poured from her mouth as vivid steam. Her skin began to crack and splinter, turning blue and purple and back to a burning shade again. I realized that the room was freezing cold. Her ragged eyes lifted across the room and met with her cellmate.

49

It was a man that I did not recognise. His dark eyes haunted mine. They attempted to sear acknowledgement into my vacant mind. It was useless. I did not know this man. I had never met this man. His eyes glimmered grimly and blinked slowly, as he allowed me to view him for the first time. He was a long haired, unwashed man whose skin had turned into a cracked mess. His eyes were crying fresh tears that froze seconds after leaving his body.

"I am… Mimic…" the cruel man whispered, his voice burning violently into my mind. "I feel your pain, Hart…"

Mimic stopped speaking and glared strangely at Raven. His glare manifested into the form of curious hatred. It was a look of self-loathing and disappointment. There was a history between the pair that I could not possibly comprehend in this moment.

The prisoners stared at one another in the cold fridge, as they tried with all of their power to survive the viciously cold temperature.

"Events that may or may not happen. The future is a road with many intersecting paths. There are so many different choices a single person can take, but if you do not help this girl, then this future of cold torture is highly probable."

"This is nothing more than my imagination," I muttered outwards. "You are just a mere…"

"I am not a mere creation of your mind, William Hart."

"This is impossible," I dismissed.

"You do not believe me? Fine. I won't waste my time on petty imagery anymore. It is time to see for yourself. It is time that you see everything that you can become."

The dream twisted violently and I saw myself writhing in a construction site. Metal twisted. Machinery contorted. My body became a colossal uncontrollable mess made of flesh, metal and electricity. I was twitching and arching and crunching and whirring. Lights flashed. Glass broke. The ground splintered. People screamed. I tried to look at their faces, but they ran away from me. I grabbed one of them. It was my wife. Adele's eyes filled with tears of pain and fear. She was terrified of me.

"I have picked you, William Hart, to save us all."

A flash of light sliced through the dream to address me directly. Its gaze burned every nerve in my body.

"It is time to discover your true…"

I screamed as I suddenly woke up. The room blurred and I shook my head violently. Adele, Izzy and Theo stood by the door together. They were scared. I tried to get up to hug them, but they moved away.

"What's wrong?" I asked.

"You wouldn't wake up," Adele said slowly, her chest heaving. "It was different this time, Will. I tried to wake you, but you wouldn't… you grabbed me." She rubbed her arm and there was a purple and yellow bruise rising on her dark skin.

"Dad?" said Theo. "You were yelling. Why were you scared? What did you dream about?"

"Yeah, it was pretty freaky," said Izzy shakily. "You were tossing and turning. Nothing we did would wake you up. Theo threw water over you in the end and you snapped out of it."

I looked down and saw that I was covered in water and the bed was soaked.

"Will, I think you should…" Adele said and touched my shoulder.

I flinched suddenly away from her and she gasped in shock.

"I'm not seeing anybody," I snapped. "I don't need to. I'm fine."

I looked at them all and I realised that it was the second time today that I had lied to my family.

"It was just a really bad dream, kids," I told them as calmly as I could manage. "I've been stressed out from work and it's affected my sleep. Daddy is going to sleep downstairs for a while."

"You don't have to do that…" Adele said softly.

"Yes, I do. I need to." This time she didn't question me. "I'm fine, honestly, let's all try and get some sleep."

I moved over to my shaken children and walked them gently out of my bedroom. I tucked Theo into bed, turned his nightlight on and kissed his forehead.

"Goodnight, number two," I whispered.

51

"Night, Dad. Sleep with the light on. It keeps away the monsters," he said sincerely. "Because, when you think about it, they aren't real. They're just shadows. It's all in your head. That's the truth. You just have to turn the light on and they will all go away."

I paused at my son's profound words and smiled as convincingly as possible...

"I will keep a light on downstairs, Theo," I said to reassure him. "Get some rest."

I left my son and moved cautiously to my daughter's bedroom.

"I'm sorry. I didn't mean to scare you," I said quietly to Izzy who was waiting in her bed. I kissed her forehead and she winced slightly.

"It's not that, Dad. I'm worried about you."

"I'm fine..." I lied again. "I'll see you in the morning, Izzy."

"Night..." she said anxiously before rolling over away.

I made the short walk downstairs and collapsed on the sofa. I rolled over and felt a cold shiver trickle its way down my spine and itch the back of my head. I closed my eyes and all the lights turned off with them.

TUESDAY

Isabella   Adele   Theo

5 – The Green Eyed Man

Theo played with his seatbelt whilst the car came to a halt for the traffic lights. He pulled the belt out and then let it go. It shot back, slammed into him and secured him in place. Once more he dragged it out, leaning out as far as he could, so that it would have maximum elasticity, before it threw him further and even faster backwards. He laughed as he was thrown back each time. With a smirk I subtly grazed my thumb over the green child safety button. The seatbelt shot back and wrenched Theo into position, the belt around his waist tightened and pinned him to the chair. Theo's limbs were wild as he struggled to be free, but the child-lock kept him in place.

"Dad! Let me out," he laughed.

"Nope. Not happening!"

I pressed the button again releasing him, and he swiftly stretched his seatbelt out again. Before he could ping the strap, I flashed my hand across the green button and he shot back into position.

"Can you please stop," Izzy said from behind me. I guess she wasn't too happy that she was being thrown back and forth like her brother.

"Sorry..." I mumbled and quickly released them both. I thought about asking her to sit in the front, but I knew she wouldn't want to be seen dead sat there in case her friends saw her.

The light turned green at last and we moved on, driving in staggered silence other than the glorious sound of raspberries as Theo made faces at the public. I reached across and shaded the windows by sliding my fingers across a nearby panel. Theo's tongue against the window was quickly hidden from society.

We reached another red light and were forced to stop.

I took the moment to look at my children in the mirror. Theo was awake and energetic as usual, his pupils wide and alive.

Izzy, on the other hand, look tired. Her eyes were almost puffy and it looked like she'd been crying. Izzy's frizzy hair was released over her face today. Whilst Adele kept her hair in a tight Afro, Izzy usually tied her hair back to show her face. She told me that she did this to stop it getting in the way of writing, however today she was letting it go. I couldn't help thinking that it looked like she was hiding.

"Your hair looks good today, sweetie," I said with a faint smile and she inspected herself in the mirror to check if anything was wrong. "Did you bring those holo-glasses with you? To return?"

"Yes…" Izzy said with an ounce of hesitation.

"Good," I replied. "You remember our deal?"

"I remember," she said absently and shook her head. "Yeah Dad, I mean, that would be good. Thank you. It means a lot."

"My pleasure. You know that I'd do anything for my family," I smiled lightly, "even the little monster over there."

We both looked over and caught Theo picking his nose and trying to subtly put it in his mouth.

"Tissue, Theo?" I said passing the same packet I'd used to help Raven.

"The light is green," he said smugly.

"And so is your snot," I grunted, before stalling the car, something I hadn't done in years. I gripped the wheel and moved on swiftly. Within a matter of minutes I was at their school. Theo left with a quick hug and Izzy gave me a vague wave and half smile as she disappeared through the gate.

I needed to sort out these dreams.

I got back in the car and took out my phone. The holo-screen lit up and I altered the connection options. The phone flashed, signalling that it had bonded with the car. I flipped my hand over the screen and choose 'Maps'. A bird's eye view of the surrounding area rose to the surface with a small black car at the centre.

I asked the phone where the 'Sprint Finish' pub was and the lights spun briefly and then revealed the most efficient route from the school. I started my journey and the system corrected my direction if I ever drove off course, allowing me to sink into my deeper thoughts without risk of hitting someone again.

This dreams had never been as bad as last night. I'd always presumed it was an invention of an overactive and stressed mind. However, I'd found out yesterday that the people from my dream were real and suddenly it developed. The dream provided new information that I had barely been able to take in.

Raven on the run, wounded and then imprisoned, which seemed logical with her current status as an apparent terrorist.

There was also this green-eyed man. I'd seen a moment of his past in startling detail, but surely this vision was merely inspired by the scene on the television?

It was all a result of an extremely vivid subconscious part of my brain going into overdrive whilst I slept.

Everything else was fantastical creation. All the destruction, death and torture was born from the remembrance of Old Street.

What about that voice that spoke to me? It was simple really. It was nothing more than my own subconscious counter-acting and enhancing the spectres in my stressed mind.

I laughed to myself. My mind was way too wild. I needed a break to relieve myself from all this mad stress. As soon as this presentation was over, I would book a holiday, as far away from everything as possible.

Except this time I'd take my family with me.

The 'Sprint Finish' came into view on the corner of the street and Mark Bolton was outside waiting smoking an electric cigarette. Bolt lifted a heavy black bag and placed it in the boot of my car. His e-cigarette flashed red as he inhaled one final drag of the device before placing it in his top pocket. He breathed out a slow nicotine-stained cloud of steam.

My mind flashed back to seeing Raven slowly dying in that frozen prison cell last night. The way she breathed out a thick column of steam was haunting...

I shook away the disgusting thought.

"Morning, Bolt," I called as he fell into my car for the first time.

"Hart," he said smiling as we set off. "Don't you find it odd hanging out like this? Me coming to your place of work, instead of the other way round?"

"We're not hanging out. We're working." I replied.

"Oh really? Does that mean you're going to pay me?"

"I am paying you…" I said uncertainly. "In a way."

"I'm only teasing. Should be an interesting week."

"I will give you that, but I honestly don't find this odd. Besides you've been round my house for dinner before."

"Adele sure does cook a great spaghetti bolognese."

"Thanks…" I murmured. "I'll tell her that."

It was just a shame it was the same meal she cooked every other day of the week. I bet the kids were getting sick of it too.

"Once we've finished business I will cook for you," I said.

"Now that will be sight for sore eyes…"

"What did you do about work?" I asked.

"Hired a kid," he snorted. "Not too bright, but a good lad. I think he's a bit scared of me. Reckon he's afraid I'll batter him with my spare leg," Bolt laughed half-heartedly. "The fear of my looming peg-leg should keep him from mucking about behind my bar!"

"Is that what's in the bag?" I said indicating the boot.

"It's a surprise. I wasn't sure what I would need to bring. So… I've brought everything."

"Everything?"

"You'll see, Hart," he said as he relaxed and looked at me. "I don't mean to be rude, but for the last two days you've looked absolutely shattered. Are you not sleeping?"

"Been having some really bad dreams. I was yelling my head off. Wouldn't wake up and scared the hell out of my family. I wisely decided to sleep on the sofa for the rest of the night."

"Sounds familiar," grunted Bolt. "I was like that once I got back from hospital. For the first couple months I was dreaming about all sorts of stuff…"

"Oh yeah? Like what?" I asked curiously.

"Take a guess," he said coldly. I glanced across at Bolt's dark expression. He looked towards the distant Circuit Road and the ruins that it held within its concrete grasp.

"Hold that thought, this is exactly what I'm looking for! Sorry, I probably should explain. I'm going to scan your brain to try and analyse your memories."

"Brilliant," mumbled Bolt. "Sounds a little bit like more psychotherapy."

"We're here," I told him as we pulled through the security gate.

The Cain Corporation building towered over our heads as we entered the car park. It used to be a derelict office block until Vincent Cain claimed it for his operations. He transformed the building into his hub for the Corporation. Each floor had a different department, which provided hundreds of jobs for the growing city. The building itself had been re-fashioned, with long panels of glass that stretched along the side. The foundations were improved which allowed for basement space. Similarly, several newer floors were built on top of the old to increase the height of the building.

I reminded myself to visit the canteen that only sold processed food to talk to Richard Glass about his progress on his holo-glasses. It would certainly cheer Izzy up if I gave her some news on the upcoming technology. It was a shame I had to meet in the canteen. I never liked the so-called food there and always made a conscious effort to go out for some un-processed lunch.

We entered the large glass doors and I pressed my hand against the wall panel to be buzzed into the building. A Cain security officer spotted us through the glass and he hit a button to let us in. The door hissed aside and the foyer to Cain Corporation opened up in front of us.

The foyer was an open space that was always difficult to fully absorb at first glance. The floor was solid white marble that gleamed against the neon lights. Two tall green glass lifts stood on either side of the room and stretched all the way up to the sixth floor. Balconies grew out from these lifts in several layers that ringed the entire room.

The lift carried us to the third floor and I walked along the balcony. I peered briefly over the edge and down at the foyer. It was a long way down. We moved through the nearest door, along a white corridor, took a right at the end and finally arrived at my lab. The sight of the familiar clouded door sent a tinge of warmth through my body. It was good to be home. The scanner above the door sent a line of blue light over my body. It was quicker than scanning my hand, which had swiftly become repetitive.

Bolt heaved his bag onto a nearby desk and gradually began to pull out its contents. There were five different legs that ranged from basic to more complex designs.

"This is the simplest," he said holding up a thin design. "Thigh, joint, shin, joint and foot. No springs. No sensors. It was the first leg I got after… everything. I wouldn't leave the house at that time so nobody really got to see it."

He dismissed one leg as un-important and picked up another.

"Once I got this I decided to run the pub again. It took a while to walk like I used to. It was important to me that nobody would notice anything different. Although for the most part I stayed behind the bar," Bolt passed me the limb so I could see the joints in more detail. "Instead of using springs they actually use a thick gel in the ankle. It balances differently as it knows when it's facing down. It's like it has its own sense of gravity. It's sturdy and feels like I'm actually making a step."

Bolt reached down, un-clipped his left leg and passed it me. I lay down the other leg and felt the new one. It was heavy and hummed with electricity.

"This is the best one, but the most expensive and delicate," Bolt began to explain. "It has more joints, the gravity gel and smart responders. Also it has this skin-like texture to it, so that it looks real. Using the nerves in my thigh I can actually move the knee and ankle. It helps with last minute adjustments when I'm walking up a curb or into a car or those magnetic trains they have underground."

It felt like I had Bolt's entire life in his hands. It was difficult to imagine Bolt without a leg when he had disguised it so well.

"You're thinking how have I done it all these years, right?" Bolt said. "I get tired very quickly. I'm usually okay for about two hours, but then this leg needs to be charged every day, which puts me out of action. Personally I find the other legs on the market are too heavy or far too expensive."

I had the contacts and resources to get him the best new leg possible, which I should be able to provide as a parting gift. It was finding the connection that was going to be the real challenge.

"First things first, we need to scan everything and that includes your body, mind and prosthetics" I told him. "It should take about an hour. Would you please lie down on the scanner?"

The scanner looked like a padded massage table that buzzed from the technology underneath its surface. I tried to help Bolt up, but he wasn't having any of it. He climbed on and the straps secured themselves to his limbs and the bed rotated swiftly against the wall.

"Could've warned me that was going to happen, Hart!" Bolt yelled.

"I wanted a natural reaction as I'm recording everything from here on in. For instance..." I reached across and chose the sedative on a nearby surface. A clear panel appeared from the wall and formed a semi-circle around Bolt that enclosed him within a formed chamber. A light gas seeped in as the glass tube sealed.

"Breathe and slow your thought processes down," I told him.

"And how on earth am I meant to do that when you have me locked into this fancy coffin?"

"Just clear your mind, no need to be tense. Feel free to fall asleep. It shouldn't take too long."

"So just do nothing?" Bolt said sleepily, his voice muffled slightly.

"Nothing at all," I said smiling.

"Well that sounds good to..." Bolt head drooped and he began to snore.

I carried the six legs, including the one Bolt had been wearing, to a table near the central computer. I activated the scanner built into the surface and a blue light began to illuminate each leg. It searched every crevice of the limbs, whilst the table tilted slightly to weigh each one individually.

Moving to my central circular desk I turned on the main hologram, which swiftly brought up my blue brain I had been looking at yesterday. The desk separated and I stood in its centre.

The desk ringed around me and its surface glinted with capabilities.

I jumped into my music library and ran my fingers over music from the last thirty years since the technological Blackout. It was such a shame that all forms of digitalised music were obliterated after the Luna Rupture in the Global War. All that survived was vinyl and tapes. I finally settled on a recent track by an artist from Kubra. They were named 'Djembe Jazz', which was a subtle fusion of west African drumming combined with soulful dead American blues and modern Kubran vocals. It was the perfect reflection of the successful hybrid of culture that had formed in the boiling sands. I smiled faintly as it reminded me of my father who had originated from the great African city of Kubra.

I selected current events and watched as six vague shapes formed on my left and soon they were identified as prosthetics. Tapping my fingers into a holo-light keyboard, I asked the scanner to look for dates and companies that each of the legs belonged to. I wanted to see what was most comfortable and efficient to find some sort of compromise.

Mark Bolton's name finally rose to the surface.

"Slow system today…" I commented to myself.

I commanded the computer to enter multitask mode. The jobs would take slightly longer, but it meant I could work on them all at the same time. Another shape formed next to Mark's name and it quickly became apparent to be his body. It was strange to see him with only one leg. I told the scanner to go over his skeletal structure, his muscles, blood and then finally, and most importantly, his nerves. Once that was finished it could move on to a detailed scan of his brain.

I touched a glowing violet button and the floor split underneath me. My chair rose up, unfurled and I settled comfortably into its swivelling embrace. I leant back horizontally in my chair as the computer worked. The hologram above glittered fanatically, whilst the surrounding ringed desk pulsed as the projectors emitted from its surface. The intuitive computer filled in all the details and the scanners began to re-create digitalised copies of Mark's body, mind and legs.

I felt my phone buzz in my pocket. It made me jump and I wished I had turned it off once I'd entered the lab. I opened up the device and it showed that it was an unidentified number. I pushed my phone into a nearby slot and a small section of the hologram opened up next to my comprehensive music library.

"System. Answer phone," I said.

There was no response.

"System. Music volume down," I told the computer and rose vertically in my chair. Again, there was silence, but as I strained closer I heard the dull fizz of static noise through my speakers.

"Hart. It's me…" said a muffled voice. "Is it safe?"

"This is a secure line," I said slowly keeping my voice down low, even though I knew no one could hear.

"Is it safe from Cain?" They asked.

"Only I have access to this line. Who is this and how did you get this number?"

"You helped me and I helped you yesterday," they explained quickly.

It was Raven.

"Sorry, you surprised me," I said. "I wasn't expecting anyone to call."

"You said I could," she said, her smug smile beaming over the line.

"I didn't think you would!" I laughed

"But yeah, I did… I am."

I noticed a small red light next to the phone call in the hologram that gave me the option to alert security.

"So what can I do for you today?" I asked.

"Do you know who I am now?" Raven said cautiously.

"I know what the news has told me," I shrugged.

"Are you going to report me?"

The red light wrinkled in my peripheral vision, like a stationary apocalypse on the way to work.

"No… I'm not," I told her.

"You should probably report me," said the terrorist.

"You don't seem like the type of person who would torch Old Street and kill hundreds of innocent people," said the Doctor in return.

I heard Raven laugh roughly. I could almost hear her stomach rumbling from here.

"You wanted to buy me lunch?" Raven asked.

"And talk to you again," I amended.

"Yes, well, you did say that too, however I'm starving for an egg and cress sandwich and a bag of chips."

"Egg and cress?!"

"Doctor said I should eat my greens."

"I guess I did offer. I just presumed you'd want something more filling…" I stopped myself mid-speech as a new notification appeared on my hologram. There was someone at the door. They had the authority that allowed them access to the lab, but the person was requesting entry.

"Hart? You there?" Raven asked.

"I'm not sure. Please hold," I joked lightly.

"What's going on? Should I go?"

"No, it's okay, just wait one moment…"

I brought up the door camera and I was able to see my visitor. He seemed to be wearing a long pale coat that tugged at my memory. He looked up into the camera and his two green piercing eyes shone down the lens. I gasped in shock as he knocked against the camera and smiled. His white eyebrows moved questioningly.

I muted and hid the phone call from view, before turning the music down even further.

"You're muted," I told the girl. "You are welcome to stay on the line, Raven. I have a visitor who may interest you."

I reached up to the door authorization and grabbed the green light that let the broken man from my dreams inside.

6 – Dream Friends

"Doctor William Hart?" The man with haunting eyes asked coyly.

"That's me," I said as strong as I could to the man who had been haunting me as long I could remember. "Can I help you?"

"I hope so. You are a Doctor after all, aren't you?" he said with a sharp smirk. It wasn't very funny, but I chuckled anyway.

He was so different to what I had expected. My dreams had showed me a dishevelled man being led through prison. His body was lean and well toned and was much younger than I thought he would be. He wore a white three-quarter-length coat that looked impossibly light as it flowed around him. He walked slowly around the room, allowing me to inspect him for the first proper time. He dressed smartly, like Quayin did, but with a white-buttoned shirt and black tie. His trousers were dark, but they weren't pristine clean. As I looked at his general appearance, I realised that these clothes was working attire. He was formal, but also military.

The man moved with a strange grace that was almost ghostlike as he drifted across the room. He placed a hand on the scanner that held the sleeping Mark Bolton. He glanced at Bolt's vitals that remained regular and oblivious to the guest in my lab. Bolt's heartbeat continued to strum naively.

"That's a friend of mine. He's sleeping whilst I carry out a scan."

"So I can see," he said vaguely indicating the hologram. "It's truly amazing the work you are doing here. I hope Lucy didn't disturb you too much yesterday."

"Only a little," I admitted. "She can be quite firm."

The man laughed at this.

"I think you're being polite, Doctor. Lucy Quayin is well known to be an abrasive person. She usually gets what she wants with the exact amount of force. I believe it's the key reason she has done so well in our little business."

He looked at me properly for the first time since he entered the room. He was the strangest looking man I'd ever met; his hair was snow white and skin was smooth and pale, which again made his age difficult to determine. The pale hair contrasted those green eyes that pierced everything they saw.

"You're staring at me, Doctor," he said bemused. "Is it my appearance?"

"Were you from Luna?" I asked cautiously as I looked at his stark white hair. All the citizens of Luna, the great city on the moon, had developed pale hair and flesh as a combination of sun deprivation and a fashion statement to contrast from those on Earth.

It was always jarring to encounter a survivor of a dead great city.

"A curious question, however, no, I'm not Lunan," he said with a sad smile. "My colleague Pierre Foshe is though. You should ask him about the dead great city if you find the courage. I certainly haven't dared ask him about it yet. You should be careful with such questions though, Doctor Hart."

"I did not mean to offend…" I said quietly as those eyes pierced my own.

"My appearance," he commented as he gestured towards his hair and eyes carefully, "is a result of a childhood incident. I'm told it was due to a technological calamity. Reckless people using reckless power. Something I cannot abide."

His voice was cold and calm, as he studied my response. He twisted a slim metal ring slowly around his finger that held an engraving of a crimson cross.

"You look like you've seen a ghost," he commented.

"Sorry. It's been a mad morning. I was just getting started…"

"My apologies," he nodded at Bolt, comatose in the glass coffin. "Would you like me to leave?"

"I'm just curious as to why you are here? I didn't catch your name… I see you have clearance from Miss Quayin, but…"

"Forgive me. I was trying to be polite and ask your permission to enter and I completely forgot to even hold an official introduction."

"It's quite alright," I said trying to disguise my nerves.

"I am here to inspect your work and I see that it is progressing well with Mark Bolton. I'm personally extremely interested in your studies in neuro-science and I look forward to seeing the results on Friday."

My heart thundered in my chest. This man didn't miss a single beat.

"Unfortunately, I'm also here to ask you some questions," he continued. "Yesterday you hit someone with your car?"

Now this was the real reason he was here. I swallowed thickly and summoned my courage.

"I asked for your name and you haven't given it. You can understand why I might be slightly nervous with security so tight in the building. It is only fair that you give me your name. This is my space and my time."

My brain buzzed furiously as I surprised myself at how forward I had been. The man's eyes glinted at my bravery. He took a seat.

"We all have many names. Here, in the Corporation, they call me Xander. You can do the same. I work alongside Vincent, but I think you already knew that."

I nodded in response.

"My personal history is none of your concern, however I can tell you details about my professional relationship with the Cain Corporation. I joined in the aftermath of Old Street. I was lost, serving time in Prima's prison, until Vincent gave me purpose. Together, we ended the incident. My work is issued directly from him as private assignments. Any information obtained is reported back as I wish. It provides an edge of freedom. Anything you say to me will likely be fed into Vincent's ear."

"You are a mercenary for hire?" I asked coldly.

"I'm not like the others in his employ. I'm more similar to a consultant on private salary, but yes, mercenary crudely covers the job description."

"Why were you in prison?" I asked shakily and Xander's eyebrows arched lightly in response. I regretted my direct question immediately.

66

"I brought an end to someone who had lost control," Xander answered simply and my mind curled darkly. "I brought myself to prison, so I could never hurt anyone ever again."

"And now you are out?" I asked further.

"I work with Vincent to ensure no-one loses control ever again," Xander said firmly and my questioning ceased. "Are you satisfied, Doctor Hart?"

"Yes, thank you," I murmured. "Should I tell you about my life…?"

"I already know who you are. Impressive education in Advanced Neuro-Science and Robotics. Very interesting family you have too. Present and past," he said and I felt my hand curling into a fist. "My questions will not take long."

I sat at my desk and moved the hologram so Xander could look at me directly.

"I hit someone with my car yesterday," I said very conscious of the hidden phone call still running behind me. "I looked after them to make sure they were okay. They didn't want an ambulance. They left and promised not to sue me."

"I have security footage of your conversation," his hand touched my hologram and footage seeped from an olive-glowing device in his ear and flowed into view. We watched as I tended to Raven's wounds. "Usually we can collect everything we need with lip-reading and body-language analysis, however your car obscured the majority of the conversation."

"We spoke about the importance of the day and the silence that would be happening later," I confirmed.

"What did she say to you?" Xander asked, his eyes drifting slightly.

"She was sad," I replied.

"Sadness isn't in her vocabulary. I think you may have misunderstood her sadness for guilt, Doctor."

"I know what I saw. The incident depressed her."

I hoped my lie was as good as it sounded.

"Are you aware of who you were talking to?" Xander asked whilst his eyes burrowed into mine.

The words escaped my mouth entirely. My brain pounded

67

with my heart and then it stopped as I realised I could just be honest.

"I didn't know who it was. She told me her name was Raven and after watching the news later, I realised that I'd aided a terrorist," I swallowed loudly. "Are you here to arrest me?"

Xander rubbed his fingers together. His head tilted and he let his touch flow onto his ring again. His nail etched into the red cross as he thought to himself.

"If this Raven character ever tries to contact you again, then you must inform me straight away. Failure to do so will result in serious consequences beyond my control. I hope that is understood. I have already sent my contact details over," he said indicating the hologram, which glimmered green.

"I understand you perfectly, Xander."

"It's been a pleasure," he said whilst getting up and began to leave the room. He turned, his coat swaying with the movement. "I appreciate your honesty, Doctor Hart."

I moved to shake his hand until my eyes settled on his ring one last time. The symbol flashed into my mind. I'd seen it somewhere before...

During a teenage research excursion, I had travelled to Lockroy, the Antarctican great city, and visited an auction house. There had been a ancient painting on sale created by Jan Porcellis in the 1600's of an immense ship in rough seas bearing the same symbol on it's flag.

"That's the Albion cross," I said quietly and Xander's face grew emotionless. "The red cross is the ancient English flag. When London became the great city Albion, their flag became black with a red cross."

"You're observant. A quality I can appreciate. Tell me, Doctor?" Xander said coldly. I stared into those eyes and I saw that I stumbled into some delicate information. "During the Fall, how did all of those people die?"

"At the end of the Global War, Albion was destroyed in a..."

"Technological calamity," Xander, survivor of the Fall of Albion, said severely. "Reckless people with reckless power. I hope you are not a reckless man, William. I cannot abide that."

"I'm an informed man," I told him as firmly as possible. "I make my decisions based on logic. This technology could change the world and I must be the one at the helm to steer it in the right direction."

"I'm really looking forward to your presentation," Xander said and smiled lightly at my answer. "It's going to be life changing."

I blinked slowly and the man from Albion was already leaving, as the double doors closed behind him.

I fell into my chair in relief and brought the hologram back up. I found the hidden call and stared at it for a while. My head told me to hang up, but my heart made me un-mute the call.

"Raven?" I asked into the system.

"Still here," she replied shakily.

"I think we need to talk."

"I should go…"

"No," I hesitated again. "I'll meet you in Central Plaza for lunch at midday."

The other end of the phone was static for a while and then it suddenly became silent. Raven had hung up.

I looked back at the hologram and saw that Bolt's scan still had another hour to go. I turned the Kubran music back onto full volume as Bolt continued to sleep. He would remain sedated until I returned.

I stood, carefully collected my coat and walked out of the lab, down the corridor, down the lift, through the foyer, out of the front door and left the building. I entered my car and drove in numb silence to Central Plaza.

My thoughts were relatively quiet, before rising to thunderous madness. I made myself calm down. This was important. I had to meet Raven again. My frightening meeting with Xander should have warned me away, but it encouraged me to strive forwards. I wasn't fully sure why, but something deep inside told me that I had to. It tugged at the corners of the brain and encouraged my course of action.

Central Plaza was busy. People streamed in from all sides of the space. There were at seven roads leading into the pedestrian area, which created an immense collision of passing people.

At the centre of it all was 'Tria Fata' fountain that was decorated with several marble statues. The monument was named 'Tria Fata' or 'Nono-Decima-Morta' after the three Sisters of Fate that controlled the thread of life according to Greek mythology. It was a faith that had emerged seven decades ago and was followed avidly by many sects across the globe. The faith of the Fates had risen in the last thirty years after the end of the Global War. It was common to thank or curse the Fates in present day. The Tria Fata fountain in Central Plaza represented the movement of birth into life and finally into death that had occurred within Prima.

The figures in the fountain's embrace were celebrating the initial construction of Prima over fifty years ago. They stood in a defiant tableau against the rest of the world. The fantastical scene occurred in the year 2051 when the central European nations decided to band together and generate a brand new city on their joint borders. The severe tensions that had been building worldwide over the last few decades were finally reaching breaking point. War was imminent and people needed to come together for protection against the violent and various invading forces that were vying to expand geographically, financially, politically and digitally. Prima was a symbol of unity in a century full of backstabbing between nations.

They had no idea that the devastating Global War and the following technological Blackout was just around the corner. It was an event that would completely change the landscape of the planet.

In the tableau, several older individuals dragged their corrupted towns and cities of various European origin towards the centre. Meanwhile, three younger individuals, two men and one woman, were starting the construction of the central complex that would serve as Prima's hub. I recognised one of the figures as Vincenzo, Vincent Cain's grandfather, who had co-founded the great city with his vast finance. I noticed the miraculous detail of the miniature marble airport, Central Plaza and Old Street. Water flowed from the fingertips of the three founders and signified the life that had grown from the merging of several contrasting civilisations.

Several other merged cities had been formed before, during and after the Global War.

Swiftly after the construction of Prima in central Europe, there was Kubra. The birth of new technology called the Core had triggered the creation of the solar and geothermal powered society within the Sahara desert that had finally begun to unite the ten nations of northern Africa. Once the Global War had struck Kubra, they had gained three more nations, Arabia, Coast and Republic, which lead to severe over-population. Once the conflict was finally over… four entire nations had been destroyed. To this day, Kubra was still the most populated great city and was now run by a democratic Capital, which managed communication between the nine remaining nations and hordes of refugees within it's vast borders.

Lockroy in Antarctica became the next great city. Directly below South America, it served as the largest port in the entire world. It became a hive of industrious activity in the frozen wasteland that provided hundreds of thousands of jobs. This city beyond the central continents had been forged due to the influx of growing mass-production businesses that needed space to expand. The tundra to the south of Lockroy held vast expanses of land for global businesses to cement their factories, industries and offices into the icy earth. It was generally regarded as a lawless and filthy city, but my own personal time as a teenager there disregarded this idea. Their culture was strange, but obeying their ways often wielded rich rewards. They had their unique law system set in place that they called 'The Code.' The entire great city was run using strict laws originally generated in ancient America, likening it to the 'Wild West in the Tundra'. This appeared to be brutal externally, but actually highly efficient internally. Criminals were dealt swift justice for their crimes and loyal citizens were rewarded richly. During my time there, I travelled to Rothschild Island to the west of the Lockroy peninsula where I saw the remnants of their greatest achievement, an immense space lift that remained unfinished. Its great pylons stretched eagerly to the sky to no avail. Construction had ceased after the need for the lift into space had very quickly died out…

A few years later, the immense city of Amazonia was born. It had rapidly harvested itself into the once colossal rainforest and signified the potent capital of the united South American nations. It was also home to the 'Shrine of Life', the tallest building in the world that was a staggering 3,112 feet high. The monumental tower stood at the centre of Amazonia and was seen as the symbol of faith towards the Sisters of Fate that had caused the creation of this 'Tria Fata' fountain. As you step inside the Shrine of Life, a wide circle of silver threads are pinned to the foundations and soared to the very top pinpoint of the building. The threads entwined and knotted to create the perfect architecture, completely immune to any seismic activity. The Oracle of Fate that lived there proclaimed the colossal building was held in position by these threads. Rumours quickly spread that these threads were actually spider webs. Scandal and critical slandering obviously followed this statement. Men of science from abroad met with the Oracle and hurriedly analysed the threads to judge the structurally integrity of the almighty Shrine.

Analysis concluded that they were indeed webs, but genetically engineered from Darwin's Bark spiders harvested from the now sunken island of Madagascar. The Shine of Life was a wondrous display of art, science and faith coming together in perfect unison.

Several other great cities had sprung up during the Global War and reached their demise by the end of it, such as Mengxiang and Albion, which were natural evolutions of Shanghai and London. Meanwhile New York had grown taller and deeper than anyone could have comprehended, however it fell and sunk the hardest of all the great cities.

Last of all there was Luna, the marvelled great city on the moon. The citizens of white skin and frail bodies that was technologically years ahead of everyone else on the planet below. They refused to share their power. Some say that prolonged the Global War, but in the end their sacrifice brought a swift end to the conflict with the Luna Rupture.

I sighed sadly. Their existence was too brief to be considered another great modern cities.

Finally there was the newest Antarctican city of Eden that was situated on the opposite side of the continent to Lockroy. It rested on the Bald Coast and viewed the turbulent Indian Ocean. The city was fully formed after the Global War by those who had become refugees from all the destruction. Since its initial founding, it had quickly become an impressive base for human advancement. Eden's primary focus was largely on protecting the Earth's health and researching new projects. It had created an impressive tunnel that allowed passage from Eden to Tasmania and further onto Australia. They were also currently beginning construction for passage to New Zealand. This allowed transport to flow from the Asian continent, into Eden and across a tunnel that ploughed through the South Pole, onto Lockroy and finally ferried across to the edge of South America.

The world was becoming more connected with each passing year.

The flickering liquid splattered noiselessly in the intense crowd. I observed the hurried crowd that seemed to completely ignore the history of the world. I sighed heavily at their ignorance. I peered around and quickly became lost within the senseless crowd.

It would be impossible to spot Raven in all of this chaos.

Suddenly the smell of grilled bacon thrilled my nostrils and I spotted a nearby sandwich bar. My stomach growled and decided it was hungry. I placed my order and sat at a table outside the sandwich bar so I could keep an eye out for Raven.

There was no sign of her yet, but perhaps I was early. I flicked out my phone. It was half past twelve. I was late. I must have missed her. I sighed as my order arrived and hunger hit me like a drum. There was a bacon and fried egg sandwich for myself, which Adele certainly wouldn't approve of, and a solitary egg and cress sandwich with a portion of chips. Hunger gripped me and I began to unwrap my sandwich. I heard the chair opposite me move and saw a quick hand grab the food.

"Thanks, Doc," Raven said as she unwrapped her sandwich.

I sat back in mild surprise, taken back by how easily she had snuck up on me. She had changed drastically since yesterday. She wore a simple blue zip hoody and styled her hair and make-up to suit the fashion other Priman girls wore. Her hair was ripped back into a vicious ponytail that hid her dreadlocks with practised skill. She also wore strange black eye make-up that flowed outwards in elegant flicks. It was a dramatic look I'd seen Lucy Quayin wear several times. Normally I would've said she looked pretty, but it didn't suit Raven and she knew it. She smiled at me crudely as I observed her disguise. It felt like she put it on sarcastically to mimic society.

"Good afternoon to you too! Oh, and can you call me Hart or William, please? Doctor is too formal."

Raven ignored me and took out a silver lighter and played with it in her hands. It had a engraving along the side, which I couldn't see. She traced her index finger along the etchings privately. I hadn't seen a proper lighter in years as the majority of smoking these days was done through electric cigarettes. The nicotine level was actually higher in the electric devices and made the subject even more addicted.

"Would you mind not smoking?" I asked. "I don't want my wife smelling it on me."

"I wasn't going to," she snapped. "It would go against the new look I've got going. Besides… it was my Dad's lighter."

"Oh right. Sorry." I said shamefully.

"I don't need your apology. You weren't there, were you?"

"No. I wasn't," I said quietly.

"Let's cut to the chase, Doc," she said ignoring my earlier request. "You're making me nervous. You knock me down, apparently clueless that I'm a known fugitive and then you let me listen in on a conversation with Xander."

I didn't have anything to say so I continued to eat my sandwich, humming with pleasure as the egg yolk burst in my mouth.

"You can understand if I'm a tad suspicious," she said.

"It's pretty simple really, Raven. I don't believe what the news says about you." I was unsure about the words as soon as they left my mouth. "I don't believe that you're dangerous."

Raven was silent for a moment and continued to eat her sandwich whilst she kept a casual eye scanning the plaza.

"Well... I am dangerous, however your confidence in me is inspiring."

"Okay... not comforting at all... so who are you exactly?"

"How do I know you aren't working directly for Cain? You could easily be part of a convoluted plan to drag me in. You pretend to knock me down, save me, buy me lunch and then you bag and tag me like the rest."

"You don't believe that."

"Are you so sure?"

"Yes, otherwise you wouldn't have turned up."

"It was free lunch," Raven shrugged. "Can't say no to a free lunch."

"I would have reported you by now. Besides... you trust me."

"Oh really? And how did you figure that out?

"Because you're eating the free lunch that could easily be poisoned."

Raven took the smallest moment to observe the food, before she continued to wolf it down.

"What do you want?"

"Something told me to trust you. I saw you and didn't see anything bad. I think Cain is wrong."

"Brave words. But I'm only going to ask once more then I'm gone. What do you want?"

"I want to know who you are, Raven."

She snorted and continued to eat her sandwich. I waited until she finished and she began diving into the piping hot chips. I expected her to gasp as they hit the roof of her mouth and wave frantically in a vague attempt to cool the meal down. She didn't flinch as the searing hot chunk of potato was flung into her waiting mouth. She scoffed the chips down and didn't even seem to register their temperature. I watched Central Plaza with her, but I couldn't see what she did. Her eyes seemed to grab small details that mine had grown to ignore with age.

"I was there when it happened," she said. "My memory is hazy, but I was there."

"In Old Street?"

"Yeah. My folks died in the explosion."

"I'm sorry…"

"Don't be. I'm better off without them," she said coldly. "After the chaos I struck out on my own. I did the best I could. Certain people were after me, even back then, so I kept a low profile. I didn't do very well. I had no idea what I was doing, but I got better over time. I took what I could from the city. I shoplifted. Food mostly…"

"This isn't exactly filling my self-confidence that you are good person."

"Why am I not in a cell right now? I am literally waiting to see any of Cain Corp walk around that corner."

I remembered my dream and how Xander had dragged her unconscious body to a cell…

"Go on," I said.

"There are people in the city like me. People with nowhere else to go after the incident. One day they found me begging on the street and said they could keep me out of trouble. I eventually agreed, which was probably the stupidest mistake I've ever made. They were good to me, but I knew I'd only get them into trouble," she said hesitantly as she worked out whether to trust me more. "The people up high have deemed some of us unfit to live. We are fugitives who ended worse off after the incident and it's easier for us to just stay under the radar all together."

"That's who Cain is looking for…"

"Yes, Xander hunts us down people connected with the incident. He's very good at catching people. He's a very persistent man. He works for Cain and his two others thugs, a big disgusting Russian called Anton Stranz and another creepy Lunan named Pierre Foshe. Listen to more news. You'll know who I mean. They want to round up anyone that wasn't identified after the incident. They think we have something to do with what happened."

"And did you? Do you?" I asked.

"All these questions will get you in a cell."

"It's a reasonable question."

"One I shouldn't have to answer."

"Fine. You were talking about your friends?

"The Outcasts found and saved me. I tried to live on the streets alone, but I didn't know how. They brought me in as one of their own. They looked after me, fed me, gave me a place to stay. Gave me jobs to do. They taught me stuff. How to fight and how to survive."

"I haven't heard of them…"

"We call ourselves the Outcasts because no one else wanted us anymore. We prefer to stay hidden. Suits us better. They move base every few months like nomads. They could be anywhere right now," she finished her chips and sank into her chair.

"But you are not with them anymore. You're living alone again."

"Like I said… biggest mistake I made was joining them. Having me around only puts people in danger. It's safer this way. I don't want anyone else to getting hurt because they want to protect me. So I looked after myself because no one should have that burden."

"And here you are. Talking to me."

"Here I am. The apparent terrorist."

"So what was your other name? Before everything. Your real one?"

"None of your damn business. These questions! Seriously? This will put you in danger, Doc. The lunch is much appreciated, but this has to stop right here. The reason I'm telling you this so you can see that our worlds are different. This must be the last time we speak, otherwise it won't end well for you," Raven pulled herself back up to look at me. "How's the brain probing going anyhow?"

"It isn't probing! It's just… scanning," I said horrified and she laughed at my reaction. "I've got a friend in to help me now. He lost his leg in the incident…"

"I'd be careful if I were you," Raven warned.

"He's a close friend. I trust him," I replied.

"You could be cracking a rotten nut there. Some things are forgotten for a reason."

"Mark remembers everything after the incident. I'm just asking him to re-visit some of his memories."

"Really?" Raven said sarcastically. "Then ask him what the first thing he remembers is. I've seen it before with the Outcasts. The survivors of Old Street are made to forget their past. It helps them adapt. Makes them normal. Most of them can't remember a thing. But when they do remember, they end up screaming that their memories hurt too much."

Raven sat up suddenly alert and got to her feet to collect a bag she had at her feet. She bent down to tie her shoelaces. I looked away and ate my sandwich slowly, relishing in the still warm bacon. She stood up casually and then began to walk away.

"What if I need to talk to you again?" I asked her.

"You won't."

Raven stepped forward into the crowd and it swiftly consumed her. I heard her voice say, "Don't worry, Doctor Hart. I'll be keeping an eye on you."

"How…" I tried to spot her in the crowd, but she was gone. The rivers of people briefly dispersed and I saw a blue hoody left abandoned on the floor.

She was gone.

I fell back into my chair and let my head roll up. Thick black clouds consumed the sun. They spread out over the sky in thick tendrils enveloping any sign of the day. The clouds flashed and rumbled slightly. It looked like it was going to rain later.

7 – Progress

"I can't believe you knocked me out!" Bolt said as he crashed into a nearby chair.

"I wanted natural results so I had to catch you off guard…" I smirked.

"You do realise that counts as assault," he chuckled darkly as he thwacked my upper arm, which stung brutally from his blow. "I'm kidding! But try and ask me next time."

"That somewhat defeats the purpose of my research…" I mumbled.

Bolt ignored my comment, rolled his shoulders and twisted his neck, before grabbing a leg from the table and swiftly strapping it to his body. He attached it with a precision that could only be gained from years of practice.

"So what did you find out?" Mark asked.

"What?" I replied.

"The test," he said bluntly. "The reason I was knocked out in the first place?"

"Oh right," I said shaking my head. I thrust my hands up and pulled down all the previous files I had laid out before lunch. The scans were, for the most part, complete. Detailed versions of Bolt's legs hovered on the far left. They rotated slowly and each of them came apart to show their constructs and components. Bolt's body hovered on the right with several options nearby that allowed me to view his functions in detail. His skeleton, muscles and nerves were all ready for viewing, however his blood network was still assimilating. His brain was also floating nearby. I highlighted it red to identify it differently from my own blue brain, which hovered next to it. I moved back to Bolt's body and selected the option to view his central nervous system. His synapses glistened instantly overhead. My next step would be to compare and contrast his body with the other two brains in my system and see how they reacted.

Bolt had been sitting in silence whilst I worked. I kept

forgetting that I wasn't working alone anymore.

"I don't know any results yet," I told him. "I went out for lunch."

"Wonderful…" he mumbled with a look of disappointment falling over his face. His eyebrows curled and his mouth opened in disbelief. "Wait. You left me in that tube on my own?!"

"It was fine. You were asleep and snoring. You didn't notice a thing."

"I don't snore," he announced adamantly.

I replied by reaching into the hologram and found the appropriate sound file. A soft rumble played through the speakers and the recorded sound waves rumbled throughout the lab. I turned up the volume. The recording of Bolt snoring filled the room making my point impossible to ignore.

"Fine. I do snore," he said sulking, "but you still shouldn't have left me."

"It won't happen again," I said, "but it was important." I looked at my confused friend, sighed, and gave him my full attention. "A member of Cain Corporation came in here asking some questions about my work," I told him attempting to leave the details out. "Once he left I got a phone call… it was someone who inspired me to bring you in here in the first place. I had to meet with them again."

"Sounds terribly vague…" Bolt mumbled.

"The less you know the better." I told him.

"If that's what you want," he shrugged. "I am here for the rest of the week, if you change your mind."

"I need to ask you some questions, Bolt," I said changing the topic quickly. "Could you sit still for a second?"

I ran the sensors through the chair Bolt was sat in. It pulled him back so that he was now lying down to face the ceiling. Bolt yelled out briefly in surprise and shot me a look of outrage for having surprised him twice now. I shrugged and laughed in response. Two sensors raised next to his head and I attached two wireless pads to his wrists to measure his pulse.

"How are you?" I asked him, as I pulled up a chair next to him.

"I am good, Doctor Hart. Other than being strapped…"

"Great!" I interrupted him to get over the formalities. "How old are you?"

Bolt sighed and shrugged. I could tell he thought this was going to be exactly like therapy.

"I'm 25," he looked at me through the corner of his eye and chuckled again. "You know I'm 35. It even says it on that bloody hologram…"

"Congratulations! Half way to 70," I interrupted him again and then softly asked him. "I want to talk to you about your legs."

"Finally…" he mumbled.

"Do you like them?"

"One of them. My one."

"And the others aren't yours?"

"No. No, they're not."

Bolt was blunt with this answer. An apology formed in my mouth but I threw it from my mind. This was work, but I needed to be careful to not hurt my friend's feelings.

"Are you happy?" I asked him.

"Hart…"

"Please, Bolt. Just try to relax and answer my questions."

"No. I'm not happy," he breathed out heavily and closed his eyes. I saw a flash of red out of the corner of my eye. It was Bolt's brain. I brought the image closer and linked the sensors on his wrists to the hologram to bring up an image of Bolt's pulse. It had returned to normal.

"I've been a lot worse," he continued.

"When do you recall being in your worst condition mentally?" I asked him as I continued to watch his brain.

"When I was first shown the new leg. They brought it in and laid it next to me. I couldn't even look at the thing."

"When was that, Bolt?"

There was a short silence as Bolt searched his memories. I watched it happen. The brain flashed once, a small dark red tendril starting to sneak up from the top of his spine and simmer into his cerebral cortex. I slowed the nerve reaction down and watched it search his mind.

81

"It was in hospital," he finally said. "I was there for a long time. All of us were."

"All of you?"

"Yeah. Me and others from the disaster were kept in the same room."

"For how long?"

His brain juddered again. The tendril circled around a spot in his brain and closed around it like a fist crushing a grape. "It was a month before the first of us were let out. It was too long in my opinion."

"When were you let out of the hospital?"

There was no answer. Bolt's heartbeat quickened and the nerve reaction sped up and flickered as his mind jittered.

"Bolt?" I asked again and turned around to look at him. He was struggling against the chair slightly, his body sweating and the veins straining against his skin.

"Hart, I can't…"

"Keep breathing deeply and remember when they gave you the leg. How long were you in there for?"

"I'm not sure. It was about two months after the incident took place when people were let out."

"You just said it was one month."

"No, I didn't…"

"I want to know when they let you out."

"It's hazy…" he said as his back arched slightly. I looked back at his vitals. They had to be wrong. I looked at Bolt again. His eyes were closed.

He was dreaming.

"Mark. Tell me. When was it hazy?" I asked him pushing him towards an answer.

"Generally," he said shakily his face twitching once. "I remember the room in the hospital. No visitors were allowed inside. They thought we might be infected. We were quarantined until they were sure they could let us go. They had so many questions, so many tests…"

"Do you remember coming home?"

"Yes," he said and briefly relaxed. I breathed out in relief and turned back to view his vitals. "I remember getting out of the taxi and walking towards the house. Sarah met me at the door. You remember Sarah?"

"She was nice. You were a great couple." I said absently as I marvelled at his capability of speech despite being in a state of unconsciousness.

"We were," he said with a smile in his voice. Bolt's heartbeat suddenly juddered and his brain mirrored the action. I turned back to face him again and I could see his eyes rolling behind his shut eyelids. "She couldn't take it, you know? My dreams became too much. She said that I was going mad in my sleep and I didn't believe her. So she recorded me one night. She showed me. I was… I was wild. Walking. Talking. Couldn't stop it. No matter what she tried. She used to try and slap me awake. Pinch me. Water. I used to wake up soaked in water and no idea why and then walk into the spare room and find Sarah sleeping there. One time she even used a tazer on me. It wasn't fair on her. I told her to leave for her own good. It was safer if I was on my own."

"I had no idea," I said quietly.

"Neither did I. Neither did…" he repeated.

"Did you feel you were safe before?" I interrupted cautiously.

"When?" Bolt asked, his eyebrow furrowing as he tried to remember.

"In the hospital? The room just after the incident?"

"What room are you talking about?" he said confused.

"When you were first given your leg?"

Bolt face relaxed as he remembered the hospital again, but then creased up at something.

"We were all there for such a long time," Bolt's body twitched again and fidgeted in the horizontal chair. "We weren't allowed visitors. I can't remember. Why can't I remember?"

I looked back at the vitals and his heartbeat was accelerating and the nerves in his brain jumped and flashed madly.

"Mark, I need you to breathe," I told him.

"There was the light and then the fire. The ground opened up. I was in the car and my brother was with me. Where did he go? My leg. I can't feel my leg. Get me out of here! Is anyone there?

Help me! It's so hot. I can't breathe. I can't see. It's so dark. I'm burning, the fire is coming, the fire is coming to kill us all."

Bolt's body thrashed violently in the chair, his fist came down sharply and cracked it. I saw him viciously clench the side of the chair. The lab security activated and the lights flickered off, plummeting us into darkness.

The sensors flashed on, searching for the source of danger, thin red lines scanning and highlighting every last surface and crevice in the room. I swore to myself and hurriedly tried to turn the security off. The red scanners deactivated before they reached Bolt.

The blue hologram lit up my hands as they flashed over the holo-board. I typed madly, panicking in the moment, unable to fix the lights quick enough

"We weren't allowed visitors," said Bolt suddenly, his voice gruffer than before, his vocal chords crunching as they became stressed. "They gave me the leg and then they sent me away. Didn't need them. Don't need anyone."

I tired to grab his arm and calm him down, but he was moving about madly in the half darkness.

"Come back, Bolt! Snap out of it," I said touching his arm.

"Let me go! Where am I? Why can't I remember where I was?" Bolt screamed. I heard a tearing sound. It sounded like stone grinding against metal. In the marine darkness I saw a piece of the chair come away in Bolt's hand and fly into the nearby wall.

"What happened to you?" I muttered to myself, as I turned the scanners in the chair off. I heard the remaining straps snap as they came away from his body.

That was enough for today. I had to wake him up.

I grabbed his arms, but Bolt was much stronger and pushed back. His hands were rough and rubbed coarsely against my skin; they were more angular than I remembered. He thrashed against my strength as I tried to keep him in place. He roared out in anguish. It sounded like a whirlwind tearing its way through a gorge; a tortured cry of pain that I didn't even think Bolt was capable of.

We both fell and he landed on top and attempted to claw at my chest. We rolled into the wall and he howled as a cupboard dug into his spine. He kicked out and connected with my stomach. I hunched over on all fours winded, clutching my belly as Bolt flailed in the darkness. His shoe clumped next to my face and I grabbed his leg and hauled myself upwards. An arm rippled across my shoulder and I crunched against a nearby table. I scurried across the room, away from my mad friend into the light of the hologram.

Bolt's brain was completely different, it throbbed in quick dark pulses and the outline was different, as though something had changed externally. The scanner struggled to keep up with the strange changes and the image corrupted and disappeared. I spotted the red emergency lights. Bolt's heavy feet clumped again and I fell forwards over my computer. His rough hands scraped my back and I tumbled into the far wall. The switch for the lights rubbed against my palm and the room was suddenly lit up by blue neon lights.

The light was blinding and I heard Mark Bolton howl again. I squinted and saw his outline next to me, staggering as he clutched his head. His whole body contorted in pain. He was still sleeping, the nightmare of his past consuming his mind. He lashed out and pain slammed into the side of my head. My eyes blurred until I saw the water dispenser in the corner of the room.

With newfound purpose, I crawled away from Mark. His fist crunched the floor and I kicked back, connecting with his body. He grunted once and I heard him fall heavily. I rushed away and quickly got a cup full of water.

"Cut power!" I yelled out to avoid damage to the system and stop Mark being electrocuted. The lights went out again and I squinted in the darkness. Silence echoed throughout the room. I hoped this worked. Water was the only thing that woke him up in the past. A hum of electricity rippled against the nearest wall that continued to irritate my ear. My heart pounded quickly due to the influx of adrenaline and my blood rushing past my eardrums. I heard a footstep a metre to my left and I threw the water out as fast as I could.

"Lights on!" I shouted out.

The light blinded me again, but this time I shielded my eyes and blinked furiously to get my eyesight back. Mark was curled up on the floor, water dripping from his hair as he remained crouched on the floor. His eyes sprang open. He staggered and his head spun around, sending soaking wet tendrils across the floor.

"Sarah?" Mark asked shakily.

"It's me, William Hart. You're in my lab. It's okay. You're safe now."

He was shaking and he fell back. His shirt was completely torn, it looked like he had scratched at his chest in an attempt to get out of the scanner. I could even see some bloodied marks welling up on his chest. His hands were dark with filth; one of them was bleeding heavily from the knuckle.

"What happened?" Mark gasped.

"You had a nightmare," I explained. "I turned off the power and threw water over you. You're back now."

"Will? I don't know…"

"Don't talk. I'll show you the recording of your dream tomorrow. That's enough. No more work," I told him firmly, but Bolt stared at me dumbly, barely able to take in my words. I clutched my searing head and pointed sharply towards the door. "Go home, Mark. We're done for today."

8 – Cloudy Skies

The rain pounded the window, turning the garden into a wet blur of opaque water. My head throbbed as it had done all the way home. Adele clasped my shoulder, gently rubbing my back and then thrust a frozen sack of peas against my forehead. The ice burned against the cut on my head. Pain sliced into my brain.

"Adele! Please be careful."

"Don't tell me to be careful when you have blood pouring from your head."

"It's not pouring…"

"Well, it's certainly bleeding." Adele touched my chin to turn my face. I dragged my gaze from the stormy sky outside and looked into her eyes that were thick with worry.

"Why won't you tell me what happened, Will?" Adele asked.

"It's just work," I told her.

"This is not work. Talk to me."

"I promise I will tell you everything after dinner…" I said walking away.

"No. You're going to tell me right now," she said grabbing my arm roughly. I pulled away and met her gaze. She stopped and rubbed my arm gently. She sat me down, unpeeled a plaster and slowly applied it to my head.

"Mark hit me," I finally said.

"What? Why would he…"

"We've had to look at his past. It's a bit rougher than I thought it would be. I asked him a few questions and he slipped into a state of delirium. He couldn't stop himself. He was re-living the nightmare of the incident and he lashed out. And now my head is bleeding."

Adele couldn't look at me straight. She struggled to find her words. I knew that losing her parents still stung to this day and any mention of the incident often depressed her.

"He's okay," I continued. "He took a taxi home and told me he'd find his own way into work tomorrow. He needs some time to himself."

Adele smiled lightly to show that she was pleased that I'd been honest with her. I couldn't help notice how tense her shoulders were...

"Go call the kids and I'll get dinner," she echoed and closed the curtains that revealed the lashing rain, before disappearing into the kitchen. I walked to the stairs holding my head as my vision swayed. I inhaled deeply and exhaled in an exaggerated sigh to get my focus back.

"Izzy! Theo! Dinner is on the table."

I walked back and fell into my chair at the table. I shut my eyes for a moment, my head bobbing as sleep scratched my mind. I groaned as I remembered that I would have to sleep on the sofa again tonight.

I opened my eyes and my family had assembled around the table. They were all eating quietly. It was spaghetti bolognese again. Adele was solely focused on her pasta, meanwhile I could see both of my children trying not to look at me as they burned with questions.

"Return those holo-glasses, Izzy?" I asked.

"Dad? You're bleeding..." she said slowly, as a drop of my blood blotted the white table cloth.

"Isabella," Adele snapped. "Leave your father alone. It's been a long day."

"Sorry, Mum," she mumbled.

"I'm fine," I said to my daughter. "Work is a bit complicated at the moment and this..." I said tapping my head "...is a result of it all."

Theo's mouth trembled as his question bursted at the corners of his mouth.

"Yes, Theo?" I asked.

"Did you hit him back, Dad?" Theo exclaimed. "I hope you did. I hope you properly hit him, because it looks like he hit you proper hard."

"Theodore. What did I just say?" Adele said.

"That I should eat with my mouth closed?" Theo mumbled.

"Yes, but also that you should leave father alone," Adele said.

"But you said that to Izzy!" Theo cried.

"Theo! She obviously meant both of us." Izzy said.

"Oh…" Theo mumbled. "Sorry, Dad."

"It's not a problem," I said and looked at him with a small smirk. I waited until Adele had gone back to eating, before catching Theo's eye again and swung a gentle fist through the air, as though I was punching an imaginary target. Theo chuckled and choked on his food slightly. I swung a second fist and knocked out my imaginary opponent. I mimed a roar of victory with both fists in the air. Izzy chuckled slightly too.

"William!" Adele snapped, her eyes fiery and eyebrows narrowing. Her frizzy hair stood out, towering over me and then she stopped. Her face broke into a smile, her teeth glinted and she launched a fake punch at my cheek. I reacted back in slow motion, leaning back in my chair to avoid her floating fist. Izzy laughed and Theo applauded the little show. I launched another fist at my wife, which she stared at in fake horror and tried to cower from it. At the last moment, she rose from beneath me and punched the side of my ribs, for real this time and quite firmly. I rubbed them and laughed with my family.

We continued to eat and I picked up my knife and fork for the first time. I said my own personal thanks to the Fates, remembering how blessed I was to have my little mad family. I shovelled down my food with the elegance of a bumbling beached whale and quickly woke up as the food filled my stomach.

From my moment of rest there was a strange sound from the front door. It was a slight groaning noise followed by a weak thud against the door. There was a pause and my family looked at me. I shook my head, regarding it as nothing and continued to eat my dinner. Another dull thud resounded through the house followed by the haunting ring of the doorbell. The familiar double tone rang slowly through the house and echoed off the walls to meet my family at the table.

Izzy got up before I could stop her. Theo remained oblivious to the mystery caller in the late stormy night. Adele touched my shaking leg. I was tense. I needed to calm down. It was nothing. It had just been a long day...

I continued to eat and let Izzy deal with the visitor. I heard murmuring as she opened the door. It continued for a while before I finally heard my daughter.

"Dad? You need to come out here quick," she cried out. I pushed myself away from the table and made my way out of the dining room. There was a heavy thud that sounded like someone falling to the floor.

"DAD!" Izzy screamed.

I ran to the front door, grabbed my daughter and pulled her away from the visitor. A body dressed in black had fallen in a soggy clump onto my hallway floor. They were soaking wet and as I looked outside I saw the storm of weather tearing through my driveway and lashing it with rain. The body groaned and tried to push up from the floor.

"Hart…" the person groaned. I looked down I saw that the gathering pool of water on the floor was beginning to turn dark red. It spread out from the person's chest, which they attempted to clutch with their free hand.

"Help me. Please. Help me, Hart."

Reaching down, I turned them over slowly, so that I could see their face. My hand touched their back and recognised the tailored jacket. I saw her face. It was pale, blood dripping from the corner of her mouth, and her eyes struggling to keep focus.

I turned sharply to Izzy. "Get your brother and take him upstairs. Once he's settled, come back down. I may need your help."

"What's going on? Who is this?"

"Do it now, Isabella!" I said firmly, which shocked her. I saw her eyes well up, but she nodded once understanding the emergency. She left for the dining room to get her brother. I tried to ignore my guilt, but the lump in my throat was too thick. I hated talking to my daughter like that, like she was a child, but sometimes it was required.

The girl at my front door groaned and grabbed my foot in desperation.

"Get it out of me, Hart," Raven pleaded. "Can't call

ambulance. Need… your help," she said indicating the hole in her chest. It was a dark gaping wound. It looked like she'd lost a lot of blood already. She barely had the energy to talk. "Get it out of me now!"

A scream slammed my ears as Adele walked into the hallway. Before she could argue with me, I dragged Raven into my house.

I glimpsed into the wild night and saw a glimmer of green and a flash of weathered white across the road. I ignored it and shut him out of my mind.

I needed to focus. Reaching out, I quickly shut the door to the storm outside and turned my attention to the bleeding fugitive from my dreams that now lay in my hallway. I looked at my wife in the eyes and kissed her once on the mouth.

"Clear the table," I told her. "I'm going to bring her in and I'll need your help. I can't do this on my own. I'll explain everything later, because we haven't got time right now. Just please go!"

Adele tried to speak, but I kissed her mouth again. "You have to trust me," I told her and she staggered back out of the hall. I saw her look briefly upstairs remembering her children, before hurrying into the dining room.

What had I brought into my home?

I bent down to look at Raven. The blood had spread and was now touching the carpet. I grabbed her arms and wrapped them around my neck and lifted the dying girl into the dining room. The table was clear and I could hear Adele rattling around in the kitchen. She rushed back and threw a towel over the table. I lay Raven down and she screamed out briefly as her wound stretched.

"Bring me all the towels you can spare," I said quickly.

"Anything else?" Adele said, an edge of panic rising in her voice.

"Some tongs. Alcohol maybe? Clean boiled water. Pain killers. Bandages, if we've got any…"

"I'll call an ambulance."

"No, we can't."

"What on earth do you mean we can't?" Adele asked sharply. "There is a girl bleeding in our dining room, Will. It is the absolute perfect time to call an ambulance."

Izzy came down the stairs with her wristwatch flashing madly on her arm. Her holo-watch pulsed red and blue to signify a lack of reception. The device deactivated entirely and Izzy started tapping it with her shaking hand.

"Dad. I've been trying to call an ambulance, but I can't get my holo to work."

"That can't be right…" Adele said. "We got you that thing for your birthday."

"Maybe it's the storm playing havoc with the signal. It doesn't matter anyway," I said cutting her off. I remembered how Raven had denied an ambulance when they had first met, "The ambulance would never arrive."

"Dad…" Izzy whispered hoarsely. She was scared. She was terrified… because of me.

"What do you mean it would never arrive?" Adele asked.

"We have to help her," I said.

"No, Will. I'm calling for help," said Adele and moved towards the landline. Her hands ran over the touch sensitive pad on the wall and she selected the emergency numbers.

"You can't," I mumbled, but she already started to call the emergency services. I couldn't let her do it. The screen flashed red and told Adele that there was no signal. I swiped my hand over the pad and completely deactivated the device. There was a fierce sequence of spluttering as Raven began to cough up blood onto the table.

"Mum, Dad, she's choking…" said Izzy who was now standing next to Raven.

"Isabella, please be quiet," said Adele. "What are you doing? Why won't the ambulance arrive?"

"Hart! Get this thing out of me…" Raven moaned.

"I know who this is," said Izzy. We turned to face our daughter who was currently holding Raven's hand. It was covered in her blood and gripped Izzy's like a vice.

"Help me, before I collapse," said Raven through gritted teeth.

I rushed over and rolled my sleeves up. I picked up one of the fresh towels and looked at the wound. It was nearer her shoulder than I thought. It was raw and gaping, but as I looked at it in the new light, I saw a glint of a metal in her chest. She'd been shot.

My mind flashed back to my dream last night. Raven climbing a ladder. A twisting storm swirling fiercely around her. Lighting crashed and she fell clutching her shoulder…

I had dreamt of the moment she'd been shot…

"It burns. You need to get rid of it," she gasped.

"This is that fugitive, isn't it? The one from the news," said Izzy.

"Yes," I admitted solemnly.

"How the hell do you know a fugitive?" Adele asked.

"I haven't got time to explain right now!" I exclaimed in frustrated confusion. "Get the painkillers and tongs I asked for, douse them in alcohol, then bring in a tub of hot water so we can work in here."

Adele opened her mouth to argue, but then she looked at the dying girl on her dining room table. She left the room without saying another word.

"Okay, Isabella. I'm going to take off her jacket. I need you to be ready to apply pressure as soon as it's out the way."

"I don't think I can…"

"You can do this. Now."

Izzy lifted the towel and I unzipped the jacket and pulled it outwards. Raven's body arched as the metal zip from the jacket dragged against her raw flesh. I pulled her top slightly and cut it with a nearby knife. I tore it open around the wound with my bare hands, so that the shoulder was now completely clear of material.

"Now, Izzy!" I said firmly and she applied pressure again, pressing the towel down tightly over Raven's shoulder, who groaned in response. Adele returned with the tongs, which stunk sharply of alcohol. She laid them unsteadily on a clean towel and left quickly for the kitchen.

"What did you use to sterilise them?" I asked.

"Vodka. It's all I had," Adele said.

"Where is it?" Raven moaned. "I'm going to need it for the pain."

Adele lifted the bottle from the floor and Raven grasped it roughly. We all watched as she necked the potent fluid.

"Okay. Raven, that's enough," I said taking the bottle of her.

"Thank you, Mrs Hart. That really hit the spot." Raven said.

"Pleasure…" Adele mumbled.

"I'm going to try and get this thing out now," I told everyone. "It's going to hurt like hell, but you need to stay awake. Would you like something to bite down on?"

She swayed briefly and I thought she was going to faint on me right there. The painkillers Adele brought in shone white in my peripheral vision and I popped them out of their packet and into Raven's mouth. Her mouth crunched on the pills and they dissolved into her saliva. Raven eyed a dishcloth next to her head. I rolled it up and carefully placed it in her mouth, which she bit down on with a grimace. Our eyes met. Hers were fierce. Ready for whatever would happen next. I didn't want to think what mine looked like, but I knew it had to be done. It was her life on the line. If I didn't get this bullet out of her, then she could bleed to death. Luckily the wound was high and out of the way of any major organs, but she needed an expert. I could get this metal out of her body, I knew I could, but I didn't know what to do after that.

Adele returned with a tub of steaming hot water. The water had begun to bubble fiercely, as though it had come straight from kettle.

"That was quick…" I said.

"Yeah it was," she said. "I wish the kettle was that quick normally."

I laughed and she did too. A nervous laugh, but it was a laugh nonetheless. I was glad Adele was by my side.

The stairs behind us creaked and I remembered Theo. I saw him crouched by the banister watching the commotion. He was quiet and his eyes looked scared. Adele moved my hand over Izzy's to apply pressure on Raven's wound. She removed Izzy, who was beginning to look pale from the sight of all the blood.

"Isabella, I want you to take your brother and stay upstairs until we call you," said Adele firmly. There was no panic in her voice anymore. She only wanted the best for our children.

"But Mum…" said Izzy. "I can help more."

"No," I told her. "I don't want you or your brother seeing this next bit. Go look after Theo. We'll be okay. You did really good."

She took Theo and dragged him upstairs. Adele came back to the table and exhaled heavily.

"I don't know how this has happened," Adele said. "But I'm here for you, Will. What do we need to do?"

Raven arched again as a sharp strike of pain surged through her body. She was sweating thick rivers of water down her face. I could see her sweat strangely sizzle slightly on her cheek and begin evaporating into the thick air. The tub of water continued to bubble and began spitting over the edges of the tub.

"We have to get that bullet out of her body and then we clean her up and send her somewhere safe," I tried to explain.

"We can't save her."

"I won't believe that. We do all we can do. One thing at a time," I told my wife. "Keep her as calm as you can."

I doused the tongs in the hot water to sterilize them. I laid them on a nearby clean towel and moved the water to a nearby surface so that the sizzling water would stop spitting on my bare arms. My hands were shaking. I wasn't a surgeon. I was a doctor of advanced neuro-science and this definitely wasn't in my job description. The lights in the room flickered nervously, presumably from the raging storm outside. I looked at Adele who was watching me; she was scared, but she was ready.

"Okay. I need you to hold her still. Hold her hands and mop any excess blood. Keep her cool. Make sure she doesn't faint. She needs to stay awake."

I picked up the tongs and moved the towels out of the way. The wound opened up. It wasn't too deep. Raven had been lucky. I pushed down on her shoulder to keep her still and held the tongs above her body. I moved forwards slowly, keeping the tongs tight and clenched. They were small and thin. Adele often used them to turn over food as she fried it. That is whenever we didn't have spaghetti bloody bolognese.

I felt a hand mop my own brow as Adele cleaned my head

from sweat. Raven nodded at me hurriedly. I didn't know how much longer she could hold on.

Moving forward again, I slowly pushed past her skin. At first the metal didn't touch, but as I drew closer I knew I would have to. I prepared myself and held my breath. Pushing the tongs forwards I found the bullet and grabbed it. The tongs rubbed and pierced Raven insides. She groaned in pain as she clamped her mouth around her gag. Grabbing the bullet, I twisted once to get it free, and then pulled it swiftly out. Raven screamed and inhaled sharply. The gag fell from her mouth and I saw her grit her teeth in agony. She tried to put her hand over the wound but Adele held her firm. The bullet bubbled lightly from the tip and as I looked at it closer, I saw that it was filled with corrosive liquid. As I clenched the shell with the tongs, the bullet suddenly split and it erupted outwards. The acidic fluid dribbled viciously out of the metal casing and proceeded to melt the metal tongs.

What the hell had she been shot with?

I threw the tongs aside and grabbed the freshest towel I could see and held it in place over the wound. I didn't know what to do next other than to keep applying pressure, but I could see the fresh blood already seeping through the towel.

"You need tape!" Raven screamed as she thrashed against Adele. "Something to seal it quickly"

"She's right," I grunted. "We need to stop external air entering her chest and keep away infection. It'll prevent a collapsed lung."

Adele rushed out the room and ran into the garage, I could hear her rummaging through my workshop. The pain in Raven's body was evident as she struggled to stay awake. Visible steam rose from her body as the sweat quickly evaporated. The lights began to whine and grow bright as their heat increased. I heard one bulb in the kitchen actually burst from the strain. This wasn't the storm. I looked to my side and saw the water again. It bubbled, fizzed and surged madly. Raven breathed fiercely to calm herself down and so did the madness around me.

Adele returned with duct tape. I grabbed the black tape and whipped the bloodied towel off Raven's chest. I cleaned it briefly with a damp cloth and ripped a small towel with my teeth. I pressed the clean material down to dress the wound and swiftly spread the tape over the material to secure it to her chest and seal the cavity.

She panted heavily and looked down at her shoulder. It had stopped bleeding. The tape was working. She looked me and smiled roughly.

"Thanks…" she tried to say before finally collapsing.

Adele and I stood over her. Our hands covered in blood, Adele still trapped in Raven's iron grasp. She was crying lightly, but she wiped her tears away now that the ordeal was over. I was dumbstruck. I looked at the girl on my dining room table. It seemed surreal that she was here covered in blood, sweat and tears. Wherever this girl went she brought destruction and chaos with her. She'd come into my home and changed everything.

Adele released herself from Raven's grip and grabbed my hand, "You did great, Will. Remember that. I want you to explain this and tell me everything, but that has to wait. We need to clean this place up so that it looks completely normal. I'll go look after the kids and you stay down here tonight. You can keep an eye on this girl and make sure she doesn't go anywhere. I want her gone in the morning as though none of this ever happened. Do you understand? Because if Izzy is right, then we just aided a known criminal without calling the authorities. In my opinion, we did the right thing, we saved her life and couldn't call an ambulance because of the storm. But people won't see it that way. First thing tomorrow morning, you're going to take her to the Priman police and say you found her like this, okay? That's what you're going to do. In the evening, we are going to sit down and you're going to explain everything. Can you hear me, Will?"

"Yes. You're right," I replied numbly. "I'll sleep down here."

"Good," Adele said shakily, her jaw tensing, as she stared at my reaction intensely. "Now help me clean up."

We worked in silence. The sizzling tongs were now covered in acid and had begun burning the floor. Wrapping them in a filthy towel, I chucked them into a spare tub and doused the entire thing in bleach, presuming the alkali would neutralise the acid. Within the next minute the tongs had found their way into the neighbour's bin. The nosey idiots were going to get a wonderful surprise in the morning if that acid hadn't fully neutralised...

The kitchen light bulb needed replacing. I took all the towels and threw them in the washing machine. I went outside, which was now drizzling with rain, found Raven's bag and brought it inside. I checked my holo-phone for service, which had returned. I couldn't bring more trouble to my family. I'd take her to the police, as I'd agreed. Adele worked to clean Raven with a damp cloth, wiping away the blood in calming strokes as if the girl was her own daughter. She rolled the girl into the recovery position to avoid pressure on the wound. She went upstairs to settle both the children and then returned with some of her old clothes that she never wore. She prepared packed lunches, as she always did the night before, and came in with food for Izzy and Theo. I looked at the lunch boxes sadly. I wished that she had prepared something for Raven as well, but I guess it wasn't something she'd be able to keep after being dropped off to a prison cell.

We cleaned the floor together. I swept and Adele mopped, wringing the bloodied mop into the bucket. All I felt was hollow and empty, as the dark blood seeped through the soap and water.

It didn't quite filter through my absent mind.

I was hollow to what had just happened.

We stepped back and the room was spotless, other than the stranger lying on our table. Adele kissed me once faintly on the cheek and moved slowly upstairs. I moved into the kitchen and found my dinner in the microwave half-finished. A minute later, it was re-heated and I ate next to the sleeping girl in my usual chair. She seemed surprisingly relaxed; as though it was the best night sleep she'd had in months. Once I'd finished and washed up, I found a spare blanket and wrapped it around Raven's fragile body.

I found the sofa again and collapsed into its rough caress. I missed my bed, lying next to my wife, but I had to do this. I couldn't risk having another dream, especially after today, and after the nightmare of tonight.

I closed my eyes slowly and the lights dimmed and turned off with them.

9 – Kindred Spirits

I opened my eyes and the lights suddenly came back on. I'd never noticed that before. My head throbbed with tiredness, as I tried to remember when I had installed that lighting feature. I closed my eyes again, slowly this time and the lights turned off. I told them in my head to stay off, opened my eyes and they remained off. I wished to see light and they flashed on, yet I hadn't said a word.

A faint glow grabbed my attention from the dining room and I rubbed away the sleep that crowded my eyelids. I could still hear the rain outside, but instead of being a tremendous force, it was now a gentle drizzle against the glass.

Raven was still lying on the table, calm and peaceful. However, somehow, she lit up the room. Her bare skin shone and flickered. Light rose over her body in soft waves. I found that she filled the entire room with a soft heat, like a Christmas fire igniting after a long frozen night.

The sweat that had once covered her was gone and replaced with a flickering shine. I crouched down next to her hands and saw her power.

I saw her gift.

Small embers of fire rose from her skin, inflamed, blossomed out and fluttered into the air before dissipating. The fire didn't hurt Raven... it soothed her. The flames flickered and floated over her head.

The black tape over her wound wrinkled slightly from the heat, but otherwise remained in tact.

I remembered my dream. Raven had walked up to that barrel of fire and it had changed in front of her. Is that even possible? I couldn't see how it would work, but here it was.

Raven had fire leaking out of her body whilst she slept.

A series of small scratches glistened along her nearest arm and streams of fire emerged from her scars. They pulsated in rhythm to her heart-beat. They flowed down her arm and fell back into her skin. Raven's face winced as the flames sank into the cut and began to glow. Her inflamed skin glistened as the fire moved inside her body.

I couldn't believe what I was seeing. I pinched my arm, but I didn't wake up. I was awake and this was actually happening.

The fire moved in and out of the small scars and wounds. They glowed with a strange infusion of colour that illuminated the room even further.

The bullet wound burned with fierce white light and I could already feel the intense heat from that single point. Raven had lost a lot of blood and the intensity at this point must somehow signify the severe damage to her body. Who knows how much blood she'd lost on the way here. She would need much more than rest and time to fully recover…

"*Hello again, William,*" said that haunting voice from my dreams.

I turned around to face the intruder in my home, but found nobody there. I walked back into the longue. The room was silent other than the sound of crackling as the girl continued to burn in the adjacent room. The sofa tickled my peripheral vision and its soft embrace tempted me to collapse into a deep sleep. It was a pleasant thought, but troubling at the same time. I didn't want to go back to sleep. I didn't want to dream again.

A lump of guilt rose in my throat as I remembered Bolt. I should have found time to call him, but with Raven's visit everything had become so mad so quickly. The last thing I needed was another nightmare tonight. I didn't want to become like Bolt…

"*There will be no dreams tonight. I promise…*" The voice curled against my ear and I lashed out vaguely to catch them. I stumbled briefly as my hand grasped at thin air.

"Where are you?" I whispered.

"*I'm right here,*" it said. "*I'm right beside you, William. I'm with you every step of the way.*"

"You're not real…"

"*A usual reaction considering the events, however, let me assure you that I am very real. I am as real as that girl on fire in your dining room.*"

"Fine…" I said quietly to the empty room. "Let's say I'm not

100

going mad from lack of sleep and that this isn't a convoluted projection of my mind. If you are real... then show yourself to me," I said slowly.

"*I am pleased with our progress tonight*," said the voice. It hummed darkly for a moment, before a pair of cold dead eyes emerged ahead. A dull crooked shape of a man began to form in the armchair opposite me.

My mouth dropped in quiet horror at the sight of the man shrouded in shadows in my armchair.

"*Here I am, William. Not perfect, but this is the best I can do right now.*"

His frame cracked and splintered, before crumbling back into the darkness. I blinked and the man had already left the room.

"*Well done finding the girl. The truth is within your grasp. Now all you have to do is take it.*"

My world fell silent and I could tell the strange figure was gone. I rolled my shoulder, itched the back of my head and uncomfortably moved away from the spectre in my mind.

The room was flickering again, but more fiercely than before. The orange colours were now replaced with a torrent of swirling crimson and black. I re-adjusted my glasses and moved back to the dining room. Raven's body was wrapped in ferocious fire. It erupted from the palms of her hands and began to spew out of new places in her body. The socks on her feet began to shrivel, as embers slipped through their seams and turned them into ash. The flames flowed along the arch of her foot, flicked off her toes and carried up her legs. They began to burn her trousers, turning them dark from the fire. A flash of red appeared at her chest and matched her heartbeat as before. However this time it moved her. The hot light flowed over her entire body. It pushed down at the table from behind her back, and created a cascade of hot flame for Raven to lie on. I noticed that the table had begun to burn and soft trails of smoke spiralled upwards. The fire was lifting her up into the air. Raven's eyes glowed and sparks started to zip and fly out of her pupils. The girl floated in the air, her body burning with natural fire.

A flash of blue caught my eye and I saw the television screen activate, suddenly flicking silently between channels, as though it was searching for something. The television continued to flicker as Raven continued to burn. My mind whirred, paused, and continued, as I used the television to search for the truth.

My phone vibrated and flashed in my pocket. I ignored it. It buzzed against my leg ferociously and I saw a growing blue light emerge from my pocket. I sensed the phone. I felt its hardware, its power and its capabilities. I felt that it could do more than it was ever designed for. I felt the battery inside its slim casing and the lights on the projectors that were causing it to glow so violently. I made it float up to me. I'm not sure how. Perhaps through a magnetic field in sync with my body's own nervous system, creating a polar opposite force that resonated between my body and...

The phone began to drop and I threw the thought of analysis from my mind until the phone began to rise again.

Raven's body was now upright and I saw fire from her back flow out in cascades either side of her body. They became thick flowing lines that began to caress the far walls, I saw her exhale deeply and the fire began to change. It flowed from a deep red to a calm orange and the heat grew less intense. I walked over beside her as she began to descend. I touched her arm and guided her back down to the table. My phone fell back down the floor and turned off to save battery life.

Raven curled onto her side, as though nothing had happened. Her skin was covered in small traces of her blood that must have emerged during her firestorm. The duct tape was now completely gone , burnt away in the maelstrom of fire that had just consumed her. Her wound was raw and ready for infection to set back in. I got a new cloth from the kitchen, carefully cleaned the wound and wiped away the blotches of blood on her skin. The tape lay nearby so I ripped off a new piece, dressed the wound and again sealed the bullet hole. Once I had finished, Raven was in a deep sleep. I pushed her stray hair out of her face and walked away from the table. I stopped. The lights were still on and bright above my head. The lights waited for me. I breathed in and turned the lights off with a flicker of my eyelids.

The room went dark and in the darkness I wavered. The sofa brushed against my shins and I swiftly fell into its inviting embrace. Sleep crawled over my mind and my body finally closed itself down.

I heard a young girl's voice in the dark. It was vague and faint. It was joined by a man's voice. I realised I knew the girl and the conversation pulled into focus.

"But I don't what to go to sleep…" the girl complained.

"It's past your bed-time," the man replied.

"Dad…" she whimpered.

"Sleep," he demanded. "It's a long day tomorrow."

"Every day is a long day. I want you to tell me about your trip. Please?"

A soft light flickered on and I saw a small girl lying in a bed. She had thick black hair that covered her small pillow. A man sat on edge of the bed and with a single weathered hand, pushed her hair out of her face.

I stared at the young girl's face. It was a young Raven, untouched by the horror of disaster or the torment of her pursuers.

"Please. I want to know where you've been," she begged, looking up towards her father.

"It is not exactly a bedtime story," he said sadly.

"I'm not tired."

"I haven't got time right now…"

"Just tell me, why did you have to go?"

"I don't want to talk about it. I can't. Not yet."

"Fine…"

"No. It's not fine. I'm sorry. I promise to tell you. Just… not tonight."

"You'll explain it to me one day, right?"

"One day, my daughter. One day you will understand everything. You'll see that everything I've ever done is all for you. I promise."

Through the gloom, I stared at the faint glowing light. The candle wavered and flickered. It highlighted the man's long hair with golden light and reflected off his steel eyes. The soft light flickered, changing my perception of his appearance and revealed his shaggy brown hair and sharp features.

A woman's voice called from downstairs. I somehow knew instantly it was Raven's mother. Something told me that her name was Akari. I smiled lightly at this information.

The light fluttered fiercely as the small girl breathed out sharply. The candle didn't blow out. The light illuminated the small girl's face. Her eyes were full of wonder as she stared at the small fire fluttering. She smiled and looked past the light to her father. I couldn't see him anymore, but I sensed him in the darkness. Through the small light I saw his hand stretch forward and stroke Raven's head gently. Her eyes closed lightly and her head fell down to the pillow.

He waited until he was absolutely sure she was asleep.

"This world is full of pain," he explained to his sleeping daughter. "Pain can make us do horrible things. Evil exists in our world when we give into that pain and let it drive us. We all do what we must to survive. We fight to live. That's all there is. That's the only lesson that I can teach you. That is all I know. That is all the Global War has taught me. I'm sorry that I wasn't there for you, but I'm here now. And, most importantly, I'll be with you at the end. Sleep well, sweetheart."

The hand flashed forward to extinguish the candle between his fingers. The room became black in an instant. The darkness was overwhelming. I couldn't see the young girl or her tormented father anymore.

WEDNESDAY

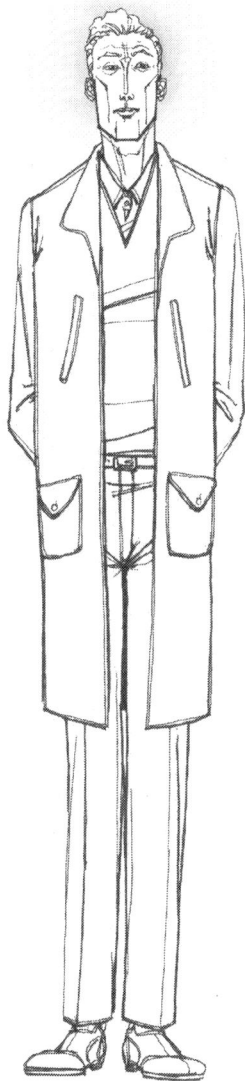

Xander

10 – Early Grave

Raven's body rolled roughly in the passenger car seat. Her face was pale, drained from blood loss. As she lifted her hand to grab the dashboard she struggled to grasp the plastic without slipping and shaking. She needed a hospital, however I knew her well enough to know that she would automatically refuse one. She coughed to clear her throat, raising a hand to cover her tired mouth.

I saw specks of blood appear on her palm.

It was amazing that she was even alive after the trauma her body had gone through. She should be dead. A bullet filled with acid had burrowed into her, plus she'd lost pints of blood and the internal condition of her body must be torn to shreds.

I pulled into a charging point and stepped out of the car to stretch my legs briefly. I popped the catch on my car by touching it with my finger. The cable from the counter extended and I guided it into the catch. It fastened quickly, faster than it ever had done before and the counter poured power into my car. I placed my hand on the cable and suddenly I could feel it. The electricity itself. There was a flow of energy pulsing under my hands. It was moving through the cable and pumping into my car. I answered the energy and acknowledged its existence.

I urged it to flow faster and I saw the counter accelerate. The dial flashed too quickly to count how much power was going in. The other dial that reflected how much money would be required accelerated in tandem. It surged over the amount of credit I wanted to spend. I couldn't afford that much. The money dial suddenly stopped, but the power dial continued counting upwards. The monetary dial remained fixed. It juddered for a moment, but then it stayed stationary. I had changed the counter. It wasn't broken, I could feel the power still pumping past my body. I filled the car to maximum energy capacity. I had never done that before, as I could never quite afford it. Reaching into my pocket I pulled out my holo-phone, which contained the data of my bank account, in order to pay.

The simplicity of the payment sent a flicker of awe through my mind. The days of fiddling around with notes and countless loose coins were long gone in Prima. Contactless payment was now the only way to pay in the majority of the continent. It made everything so much easier. It was incredibly easy to change your finances on the move.

A new thought bounced through my cognition and I pressed my palm against the touch pad. I looked back towards the monetary dial. It juddered again for a moment and then flashed back to zero. A single red light blinked next to the pad. It was an alarm. An impulse flew through my hand and flashed sideways to disrupt the signal. The red light fizzed once and then the bulb burst as I cancelled the alarm. I stepped back in surprise, unhooked the cable from my car and it fizzed automatically back into the counter. With a flicker of my eyelids I caused a power-cut in the fuelling station.

I drove away, shaking, trying to push away the reeling thoughts that were surging through my head. I looked back and the lights came back on in the fuelling station. The back-up power had kicked in and my corrupting presence had gone by hopefully unnoticed.

I cursed as I saw a man walk out of his booth. I had presumed the entire station had been un-manned and completely self-service. Why was he there? Perhaps he was working as security or he lived in the building or…

The man spun around confused on the spot. He scratched his balding head and moved over to the malfunctioning fuelling point I had just left. Power cuts were extremely rare in the city. They hadn't occurred in over a decade, so it would surely be reported. The man rushed back inside and disappeared from sight. I waited for another alarm as he reported the power cut.

I screwed my forehead in frustration. This couldn't happen. I couldn't let this happen. I had no idea what was going on or what I was doing…

Nothing happened. No lights, alarms or signals triggered from the buildings. I didn't feel him send any signals out.

Or perhaps I was somehow stopping him.

My mind buzzed with possibilities and then shrank away scared. How did I know he wasn't sending signals out? I was working on impulse. I barely knew what I was doing…

"Hart?" Raven asked weakly as she began to regain control and consciousness.

"You're awake," I sighed with relief. "I was worried that I'd lost you."

"Be careful and don't rush what you can do," she said faintly.

"What are talking about…?"

"Don't lie to me, Doc. Don't you dare play dumb with me. I saw what you did to that station back there. You know exactly what I mean…"

She raised her hand and stretched it out. Her eyes strained for a moment and then a faint light appeared. A small flame flicked out of her palm and floated away as she grew tired again.

"How did you…" I asked in awe.

She snorted once and shrugged.

"Helpful, Raven," I tensed with frustration. "Real helpful."

"No need to be sharp," she snapped. "I don't know how it works. It just happens."

"If I only had the time to analyse what you can do…"

"Seriously? You're such a nerd. Alright then, okay, humour me. How do you think I can do this?"

Raven raised her hand again, strained until sweat dribbled from her head and then clicked her fingers. A spout of flame flickered and flashed into the air.

"Wow," I said in awe as the flame flickered out of existence. "Well for accurate results I'd need to scan your body properly. Same drill as usual. Body, mind, nerve, but also a detailed account of your blood. I doubt you have hospital records?"

"Don't be stupid," Raven mumbled.

"So, as we know absolutely nothing, we'd have to look for the source that makes all of this work. There must be something. The combustion triangle figures that fire needs fuel, oxygen and heat to form a chain reaction in order to exist. I mean, well, I doubt that you will let me scan you?"

108

"Sure. Why not…" she shrugged.

"Really?" I asked, excitedly.

"No, you gullible idiot," she smirked.

"Well then…" I huffed lightly. "As we're living off pure speculation, perhaps your body converts excess oxygen, which is fuelled by a component in your blood and then it's ignited by friction via clicking your fingers?"

"It's funny listening to you trying to figure this out. Don't stop. You're making the pain bearable."

"What you can do is amazing! Have you seriously not thought about how you can do it?"

"Not particularly. I haven't got the head for it like you obviously do."

"But how did you get this? When did you first know you could do this?"

"Same as you, Hart. The same as you."

"I'm sorry?"

"You apologise a lot. You know that, right?""

Raven's arm twitched roughly and she swore, grasping it tightly. I looked at the twisted angle it formed and gasped as I realised it was broken.

"You could have mentioned that last night!" I said.

"I was a little busy trying not to die from that thing in my shoulder."

"That thing was barbaric," I mumbled. "I've never seen anything like it."

"It was an Mengxiang acidic round."

"From the Global War?" I asked incredulously. "They shot you with a corrosive bullet from the torched great city? I didn't think weapons like that still existed."

"They obviously do," she said, indicating the hole in her shoulder.

"You must have really got under their skin."

"Hilarious…" she grumbled and tapped her wound vaguely. "Cain isn't fond of me. They stopped chasing me. They were trying to destroy me."

"You mean kill you?"

"No," she said quietly. "After everything... that's too simple."

I looked out the window at the rush of oblivious people. They knew nothing of what had happened last night and the madness that I knew would follow. They should consider their ignorance to be naive bliss.

"Your wife told you to take me to the police," she said coldly.

"You heard that?" I said.

"Yeah and I know you saw me on fire last night. So now you finally know why I can't go to the police."

"Cain will finally get you. He wants you because you can do this?"

"There's not much I can do to stop him right now," she groaned.

"No. There's not," I paused. I looked at the half-dead fugitive and remembered the dreams that had been haunting me. This wasn't the end. I couldn't let it be over after everything I had already risked. I placed a gentle hand on Raven's shoulder.

"So where are am I taking you?" I asked. She attempted to smile in return, but gave up from the effort.

"There's only one place I can go now," she said. "Take me to South Bridge."

I nodded. I knew the bridge. It was a recent project that would cross the southern river and bring in a new lane of traffic that would lead directly to Circuit Road.

"There might be someone there..." Raven said and moved in her seat so that she could look out of the window.

"Family?" I asked quietly and remembered the young girl and her father last night.

"I told you already that my parents are long gone."

"Sorry..." I said giving her a sideways glance.

She didn't even bother telling me to shut up. She just looked at me before continuing. "South Bridge is as close as I'll get to having a home and family these days."

"That's where the Outcasts are? Your old work colleagues?" I asked.

"That where they were. Hopefully they won't have moved on, but it's highly likely. The last time I saw them was over a year

110

ago."

"A year!"

"If they have moved, then there is usually an sign of where they went," she said numbly.

"You sure we can't stop off at a hospital? You could pretend to be my adopted daughter?"

"It would never work. Too many witnesses. Plus you're too nice. No one would buy that you raised me. We head for the bridge," she said and gripped the seatbelt to pull herself upright. "All sorts of people live with the Outcasts. Might be a surgeon handy. Who knows…"

"South Bridge it is." I said and pushed my foot down on the accelerator.

I turned the car into the next junction and pulled away from the centre of Prima, heading south through the suburbs and into the outskirts. I rarely came this way and I couldn't remember ever stopping at South Bridge itself.

The car hummed as normal. I could feel it as I had felt my phone and the fuelling station. My mind recognised a certain connection between devices. I could sense the on and off switch, but that was all I understood. Even now the path to completely deactivate the car formed in my mind's eye. I blinked the dangerous thought away. That would not be happening whilst I was driving in three lanes of traffic.

This power was mostly impulsive and beyond reasonable thought. The logical solution would be to ignore it, otherwise I'd end up like Raven with an acidic bullet in my shoulder and nowhere to find sanctuary.

No wonder she came to me. I was the only person who had shown her a single moment of kindness. Perhaps I should've driven away from her unconscious body whilst I had the chance...

No. I'm not like that. It wasn't in my nature, but then again, if I had, then none of this madness would've happened.

Without Raven I'd be at work staring obliviously at my holograms. She'd given me the idea to ask for Mark's help. She had kick started this week and shown me that there was something bigger going on and my head couldn't ignore it anymore.

There was information that had clearly been covered up. After the Old Street incident, Vincent Cain had swarmed in, consumed all the vital data and dealt with a terrorist threat that we didn't even know existed. Within half a year, Cain Corporation had become a massive power within Prima, which itself was one of the largest great cities in the world and the centre point of the scattered European continent.

Cain controlled so much more than anyone realised.

Point and example, after the incident it took months before any survivors emerged from Cain's hospital and custody. Survivors like Mark suffered serious physical and psychological damage and they were helped without any of us knowing the extent of their treatment process.

Innocent people like Raven who were forced to become criminals in order to protect themselves and survive.

Meanwhile the general public didn't even know what these terrorist crimes were anymore. What were they actually guilty of? Surely Cain had the people responsible for the blast by now.

Putting everything together, it was extremely clear that Vincent Cain had everything exactly where he wanted. Under his oppressing thumb.

There was also the figure haunting my unconscious mind for the last few years. These disillusions were growing in startling detail and connecting with reality. I remembered Bolt and how he had reacted so fiercely to his own dreams. Perhaps the same figure was haunting him? My memory bounded to my conversation with Raven in Central Plaza. She had mentioned several Outcasts suffering from the same wild dreams.

The back of my mind itched violently. I smoothed the back of my hair and wiped the sweat from my neck. I felt Raven staring at me curiously, before rolling over to look out the window.

It was utter chaos. All of this was madness and my head couldn't grasp at the events unfolding around me yet.

I needed my home and my family.

The house had been empty this morning. It was so silent after the storm last night. There had been a note. Adele had written that she was taking the kids to school. She never did that.

The house had been clean when I woke up. The kitchen smelled strongly of disinfectant and the floor had been mopped again. Two piles of clothes lay on the floor of the lounge. Work clothes for me and another pile of fresh clothes for Raven from Isabella's wardrobe.

We had woken up without sharing a word. Raven left to get changed and then I walked her to the car. The rain coated the streets and left an echo of sound when we left the house.

The feeling inside my chest had still been hollow and empty.

I thought about my house. My family. I thought about the spare sofa downstairs…

"You could stay with us?" I said slowly.

"We both know that can't happen," Raven replied without looking at me. Her breathing had become ragged and hot breath started to cloud up the window.

"Please, Hart. It hurts to talk. Let me be. I've lived through worse than this…" Raven mumbled.

"No you haven't," I said back to her. "You can't have ever been worse than this, right?"

Raven didn't answer, which left me doubting the question and myself.

South Bridge loomed into view. It was still way beyond construction. The initial struts stood up as sharp metal pillars in the river that still needed to be fully connected.

Raven pointed faintly at a junction to the right. I slowed the car and moved into it easily. There was no traffic anymore, as we moved along the side of the construction site. Raven pointed towards the waterfront and the river consumed the entire view. The early morning sunlight sparkled on the dirty waves. She raised a weak hand to tell me to stop. My hand touched down to the blue button and activated the handbrake, bringing the car juddering to a halt.

Raven stretched forward into her bag and gasped suddenly. "You're a lucky man, Hart."

I looked across and saw a packed lunch that Adele had placed in Raven's bag. It was filled with all the same food she gave the rest of my family everyday. There were some cucumber sandwiches, fruit, chocolate, a bottle of water, several packets of crisps and a tub of leftovers. It was, of course, spaghetti bolognese. She'd also packed a dishcloth, the rest of the duct-tape, painkillers, bandages and a small contactless gift card that could be used to pay for groceries.

It looks like Adele had already known that we wouldn't go to the police station.

"Adele isn't good with farewells," I told her.

"Are any of us?" Raven replied.

I saw her lip tremble. Her body shrank forward, making her thick hair fall over her face. I thought she might be crying, I couldn't tell from here. I opened my car door and quickly moved round to help her out. She gently shrugged me off and planted both her feet on the muddy ground. She seemed stable and began to slowly walk.

We followed the side of the construction site towards the riverbank. The river was directly ahead, but there also a slope that dipped downward. It travelled alongside the site, until it was actually underneath the water level. The mass of filthy water was only held back by a concrete wall. The filthy slope dipped down slowly and the half-finished bridge towered over us.

"Goodbye, Hart. Thank you for everything," she said with a half smile. "This power you now have. We call it a gift. Don't use it. You will only end up even worse than I am right now. It will only bring grief to everyone you know. Show it to anyone and they will share the same fate as you. Walk away. It will be better if you never see me again."

She walked down and stumbled slightly until she hit the wall of the site. She followed it further until a series of pipes were in front of her. The pipes must lead into the river and flow downwards into an unknown network of tunnels beneath the construction site. I admired the location. No one would ever even think to look for a company of lost survivors under the southern river.

Raven grasped one pipe and breathed out heavily, her lungs wheezing with the effort. Raven coughed again, but made no effort to hide the blood that clumped against the wall. Looking briefly down the pipe, she threw her bag into the abyss. The pipe was small but she would fit through it if she crawled. Seeing her condition I realised that it didn't matter. Raven would most likely bleed out or collapse with exhaustion before she found what she was looking for.

"What if no one is there? You might not find anything. Perhaps I should come with you just in case," I called after her.

"Don't follow me," she said sharply. "You've already seen too much." She tried to lift herself into the pipe, but her limbs failed her and she fell to the muddy earth. I raced down the slope to catch up with her. I hesitated for a moment and then picked up her body. She was heavier than Izzy was. Raven didn't struggle, she didn't have the energy anymore. I carefully placed her feet into the pipe with a sense that I was sending the girl to her death.

"I have to know something," I said. "Just in case we never see each other again."

"Which is highly likely," Raven sighed. "What is it?"

"What is your name? Your real name?"

"After everything… that is what you want to know?"

I nodded slowly and waited patiently for a reply. Raven didn't give me an answer. I sighed and helped her further into the pipe, making sure her legs went fully inside.

Raven touched me weakly on the shoulder, which I think signified a small amount of appreciation, before crawling away into the dark of the pipe.

I heard a faint echoed cough and then there was a sharp click. A flame flashed up in the palm of her hand and lit up the entire pipe with a soft flickering glow. Raven's body was already covered in filth but she smiled despite the situation. She smiled despite the fact she was about to doom herself. The honest smile reminded me of the little girl I'd seen. A girl that was once untouched by disaster.

"My name is Jess," she said before closing her fist slowly and extinguishing the fire.

11 - Speak of the Devil

The hollow feeling in my chest left me so unaware that I barely realized where I was going. I hardly noticed driving through the traffic-filled city. I couldn't remember parking my car or even entering the building. My mind was so distant, as it whirred at the events of the last day. It was only when I got out of the lift that I realized I'd made my way to the lab.

Bolt was nervously waiting outside and moved forwards quickly when I approached. I'd forgotten about the incident with Bolt yesterday. His nightmare that had sent him sprawling around my lab felt like a lifetime ago after taping up a twenty-year-old fugitive's chest.

"I tidied up the lab," he said hurriedly. "Don't worry. Everything is back to normal, but…"

"We can't ignore this, Bolt. We should talk about what happened yesterday," I said.

"I've already gathered you want to see the back of me. I just wanted to say goodbye," he mumbled before making to walk away.

"Mark," I called and he turned to face me. The bags were heavy under his eyes and I wondered whether he'd had another dream last night. "I've been through hell and back last night and honestly I can relate to these dreams you've been having…"

"It doesn't matter," Bolt said cutting me off. "You should know that you have visitors in there."

Bolt raised a tired finger towards my lab door. He was right. I could hear the hum of voices from the other side of the glass.

"Who the hell is it now?" I asked him impatiently.

"It's that uptight blonde woman. But she's got company this time. They went in about ten minutes ago. I thought I'd wait and give you the heads up, before I headed out."

"Greatly appreciated, but can you please wait until I've dealt with her?" I asked sincerely and Bolt gave me a hesitant nod.

The glazed glass door hissed and began to slide open. I

glanced at the pad and read that Lucy Quayin had opened my door.

"Ah, Doctor Hart! I am so glad you actually decided to join us at Cain Corporation. Better late than never. I suppose," Quayin crooned.

She was repulsively rude as usual, as she stood in her a cream suit, clipboard in hand and heels piercing my pale floor as though she was the cold centre of the universe.

"You look awful," she said.

"Long night," I replied.

"How unprofessional."

"It was productive nonetheless."

"You are aware that you have a presentation this Friday? Remember? It's the one that has your future in the balance?"

"I'm confused… is there a presentation that doesn't have a balancing future? Because I'd love to attend that party," I said jokingly and Bolt chuckled too. Quayin remained statuesque. "But, yes, I am well aware of my upcoming deadline."

A hand suddenly appeared at her shoulder and firmly pushed my employer aside.

"I will take it from here, Lucy."

Miss Quayin's face fell instantly at the sound of her first name. It instantly crushed her authority as Vincent Cain stepped forward to take her place.

His face was stunningly familiar, which was a gift from seeing him on the projectors so regularly. His swept back blonde hair was in order, reflecting the rest of his figure. His eyes were gun metal and secure. His posture was commanding and his position uncompromising. Vincent Cain was in charge. My lab was now his lab. The mere fact that he had come in person filled me with a strange fear. He could have easily conducted a meeting through the holo-projectors.

I shuddered slightly at his looming presence.

"Here you are… the prodigal employee," he said with a glimmer of a smile. "It's a pleasure to finally meet you in person."

"You flatter me." I replied bowing my head lightly without even thinking about it. "The pleasure is mine, Mr Cain."

117

He seemed pleased at my answer. His head tilted to show his joy. It was as though our first encounter could not have made him happier.

"You give respect where it's due, Doctor Hart," he said approvingly. "This interaction is all so familiar, don't you think? Are you sure we've never met before? Not in passing or anything like that?"

The question was peculiar, but nonetheless more pleasant than I had been expecting. I searched the back of my brain for any form of meeting, but nothing occurred to me at all.

"Never," I said honestly. "I can't think of anything."

"Excellent. I love creating fresh first impressions!" Cain replied showing the white of his spotless teeth. He waved for me to come inside my lab. He sat in my chair at the ringed computer and looked up at the hologram.

"Your work is truly astonishing. You're a real asset to my business," he hummed. "Please come in, don't be shy."

The holograms wavered above him. Everything was there: all the scans, entrance details and all recent activities. They could see everything. At the corner of it all I saw the notification of a call with an un-identified phone call. Next to that was the recording of my conversation with Xander yesterday.

"These are my associates; Foshe and Stranz," he said indicating to the side of the room. "I'm sure you've seen them here, there and everywhere."

"I have," I said finally taking my eyes off Cain to notice everyone else.

Stranz was much larger than he looked on television. His great bulk easily filled the lab door. His frame consisted of an elephantine bone structure, layered with seismic muscles and any room to spare on his huge body had an excess layer of fat. I'd never seen a man so built in my life. His eyes were bored and tiny compared to his massive head. His small pupils dilated and narrowed across the lab, as he spotted me staring at him. They flitted briefly towards Lucy, sullen and quiet at my side, before retracting his fierce gaze towards me.

Foshe, on the other hand, was distracted in the corner. He was fiddling with a panel next to the tube scanner. Foshe's silver hair hung down his back. His scalp was starkly white at the crown of his head. He did not pay my presence any attention.

"And I know you have already met Xander too," Cain continued waving another hand absently at the far corner. "I hope you're already well acquainted."

Xander leaned motionless against the wall. His presence caught me by surprise and his green eyes shone out in sharp response. They were different today; lines of tiredness hung under each pupil and blood red veins tinged the corners of his eyes. He blinked slowly.

"No need to introduce, Mr Bolton. I am already well aware of who he is," Cain said as he grabbed Bolt's file from the hologram and spread it out before him. His metal legs filled the air.

Bolt stared at them dumbly. It hurt him to see his affliction in public view. He had wanted these scans to remain private and now Cain was running his hands through the intricacies of his past.

"I was just going actually…" said Bolt as he moved to collect his bag filled with his prosthetic legs.

"That's a shame," Foshe said suddenly. "It would be great to get to know you better." He stepped between Bolt and his bag. They eyed each other curiously. Foshe looked much older than I thought he would, especially for someone who worked beneath Cain, who was in his early-thirties. Foshe's face was lined, his hands were crooked and weathered.

"I mean for someone who doesn't even work here… you have already helped the Doctor so much," Foshe continued. "As a result… you have helped us, Mr Bolton. Your company is therefore much desired."

"Have we met…?" Bolt asked slowly.

"Why? Do I look familiar?" Foshe replied staring back at him. Foshe's long nose sniff as his nostrils flared out. "Come now, Mark. Why don't you sit down?"

"I'd prefer to stand," said Bolt as he leaned against the wall. Wincing as his prosthetic twisted slightly. "What was your name again?"

119

"Foshe," crooned the old man. "But you can call me Pierre. See? This is good. I feel like we're friends already."

I heard Stranz laugh deeply across the room. I could feel the vibration of his laughter underneath my feet.

"I found Anton in Russia near the ruins of Moscow," Cain hummed with a small ounce of admiration. Anton Stranz shifted his humongous weight in response. "His combat experience is simply priceless. I just had to have him in my employ."

"So what do *you* do?" Bolt asked Pierre Foshe bluntly.

"Pierre was a lead scientist from Luna," Cain announced calmly before Foshe could argue back. "Which explains his pale complexion and odd demeanour. The Lunans were always a strange folk. Imagine living on the moon in that shining great city and circling around us dirty Earthlings again and again. Do you want to know my theory? I reckon that lack of gravity messed with their minds."

"My mind is perfectly sound, Mr Cain," Foshe commented dryly. "But what about yours, Mr Bolton? Are you sleeping well?"

"I don't know you," Bolt answered bluntly.

Pierre Foshe strained himself forward to look at Bolt's face closer. Foshe's pale sun-deprived skin stretched as he smiled. His teeth were yellow and black, presumably from many years of smoking. He licked his cracked lips once.

"That's what we like to hear," Foshe said. "Because you really don't want to get to know me personally."

"Come along, gentleman! Let's find some decorum. There is no need to bicker in front of the esteemed Doctor," called Vincent Cain.

"It's okay, Mark," I called out to my friend. "You should stay. I still need your help."

Bolt looked back briefly at Pierre Foshe's false smile. He moved away and the old Lunan continued to fiddle with the panel he'd been working at.

"Very well, Will," Mark said. "But after Friday I'm out of here."

"Ah yes! Our little presentation," Cain said. I felt the others straighten and await his next word. He looked at the forgotten

Miss Quayin, who stepped forward eagerly in order to be brought back into focus. She hugged the clipboard to her chest.

"Bring me the schematics of Doctor Hart's entire progress at the Corporation," Vincent told his employee.

"Of course, Mr Cain," Lucy replied quickly with a small stutter.

"Oh and Lucy? Would you check on security whilst you are downstairs? Can't have them dawdling can we?"

"Already done, as I do every morning, sir."

"Perhaps you could pop downstairs and see why in the name of the three Fates that research and development aren't living up to their job description?"

"I will endeavour to push the development process…"

"We are Prima. We are the greatest city on the planet. Would you not agree, Miss Quayin?"

"Yes, of course, Prima will always be the…"

"Then, tell me, why is Doctor Hart the only employee showing any signs of Priman promise in the science division of my Corporation that I have left specifically under your supervision? Well? Do you have an answer for me?"

"The holo-technology downstairs is performing at…"

"The great city of Eden is making us look like children playing with glowing magnets! They have holo devices streaming out of their eyeballs. Literally. Compared to their progress… our regression is pitiful! And that is entirely on your shoulders. Get downstairs and turn those fools into functioning adults. Is that clear?"

"Is that everything, Mr Cain?" Lucy Quayin asked quietly, tension rising in her jaw line.

"Just get the schematics," Cain commanded. "Do you think you can manage that single task?"

"I can manage that small task, brother," she said hurriedly.

The room suddenly went ice cold.

Stranz stirred roughly and the floor swayed from his gargantuan motion. His mouth dropped open and then he lowered his gaze. Foshe raised a crooked eyebrow. Xander's emerald eyes moved to the conflict between Cain and Quayin. He looked at the siblings in the centre of the room. This seemed to be news to everyone in the room or at least an extreme surprise that she had dared to mention her blood relation to her boss. Lucy quivered, lowered her clipboard and bowed her head. Vincent's face remained the same. He stood slowly. Those gun metal eyes of his focused entirely on his sister.

As their eyes met, I saw the resemblance for the first time. Their blonde hair was the same. Their nose was the same. Their cheekbones and jaw line were entirely identical.

"We are family in blood alone. You seem to forget your rank here," Vincent said.

"Apologies, Mr Cain," Lucy replied quietly.

Vincent raised a single hand towards his sister's face. I didn't know if he was going to slap her or stroke her cheek. No one in the room stopped him. His authority was total.

"Accepted," he said with another glimmer of a smile and pinched her cheek. "Leave."

She left the room as swiftly as possible, the click-clack of her scurrying heels resonating down the corridor and all the way into the lift. I could almost imagine her crying in despair as she descended to the bottom floor.

Cain returned his attention back to me. Those cold authoritarian eyes met mine and I found myself scared at what this single man was truly capable of...

"So, Doctor Hart, you're looking for a connection? This concept seems quite plausible," he said looking back up to the hologram above him.

"You understand my work?" I said with slow amazement.

"I know a few things on the topic of the nervous system," he replied cutting me off. "Especially the brain."

"Were you educated in science?" I asked.

Cain smiled, his cold eyes piercing my query. He wasn't going to give anything away about his past. "A friend taught me about it," he said towards his elderly employee. Foshe raised a gnarled hand in acknowledgement. He was still busy tapping away at the panel.

"Hello?" Cain asked impatiently. "Can you hear me? How are

you doing over there, Pierre?"

"Almost done actually," Foshe finally replied. "I'm collecting everything to be transferred once we're finished."

"Excellent. I hope you don't mind, Doctor. I know this could have all been done remotely, but this is much more fun. Reminds me of a time, before everything was so digitalised. During the Blackout and the many years that followed, everything was personalised again. Those are the years I was raised in, where communication was vital to survival. I'd like us to be able to communicate like human beings should. Ah yes... those were the days! That is why we are here, Doctor. Your work may bear some connection to something we are working on upstairs. You don't mind me taking a few notes? And... I do mean all of them."

"Not at all..." I said through gritted teeth. I was unable to stop this juggernaut of control whilst I was working in his building and using his machines.

"Perfect," Cain said. "Where were we? Of course! The brain. How could I forget? So Foshe showed me how to physically tap into the noggin, however Xander has given me a few lessons on what happens on the inside."

Xander didn't answer, but his body shifted in acceptance of the statement.

"Silent as usual, but wise beyond simple words," hummed Cain. "He barely speaks to us, but he is absolutely fantastic at his job. Did he speak much when he came here yesterday?"

"Quite profoundly actually," I replied. "We held lots of rapport."

"Remarkable," Cain said. "I guess he must like you."

Vincent grabbed the red brain that hovered above him. He held it in his hand and began to inspect it from several angles.

"What a lovely brain you have here, Mr Mark Bolton. Grow it yourself?" Cain asked playfully. "I would recommend seeing a doctor, it looks quite stressed to say the least."

I felt him as he finally moved past Foshe to look through his bag. Pierre Foshe's shoulders lifted as he laughed to himself.

"Well... I'm impressed with it. Keep up the good work, but try to relax. This strenuous mental activity isn't healthy for anybody," said Cain, moving away from the main computer and stood beside a nearby table. We both looked at the deep scratches at the side of it. Vincent Cain suddenly lay down on the table.

"Scan my brain," he commanded. "I'll show you a few personal notes that might help you out."

Stranz moved sharply and I felt the floor bend as he stood beside me to address his employer. His body was hot. I could smell the sweat from him even as I stood a metre away.

"Are you sure that you trust him?" Stranz said firmly. His tone was deep and gravelled with the edges of his foreign accent emerging in his vowels. I imagined his vocal cords were like boulders being scraped together as he spoke.

"I can look after myself and, yes, I do trust the kind Doctor," Cain said as he loosened his collar to allow the scanner access to his head. The scanner wrapped itself around Cain. Straps formed around his limbs. He lay motionless, ready for me to activate the machine. "You wouldn't wish me any harm, would you?"

I stared at the panel. I could change the diameter of the scanner around his skull to zero, crushing his head in an instant. I could retract the straps and break his limbs. Cain's eyes bore into mine. I felt Stranz hot heavy breath leak down the back of my shirt.

"Not at all," I said numbly.

"I'll be watching you," said Stranz. Cain looked at him impatiently in response, already fed up of his interference.

"Stranz, could you watch the door? I don't want anyone poking their nose in and taking a photo of me spread out like this."

The doors swung open and Lucy Quayin, or perhaps her surname was actually Cain, entered breathlessly with the schematics.

"Talk of the devil," laughed Vincent. "In fact, I have better idea, Lucy leave the papers and take Mr Stranz downstairs. Show him the pretty sights, get him some exercise, play fetch, you know how it is. Make our presence known and scare some people. It's always good to keep employees on their toes. Go on, kids. Go ahead and have fun."

Stranz reluctantly moved away from the scanner and ducked under the door as he left the room. Lucy looked flustered, nodded sharply once and exited without a single word.

"Family…" Cain sighed with disappointment as he settled into the table. I activated the scanner and the blue light emanated and began to filter into Vincent Cain's head. Most people were usually un-nerved by this. He simply closed his eyes and let the machine work. I felt the table hum under my hand. I could still hurt Cain. The sick temptation tickled my senses.

I sensed how fast the sensors were working. I found them. The power ran under my hands as it had done at the fuelling station. The power began to flow faster. I accelerated the scanner. Cain shifted slightly, but I continued anyway. I looked down and saw the scanner receive more results faster and more efficiently than it had ever done before.

"Where would we be without family?" Cain asked.

I paused for cautiously before answering him. "We'd be dead, Mr Cain."

"That's right we would! I'd never thought of it like that. Imagine growing up without Mum or Dad. That would be endless fun! Stay up as late as you like. Eat what you like. Never go to school. Do whatever you want! However, sadly, you are completely correct. We don't have a choice, but to exist alongside our family."

"Yes. I hope you don't mind me saying this, but you are not what I expected, Mr Cain."

"People comment that I have a way with words. Do you agree?"

"You speak your mind. That is all. It's actually refreshing."

"I do indeed. Have you figured out why yet?"

"There's no one to correct you."

"Almost. There is no one around brave enough to correct their boss."

"Or stupid enough."

"Quite. You have family, don't you? A wife? Two children?"

"You know he does," said Bolt quietly.

Foshe moved away from the panel and touched Bolt's

shoulder, his nails digging slightly into his skin. Bolt clenched his fist and resisted the urge to punch the Lunan in the face.

"Mr Cain wasn't speaking to you, Bolt," said Foshe.

"Don't call me that," Mark replied. "I don't know you."

"What will you do? Tell me, Mr Bolton."

"Take your hand off me."

"What are you going to do?"

"I'll break your smug face."

"I'd like to see that."

"Mark," I said quietly. "Stop it."

Cain smiled at the bickering pair and moved his lips to bring compromise. "I do know his family, yes, but I would prefer the Doctor to tell me about them. We were just starting to relax into conversation, before you both interrupted us."

My skin crawled as I continued to work over the scanner. I had to tell my boss about them. I had no choice. I didn't want to know what would happen if I didn't answer.

"Adele. Isabella and Theodore." I told him.

"And how old is Isabella?" said Cain.

My hands froze over the scanner and it began to slow with my thoughts. The hairs on my arms spiked as he enquired about my daughter. He was asking about Izzy. She was a similar age to Raven. Was he indirectly asking about Raven? Why else would Vincent Cain even care about my personal life?

I looked over to Bolt. His eyebrows furrowed and I could see him wondering what I had done to annoy Cain. In hindsight, I had recently helped a fugitive, hid knowledge of her whereabouts, lied, saved her life, kept her safe and then set her free.

"Mark, get in the tube again," I snapped at him asserting some authority back into my lab. "I need to re-scan your brain after the activity last night."

Mark froze. I had never spoken to him that way before.

"Yes, Doctor Hart," he grunted. "Whatever you wish."

There was a cold silence as Cain waited for my answer.

"She's sixteen," I mumbled.

"They grow up so quick these days. Well, not really, we all grow at the same rate, but you get my drift," he laughed. His

126

shoulders shrugged against the working scanners, making them slow down but I didn't dare tell Vincent Cain what to do. "Pierre, would you help Mr Bolton into his glass cage? Sorry. I meant tube."

Mark got into the tube and Foshe activated the scanner. The door shut fiercely behind Bolt before he'd barely got in. I tried to restrain my anger at the men who had taken control over my lab.

"I'd hate to waste your time, Doctor," said Cain. He opened his eyes as the scanner finished and the results began to collect on a near panel. "I have Pierre, so I thought I might make him do something useful."

"Not at all," I said. "It's unusual to have some assistance for once."

The scan of Cain's brain was complete. The scanner shrank back into the table and he sat up sharply. He stretched over to the panel and flicked the download towards the main computer. He shouldn't be able to do that. It was my system. He refastened his collar and shot me a vicious smirk.

It was his company. His technology. Of course he had access to everything. It hit me that if I had made a move to hurt him, then some sort of hidden protocol in the system would've counteracted me.

He made his way back to the centre of the room. He grabbed his brain, highlighted it green and then threw his arms out wide to increase the size. It swallowed him, leaving him standing in the caress of his own synapses. His eyebrows furrowed as he searched his brain. I felt utterly useless, as he pointed at a spot in the hologram.

"Here," said Cain. He looked over his shoulder at the green eyed man. "Isn't that right, Xander?"

"No," he said simply and moved over the join his boss. He limped slightly on his leg, winced briefly in pain. He indicated another point very close to the base of the skull. "It's there."

"Oh, that's the other place, isn't it? Slip of the finger," he laughed as if this was some sort of inside joke between them. Xander laughed too, but his cheekbones did not lift. "So, yes, here is where I believe you will find the connection," Cain

127

continued. "The link between the past and present. It isn't where our memories are kept; it's more like the focal point of where we interpret those memories."

"How do you know this?" I asked in bewilderment.

"Time in the business. It's simply experience working with lots of people with difficultly using their faculties of memory. A result of the incident. We have helped people adjust to reality after disaster has damaged them. We have fixed their minds, but you plan to fix their bodies. As you probably guessed, we've been keeping a close eye on your work, William. So if you need anything, then just ask for it. I am right upstairs, okay? We are hoping for great things to come from you. We value you as an employee, so don't make me doubt that value. It would be a shame if that value were misplaced, as I am invested in your future."

His voice grew quiet for moment and he drew himself closer to me.

"Your work might even personally help me out one day," he spoke quietly. "Look at the scan, I think you will see what I'm referring to. I will continue to support your work when required, despite my sister's unsubtle opposition. So do not prove me wrong. It's time for us to go." Cain looked across the room and watched Foshe tap on the glass of the tube that was now scanning Bolt's body.

"Calls us if anything strange turns up in your conclusions, Doctor," said Foshe before leaving Bolt alone. He tapped the panel and the tube allowed Bolt to step out. "We'll see both of you soon. I can't wait for the presentation. It sounds like it's going to be sensational. So long, Bolt," Pierre Foshe crooned, before making his way out the room.

Mark rubbed the back of his head deeply. "Foshe…" he murmured faintly.

Vincent Cain laid a single hand on my shoulder and left without another word.

I relaxed as soon as I thought the room was empty, but then I heard Xander clear his throat. He adjusted his wounded leg. My eyes darted down and spotted a speck of blood on his clothes.

"Yesterday I asked you about the fugitive called Raven."

"I remember," I said slowly.

"She did this to me," he said, indicating his limb. "Which is a very difficult thing to do. She won't get the chance to do it again."

I swallowed roughly and nodded numbly to his statement.

"Is it broken?" I asked him and indicated my scanner. "It would take me seconds to assess the damage."

Xander held up his hand to silence my suggestion. I didn't dare ask what Raven had done to him. I had no idea how she would have managed it either. The man survived the Fall of Albion as a child… it must be very difficult to catch him off guard.

"Have you heard from the fugitive, Doctor Hart?" Xander asked.

His green eyes pierced mine and I inspected the tiredness that hung from them. It looked like he had been up all night. Xander was inspecting my own face just the same. I thought about giving him some inclination of truth and then I remembered my dreams. They had told me to beware of the man with green eyes.

"No," I lied. "Nothing new."

Xander breathed in sharply and walked past me through the lab door. "There is mud on your shoes," I heard him say as he finally left. "It makes me wonder where you have been this morning."

The man walked succinctly. There was no way of knowing if he was truly hurt by his injury, as he finally left the room.

I stared down at the thick line of slick brown mud on my shining black shoes. The mud had been picked up from the bridge. Xander didn't miss a single thing. What did it mean? Did they know everything I had done? Were they just playing with me?

I held my head in hands and became aware of how much they were shaking due to the lack of sleep that was hitting my body like a hammer. My adrenaline had run dry and my mind was exhausted. I had no idea how I had come out of that encounter unscathed.

"What the hell is going on, Will?" Bolt asked. "That creep asked if I knew him, and I don't, but…"

"But you do know him?" I asked.

"Maybe. I don't know," he sighed and shrank back into his seat. "I feel like I've seen his face before, like it's burned into the back of my mind."

"Perhaps he helped you adjust after the incident and you just don't remember him? Perhaps they fixed your mind and this could be their way of checking your memory."

"I would definitely remember a man from Luna looking after me, wouldn't I?"

"You would think so…" I said absently.

"I thought the Lunans were all dead?" Bolt asked. "No-one survived the Luna Rupture. Their whole city got vaporized!"

"I don't know, Mark," I said and hesitated as I registered the look on my friend's confused face. My head rolled back and looked straight at the floating hologram above me. Vincent Cain's brain still illuminated the room.

"I don't know what to think anymore, Mark," I said quietly.

"You can talk to me," Bolt said. "I'm your friend and Vincent Cain's crew just came in here and shifted through all your work. That's big."

"Too big…"

"What did you do, Will?"

I felt the truth tug at my tongue. I could tell him everything, but it would only cause more harm if I dragged Bolt further into my mess. I'll tell him everything… but not today…

"We need to finish this work, but I'll need your help to do that," I said.

"You've got it. Don't worry. I want to see what comes out of this."

I nodded in response and shrank the brain into the palm of my hand.

"Bolt, can you complete the scan you just did in the tube and send the file over?"

"Of course," he said uncertainly. "I mean, I can try and figure it out, just give me five minutes…"

"Never mind," I said, forgetting how technologically inept he was. "I'll do it later. Just hang tight for a moment."

The synapses of Cain's brain flashed and I looked at the two points Xander had pointed out. The first was a dark smudge at the base of Cain's skull. There was no activity here at all. It was a dark absence that I had never seen in a brain before. Meanwhile, the second point flashed normally, but it seemed irregular and impossible to follow. I would need to compare it to the other scans.

Unfastening my tie, I moved over to the table scanner and laid down. I felt the machine hum underneath me. I'd never scanned myself before, as it was impossible to do without access to the panel. However I could now feel the panel. I could see the switch in my mind's eye. My head twitched and the scanner activated, moving even faster than earlier. I felt the scanner move along my head. The blue lights leaked into my mind. I felt their energy sources. I saw the neon bulbs and how they functioned to create analysing light. I saw the information being absorbed from my head and into the machine and back into my mind through my power. I did this through my 'gift' as Raven had called it.

I opened my eyes and felt more awake than I'd ever done in my life.

The scan was complete in only a minute.

"Will! I managed to figure it out," Bolt exclaimed. "Did this work?"

Bolt sent a new file of his brain to the main server. As I sat up from the scanner, I felt a small response from the central unit that proclaimed that he'd done something digitally useful.

"Not bad work. Only took you five minutes?" I said.

"C'mon! That was difficult. No need to congratulate me or anything."

"Oh I'm sorry! Congratulations. I keep some sweets in my drawer over there. They're only for really good patients though."

"Really? Do you have lollypops and everything? You really are a proper Doctor?"

"No, I don't have lollypops! That was sarcasm."

"Obviously. But it still sucks that you don't have any."

"We'll get some sweets on the way home, you big child!"

I highlighted the newest scan of his brain in a darker tone of red and made mine darker blue.

I compared the scans and saw that at the same point where the dark smudge existed within Cain, there was a small flickering light in Bolt's brain. My computer did not recognise the synaptic signal that was emitting from this point. However I also noticed that every time the spot at the base of Bolt's skull lit up the other point did as well. Every single time, they ignited at exactly the same time. It shone as bright as a florescent light and stayed connected for a fairly long time. I looked across to my own brain and the same thing happened. Both spots lit up at the same time.

This might be the bridge I needed to make my work a reality.

"What I don't understand is why do they need you?" Bolt asked. "They seem to know all of this already. I mean, look, they can clearly scan their brains and they probably have all this technology and information upstairs anyway. So what do you know that they don't?"

It was a good question.

"We need to match the electrical signal of this synapse here," I said pointing at the second point in the centre of the brain. "This point in all the scans lights up whenever we connect to the past. If we make that link permanent…"

"…Then you will have your connection?"

"Hopefully. This is all theory, but it should at least trigger a strong emotional response in the brain once activated. I reckon this could reactivate lost memories as a side effect to my technology."

"That doesn't answer my question."

I pushed the two brains aside and brought my own into view. Bolt gasped slightly. The spot at the base of my skull wasn't a dark smudge or a flickering light. It was a volcano of activity. The base was the heart of the commotion that was erupting across the brain like lava spilling out of a mountain. It made the hologram bright and filled almost the entirety of my head. It activated the mass of synapses unlike anything I'd ever seen before.

It was proof that this gift I was experiencing was real. It was alive. The proof of it was floating above my head. I wish I could have Raven here and scan her brain. If she has full control of her gift, then her mind must be even more on fire than mine was. Although that level of mental activity must exhaust the body at an alarming rate…

I looked back at the scan of Vincent Cain. The dark smudge latched onto the point Xander had pointed out. Something had happened to Vincent that stopped him activating this part of his brain.

Now I knew why they needed me. I physically had something that Vincent Cain did not. That was why he needed me.

"I have something they don't Bolt. I can do something that they can't. I can see the connection that they can only dream about."

"What are you talking about?"

"We're done for today. I think we both need to clear our heads and there is very little we can physically do. I'll set up all the computers to run through the scans, which should find the result we're looking for by the morning. Give me a few minutes and I'll be at my car outside. We could go for a pint at the Sprint Finish?"

Bolt looked at me in disbelief at my sudden switch of moods and then his face broke into a grin. His shoulders dropped and he spread his arms out wide. Drinking was his business and it was definitely something he could help me with.

"It would be my pleasure, Hart. I'll call the spotty kid I hired and get him to set up two pints for us! Are you seriously saying that this will help you? A drink?"

"I can't think straight. Look at that scan of my brain. That is evidence that I need to relax. Plus I always think best with a pint in my hand."

"Now you're talking my language!" Bolt said before grabbing his bag and walking out of my lab.

I couldn't even begin to fathom how all of this worked, but I could see what I needed to do next. I needed to build the bridge and to do that I would need Bolt even more. The two points in his head were sporadic. Mine seemed always active and Cain's seemed completely inactive. Bolt was just the right person I

133

needed. He was someone whose connection was faulty but had the potential to be fixed.

I wasn't sure what his faulty connection actually meant yet. I speculated it either meant that Bolt had a sporadic gift or was, more likely, severely affected by the mental trauma he'd experienced three years ago.

I set the computer the overnight task of analysing the electrical signal being outputted by the secondary point in all three brains and asked it to relate to any previous scans within the Cain Corporation system if it had time. Hopefully I would find a matching result.

I left the lab and felt the machines hum smoothly as I walked past them. I breathed in deeply and found the point where the power entered the room. With a twitch of my head, I rerouted more power so that the computer would have sufficient energy to work through the night. I turned the lights off with a flicker of my eyelids and shut the door behind me with a wave of my hand.

12 – Homely Delights

The door creaked open as I stumbled into my home. The alcohol had gone to my head much quicker than I thought as I staggered across the hall. I hung up my coat and groaned as I saw I'd left the door open. I fell against the wood lightly and the door clicked shut. I breathed in deeply. I wasn't drunk, not at all; I definitely wasn't even remotely tipsy…

"How many?" Adele asked in a spectacularly cold tone. I swore in my head and turned to face her. She wasn't impressed.

"Just the one," I answered.

She crossed her arms and ached her eyebrows.

"William," she said firmly.

"Adele," I replied. "That is your name. Did I win?"

"Yes, that is my name. And, no, you didn't win anything," she said.

"I swear I only had one drink."

"I love you. You know that right?" Adele said sweetly.

"And I love you too?" I said giving the appropriate response. Adele still didn't look convinced, so I sighed deeply and rubbed my eyes.

"Fine!" I said. "I might have had two drinks…"

"William!" she retorted.

"Or three," I mumbled. "It gets somewhat blurry…"

"You're ridiculous. This isn't funny," she cried. "You're meant to be a grown man and setting an example for…"

"It's been a rough few days," I said firmly and her eyes softened at last. The week had been rough for her too. Last night must have been hell. "Thank you for earlier. Raven was very grateful for everything you gave her."

"I don't know what you've got yourself into, Will. But never bring it back to our house ever again," she said stroking my cheek, but not looking into my eyes.

"I would never do that on purpose." I said in defence. "She found her own way here."

"I don't care. Never again," she said sharply and looked into my eyes. They were the same chocolate brown that I couldn't help melting into at each glance. She always won me over. Her eyelids were puffed out. She must've been crying. "I love our family. I thought you did too."

I staggered back shocked. Everything I had done this week had been for them. I'd gone above and beyond to protect them all...

The house creaked and we both looked round to see Izzy descending the stairs. It felt like I hadn't seen her in weeks. My heart tinged with guilt as I remembered how Cain had enquired about her. It had been a cruel jab at my personal life.

"Everything okay?" Izzy asked looking between her parents. She stopped halfway up the stairs in fear of interrupting an argument. I decided to move on and change the subject.

"How was school?" I asked.

She ran down the stairs and gave me a quick hug and then retreated quickly to lean against the stairs. It was rare for her to hug me first. I would usually have to approach her or go to her room after work.

"Remember those holo-glasses?" Izzy said.

"You were learning about Eden. You returned them yesterday."

"Well, I didn't exactly return them and they may have broke last night, but don't panic, they are now somehow fine. It's weird, like, I found them this morning outside my bedroom door and they were fixed. So you didn't fix them?"

"I didn't touch them. I had no idea you still had them."

"Weird, but I guess that's good. Anyway... my point is that I tried to return the holo-glasses today, but they let me keep them."

"But why would the school do that?"

"I told them how I'd been researching ancient aquatic life. Eden has all sorts of animals that it looks after. I definitely want to go there when I'm older. I told my teachers I wanted to look beyond whales, as I really like the idea of mammals in the water. It's like they don't quite belong, you know? The fish belong in the water, but the mammals mostly live on the land, right? So, basically, I asked them about other types of animals and we got talking about molluscs and crustaceans. Snails and crabs. That sort of thing. Maybe if I get time I'll also look at jellyfish and squids as I know nothing about them, but I hear they are really old. They said they were impressed and that I can keep them for the week and tell them what I find out."

"That's really fantastic, Izzy," I said unable to hold the pride from my face. "Well, I haven't been to Eden, but I've visited Lockroy in Antarctica. I was nineteen, just a few years older than you, researching and exploring with a few friends from university. It's the largest port in the world and they would bring in every single type of aquatic creature you can think of. Some were fished, hunted or sold as pets, but they took care of a few of the larger specimens. I am sure I could find my old notes somewhere in the attic. We could have a look together?"

"Yeah, sure, that would be great..." Izzy looked briefly at her mother and then met my eyes. I already knew exactly what she wanted to ask me. Her tangent on the topic of the great Antarctic cities had been a mere ice-breaker for the real conversation.

"What happened to Raven?" Izzy asked concerned.

"Isabella!" Adele retorted. "This is not a topic of conversation we are having."

"You can't be serious? Mum, I want to know!" Izzy said. "I deserve to know. Her blood is still on my clothes and whenever I close my eyes, I can't help but think about the way she..." Her throat got caught into a sob at the end of her sentence.

Adele raised a hand to speak and then dropped it reluctantly. She left us in the hallway and joined an innocent Theo in the lounge. He was tying his two shoes together, which caused him to topple over as he stood up. Adele caught him as he was about to fall and lifted him up. They laughed together and moved into the kitchen.

How wonderful it was to live in ignorance as Theo did at the moment.

Izzy looked at the floor and I moved forward to hug my daughter properly. She hugged me back firmly, but she didn't sob or cry. She remained strong. I kissed her forehead and whispered

137

into her ear.

"Raven's safe. That's what matters. She came here looking for safety and we helped her. We saved her life."

"Where is she now?" Izzy said into my chest.

"I don't know," I said and remembered the last time I saw her. Her body disappearing down the dirty pipe under a construction site. Izzy didn't need to know that. "But she is strong. You saw that, didn't you? She can look after herself."

"I guess you're right. She was a bit blunt and angry, but I think she's got a good heart, you know?" Izzy said and I wondered briefly how she knew so much about her personality. Had they spoken when I was asleep?

"Dad? You smell of beer," she suddenly said, unable to stop herself from wrinkling her nose.

"Dinner's ready!" Adele's voice suddenly rang through the house.

Izzy smiled before disappearing into the kitchen. I fled quickly into the downstairs toilet to gulp down a glass of water. I continued on to wash my face and dry it in an attempt to sober myself up. My family was waiting for me to eat. I focused on that and left the bathroom.

They had started eating without me, which was unusual as Adele was usually so adamant about starting together. I joined them and paused as I saw the meal. It was not spaghetti bolognese. It was steak and chips. I stared at my family in awe. The kids were munching their food and Adele was delicately tucking into her steak. I dived into the meal and had never tasted something so good in months.

"How was work, dear?" Adele asked.

I paused before answering. I never gave them a full answer, but perhaps it was time. I smiled smugly.

"I had Vincent Cain visit me at work."

"Excuse me?" Adele choked.

"Vincent Cain…?" I said slowly to make sure she understood me.

"Yeah, we know who Cain is," said Izzy with a marvelled smile. She was in shock like her mother. "Why'd he visit you?"

"Well… why not?" I replied indignantly.

"Because you're you," Izzy replied simply.

"I am me?" I asked.

"Yes. Exactly." Izzy teased.

"So what?" I asked again.

"So you aren't important enough," she said jokingly, before stopping herself. "Wait. Are you actually important at Cain Corp?"

"Mr Cain likes my work. Apparently," I said simply.

"I like your work!" Theo announced, desperate to be included.

"Theo," I said sweetly and looked at my son lovingly. He had gravy on his face. I stretched forward and used a napkin to wipe it off. "You have no idea what I do."

"Nope," he said. "But you do it lots! You are always off doing it. So it must be good!"

I rubbed him on the head. I looked back at my girls and shrugged. "Well, I've found what I'm looking for at last. Now it's up to the computer at the lab to analyse it all overnight, hence why I left the lab early to go join Bolt at his pub. There was nothing else to really do and we both needed to clear our heads."

"Clear your heads? Really?" Adele said.

"Okay, fine, you're right, alcohol doesn't clear the mind, but it certainly distracts it from the greater issues going on. Work has been tough for me. Plus Bolt has been having really bad dreams."

"Just like you, Dad." Theo said cheerfully.

"Yes, actually…"

Theo's naive statement rang heavily through my head. He was right. They seemed very similar to mine and I pondered after the man shrouded in darkness I'd encountered last night and how the same spectre might also link to Bolt.

"I hadn't considered that fully, but yes, he has been having dreams just like me. Thank you Theo. That's actually very helpful.

"Really?" Theo said. "You hear that, Mum? I helped Dad!"

"Yes, that's right, well done," Adele said with slight impatience. "You were saying, Will?"

"So, I have to wait until tomorrow to see if I have any promising results from the computer, if I do… then we should be ready for the presentation."

Adele continued to eat her dinner and seemed to absorb all this new information. Theo nodded in amazement, but I could see he didn't fully understand. Izzy's eyes narrowed.

"But you said that your presentation is on Friday?" Izzy asked.

"That's right," I replied.

"But it's Thursday tomorrow, right?"

"Your point being…?"

"What happens if you don't find anything by tomorrow?"

I looked at her firmly. She was old enough to understand the importance of what was happening now.

"It means that I will no longer be employed by Cain Corporation and I'll have to look elsewhere for a job."

Everyone stopped eating. It was the first time I had said that out loud. There was a strong chance that I would soon be unemployed and that affected everyone in the room. Adele put down her cutlery and gave me a small smile. Even Theo noticed the change in atmosphere and bit his lip.

"My school is looking for a new science teacher?" Theo said. Adele laughed lightly and winked at our son.

"That's very sweet, but his days of lecturing students is long gone. I know for a fact that you wouldn't want to go back into teaching. Not after losing the university. It would only bring back bad memories for us all. I wouldn't want you to do that." She rubbed my shoulder firmly. "You will find what you're looking for, dear. You're bright. You'll figure it out. Besides… I can take more hours on at the estate agent."

"You work hard enough over there and looking after the house and the kids…"

"There are some new houses popping up around the new dockyard and, who knows, they might actually finish that South Bridge this year. I reckon they will renovate the whole area. They are going to need people to sell."

"Thanks, but I couldn't ask that from you," I said thinking about the dangers that might surround that unconstructed bridge to oblivion.

"I'm your wife," she said softly. "We're in this together. Equal in measure to the end."

I smiled back at her. Adele's eyes twinkled and she turned her cheek away blushing. Just like she had done when we first met. I touched her leg lightly. "This food is delicious by the way."

"Thought I'd try something new," she said.

"I like spaghetti bolognese," I lied.

"No you don't," Theo interrupted.

"Thank you for your contribution, son," I said with a smile.

"You don't like my bolognese?" Adele cried and swiftly removed my hand from her leg.

"I didn't say that."

"Why didn't you tell me?"

"Because I love you."

"You can be so gross sometimes," Izzy mumbled.

"Thank you, wonderful daughter of mine," I laughed dryly.

I looked back at my wife, but she had gone back to eating her food. I think she secretly knew I wasn't keen on her bolognese. I think she'd known for a long time and kept serving it to continuously bug me. I guess I would never know. She swallowed another mouthful, finished her meal and then turned to me suddenly.

"So what did happen to Raven?" Adele asked.

"Mum!" Izzy said surprised.

"We're all mature enough to know what happened after last night," she continued. "Even Theo is."

"I am?" Theo asked. "Cool!"

"You heard those noises last night, Theo?" Adele asked her son.

"Yeah…" he said slowly, before looking at me uncertainly.

"Your father saved a girl's life last night. She came here very hurt and he saved her. It was only later on that we found out she was a bad person, but that doesn't matter. Because we always help hurt people, don't we, Will? It doesn't matter about their bad history."

I didn't believe Raven was a bad person, but this wasn't the time to argue details with my wife whilst she was backing me up.

"Yes. Always," I said.

"Thank you for your help, Isabella," she continued. "You helped more than you know by being very mature, calm and sensible about it all."

"I was scared," mumbled Izzy.

"You were brave," I said as firmly as I could.

"I haven't been able to stop thinking about it all day," Izzy said downcast. "The hole in her chest…"

"Izzy," Adele interrupted. "You forget about your brother."

My daughter smiled as bravely as she could, but I saw her lip tremble slightly and her eyes watered up. She sobbed as she spoke again.

"Thanks, Mum."

"Our pleasure, sweetheart," said Adele. "So where did you take her this morning, Will? And there is no need to lie to us, because you think you're protecting us, but we need to know. Where did you take her?"

I thought for a moment and decided to be as honest as possible.

"In case I get in serious trouble one day and you all get asked about it, I'm not going to tell you where I took her. All I'll say is that she directed me to meet some old friends that could help her properly. Give her the medical help she requires. I dropped her off and that was that. We went our separate ways."

"Okay. Thank you. It's not ideal, but it seems like the best solution given the circumstances."

I looked at Theo and he remained clueless. Suddenly he got off his chair and ran round the table to hug me. He landed in my lap and wrapped his arms around my neck.

"My Dad is a hero," he whispered.

I hugged my son tightly and nodded to Adele, who began to take the empty plates away. I felt the room sway around me. Blinking, I tried to focus on the ceiling, but it swam furiously. My head rolled and I stared at my blurred hand on the table.

Perhaps I shouldn't have drunk those pints. It had hit me much harder than I thought it would. Meanwhile I bet that Bolt was absolutely fine, sat in his armchair above his pub with a smug grin and another beer in his hand. Some of us aren't lucky enough to own a liver of steel like Mark Bolton.

Adele chortled and raised both her eyebrows. I wasn't that drunk. Was I? Surely not. Before I could say a word to argue against her eyebrows, I noticed that the table was empty of crockery.

My wife left the room first. She took Theo away with her who smiled at me over her shoulder.

"Dad?" Theo said. "I hope you have sweet dreams tonight."

"I'll try my best, son. Goodnight."

I glanced over at Izzy, but she was in a world of her own. She stared out of the window with a blank expression, her mind whirring on some unknown project. Maybe she was thinking about aquatic mammals again, but judging by her newest rant it was more likely to be molluscs.

I left her to her thoughts, made my way into the kitchen and grabbed myself another glass of water. The ice-cold fluid surged down my throat and dragged through my oesophagus. I sighed deeply as I felt fresh energy slip into my faded head.

Izzy cleared her throat, walked up and hugged me for the second time.

"I'd like to hear about Lockroy some point," she said and stepped back to lean against the kitchen counter. "That actually sounded pretty interesting."

"Sure," I smiled. "I guess we don't talk about my past that much."

"True," she shrugged. "You know, I was thinking, surely if Lockroy is this massive shipping and fishing city, but Eden is in favour of protecting ancient sea life…"

"Yeah… they've had their moments of conflict. Political and otherwise."

"Eden was formed after Lockroy, right?"

"Much later. It's our most recent great city. It's clean from the damage of the past. From what I understand, Eden is completely unique. Lockroy, fundamentally, is old fashioned. It lives on archaic laws and thrives on industry. The cities have some serious conflicts for… obvious reasons…"

"You mean the Global War?" Izzy asked in quiet awe. "I

know that Eden is full of refugees, whilst I think Lockroy was involved in the War? Sorry. They really don't teach us much about it at school."

"It is not worth learning about."

"Surely it's important to learn our history? It was, like, almost a decade long and it was only thirty years ago…"

"Modern history is horrific, even worse than World Wars in the twentieth century. Sometimes it's best to forget the horror and the mistakes we made. The world is better now. People just want to move on."

"But we live in Prima! The first great city. I've always wanted to know about the others that didn't make it through the…"

"Trust me, Isabella. If I was to sit down with you and tell you about the Fall of Albion or the flooding of New York or Lockroy's betrayal or the Luna Rupture, it would only give you worse nightmares than mine…"

"Okay, fine, but can you tell me more about the worldwide Blackout? We were taught a bit about that at least."

I bit my lower lip. This was a conversation I knew would eventually arrive. I had no idea it would be during such a troubling week. Maybe that was the exact reason Izzy felt brave enough to finally ask about it. I wondered whether every parent faced this same conversation with their children.

"Alright, but only because it marks the end. And don't go telling all your little friends or your mother, okay? This is between me and you."

"I promise. I won't say a word."

"So what do you know?"

"Well… the Blackout occurred in the last recorded year of the Global War. I don't actually know when that was. There were three main sides to the fight and everyone else was forced to join or they got caught in the crossfire. Amazonia and Luna did their best to stay out of the fight. Prima worked with Kubra to hold their own. And I know that Albion and New York were fighting against Lockroy and another great city in the east. They don't teach us the name of it though…"

"The Global War started in 2061," I confirmed. "The eastern

great city was called Mengxiang."

"And what does the mean?"

"Dream," I hesitated before continuing. This wasn't something that Izzy was meant to be learning, but I knew that it was fundamental for her growth into an adult. "There had been extreme attacks on cities before the Blackout. Albion had just been completely blitzed and Mengxiang was suffering against an airborne acidic virus infecting the city. We don't know who fired first, but in 2069, in some form of retaliation there were suddenly hundreds of bombs in the air. They were nuclear devices and more evil creations created by desperate minds during desperate times. I remember looking up as a boy and seeing them. Burning dots of fire and rage burning through the night sky. Some aimed west for Albion and New York, east for Mengxiang or South for Kubra and Lockroy, while others were firing directly at us in Prima. We were all marked for death."

"Luna saved you. We got taught that. They made something that could stop it all."

"Their weapon was called the Rupture. However our Priman schools only teach half the story. There had been fighting for years inside Luna. A civil war that was ripping the streets apart. Everybody wanted to live on Luna, the shining jewel on the moon. A technological paradise away from the rotting warring Earth. That was the problem. Overpopulation. No distinct leadership. A nationless great city constantly struck in endless debate that refused to join in with the Global War. Something happened. Something changed that we will never discover. They fired their worst weapon, the Rupture, at Earth and very single missile was blown out of the sky."

"I don't understand," my daughter asked. "Why is that bad?"

"They didn't save us, Izzy. There are no heroes in this story. Luna didn't save Earth. You see... I was only a boy when the Blackout happened and there are no words that can fully explain it. Imagine your life without technology. No communication, light, automatic heat or transport. Nothing. Everything we had built, all the amazing technological advances, were completely erased with a single abrupt action. The entire planet was sent back

145

a few hundred years. All of our various technological feats were utterly destroyed and wiped out of existence. Every database, every single byte of information was entirely erased. As a result, we had to survive on our own in Prima for several years until when we rebuilt some of our systems from scratch. I can still remember curling up in my mother's arms every night to try and keep warm. I can still hear my father fighting for rations so we could have enough to survive the endless winter. Eventually, the power began to get restored. However, worldwide communication is something we wished we never got back."

"That's horrible. This is what they don't teach us. This is the real Blackout. There was this whole period of time. There are years where we have no idea what happened."

"It is for the best."

"Tell me. I want to know."

I looked into my eldest child's pleading eyes and smiled sadly in response.

"Luna died when they fired their Rupture, because the vacuum of space murdered the majority of the riotous over-population and ripped the city apart. The time alone up there without provisions killed most of those who remained. It's now extremely rare to meet a Lunan today."

I watched my daughter hollow reaction as I continued.

"On Earth, the Rupture disrupted the magnetic poles of our planet and the tectonic plates shifted and flooded a vast number of island bound nations. A seismic shift in the Atlantic sent a cascade of water into the remnants of the island bound Albion at the edge of western Europe. Only a few hours later, the surviving remnants of New York struggled to survive a tsunami that ploughed into the east coast of America. Over to the far east in Mengxiang, the dream for a better future was swiftly eradicated. Due to the lack of medical supervision, their acidic virus had mutated and silenced them all forever. Lockroy made the cruel, but logical decision to ignite Mengxiang and precisely burn the disease out before it could spread. To this day, the great empty city is now under permanent quarantine, until we are absolutely sure it is safe."

Izzy's mouth dropped slightly and nodded that she wanted me to keep talking.

"The fighting continued and, if I am honest, I don't know exactly what battles were fought during the Blackout. There is no digital way of tracking what actually happened in those years. It becomes difficult to track who fought who and why they were even fighting in the first place. That's the primary reason why you don't know about it. Once Prima's communication came back online, we demanded a world-wide ceasefire and the fighting came to a brutal halt. And here we are in 2101. Thirty years or so later and we make sure our children don't learn about the horror that we dragged the planet through. I'm sorry, Izzy. We stayed silent to make sure you were all kept safe. My generation now work to create this fresh clean slate. With any luck… your generation won't screw it up like my father's generation did."

"I don't know what to say…" Izzy mumbled, clearly aghast at the torrent of information I had just given her.

"There is nothing that can be said. Just remember your promise. I could get in trouble with your school for talking about this."

"Yes, of course, I won't say a word…"

I hugged my daughter gently and kissed her forehead. I felt her arms hold me tightly around the waist.

"It's been a long day, Isabella," I said and let her go. "I think we should both get some rest."

"Okay, well, thank you, goodnight, Dad. You didn't have to tell me, but I am glad you did."

My daughter quickly left the kitchen.

I swallowed roughly and pondered briefly at the dark truth behind the Blackout. I felt that I was right to tell Izzy, but it would take a long time for it all to sink in. Sometimes the truth was an immensely difficult thing to fully understand…

The microwave pinged and a hollow blue light shone out of it and made me jump. Inside was my dinner, reheated by Adele and ready to eat. I grabbed a tea towel, some new cutlery, and clutching my towel-covered hand around my piping hot food, I left the kitchen for the lounge.

I watched the news for the next hour, before I was lethargic. The television showed me the continued construction of Circuit Road around the Old Street blast zone and a small snippet of work at South Bridge. There were also highlights from the anniversary of the incident and, of course, the continuing hunt for Raven and other individuals from the Outcasts. I saw images of a lean brown-haired girl with white bandages laced around her muscular arms and a lanky adolescent boy wearing glasses and baggy clothes. The news released further images announcing the capture of an older Kubran with dreadlocks and a twenty-year-old named Julian Issumatar, whose smug-shot showed off his tanned skin and thick black hair. The juvenile was responsible for a long series of thefts, vandalism and aiding extremists.

Grunting, I pulled my slim phone out of my pocket and placed it on the table. As my hand lifted away I felt the machine judder. The device did not light up. I willed it to move again, but nothing happened. With my hand stretched over it, I felt a buzzing sensation on the inside of my palm. It connected with the phone. I could feel the power contained within the small battery. It yearned to touch my palm and become one with my body. It wanted to be controlled by me.

I laughed at the impossible. The buzzing sensation stopped and I became detached from the phone. It stayed cold on the table.

It was time to face reality. This gift was real. All I had to do was accept it and then it would become a permanent part of me. This concept was much easier said than done. My entire life and education had been focused on looking at the absolute truth in life through science. However this power defied all logic and analysis that I could throw at it. I would have to forget my analytical mind for this to function efficiently.

I closed my eyes and stretched out my palm blindly. I tried to find the phone's power, but I couldn't. My body wouldn't connect with the insane thought.

No.

I had a family; a wife, daughter and son, who I loved with all of my heart. The feeling of love and protection I held for my family wasn't quantifiable. It existed within me. This was a similar notion and I wasn't going to let a contradiction of thought stop me from discovering the truth.

I could feel electrical energy around me. I could feel connections within the machines. I could control technology with my mind. I could do this.

I was William Hart and I had a gift.

My eyes opened and the phone rose next to my face. I jumped back in shock, but kept my palm outstretched. I could feel it. I could feel every part of the phone, like it was part of my own body. The energy core was a part of me as much as my own beating heart. It surged and pulsed and I let it fly free from its casing.

The screen flashed and cracked and twitched. The casing began to shake and a burst of electricity poured out from the battery, wrapping itself around the phone. The glass splintered. The rupture ripped my phone apart and sent the pieces flying across the room.

I heard a door open suddenly upstairs and heard the rushing of feet come down the stairs. I could still feel the remains of the phone, even though it was now broken. I stretched out my palms and brought them together. Every single last piece of the phone came surging back. The energy that had just wrapped itself around the machine began piecing it back together before my very eyes.

"What's going on?" Adele said behind me.

I stood slowly and turned to face my wife, keeping the reforming phone held behind me.

"Nothing! Just…" I struggled to find the words and then I saw that a lamp had been knocked over by the small explosion. "I think a bulb burst."

Before Adele could walk over, I sent a surge of electricity shooting into the lamp's bulb and made it burst. Adele jumped back in shock from the sparkling light.

"Yeah, I'd leave it alone if I were you," I smiled.

Her gaping expression turned to humour as she laughed lightly and fell gently into my chest. I dropped the phone on the sofa and we embraced. Her head sank into me and I kissed her hair. Adele looked up and kissed me. Our lips parted and she continued to kiss me, much longer than usual. Her tongue touched my lips and then she began to kiss my neck.

"I missed you, Will," my wife said. "Leave the sofa and come back to our bed."

My heart jumped slightly and I pushed her back lightly.

"But my dreams…" I said slowly.

"Stuff your dreams," she replied. "I'll keep some water up there for you. I'll wake you up the moment I feel anything is wrong."

"Only if you're sure. I don't want to hurt you again."

"You won't. I trust you. Nothing you could do would scare me."

I hesitated as I felt my gift flow through my body and the impulse to tell Adele everything dug at my mind.

"What's wrong?" Adele asked.

"It's nothing," I lied. "I'm just worried."

"Don't be," she interrupted. "I miss my husband. So turn off that head of yours and join me upstairs."

"I'll be up there in a minute, okay? Keep the bed warm for me," I said.

"Don't be long," she replied softly before walking away and upstairs.

A glint caught the corner of my eye and I saw the phone start up again. It beeped and welcomed me. I picked it up, threw it up in the air and caught it again. It felt brand new.

I felt brand new.

13 – Sleep Talking

"Are you there?" I asked the darkness inside my mind.

"I'm always here, William," it instantly replied.

"Okay…" I said nervously. "So let's have a conversation."

"How sophisticated of you to engage me like this, William," said the voice from the dark. *"And where would you like to talk?"*

The darkness dissipated and was replaced by dim lamplight and a surprisingly comfortable sofa. My home was far too familiar, no; I wanted to talk somewhere more succinct.

I blinked and my living room vanished and was replaced with my pristine laboratory. The hologram at the centre of the room activated to greet us.

"Actually…" I murmured. "I think that I spend enough time in this place."

"You resent your time at your work place?" It asked.

"Not at all… but we all need a break from work now and then."

People rushed past me, destroying my lab in seconds, I looked back and forth through the mass of people and at the brick covered ground that was intricately generated across an open area. I stared at the tall fountain that towered over me. I smiled at Central Plaza and quickly became familiar with the sandwich bar nearby. There were two people sitting down and eating their lunch. I gasped in shock as I observed them both. Eating an egg and cress sandwich was a girl with mixed Eurasian heritage dressed in a hoody. Sat next to her was a forty-year-old black man wearing glasses who was chomping his way through an egg and bacon sandwich.

It was me. My eyes looked casually around the Plaza and I smiled as I saw how happy I was eating my sandwich. I shook my mind against the bewildering confusion.

"This is so strange," I said. "Did you know it's impossible to see an accurate representation of yourself? Whenever you see a photo or look in a mirror, you see a reflected image of yourself.

Even if you could flip the image, then you would still only be seeing a two-dimensional image of the truth."

"And what is the truth?" It asked me.

"You'll never meet the tangible three-dimensional version of yourself that you can interact with."

The voice chortled once and sighed out deeply. *"Until you met me,"* it said.

"Yes. That's right," I replied.

The image of myself disappeared and I realised that I was the one actually controlling where we were going.

"You wanted to choose where we talk," it said. *"What's next?"*

Blinking again I found myself looking at the construction site around South Bridge. My vision focused on the pipes under the water's edge as I watched myself lift Raven into the sewer's dark grasp.

"Why don't you choose?" I asked him. "Let's go someplace that you are relaxed and feel at home."

"...if you insist..." it said hesitantly.

My mind warped and I felt myself transported a long distance across Prima. We moved over the great city and landed in the mountains that overlooked the metropolis. We drifted towards an elaborate home set into mountainside that absorbed the vista of Prima. I gasped as I fell through the building and onto the floor. I looked around to see a circular room surrounded by tall bookshelves. A staircase led upstairs to a bedroom, whilst a wide window overlooked the great city. The window was the size of the entire wall and created a breathtaking view. Low clouds hugged the neighbouring snow-capped mountains and dropped down into civilisation below. From here... you truly saw the scope of the great city. I could actually begin to fathom that over 45 million people lived there. The lights of Prima shone like the dazzling constellation of stars found in the night sky. I smiled. Each of those lights was accompanied by a human life. Every light represented an entire person that was full of hopes, desires and dreams.

At the centre of the room there someone sitting in an armchair that looked out of the window.

"This is where I work," it said from the chair. *"This home has belonged to my family for generations. From here, my father founded Prima. As a child, I watched him build the greatest city in the world. As an adolescent, I watched him die for this great city during the Global War. Once I reached adulthood, I was taken down before I could assert my own control over Prima."*

I made my way forwards to finally look at them properly. The armchair turned slightly. Their cold dead eyes squinted to see me and, as they leaked open, the rest of their body attempted to form itself. The person was male. I'd never been fully sure through the transparency of the dream about the person's gender, but I discovered the truth as the man emerged. His skin crinkled into view. It looked more fragile than rotting newspaper. His hair hung down as small white wisps from his balding head. His frame was skeletal and twitched as I looked at him with curious eyes. He blinked. A dark suit formed itself onto his body, but it hung from his wretched limbs. His skin was liver spotted and wept with exhaustion. I could tell instantly that this man was dying.

"No, this is where you did your best work," I said. "Your age has weakened you. That's why you can only get to us whilst we sleep. Our minds are relaxed and open for you to break into."

The old man attempted to smile, but the muscles in his face gave up before it could take shape.

"Clever boy," he croaked. *"I see your doctorate isn't just for show."*

"Show me the truth," I said. "I want you to show me where you really are, old man."

The walls began to crumble and the books aged, pages tumbling over us both and disintegrating into dust. The building crumbled and burned. It was blasted into oblivion and left as a desolate ruin on the mountain. Years passed in seconds and the observatory dissolved. We hurtled forwards, off the mountain and blasted deep into the populated metropolis. Bright lights and clean sheets replaced the neon world as we moved again. Rows of white beds in shining metal frames suddenly lay either side of me. Straight ahead was the only occupied bed and I knew exactly who it was for.

"How do you like my home?"

153

I looked at him lying in his hospital bed. His mouth did not move when he spoke, which was distinctly strange. A series of tubes threaded down his oesophagus and trachea that stopped him speaking and automatically breathing. I became aware of the dull throb of varied machinery surrounding the bed. They fed into his body through a series of tubes, wires and cables that allowed him to breathe, eat and exist.

"It's not too shabby," I admitted. "It looks like you get all the sleep you want. Also you don't have to worry about eating or drinking, the intravenous drip must sort that out. Finally, you can defecate yourself without worrying about walking to the toilet."

"I'm glad you see the positive side of my situation," he spat into the back of my ear. It was truly unnerving hearing him, but not seeing his mouth move. Having his voice constantly curl into the back of my ear unnerved me. I decided to not look at him.

"I unnerve you, William?" He asked. *"You were the one who wanted to see me."*

"What is wrong with you?" I asked.

"You're the Doctor. I was hoping you could help me out with a diagnosis and solution to my problem," he chuckled.

"I'm not that kind of…" I tried to say.

"Oh, but you are, William," he interrupted. *"You're exactly the type of Doctor I need. It's the reason I sought you out."*

"Well… if we ever truly meet then I'll see what I can do," I said.

"You'll help me?" He suddenly asked.

"If I can…" I mumbled.

The body twitched and the dying man's face formed next to mine. Darkness assembled to create dead eyes, crinkled skin and a shapeless mouth. It wavered in the air struggling to remain in tact.

"Given the opportunity, do you promise that you will treat me, Doctor Hart?" The man asked.

I looked into his grey eyes, as I realised that was the first time he'd called me Doctor Hart instead of William. Something was not right here, but I couldn't deny help to someone who was truly sick. It was exactly as Adele had said to our children… we always help hurt people. It didn't matter what he'd done in the past or what had happened to make him become like this. It was my duty to help him if I could.

"Of course I will."

"You have to promise. Yes. You must vow on your family. Promise on the lives of your wife and children that you will help me, Doctor Hart."

"Sure, I promise on their lives that, given the chance, I'll do everything I can to help, okay? Good enough for you?" I asked.

"I'll remember that," the dead face said before it faded into smoke and returned to the empty voice behind my ear. *"I look forward to the day we meet in person. Although I might be considerably unconscious for our encounter."*

I decided to move on. It was important I found the answer I was looking for before this man grew bored of our conversation.

"I was initially thinking that dreaming with you was a one way street and that I have to take your torment, but I don't. I am stronger than you, old man."

"Not by much, Doctor," he sniggered. *"I can't do much to stop you right now for a variety of reasons."*

"How are you enjoying my alcohol consumption this evening?"

"It's dreadful. It makes this entire process much more difficult."

"I apologise. I honestly didn't realise it would affect you."

"It's not like you did it deliberately… or did you, William? Now there is an interesting question. Perhaps this was your plan all along," he said bluntly. *"Anyway… it's not just your drinking that has put me out of complete action tonight. My heartbeat is much slower than usual."*

"You should get your nurse to check on that," I commented.

"She isn't too happy with me in all honesty," he laughed darkly. *"I think she has done something to one of my machines. If only you were here in reality, William."*

"Have you been haunting her too?" I asked.

"We all have to pass the time somehow."

"You're a telepath, aren't you?" I asked.

"Oh, a label!" He exclaimed. *"My turn now. So… if I am a telepath, a being who communicates with thoughts, then that would make you a techopath. Would you agree?"*

"I suppose it would," I said smiling to myself.

"You like your label, do you? You know, they used to call me Mind-Walker... but that was during the Blackout, which was my time to thrive. I liked that. It made it sound much less... intrusive. So if you must give me a name, then I suppose that will suffice."

"Very well... Mind-Walker," I said sardonically.

"I can sense your pitiful excuse for derision, boy," he hissed as his voice drove into my ear like a weevil trying to dig it's way inside of a corpse. "Be careful who you mock."

"What do you want from me?" I demanded in order to make the pain cease.

"I see that we have finally come to the crux of our conversation," he murmured. "Our work together is almost complete, William. You have done exactly as I have recommended. You found your truth and discovered your gift. I am unable to personally teach you how to achieve enlightenment in my current state, so I had to introduce you to someone else who could assist you."

"Raven," I whispered. "Where she is now? Is she alive?"

"I honestly don't know. She is now beyond my sight, but I have connected her with an old friend from Old Street incident to keep her company. Anyway... she doesn't matter anymore... all that matters is that you enjoy your gift, William. Embrace the power within you and feel free to use it. Do you think you can do that?"

I was getting the answers I needed. All I had to do was keep him talking and keep him happy for a couple more minutes.

"Do you torment everyone with potential power?" I asked in humour. "Or is it just me and Raven?

"I meet lots of people, William."

"Like Mark Bolton?"

The voice stopped and I saw the man in the bed flinch. His mouth adjusted slightly against the pipes jammed into his throat.

"I meet lots of people," he repeated.

"But you can't do this to everyone, can you?" I announced at last. "At first I thought it was to do with people's gifts and they somehow act as a beacon so that you can spot that specific person in an extremely crowded world of minds."

"You ask far too many questions," he spat at me.

"But then I saw that it was more than that. I realised that you

156

can only do this to very small set of people. So now we've arrived to the crux of my enquiry with my one last question that I definitely deserve an answer to. Why can you do this to me?"

"Well, in a way, you are correct. The gift helps me notice you, but under the right conditions and when I'm healthy, I can do this to anyone I please. Do you hear that, William? I think I can hear your wife. I believe she is having trouble sleeping."

A faint groan echoed across the expanse of my mind. I felt a soft arm rub against mine, as my wife rolled over in her sleep next to me.

"Leave her alone," I told the telepath.

"And what about your children? When we are young we are all so susceptible to nightmares. It's the penalty of having such vivid and free imaginations."

A pair of piercing screams shattered the surreality of our conversation and the walls of the hospital reverberated for a moment.

"Please stop this…" I cried.

"I could even stretch even further and do this to your extended family, but, oh, wait, I don't have worry about them, do I?" He said cruelly.

The memory I dreaded most flashed before our eyes.

"You have no right to look at my memories," I said feeling the anger curl around my fists.

"You stepped into my mind, William," he said indicating the bleached white walls around us. *"I am merely stepping back into yours."*

"No, you're lying. You're just making me hearing that. I know this because they're not going through the same experience as I am. If you could do this to anyone, then you would have been out of your hospital long ago with the help of some poor nurse. Oh and I bet you've tried that and shattered their minds, but it never works, does it? So you've had to think outside the box. You've picked an individual with a certain inclination towards technology to help you out. Doctor Hart, who has the potential power to turn off all those machines that keep you comatose. The problem is that you're a weak old man with little life left who is in dire need of help. So I will not be asking you again, why can you do this to me?"

"It's rather simple. It is because your mind is weak, William. You've been damaged."

The old man in hospital croaked roughly, twitched and then opened his eyes. They filled to the brim with darkness. The force of his gaze threw me out of the hospital, back out of the observatory, smashing through the construction site, into Central Plaza, stumbling past my laboratory, flashing into my home and falling down and down, further and further until I dropped suddenly into my bed.

I awoke suddenly from the sickening sense of falling in my sleep. Adele woke up violently and slammed the bedside lamp on. The brightness was blinding and I blinked to get my vision back. By the time I opened my eyes, I saw Adele grabbing a jar full of water. Before I could yell at her to stop, I was already drenched in ice-cold liquid that soaked my body down to my underwear.

THURSDAY

Raven

14 – Powerful Temptations

I looked at the digital clock on my car dashboard, its neon light shaking in time to the pounding engine. We wouldn't get there on time. Once again I was stuck in several lanes of traffic, between two Pruckers and there was another red light preventing me from getting to my destination.

I looked back in my mirror and saw Theo fidgeting absently with his seatbelt. Meanwhile Izzy was anxious and growing increasingly worried..

Her biology exam was today, which was the primary reason why she'd become so fascinated with marine life at Eden. It was the exam she believed would truly change her future. It determined her final grade and defined which universities she could apply for. She might even be able to study Marine Biology at Eden University, which was truly for elite aquatic minds. Her lip quivered as she looked at the heaving traffic.

We only had five minutes to get her to school on time.

How had this happened? I couldn't blame Adele for allowing me back into our bed. My conversation with the Mind-Walker had put my mind at rest and he had left me in peace for the rest of the evening, or perhaps he made me oversleep as punishment for our direct conversation. Everyone else had also been fast asleep and once we all awoke, the home had become a hurricane of motion and flying bodies as we all scurried out of the house.

Now we were sat in traffic and there was nothing I could do about it.

My grip tightened on the steering wheel and I closed my eyes. I suddenly felt the electricity flowing inside the traffic light ahead. It stretched up the column and surged into the bulbs. The connection was there. I could change it. Yet, I knew that would do little good, as I would have to change the entire crossroads of traffic lights. I broadened my search, moving through the power lines that burrowed under the street between each light. I mapped the system in my minds eye, struggled with the concept and then lost the whole map in an instant.

I grunted with frustration and opened my eyes. The lights were still red. I felt a buzz in my head and there it was, subconsciously, the map developed, the dots joined and the connection lay there. I flicked the switch and the power grid lit up in my mind. The traffic light turned off completely. A man in a nearby car leant out his window in confusion and waved a hand at the light. I focused and turned the light green, which triggered a chain reaction of events that made the rest of the lights in the crossroads stay red. My lane of traffic surged forwards and already I could see the next light. I turned it green so that my traffic continued to power forwards. We moved into the final stretch of Circuit Road. The usual cold shiver tickled my spine as the remnants of the incident rippled past my peripheral vision. I had to stop getting distracted, I had to move quicker. I had to get my daughter to school on time.

I checked the mirror and Izzy looked out of the window, staring at the apocalypse alongside Circuit Road. Her eyes were hidden, but the window was quickly becoming steamed up. She was clearly upset. I stared ahead again, viciously, we were moving too slowly due to a convoy of wretched Pruckers blocking all three lanes ahead. I grabbed the first vehicle with my mind. Remembering my phone's energy source last night, I found the vehicle's battery and sent a surge of energy out and into the engine. The battery blasted out and I saw a plume of black smoke rising from the bonnet. He quickly pulled aside. For the next truck, I found that it was low on bio-fuel, so I made the engine work needlessly harder so that the rest of the fuel was used up in seconds. The truck chugged to a halt, blocking my path. I felt the wheel, axis, pivot, motor and I sent the network spiralling into rapid motion. It moved so fast that the friction caused it to burst and the axis collapsed. The Prucker lost its traction and skidded to the left.

My engine purred in delight as I pressed down on the accelerator and fled past the truck. I saw the next distant red light. It changed to obey me. The road was open and the end was in sight. I let the car go wild. The engine roared into life, like never before, it pounded through the fuel and soared faster than it was

161

ever designed to go.

There was a flash in my eyes as a speed camera caught me. I raised my right hand and clenched it in a sudden fist. The camera imploded at my grasp. I sent an extra burst of electricity from the power lines and into the remains of the camera. The metal work melted under the high temperature. The data of my presence and sin of driving too fast were safely erased.

Within moments, I'd pulled up at the school and Izzy sent me a quick wave before running as fast as she could to her exam. We'd made it with a minute to spare. Theo waddled out of the car, oblivious of the disappearing time and waved a sleep-filled goodbye as he slipped through the school gate.

I fell back in my chair. My heart pounded with adrenaline. My hands were shaking with excitement. For a moment I felt a hint of regret at affecting everyone else's day by halting other traffic and wrecking those trucks. But then I remembered the look on my daughter's face when she realised we were going to make it. My family was more important than other people's journey to work. They would get over it. Besides… those Pruckers had been bugging me since the day I'd moved here. It was definitely time to teach them a lesson.

The traffic network was still active in my mind and I saw that I hadn't changed any of the lights back to normal. I laughed harshly and let go of the map. The traffic system came back under control of Prima and allowed everyone to drive once again. Everything was back to normal.

I looked at the clock. Bolt would be waiting for me at work if I didn't get a move on. The handbrake released and I moved away from the school. The road opened up and I slowly drove past the sizzling speed camera that I had destroyed only moments ago.

I turned the radio up and relaxed into my seat. My head fell back into the headrest and I sat cross-legged in the chair as my gift stretched over the pedals to propel the car into motion.

After half an hour of traffic and the usual flustering security checks, I was sat in my lab once again with Bolt.

The three luminescent brains hovered above us. They rotated slowly and taunted us. The answer was right there but it was no clearer than it was yesterday.

I'd left the machine to work overnight, but all it had done was confirmed my theories about the two spots in the brains. The point at the centre of the brain was a place that reacted to memories. Meanwhile the other, at the base of the skull, was an undefined place that existed in all of the brains. Its mystery grew as I looked over Vincent Cain's brain and saw the dark smudge where there should be working synapses. The connection between the two spots was still unbridged.

"What can I do, Hart?" Bolt asked.

I looked at him speechless and glanced back at the brains. There was nothing that I could do to solve my problem. The presentation was tomorrow and I still didn't have an answer, other than a mass of un-confirmed theories.

I stretched my palm. I could feel the taunting machines hum all around me. If I had another month with Bolt, then I could record several different memories and see which one made the second spot in the brain react and find a way to keep this synaptic connection active permanently. It would be working through a process of elimination, until I found the exact synaptic frequency that triggered both spots in all the brains. However I didn't have a month. I had one day.

"Hart?" Bolt asked again slowly and realised what was happening. I didn't have an answer. I didn't have the cure for his leg that I had promised.

I felt the buzz of power on the hairs on my arms. They stood on end, pointing at all the machinery around me. Tempting me. I could use my power. I could use my gift.

I remembered Raven's warning and I knew that I shouldn't...

"There might be a way," I told Bolt and pulled up a chair and signalled for him to sit. "This isn't easy to explain..."

"There's nothing left, is there?" Bolt asked me.

"No. Mark. There isn't..." I said quietly in response.

"I gave up my week for you, because you said that you could help me," Bolt said roughly. "I get what is happening. The presentation is tomorrow and there's no way you'll be ready in time now. Now, after everything, you are just going to give up

163

because there is nothing left?"

"There is a way to finish the project," I said. "I can still do this, but you're going to have to trust me, even more than before…"

"I'm not one of your kids. I'm your friend."

"I didn't say you were a child," I said.

"I'm done with you talking down to me. You're my friend, but…" Mark rubbed his forehead once again, stretching the stress lines that etched into his forehead. "I can't keep believing in your dreams. You're getting my hopes up and then crushing them each day. I know I'm sounding like a broken record, but I'm fed up with false promises. I can't do this anymore. I'm out."

Bolt pulled himself up, gathering his belongings and began to leave the room. I had to stop him. I had no choice but to tell him the truth.

"I can control technology with my mind," I said. Bolt stopped and looked at me quizzically. His eyes flickered with recognition and then faded.

"You're stressed, Will," he said dismissively. "I would be too with all of this madness. It's time to let go of your work."

"You don't believe me, don't worry, that is perfectly understandable. I wouldn't believe me either. Just give me five minutes of your time…"

"I've given you that and more. Have you forgotten that we've been doing this for four days now?"

I had to say something to keep him in the room. Without Bolt I would have no way of achieving my goal.

"Do you want your leg back or not?" I asked bluntly.

It was a harsh blow and my guilt swelled as I saw the hurt on his face.

"Five minutes…" Bolt mumbled.

"That should be plenty of time," I said. "Please can you lie down on the scanner?"

"At least I don't have to go back in that bloody tube," he said.

"Sorry about yesterday. I shouldn't have spoke to you…" I said.

"Four and a half minutes, Doctor," he interrupted me. "If

164

we're not done, then I'm walking out that door."

Making my way to the centre of the room, I stretched out my arms and for the first time I let myself go in my own lab. I activated the scanner and accelerated it as I had done with Cain. I focused solely on the two spots in the brain. I asked the machine to multitask and scan each individual point multiple times. It juddered. It had never been asked to do that before. I demanded that it continued regardless. It started to burn with energy that it didn't have and began to fail. I fed it more from power units feeding into other parts of the Corporation and it coped. If it could cope with the strain just this once, then it would never have to be used again. A sudden weariness swept over my body that I hadn't felt before, but I powered on, urging the machine to do the task it wasn't designed to do.

The results came in faster than they ever had done before. Ten times faster. Twenty times faster. We had to do a months work in three minutes. I recorded the two points in Bolt's brain and observed them reacting every time his brain clicked onto a new thought. The mysterious secondary point at the base of the skull was partially active and results were coming in thick and fast. In the hologram, I saw that his entire brain was glowing as it had done after his dream a few nights ago. Slowly but surely Bolt's faded secondary spot began to glow once again.

He was thinking about what I had told him and relating it to himself.

The secondary spot at the base of the skull must be where our power came from. Mine glowed bright with recognition of my gift. Bolt's was faded and damaged somehow by the Old Street incident. Meanwhile the dark smudge that lay inside Cain's brain showed that his power must be completely inactive.

It wasn't time to focus on that. I had to work onwards. I compared the two points and looked for matching wavelengths. I used my own brain at its highest activity as a point of comparison and made the computer look through the results, whilst comparing them to Bolt's brain now, when he was dreaming and whilst it had been completely inactive at the start of the week. I would find the wavelength. I would build the bridge I needed.

165

The computer triggered a response reading that insufficient data was available. I would need to compare this connection on a much grander scale. I dived into the Cain Corporation database and collated every single neurological scan of the cranium that had ever taken place in the last thirty years since the Blackout. Dozens of results rose to the surface. The door in my mind opened and the system re-directed me to every hospital within Prima. Hundreds of results appeared. It wasn't enough. I needed more. The systems sent searching tendrils of connection that spanned across the digital world. I connected with databases within several other great cities including Amazonia in south America, Kubra in north Africa and Eden in the extreme south of the planet. Tens of thousands results exploded into the computer. I accessed the computing power of every single device in the Cain Corporation and used them to back up my computer. My machine juddered ferociously. It demanded more. Other largely populated cities sparked into the web of connection and comparison. The immense cities rose one-by-one, travelling from the furthest west point of the ravaged American continent and moving eastward to the underwater remnants of Indonesia.

San Francisco, Chicago, Rio, Lockroy, Madrid, Johannesburg, Cairo, Mumbai, Guangzhou, Seoul, Melbourne and finally Lupo joined the mix.

My mind flickered with surprise as an immense archive of data from Lupo slammed into my system. My jaw dropped momentarily in awe as I sensed ancient information flooding into my search engine like a tsunami of data.

Lupo was a lunar communication base on the dark side of the moon. It had the largest satellite dish ever created and was used to broadcast swiftly to Earth and to other smaller bases on other planets. After the Luna Rupture, the population of our planet had grown against the idea of living in space. After seeing the disaster that afflicted a lunar home, the residents of Lupo and the survivors of Luna had swiftly abandoned the moon altogether.

Interplanetary travel existed, but it seemed highly impractical, dangerous and entirely pointless as the moon didn't provide any form of useful export.

Until now…

It appeared on the hologram that the inhabitants of Lupo had salvaged an entire library of lost information that should have been destroyed during the Blackout. There was nothing more valuable than knowledge, especially the volumes of information on our technological history that was lost during the Global War. It was no wonder Lupo had kept their discovery a secret or perhaps no one even knew that it existed. Excitedly, I accepted the data and millions of results flashed into sight.

I sent commands across the room to start construction of a limb. I would start with something relatively simple. A thigh. Knee. Calf. Ankle. Foot. There wasn't any time for toes or muscle fibres yet. We didn't have components in the lab, so I demanded that development downstairs sent components with the utmost urgency. I overrode the programs of priority and demanded the network sent metal, wire and fibre immediately.

In the meantime, I found the bag containing Bolt's old legs. Using cabling that ran along the floor by the desk, I picked up the bag. Sweat began to trickle down my head in a thick stream. I opened my eyes and focused on the cabling, sensing the power surge through them. I lifted them like tentacles, wrapping them around the bag and slid it across the floor.

I brought the bag into the construction station in the far corner of the room. Placing my hand on the desk, I sensed the machinery that lay waiting. There were claws, pivots, nut, bolts, mechanical screwdrivers and so much more. I used them to pick apart the old legs, completely dismantling them into their core components. Next I referenced the scans of all the legs I made a few days ago, combined with the countless of fragments of data that my system had just assimilated, synthesised a new model subconsciously and left construction to complete the job.

Returning my eyes to Bolt, I found him lit by an ominous blue glow. The scanner had grown, joining with surrounding components to form a new and more effective machine.

Bolt's hands were tensing and his skin grew white around his knuckles. I would be feeling nervous too if that amount of fast working metal was moving so close to my face.

167

I looked up and saw that the scanner had finished its job. Nervously, I switched the scanner off and it began to unravel itself from around Bolt. It attempted to fold away, but its new enhanced bulk struggled against its old programming. I turned the machine off completely and it lay motionless either side of the table.

Bolt's red brain hovered above us. The two points were lit up brightly, frozen at a single moment. Both points were perfectly in sync and consequentially fired up the majority of other synapses in the brain. At this point the person was using more of their cranial capacity than usual. The computer had drawn a dark line following the strongest synapses that connected the two points. I reached out and grabbed the synapse connection. The dark line hovered in my hand.

The bridge was complete. The computer finished analysing its ensuing global results and announced the exact electrical wavelength that made the brain connect. I compared it quickly to my own brain and ran a quick simulation. The wavelength reacted and the two points instantly matched up again.

I picked a random brain from the millions of results. Data entered in the year 2079: A twelve year-old child, female, born in Guangzhou in the south of the reformed People's Republic of China. She was homeless and brought into her local hospital ten years ago for a scan of her brain after collapsing in the street with a seizure.

Her brain connected instantly.

I accessed the ancient archive. I found a seventy-five year old man with terminal brain cancer who used to live in London, before it was upgraded into the great city of Albion, which was later destroyed during the final moments of the War. I was informed that this scan had taken place in the year of 2021. My hands shook with excitement at the prospect of picking a man who was completely lost in the expanse of time until now. Tentatively, I asked the system to apply the bridge and see if this ancient brain would still connect.

The computer buzzed momentarily before illuminating brightly.

I had done it. I had found a way to connect constantly with past memories, stimulate the majority of the brain and make it more susceptible to connect to external objects. With this wavelength I should be able to connect the two plugs I had created. I could now apply the nervous system into a machine.

Technology currently existed to control prosthetics with the remaining nerves in a limb, but with my discovery the prosthetic would actually feel real. The new limb would feel alive and a real part of the patient.

Reaching across the desk I found the hollow nerve plug. I plugged it in to the computer and allowed the wavelength to register. I ran over to construction and collected the newly constructed leg. It had come out even better than I expected. It combined all the best parts of Bolt's previous legs and made them into one.

"Will. It's been seven and a half minutes. I'm leaving now."

In all the commotion and excitement I'd forgotten that Bolt was still waiting for me.

"But I've done it. I've finished!" I said. I held up the leg so he could see it and he fell back against the table exhausted.

"I... I really don't understand..." he said. "I should go home..."

"I promised you a leg, didn't I?" I said. "So you can at least take this one away with you. Why don't you just try and put this on?"

I hurried over and Bolt slowly undid his leg with resignation and I saw the remains of his leg. It was hairless and well healed over the years, but I could still see the white scars etched into his flesh.

I removed the nerve plug from the computer and it came apart in two pieces as I had designed. I grabbed the two halves of the nerve plug and fastened one to Bolt's leg. It hummed as it activated and synced with the nerves in his thigh. Next I collected the new leg, pressed the other half of the nerve plug into the wires and waited for it to activate. I slowly pressed the two halves together, completing the nerve plug. Bolt helped me with the straps and we attached the new leg to his body.

169

"It's a great leg, Hart. But I'm sorry. I don't feel any different," he said.

"Bear with me. It's just got to connect."

I sensed the nerve plug trying to bond and saw my fault instantly. I hadn't found a way for the new leg to connect with the nerve plug yet. I found an electrical circuit for one of the leg motors and extended the wires and fed them into the nerve-plug. I would have to create a socket later.

"You may feel a slight tingle," I told him.

The nerve plug activated and sent a sudden shock rippling through Bolt's body and made his eyes widen. He gasped, swore and kicked out his legs. He kicked out with *both* of his legs. We stared in awe as Bolt began to rotate his new ankle with ease.

"I… I can feel it, Hart," he gasped. "I can feel it."

In an instant he stood up, he swayed and in a single moment he was completely balanced. He laughed to himself and reached down and touched the new leg. The prosthetic shuddered as it was touched. He began testing the foot on the ground.

"I can feel the floor…" Bolt murmured. "It's freezing cold!

Reaching out with my mind, I connected with the leg myself. Everything worked perfectly. I sensed the nerve-plug. It was connecting smoothly with his body and to my surprise I also gained a vague glimpse beyond the plug and into Bolt's central nervous system. My mind struggled to take in the millions of nerves, so I pulled away before I got pulled into the complex network of the human body.

I tried to create a socket for the nerve plug in the leg whilst my friend adjusted to the limb, but Bolt's nervous system immediately took over. My gift couldn't alter this technology. Bolt was in complete control of the leg now.

Bolt began running across the lab. He jumped on the scanner and kicked the machine that lay crumpled there. His new foot dented from the force of the blow and Bolt yelled out in pain and laughed with joy. He grabbed the metal foot and run his fingers along the metal groove that he'd just created. He tripped, but landed perfectly and skidded, causing a deep scratch into the lab floor. He laughed and collapsed back onto the table.

"You did it. You actually did it, Hart!" Bolt cried.

Bolt stared at the leg in amazement and gripped it with both hands. He bent over double and began to kiss the leg, laughing as he felt the caress of his own lips on the metal. His hands fell down on each leg and tapped them both repeatedly. One had a faint slapping sound of flesh on flesh and the other pinged as flesh hit metal.

Bolt's head suddenly creased with confusion and looked out of the window in my lab at the dark speck of Old Street on the horizon.

"I don't understand..." he murmured under his breath. He stared out the window and I found myself in awe of my friend who was complete once more.

"I'm going to call Quayin and say we have something," I said.

"How can someone just forget months of their life?" He asked.

"Hold that thought, okay? I just need to contact my employer. I won't be long. Hold tight."

I ran back to my computer and tapped the quickest mail I could to Lucy Quayin. The mail disappeared into the network and appeared on her holo-glasses.

"Can we order lunch up here?" Bolt asked strangely.

"Yeah. I think so," I said. "We can do whatever you want!"

"I could kill for some pizza right now." Bolt admitted.

"Seriously?" I asked.

"Why the hell not? You've just had the breakthrough you've been waiting for your entire life!"

Bolt was right. I should celebrate. I laughed and quickly found my mind connecting with the computer and ordering food online to be delivered to the office.

My reflection shimmered in the nearby window. My eyes were fresh from adrenaline, but my face was profusely sweating. I felt slightly faint, as though I'd done a full day of work. I rolled my shoulder to release some tension. Using my gift had made me weaker. The answer hit me suddenly. Whenever I had been manipulating objects, turning them on and off and telling them to work faster, I was absolutely fine. However I grew tired whenever

I attempted to do something beyond the initial design of the machine.

Everything has a limit. Everything has an end. My gift required fuel from my body in order to work in extreme circumstances.

So what would happen if I pushed my body too far?

15 - Discovery

"I remember the fire…" Bolt gasped to himself.

Heaving myself away from my drained reflection, I turned to face my friend. He was stretching out his new leg. He pulled his trouser leg down, covering the metal limb and moved his new ankle around in a circle. I could see him imagining that he had his leg back, but then his eyes travelled down to his bare metallic foot. It twitched and he flinched. He looked at me with confused eyes.

"I was on my way to see my brother," he continued. "Did I ever mention him to you?

"Very briefly in your dream…" I said quietly.

"Did I say what happened to us?"

My mouth moved to form words, but didn't find any to heal his pain.

"I don't talk about him very much these days. Maybe it would help. I don't tend to think about what happened, but I should. I guess that it might help let go of some of it."

He cleared his throat and mopped his sweat away.

"I was driving when the tremors hit us. My brother's house was at the end of the road. The first tremor was fine. It just felt like a strong wind."

"You don't have to tell me…" I said.

"I think I do. For the first time, I'm seeing what happened properly. It's like some sort of fog is clearing." Bolt stood on his new foot again and began to pace around the room.

"The sky just… screamed," he said. "The road cracked in half and my car dipped down into this huge hole. I tried to get out, but the metal in the car was becoming too hot to even touch. The plastic melted. The ground widened and the front of my car fell further in."

Bolt stopped walking around the room.

"There was a bright flash and this searing heat rushed by and a screaming sound followed it. Then the ground tightened. The car began to crush and it broke my leg. First, there was a tearing pain that made me aware of my bones cracking and then there was suddenly nothing. There was no pain. Just… emptiness. I couldn't feel my leg and that was somehow worse. I'd lost a part of myself and it made me panic. I was doing everything I could to get out, but every time I moved I burned myself on the car. I tried to pull my leg out, but when I looked down I saw the white of my bones sticking out of my trousers. There was blood everywhere. My blood…"

Mark remained still, his body numb with shock as the incident echoed through his mind.

"It sometimes hurts again. It's a relief in a way, but then I remember there's nothing there anymore. I'm feeling pain and movement where there is nothing. And now…"

Mark tapped the metal leg again and shook his head in disbelief.

"The next thing I know, I'm being hauled out of my car, I look up and it's my brother," he smiled and sat back down at last. "James Bolton, smaller and a few years younger, a computer programmer, so, yeah, I'd reckon you would have got along great. Imagine that? If it had been him instead of me? You would have someone better to help you out here."

"There's no point dwelling on what could have happened…" I said.

"I suppose, but you can't help thinking, you know?" Bolt replied.

"So did they find you in the car?" I asked.

"Not quite… James looked terrible when he found me. He had this gash in his head, I blacked out for a bit and somehow he had managed to drag me out of there. I don't remember that at all or how he managed it when I'm twice his size! I always thought that he must have had some help…"

Bolt scratched the back of his head for a moment. I thought about stopping him, but it was important that my friend got this out of his system.

"We made it to the side of the street and into a corner shop. He told me he'd be right back. Stupid idiot. Before I could stop

174

him, he'd run back into his house at the end of the street."

Bolt reached down and removed the straps that secured his new leg. He left the nerve plug on, as he had no idea how to deactivate it. I rushed over and helped him remove it. There was a sharp release as the nerve plug deactivated. I heard him sigh heavily the moment it was gone. He nodded to himself and I saw a glimpse of a tear in his eyes.

"A final flash of light filled everything. The fire was so intense it tore everything down. It shattered windows and ripped buildings apart. The fire took away everything. My brother didn't stand a chance. I remember seeing it sweep down the street and turn people to ash in a second. They ran but there was nothing they could do to stop it. My brother and all of those people died right there in the fire. This horrible scream followed, which deafened the sounds of pain. There was the fire first and then the thunder arrived afterwards. The light burnt my eyes and the sound blew my ears. The power of it threw me further back into the shop. And that's it. That's all I remember. Reports told us that everyone had either been killed or blinded, so any of us who did make it couldn't see or hear anything for the days to follow. I was told, much later, that they found me in the next room. All huddled in a corner, amongst the rubble. They found me hiding from it all like a coward..."

"You are not a coward. You survived a horrific event and that takes more courage than anyone can imagine," I said quietly. "I'm so sorry Mark..."

"I've heard that word, *sorry*, so many times now that it's lost all meaning," he murmured. "You've helped me today. You've given me something back that I'd lost. It's not the same, but I feel better. What you have done means more than words. Actions weigh much heavier in my eyes and one day I will find the way to thank you. I promise you. I will repay this debt."

"There is no debt, Mark..."

"You don't understand what you've done. There is a debt to be paid and nothing you can say will change my mind."

I nodded in agreement. I couldn't debate this with him, not when he had just revealed the darkest moment of his life. He had

175

been truly damaged, more than I'd ever imagined. Giving him back his leg was fixing some of the damage at last and somehow making him stronger.

Perhaps Vincent Cain was right to hunt down those responsible? What am I thinking? Of course he was right to. Whoever caused that explosion deserves to be punished.

A pang of guilt seeped into my heart. I had helped one of the terrorists. I had saved Raven's life and now she could be anywhere. No. I couldn't think that way. I didn't know if Raven was responsible for the incident.

Everything was mere speculation. I had no way of knowing right from wrong here. I had to face the truth. I helped someone that Cain believed was responsible for the incident.

If that is true, then in the public eye I am partly to blame. I looked at Bolt and kept my mouth shut.

"Whilst I was in your scanner, I was thinking about what you told me. You know, about how you have an ability to do things with technology. I thought you were mad, but then you made this," he said pointing at the new leg. "I saw you controlling the whole room by just standing there, sweating and flinching every now and then. You weren't even touching the hologram as you normally do. And… all I could think of was that Lunan from yesterday."

"Pierre Foshe was just a sun-deprived creep," I told him.

"No, he wasn't. He asked if I knew him. I said no, but I do know him. The more I think about it, the more I remember…"

"The hospital," I said cutting him off. It made sense. They recovered Bolt and brought him to their private hospital until he regained his senses.

"Yeah, after the incident. I remember seeing him. Foshe was there at the hospital. There was this pain." Bolt reached back absently and touched a spot at the back of his head. I moved forward and grabbed his hand.

"Why did you do that?" I asked firmly.

"Do what? I was just scratching?" he replied.

"Hold still. Can you point to where you remember the pain was?" I asked.

Bolt slowly placed a single finger on a spot at the back of his skull. I pushed his hair out of the way and found it.

"There is a small scar here. It looks like an incision to the back of your skull," I told him.

"He did something to my head?" Bolt asked in disgust with a dark fury building in his voice.

I looked left at the main computer and saw Bolt's brain still hovering with the dark bridge illuminated between the two faded points.

"Of course, the scan. Yes. Look at your secondary point, the one at the base of your skull; it's right beside the place you just pointed at. It's been disconnected somehow. I believe from the scans I've seen that is where our abilities are kept or analysed or...."

"Our abilities?"

"I really don't know what else to call them."

"Are you saying that I can do..." he paused and opened up his palms as I did. "What you can do?"

"I think you can do something different. I think you already have."

"Okay... and Foshe took it from me?"

"Yes. It seems to be possible," I nodded. "Have you ever heard of lobotomy?"

"Yeah, once actually. I was watching this documentary about frontal lobotomy with a bottle in front of me. Isn't that where they stick a needle in your head and turn you off?" Bolt asked.

"In part, yes. They used to put a spike through your tear duct and hammer towards a point between the two halves of your cranium. There's a specific point there that deals with over using your emotions. Hit the point correctly and the subject calms down."

"I've never heard that," Bolt murmured.

"That is the purpose. Unfortunately the failure rate was too high, the spike can go wrong and your subject becomes dysfunctional. They are awake, but unaware as their mental functions cease to work. This effect is usually somewhat permanent. It was made illegal a long time ago. Although, before

177

the Blackout, I heard reports in Kubra that they had technology that would use solar lasers for the same effect. They used it on war criminals in their prison, Inferno, as punishment. They'd calm them down or erase their memories to rehabilitate them into Kubran society."

"It all sounds barbaric to me. Glad they forgot how to do it. So, wait, you're saying they did that to me?"

"No, not quite, but I think this is a much more precise format. They targeted a point nearer the surface. They cut into the back of your head. A researched specialist could alter it efficiently."

"They took something out?"

"Memories are easily faded, especially after the trauma you went through. It would've been very easy to confuse a patient about what happened in the weeks to follow the incident. Your gift, on the other hand, I don't think they can actually take that away. It appears that they just damaged the nerve clusters that allow it to function."

"So let me get this straight. After the incident they took the survivors into a private hospital and then people, like Pierre Foshe, stuck a needle into us and mucked about with our heads? Why? To makes us forget the event and shut down these powers?"

"That seems likely given the evidence on these scans."

"Well, we have to say something!"

"To who? To Vincent Cain? He rules this great city. Besides… what evil has it really caused? None. They turned off all of your gifts. They've prevented an outbreak of people with powers. Imagine what damage that would've caused to Prima."

"People deserve to know the truth."

"They wouldn't believe us for a second," I told him. "Even if I showed them what I could do, I would be shut down by Cain within the hour. Everyone we know would be in danger."

Bolt hesitated as he realised I was right.

"So the incident caused people to gain powers?" Bolt asked slowly.

"I didn't say that," I said.

"You were insinuating it. Cain mucks with our heads to make

sure we forget it all and that stops us from having powers. We saw something that day that gave us all these abilities."

"I didn't get mine through the incident."

"You sure? Where were you when it all went down?"

"I was away, on holiday, on my own."

"You were on your own?"

"Yeah. Adele agreed. I remember that we'd been arguing lots and that I needed to take break from everything. Bad time to go abroad…"

"Definitely. Well, if you weren't here, how did you get your ability?"

"I'm not sure. Someone else showed me. Someone else who had a gift."

"And who on earth was that?" Bolt asked incredulously.

Suddenly I felt the door panel activate and the door began to unlock. I was fed up with people entering my lab without my authority. I locked the door with my mind and overrode any higher commands that would overtake my authority.

I looked at the glass door and there stood the fixed figure of a woman silhouetted on the other side. I didn't even have to look at the hologram to know who it was.

"Doctor Hart, I have no idea how you have done this, but open this door immediately," Lucy Quayin cried petulantly.

"Just a second! I believe it's broken. I don't think it's used to all these commands going through it." I winked at Bolt, who chuckled and signalled that we would talk later. I nodded to him and signed for him to put the leg on.

"Bear with me, Miss Quayin, whilst I fix it from here."

"Time is short and we need to talk," she said firmly.

I stretched out my palm over the door panel and sent a surge of electricity shooting out her side. Lucy cried out as her panel fizzed and shot out a stream of sparks out at her. That would teach her.

The door finally swung open and a flustered Miss Quayin stumbled in on her ridiculous heels to get away from the small column of smoke emitting from the door panel. I de-activated the power to the door behind me, stopping the stream of sparks

179

before any sprinklers or maintenance staff came to give it further inspection.

Quayin restored herself next to Bolt who was happily sitting on the scanner with both his legs swinging back and forth.

"Doctor Hart, the commands coming from your system today have been quite…" She stared at the mass of information that streamed all across the hologram and filled the majority of the ceiling with information. Her gaze stopped at the dark bridge shimmering across Bolt's brain. "Extraordinary."

"I apologize, but you asked for results. I only had a day left and, after the several intrusions this past week, I felt it was time to take matters into my own hands."

"Well, yes," she said flustered. "But that does not means you can hack the system, steal computer processing power and over-prioritise yourself over other projects."

"Would your brother agree with your continued intrusion on a project that he has personally endorsed?" I said daringly.

She wide shapeless mouth opened, her sharp red lipstick contorting with her lips, emphasising her inability to find a retort. She was unable to believe I had spoken such words against her.

"I have completed the project, Miss Quayin," I told her triumphantly. "And I know how much Mr Cain has an interest in this project. I think he would agree with my actions to prioritise my project over those going on at development."

"That doesn't excuse your hacking," Lucy complained.

"Did you bring what I asked for or not?" I asked.

She stared sharply and for a moment I thought she was going to slap me.

"They are outside," she spat.

"Then please stay and I'll prove to you that I am completely prepared for your presentation tomorrow. Mark? Would you mind retrieving the items outside?"

"Of course, Doctor," he said smugly and hopped off the counter and half-ran out the lab door.

"For your sake this technology better work, otherwise you will be out of here within the hour," said Lucy.

"You have already seen it working. Mark is wearing my nerve

plug right now, aren't you?" I asked him as he re-entered the room.

"I am," he said lifting his trouser leg to reveal his limb. He was pushing a trolley that contained all the components I'd asked for, however there was another item of interest. I'd sent a scan of Mark's leg downstairs earlier this week to create his leg in advance. There lay the perfect prosthetic. Cable and springs interlaced and created muscle fibre that covered the skeletal structure. This model also had toes and an arch in the foot.

"Mark. The leg is yours," I smiled. "Try it on."

He carefully picked it up. The entire limb flashed as projectors lit up all along the entire leg. A fine layer of skin covered in hair simmered over and perfectly camouflaged the intricate mechanics of the leg. Lucy stood cross-armed and watched him. He hopped back on the counter and moved with swiftness that only years of experience could give him as he changed the two limbs around. The new leg fastened and the nerve plug activated easily with a glimmer of blue light. I saw the ripple of energy echo through his body and the small dark hairs on his arm stood sharply on end. Mark laughed as he began moving his toes one-by-one. They wriggled and swerved, as he stretched the new arch in his foot.

"That only proves heightened nerve control," said Lucy. "Impressive nonetheless, but not what you promised. Mr Bolton clearly has experience animating prosthetics with his remaining nerves. Where is our metal skin?"

"Patience." I said and led her into a nearby chair. Bolt stretched out his new leg and tried not to laugh as Lucy's heel impaled his new metal foot.

"Watch it!" Bolt exclaimed.

"What?" Lucy cried and then she looked down and saw her heel piercing Bolt's foot. She wrenched the heel out and gasped slightly as Bolt's metal foot flinched from her touch.

"There's a right arm in the trolley. Would you mind getting it, Bolt?" I asked him.

"Of course," he replied.

I made my way back to the main computer and found the other nerve-plug I'd created and filled it with the wavelength that

181

formed the bridge I'd worked so long to create. The machines whirred around us. The power buzzed all around my arms and made my senses heighten.

The temptation to use my gift was so strong.

Once the nerve plug was prepared, I wired the device into the right arm lying on the table. I looked at Quayin and wondered where to strap the device. She still had her own arm so perhaps I should just cut it off. I realised that it didn't matter where I placed the device, but it would be most effective where the external signal of the central nervous system was strongest. Bolt was fine to use it on his thigh as he was now used to sending nerve signals to prosthetic limbs through there. However, for any future subjects, the back of my neck where the skull met the spine would work perfectly.

"Your job is on the line here. It would do you well to remember that, William," she said coldly.

The nerve plug activated with a flash of blue at the back of her head and she suddenly gasped as the signal rippled through her body. All three of her arms twitched. We watched as both of her right hands moved at the same time. Like Bolt, she tested each metal digit one by one, which moved in time with her own hand. She grasped the table and breathed in with sharp shock. It was working. She could feel it. She curled both hands into a fist and closed her eyes.

"Are you satisfied, Lucy…?" I paused.

The metal hand was moving on its own. Her own hand remained motionless, but the metal hand continued to stretch. Quayin opened her eyes and the metal hand rose on its fingers and begin to walk along the table. It wavered on two fingers, as it learnt how to balance and then walked along the surface on two digits with a faint click-clacking sound.

Lucy's eyes glinted with a strange menace as I saw her imagination soar through the possibilities that this technology could give her. The nerve plug shimmered dark blue and I saw her eye twitch with the effort.

A glimmer of water wrinkled along her right eye.

"Yes, I'm very satisfied," she said before curling the new hand into a fist and bringing it sharply down on the table. I deactivated the nerve-plug on the back of her neck and the metal hand fell limp. She rolled her neck and I took off the straps.

"Metal skin…" she said whilst stretching her own palm again. Her eyes unfocused momentarily and fixated loosely on the floor. She seemed somewhat lost on an absent thought fluttering through her head. The moment scattered and Quayin restored herself. "Congratulations. You have achieved the impossible. This is satisfactory, but you will need much more to impress the crowd tomorrow. Do you have anything bigger?

"Bigger?" I asked.

"Of course. You will need something that a client could operate during the presentation. These are respective buyers coming from all over the world who want to see our future. They want to see all of your work's capabilities. We shouldn't limit their imaginations."

"You don't even want the prosthetics, do you?" Bolt said catching on before I could.

"I want much more than that," Lucy confirmed. "You are so short sighted, William. It's painful to watch. If you won't submit to our demands, then what is yours will become ours."

"The nerve plug is mine," I told my employer.

"Yes it is, but I will not be limited by your small vision. The opportunities that will emerge from your metal skin and nerve plug will be something entirely different to your prosthetics."

"This is my life's work."

"Show us more tomorrow or your work will end right here. You must produce results, otherwise everyone of importance will agree that the nerve plug must belong in more capable hands. However, I will give you another option to whet your appetite. Give me the nerve plug right now and I promise that you will be paid a royalty every time we manufacture the device. You'd never have to work again! This way you can pass complete ownership to me and we never have to worry about it again."

"A retirement payment?" said Bolt.

"Please stop interrupting or security will escort you off the premises. You are only here on a temporary basis and upon my authority after all. You should be happy. Doctor Hart has given you your leg back and I will let you keep that for free, okay? Good. Now do not get involved with matters that you do not comprehend."

"You want me to leave?" I asked. "Right now and give everything up? Leave my technology and you will pay me for each nerve plug?"

"That is exactly what I am saying. Wouldn't your family like that? You would easily become the richest civilian in Prima. Not an easy feat..."

"Perhaps you don't understand, but this is my life's work. I want to use this nerve plug to help people feel complete again."

"If you do not desire any more interest in the project beyond your pathetic limb reconstruction, then you will have to leave."

"This can't be it. It's too simple and easy. There must be more. What do you get out of this?"

"This project will become mine when you leave, William. My brother does not have control over everything in this company. He is too busy hunting down his fugitives with his private little army of soldiers to know what's really going on in his own company. Sometimes technology simply slips out of his control."

"You're trying to work over Vincent Cain?" said Bolt

"Your own brother!" I laughed in her face. "It won't work."

"Thank you for your support, gentlemen, but it is already happening. Unless you give Vincent military results tomorrow, he will be forced to cut you loose and give the research, the buyers and the future to the reliable hands of his hard working sister."

"I guess that means I'll be working overnight," I said sharply.

It was Lucy's turn to go silent. She hadn't expected that. Bolt coughed roughly and looked at me confused.

"You'll never finish your work in time," said Lucy.

"You can't be serious?" Bolt asked.

"All of your work will become mine," said Lucy coldly. "You have less than a day to achieve satisfactory results for Vincent. Those satisfactory results mean much more than limbs. That means something new. That means military results. Revolutionary results that people will want to buy. That means building beyond

184

your moral comprehension."

"You can't give them weapons," said Bolt. "You said it yourself… you built this for prosthetics, not to fall at the demands of the highest bidder. This is yours, Will. Don't give in."

"It's what needs to be done," I told them both. "I want to make sure the technology gets used correctly. I believe that prosthetics are the future, but some people want more and I have to submit to that."

"You are really going to do this?" Lucy Quayin asked. "You can't win this fight. It's pointless even trying."

I thought of my family waiting at home and I knew I was doing the right thing. I had to keep control of this technology. I imagined my children becoming adults in a strange new world that had become altered by their father's technology. It was exactly as I had told Izzy. They needed a fresh clean slate. We have to keep the world safe and not repeat the horror that my parent's generation inflicted. I had to keep control, even if that meant producing a product that I didn't agree with.

"I will never give away control of this project," I told my employer.

Lucy Quayin laughed and her nostrils flared with hidden fury. She turned on her heels and clacked her way out of the room.

"See you tomorrow, Doctor," she hissed. "Good luck creating the future in less than twenty-four hours."

"You can't do it," he stared at me in disbelief. "You can't give her want she wants."

"I don't have a choice," I said quietly. "I need action in order to save my work. I have to give them something beyond my original intentions; otherwise I will lose everything. Thank you for all your help Mark, but I won't need you any more today. Come in midday tomorrow, so we can work out your place in the presentation tomorrow. We will make sure the world sees the true potential of this work. They will see that it should be used to complete people, not enhance them."

"You can't do this…"

"I am doing this," I told him sharply. "I don't have a choice."

185

16 – Moment of Clarity

My father drove our car with controlled tenacity as he tackled the difficult road ahead. His skin glistened slightly with sweat. He rubbed his eyes and I wondered if he was getting tired.

I breathed out heavily and the window steamed up. With my finger, I wrote my name slowly through the thick condensation.

William.

The rain was getting heavier by the second and the wind rattled the oak trees nearby. Peering out at the slur of the leaves, I watched as the torrent of air snatched them from their branches and splattered them across the road.

From the backseat of the car I pulled my seatbelt out so that I could look through the front window at the autumn storm. The car wipers lashed fiercely, wiping away rattling water and clumps of leaves. The setting sun burst through the clouds and pierced my eyes with sharp beams of light. Our headlights flashed on in an attempt to power our way through the dying dusk.

There was a bump in the road and the car swerved suddenly causing my mother to swear absently. Her hand clutched the car seat until her knuckles became white. Her breath steamed up the inside of the windscreen to further obscure our vision. She wiped the glass with her sleeve before changing her mind and turned the heating up in the car.

A glint of a green light caught my eye and illuminated the dashboard. The temperature outside had plummeted below zero.

Words tried to crawl their way out of my mouth, but I stopped them. I didn't want to distract my parents whilst they were driving us home.

We bounded our way over a long bridge, suspended over a cascade of dark water. I tried to hear the rushing river far below, but it was swamped out of earshot by the rattling air conditioning, the splattering rain and the drone of the radio.

I breathed out heavily again and allowed the letters of my name to disappear under my hot breath. I wiped the glass with my hand and looked at the reflection of my fifteen year old face.

The sound of a horn blasted through the air and I flicked my head back to the road. A set of burning bright lights blinded us. I heard the screech of tyres as we swerved to avoid the other car. My father slammed his foot down to brake and our tyres squealed over the wet road.

The car twisted and we slammed through the side of the bridge.

The rain was howling. The world was spinning. We were falling. I glimpsed the rushing river rising to swallow us whole. The water crashed into us, surrounding us and drowning us. We sank quickly into the deep dark heart of the river. The lights inside the car blinked out one by one, silenced the radio and the darkness consumed the confined space.

The car slammed into the riverbed and the force flung our bodies forward. The water rushed and pounded against the glass as the car contorted against the current. I heard my mother screaming and my father struggling in his seat. I gasped as my breath became tight. I couldn't move. I couldn't breathe. I felt water already spilling into the car, it was cold and thick with grime, and already crawling its way up my leg.

My hands scrambled into my pocket and dug out my touch-screen phone. The screen shone with dull blue light and illuminated my parent's faces. They both looked back at me, their eyes full of fear and numbed by the shock of the crash. My mother's head was bleeding heavily and her eyes faded with the pain. She must've have hit her skull against the dashboard.

My father's eyes narrowed as they looked past me. I undid my seatbelt and shone my light against the back window.

The light revealed thick cracks that splintered the glass in blue crooked lines. They shimmered as water spat through the fractures as the river tried to force itself inside the opaque window. I could see the pressure building against the fissure. The glass was going to break. I gasped in deeply to take the biggest breath I could as the dark river destroyed the window and erupted inside the car.

17 - Breakthrough

I woke up and became disorientated in the darkness. My heart pounded fiercely as panic took hold of my body. The memory of my parent's death slammed through my mind and I began to hyperventilate.

A blue light above clicked on.

I lifted my head off the cold surface and stared at the blurred series of blue lines that formed a sequence of numbers. I squinted and read that it was nearly midnight.

I released a sigh of relief as my mind recognised my surroundings. The lab looked so different in the half-darkness. The blue clock lit the edges of the wide workspace. The walls were far out of sight, but I could see the circular desk surrounding me. The scanner was within sight too. The sprawled mess of new machinery still wouldn't slot back into the table and sparked briefly in the darkness. The splattering of light illuminated a stack of cardboard boxes that I had ordered earlier from a pizzeria in Central Plaza. The aroma of the leftover food struck my nostrils and made my stomach rumble. If I remembered correctly there were still a few slices and crusts left of the pepperoni pizza.

The exhaustion must have hit harder than I thought. It was never my intention to fall asleep at the lab, but I'd been constantly working since Bolt left. My gift had taken its toll on my body at last, as I predicted it would.

The clock reminded me that it was too late now to go home.

Adele was going to be angry. I'd forgotten to call her to explain that I would have to work late. I dug out my phone and saw there were five missed calls. I swore under my breath and saw there was a text message waiting for me. I selected the green icon and the messages expanded on the holo-screen.

"Okay. I was just worried. Love you," Adele's message read.

Confused, I swiped upwards and saw my previous messages. It seemed I'd managed to get a message through to her saying that I would sleep at work. It was sent at half ten and I couldn't remember typing it...

I moved out of my central desk and fell against the scanner. I felt weak, as though I'd just completed a half marathon. Burrowing through the boxes, I grasped a couple slices of pizza and munched on them furiously. Swallowing desperately to rebuild my energy, I ate everything. All the slices, crusts and leftover crumbs in the corners. I licked my fingers and savoured every iota of sensation against my taste buds. My stomach was satisfied, but I coughed fiercely through my dry throat. I made my way to the water dispenser and clasped my mouth against the nozzle. The water was cold and refreshing. My throat finally cleared and my mind began to fully wake up. Rubbing my fingers together, I pressed some of the water into my eyes.

A buzz tingled along the back of the neck, making the hairs stand on end. Moving through the half darkness I found the source. It was the nerve plug I had created for Lucy Quayin earlier. A wire stretched from the plug and up into the mass of machinery that resembled all the work I'd been doing for the last ten or so hours.

Quayin had wanted more, so I had created more. I made an entire body using the materials I had from development. It had arms, legs, joints, chest, head and everything you'd expect from a humanoid structure. Using the nerve plug, a person would be able to control the exoskeleton remotely. There had been technology of a similar nature before, but this would be faster than anything else. They would also be able to feel everything the exoskeleton touched, creating an entire new body of metal skin and allowing instantaneous reactions by the user.

I'd also created a few functions that weren't human. The joints of the exoskeleton moved in ways that humans did not. All the joints revolved 360 degrees, such as the torso or the head. I had tried it a couple times and had become very disorientated as my head turned all the way around for the first time. After that, I had become elated with the new levels of movement available in the body, however if you didn't believe you could do the new movement, then it would simply not happen.

189

I also designed a few inhuman creations by drawing up a quick design of a lizard and a spider. They showed that with practice, the user would be able to handle a body with multiple limbs. The lizard design had an extended neck and a long tail that the user would have to control as well as the four extra limbs. Meanwhile the spider design had eight limbs and two smaller pincers at the head. Both new designs had the capabilities to climb up walls and move with extraordinary speed. The idea had come to me when watched Lucy controlled the metal hand remotely and made it crawl across the table. She effectively, at that moment, had three arms and controlled them all easily within the first minute of using the nerve plug.

Finally I'd researched technologies that Cain Corporation already had available such as prototype chemical, electric, magnetic and laser weapons, an unmanned aircraft capable of switching between hovering and flying with high-powered jet engines and a new type of multi-limbed all-terrain-vehicle. I knew little to nothing about these projects, but I'm sure Vincent would pick up any questions if there was any interest.

If this didn't help me keep my job, then I didn't know what would.

The hair on my arms suddenly stood sharply on end. I flicked my head towards the door and saw it illuminated by several torchlights. I grabbed the nerve plug attached to the exoskeleton and retreated carefully into the darkness of the room. The light outside tried to activate the door panel, but my earlier interference only allowed access to me.

The blocked door provided a moment to gather myself, as I headed toward the tube. I ran across the lab and waved it open with my hand. It slid open and I jumped in. The door slid close and I shaded the glass. My visitors wouldn't be able to see me now. I turned off power to the tube and waited in the darkness for the intruders to enter my lab.

I felt the door slide open and through the blurred glass I heard the muffled sounds as several bodies entered the room. I counted four lights zip past the tube. I held my breath and stayed still.

"It's clear," one of individuals called out and I relaxed slightly.

"Stand down," replied a sickly voice that I knew instantly. She entered my lab with the usual grind of her clacking heels.

I grinded my teeth in anger and I sent my focus across the room. I had to know if I was right. My exoskeleton laid waiting in the dark and I sensed the spark of power still alive in the machine. I sent a small slip of stored power into one of the eye sockets that held a camera. Normally the user would need a visor to see through the cameras, but I did not restrict myself. Confidence was the key. If I believed it was possible, then it could happen. My gift seemed to be limitless in this way. As I closed my eyes, I found the picture of the lab there, waiting in my mind's eye. Glancing at the shaded tube, I checked that I was safely hidden. The right eye of the exoskeleton then looked at the other inactive eye. I smiled at my work. At least it would function efficiently for the presentation tomorrow.

Lucy Quayin was silhouetted in the half-light. A large man that dwarfed her in size moved roughly past and walked straight towards me, I juddered backwards and felt the exoskeleton do the same. I kept my focus and forced the external body to stay still.

He approached the body with his torch, shining the light into its face. His thick muscles swallowed each other as he peered forwards. Heavy rivers of sweat leaked from his forehead and down the folds that surrounded the small eyes buried in his face. The last time I'd seen Anton Stranz was in this same lab with Vincent Cain. It would seem the alliances lay more strongly with Cain's sister.

"So, is this it?" Stranz asked, his thick features stretching to form words.

"No," answered Quayin shortly and she moved over to join him.

The sound was muffled and I realised I was hearing their voices from inside the tube, so I sent another surge of power to activate the audio in the head of the external body. My forehead creased with effort and I forced myself to ignore the clacking of Quayin's heels from my own ears and hear them through the exoskeleton's mechanical ear instead. Breathing deeply, I relaxed my body and sent my full focus on the scene happening outside.

191

"It's much smaller. The size of a fist," she told him. Stranz raised his hand and it looked about the same size as Quayin's whole head.

"Much smaller than that," she continued. "It glows bright blue once activated and will have several black straps attached. Earlier it was right here." She traced her manicured hand over the scanner and tapped it with her nails. The guards around her watched her think. There was Stranz and four others in total. I couldn't tell if they were men or women, but they all seemed loyal to Quayin's personal cause.

"If we can't find it, then we will take his hard-drive and copy the information. He had an extraordinary amount of data that I want to be able to access. The man had results from Amazonia, Eden and Lupo. That is unprecedented. It is therefore vital we copy it and leave this place untouched. I don't want Vincent knowing that anything has gone missing from his beloved pet project."

"Won't Mr Cain know anyway? He keeps track of any unusual results in the machines in this lab," Stranz mumbled.

"Vincent isn't a god!" Lucy screamed, which made her guards stir uncomfortably. "The sooner you all realise that he doesn't have eyes everywhere, the sooner you can get on with your lives. I am the one in charge here. I am the one that pours everything I have into Cain Corporation. I am the one who looks after everything, whilst he is off hunting terrorists that have long fled Prima. Without me, this business would have collapsed long ago. Vincent doesn't care what his employees do, but I do."

Lucy moved between each of her loyal servants.

"You all came here tonight for me," she purred and stopped in front of Stranz and laid a small manicured hand on his huge chest. Stranz smiled sickly and his small eyes glittered in the marine luminescence.

"Forget Vincent. He is nothing but a mere man. Work for me and you will have power beyond anything Vincent could ever promise you. We will control the next step in technological history."

She lowered her voice so that only Stranz and my amplified

audio receivers could hear her...

"You'll have all of this and I will be at your side every step of the way."

"You heard Miss Quayin," Stranz roared to his colleagues. "Find that nerve-plug."

I nodded to myself in the tube; of course she wanted the plug. Once she mass-produced the device and claimed it as her own then it would completely take me out of the equation. However, luckily for me, I only made two plugs. One rested in my pocket and the other was safe with Mark Bolton inside his new leg.

I couldn't let them have the computer hard-drive either. All of my work was on there. With that information they could claim the research belonged to Quayin all along. Also, who knew what other lost marvels she could find in the Lupo archive?

I had to do something.

Lucy was currently working with two other soldiers at the main computer trying to breach the hologram. She ran her hands through the air desperately to get past the clock screensaver, whilst her guards fiddled with the panels below the desk to find the hard-drive manually.

Stranz and the other two soldiers continued to search the room. They gathered around the exoskeleton, planning to search inside the machine to find the plug. Which was exactly what I was waiting for. All I had to do was scare them away and I had the perfect tool to do it.

The stored power slowly streamed throughout the skeleton, the left eye activated first followed by the entire body. I grasped control of the exoskeleton in my mind and felt the entire body. It was like I had performed mitosis and my long lost metal twin was standing across the room. I began to feel the guards probing fingers search through my metal bones and wire veins. Stranz's sausage fingers were currently laced around my neck. I collected a sudden burst of energy and sent a stream of fiery energy pouring into my new neck. Stranz fell back in shock and shook his burning hand. I turned my metal head to face him and turned the lights on in my eyes. The space lit up in brilliant white light, blinding Stranz, and allowing me to see in perfect quality. He

193

raised a smoking black hand to shield his eyes.

"What did you do?" Quayin shouted.

"I didn't do anything! It just turned itself on," he continued.

"Then the plug must be inside it," she said.

Thick laughter rose in my chest and I pressed my lips together in order to stifle any noise coming from into the tube.

"Pry it open. I want that nerve-plug," said Quayin.

Stranz and the other four guards moved towards the machine. They fanned out in a semi-circle and blocked my creation against the wall. Lucy Quayin remained unfazed as she stood by the main computer.

"What are you waiting for? Destroy it!" Quayin said fiercely.

Stranz moved forwards and I fully activated the exoskeleton. It took two sharp steps forward and a stream of electricity flowed through its body and activated all external signs of life, illuminating the skeleton in thin blue lines. It weaved to the left, pushed a quick metal foot against the wall and jumped off it. A heavy clang sound resonated across the lab and made the first guard stagger back. I landed heavily and slammed a quick jabbing fist into his protected chest. He hunched as the metal bruised his ribs. Grabbing the next guard, I lifted them by their arms and through my cameras I saw the squirming face of a woman in her thirties. I threw her across the room and she skidded into the far wall. Stranz's great arms wrapped themselves around my body and lifted me up in the air and slammed down to the ground. Stranz loomed over the machine and filled my vision. He was easily twice the size of the exoskeleton. I tried not to think how small I was next to him normally. He lifted his boot over my face and I grabbed it with both hands and pushed my metal body to the side. I lashed out with a sharp kick into his kneecap, which crunched sharply. There was a mighty thud as Stranz crashed to the floor.

There was a double click and I saw the remaining two guards raising their guns at me. From the tube I stretched out my subconscious to try and deactivate their weapons. The skeleton and I both raised our hands at once and I wrapped my focus around the nearest gun and broke it apart. The gunpowder inside

194

one of the bullets ignited fiercely. A sharp bang filled the room and the man screamed as the fire broke his gun into pieces. The remaining man fired several bullets and I felt two sting the skeleton's chest, but another slipped into my neck cavity and ruptured the fibres there. The skeleton flailed about roughly as I struggled to regain control.

Stranz got back up and kicked it onto its back. He smiled roughly and spat downwards on the camera lens.

"Only a machine," he grunted.

Electricity fizzed through the battery and I sent it shooting out the skeleton's right arm and streaming at the man who had shot at me. He went flailing backwards through the open lab door. Stranz kicked my metal head, but I sent out another kick toward his calf. It caught him and made him lose balance slightly. I sent another surge of power through my left fist and then my right. They dazzled with white and blue electricity. I hit Stranz once in the chest and he caught my other hand before I could hit him again. It was the grotesque burnt hand that I had scorched earlier. He grasped my metal fist, refusing to fall down. The electricity flowing through my arm fixated on his charred hand and burned into his flesh. He roared in pain. I pinned him against the wall and slammed a metal fist into his chest again and again and again. Stranz dropped to his knees and I placed my left hand on his forehead, firing a rasp of power into his head. He finally fell to the floor in a rough clump.

I looked at a wordless Lucy Quayin, who was unsure whether to hide or run. The metal man picked up the three remaining guards and tossed them one by one out of the still open door. It moved over to Stranz and dragged him by his leg to join the others.

It took a small moment to check that they were all still alive.

The tube door slid open and I stepped out. My eyes were fading and hands were shaking. I walked behind my exoskeleton and lay a single hand on its shoulder and moved round to face Lucy Quayin.

"This is my work," I told her. I pushed a hand into my pocket and pulled out the glowing nerve plug. "This is mine."

Her speechlessness slowly transformed into hatred, her eyebrows curling with fury. Her makeup was smeared. The black eyeliner dragged out in cruel lines and her prudent red lipstick that she had put on so meticulously earlier, now dripped down her lower lip like running blood. Quayin's white teeth snarled at me.

"You are going to pay for this," she said.

"And you are going to pay for breaking into your brother's lab," I replied. I activated the nerve plug and controlled the exoskeleton with the device for the first time. My plan was to make sure she believed that I was using the nerve plug all along. I couldn't have her finding out about my gift. I raised the nerve plug and made my metal twin point at her whilst I pointed.

"Get out of my lab," I said coldly. "Tomorrow I will make sure Prima sees who you really are. A manipulating woman, who uses her employees to increase her social status. A traitor who would happily use one of her brother's most loyal soldiers to betray him. Cross me again and I will make you leave Cain Corporation. Permanently. Counter my presentation and you won't be having words from me. No. You'll be having words from my metal friend and you've seen what he can do."

She looked nervously at the skeleton and then back at me. She tilted her head slightly and then stumbled out of the lab on awkward heels. I looked down and saw that one of them had broken in the panic. She left with only a single click with no clack in her heelless footsteps.

I waited until I was satisfied they had all left and looked at the skeleton. I felt myself let go. I didn't have to use my gift to connect to the machine.

Yet... I could still feel it through the nerve plug.

The device buzzed violently in the palm of my hand and connected vibrantly to the entire exoskeleton.

A burst of pain surged into the base of my skull.

I could hear them screaming briefly before being swallowed by an endless cascade of water. The force threw me backwards and knocked the held breath out of my body. The water filled my mouth and forced its way down my throat. I grasped out desperately. We were drowning. I couldn't breathe. I couldn't...

I blinked slowly and the lights of my lab fluttered. The pain spiked at back of my head.

Intense heat burnt at my flesh. I screamed out in exertion. I pressed my sweating palms outward against the shell of searing boiling hot metal. It was the only shield stopping the flames. There were people with me. They needed me. The fire was getting stronger and fiercer by the second. I couldn't hold it back any longer...

The lab suddenly faded. The pain subsided.

I stared at the nerve-plug in fading horror as I tried to comprehend what it had just done to my mind. I pressed my hand against my face and saw that my nose was bleeding heavily. I swore faintly as the floor rushed forwards to meet me.

18 – Fire and Water

The ground crunched into her face. The rubble began to rain down and she curled into a ball to protect her head. As the dust settled, she pushed her thick dreadlocks out of the way, allowing her sharp eyes to assess the situation before pushing herself back onto her feet.

The girl was in an underground cavern that was occupied by a vast series of coloured tents. The tents interlaced with each other and formed large rooms and corridors. The city of fabric that held a community of Outcasts within its embrace was now under attack.

She stumbled away from the breaking wall behind her that had just blocked one of the few entrances to the cavern. She made her way to her nearby crimson tent to collect herself. She closed her eyes to ignore the screams that were already echoing across the encampment.

Raven was wearing laced boots, dirtied combat trousers and a crumpled grey vest top. Her hand clutched her shoulder as she checked whether the bandaging around her bullet wound was still secure. She raised her hand and saw that it was already speckled with blood. She swore crudely to the Fate of death, peeled the bandage away and peeked at the wound. Her flesh was laced together by eleven stitches, but one of them had split in the explosion. She licked two of her fingers clean of blood, dried them on the inside of her vest and grasped the stray stitch. Raven gritted her teeth as she pulled the stitch taunt. She sent a burst of fire out of her shoulder to swiftly cauterize and seal the wound once again.

A solitary scream echoed one hundred and twenty seven metres away. Their heartbeat rushed sporadically allowing Raven to sense their exact location. It was a woman and Raven could tell by her fluctuating heat signature that she was clearly afraid of the impending danger. Raven peered around the tent and spotted several soldiers entering the encampment from another entrance.

Her palm ignited with fire and she slammed it into the canvas wall. Tracing her palm upwards, the tent split open and clambered inside. Eyes dancing around her room, she quickly gathered everything she would need and threw it into her rucksack. She grabbed rope, flint, bottled water, her silver lighter, quickly rolled up her hammock, gathered some remnants of clothes and collected a single photograph. Her palm splayed open and the rippling fire that was already cascading up the tent dissipated and flowed into her body. With the fire extinguished, she grabbed her weathered jacket that lay crumpled on the ground, threw it around her, grabbed her rucksack and ran out of the tent.

The Outcast encampment was on fire. At least fifteen tents by the far entrance had already become rising columns of flames. Raven's nostrils flared as she sensed the raging inferno nearby. As she ran forwards, she felt her lips smile. The fire was inviting her to come closer. It was demanding to grow. It craved her control. It demanded to eat more.

No…

She was not going to fall for that old trick again. The soldiers were taunting her. They were using the fire to attract her, like a moth to candlelight. They knew that she would run straight to the point where she could use her gift the most.

Another explosion blasted high above her, raining down destruction and a series of long abseiling ropes. Raven's looked into the newly formed entrance and was suddenly blinded by bright lights.

It would seem they had learnt new tricks after all. They weren't taunting her. They had been distracting her.

One by one, soldiers dressed in black descended the ropes and surrounded her. Each of them raised their guns and she remained perfectly still. She waited. She knew there was no escape.

Not yet.

Her eyes flicked into the pupils of each of the soldiers. There were twelve of them. Their heartbeats bounced out in different rhythms allowing her to gauge their age and confidence. There were seven men and five women. Raven grunted at the gender

199

inequality of the group.

She judged the strength of their heartbeats and the temperature of their bodies. It was a skill she had honed after having a gift for so long. She could discover so many facts about an individual just by sensing their body temperature. Some were warmer than others. The heat flowed differently. Raven didn't fully understand it and neither did she care to.

All she knew was that was damn useful when surrounded by gunpoint.

Her eyes flickered strangely. Darkly. An invisible and inaudible voice hummed in her ear and fed her thin threads of information. She grimaced in disgust and nodded roughly. Aspects of their lives were force fed into her mind. Aspects she didn't want to know. Aspects that suddenly humanised the group of people she was about to destroy.

They were all in their thirties, except for two men who were nearing forty five. Her gaze settled on the man who had been chain smoking for the last twenty-seven years and was the eldest and most experienced in combat. He was called Jared. He was forty-four. He'd fought during the Global War and shot down seventeen Lockers that had tried to raid Prima in 2066. She smiled wryly, Lockers was the common name used for folk who live in savage Antarctic great city. Jared later tracked down their Lockroy encampment and cut ten throats before setting fire to the barracks. Jared had watched as the remaining thirty-two Lockers burnt alive or ran out into the darkness all aflame and screaming…

Raven flinched with utter disgust. Why did he tell her that? She hated that damn telepath. That was information she really did not want or need to know.

She glared at the veteran. She had to take him out quickly. He was ruthless and inspired confidence in the others. Break him and she would shock the rest that he'd gone down so easily.

The trick to surviving these encounters was to mentally break the group and exploit their weaknesses.

Her vision moved beyond the men and fluttered to the flaming tents. It was difficult to tell from here, but she could sense at least twenty unconscious bodies. Whether they were Outcasts or soldiers was beyond her senses…

She watched as many of her associates tried to run away and were shot in order to disable them. They were electrocuted, grabbed in nets, gathered, and paraded out of the cavern. The fires spread from tent to tent, burning away livelihoods and homes. Raven spat on the ground, which sizzled violently, causing the soldiers to tense up with fear.

She should never have come back.

The soldiers still did not make their move. They must be waiting for orders. She nodded her approval at their patience and then decided to raise their body temperatures by several degrees. Raven sweated slightly from the effort of the activity.

Her eyes bored into the youngest individual. Paul. He was thirty-one. He was single. No. He had a cat. What a stupid fact to be told. She mentally shrugged. It was something she could try and use against him at least. Raven smiled as the gun began to shake in his hands. She winked at him and his pupils widened in horror.

Through the smoke, a figure finally emerged surrounded by his guarding troops. His blonde hair shone in the firelight and his gun metal eyes bore directly into Raven. He swaggered his way into the cavern, as though he owned everything that he touched.

"Oh, how wonderful!" Vincent Cain cried. "You waited for me? Really? You shouldn't have."

"I couldn't let you miss the show," Raven replied simply.

"And I thank you for that," he said. "Because I've been waiting for this one-on-one meeting for a very long time. We left on bad terms last time we chatted. I don't know about you, but it's like there's a hole inside me, just below the collar bone…"

"Yeah, yeah, I know," Raven interrupted. "The hunt is over. You've won. Great job. Are you going take me in or not?"

"You would like that, wouldn't you?" Cain asked.

"Yes, I would," she replied. "So shall we get on with it or what?"

"You see…" he said and stopped outside the circle of his soldiers. Raven swore under her breath. She'd been hoping that she could take him hostage and use him as a human shield. "I was thinking about it on the way down here to your scum hole and I realized that my life would be better off without you. I thought we established that when I fired that Mengxiang round into your chest. I thought the acid would have finished you off. So. You know what? I reckon you'd be much less trouble if you were dead."

"You know…" she said. "I was thinking exactly the same thing about you."

Raven turned suddenly and punched Jared directly in the chest and felt his forty-five year old diseased heart shuddering under the force of her blow. As he stumbled, she threw her elbow backwards into Paul's young malleable jaw and grabbed the wavering gun from his hands. She fired a single round into the foot of the next experienced individual in the circle. He was in his prime. Gregor was thirty-five, wasn't married and already had his gun aimed at her head. He fell down crippled, moaning through the pain, but managed to fire several shots that whizzed past her ear. She found the friction of the hammer that had just sliced into the gunpowder inside of his gun, amplified it and ignited his ammunition. Gregor's gun exploded and sent him flailing backwards. Stray shrapnel caught his nearby associates; whilst the rest of the soldiers finally raised their guns to try and kill her. Raven rolled before they got the chance and grabbed the most vulnerable individual out of them all.

The dark voice told her that Marie had two kids waiting for her at home and had been married for ten years.

Raven swore to the Fate of life quickly, cursed this cruel humanization, and ignited her palm inches away from the mother's throat.

The remaining eight soldiers all clenched their fingers around their triggers. The youngest individual, Paul, held his jaw with one hand, before pulling out a pistol. All nine trained their guns on Raven and her captive… but not a single one of them fired a bullet.

"Do you really want to do this?" Raven asked them all. "I can keep going. I'm serious. I won't stop until you're all burnt to ash."

"Wonderful show, Raven. Simply splendid!" Cain applauded vaguely before indicating the captive woman. "Would you let Marie go, so we can go back to the bit where we shoot you in the head?"

"Marie and I are just getting to know each other that's all…" she replied.

"I can tell you're lying," Cain said. "At first I thought you two were just hugging, but then I realised that you're holding her captive. You know how I figured that out? Because you punched old Jared in the heart and made Gregor shoot himself! Clear signs of aggression on your part and clear signs that some folks are getting fired this season!"

"Don't forget Paul. I think I broke his jaw," she smiled sickly and Paul looked in horror and flicked his nervous eyes to Cain.

"And how on earth are you on a first name basis with our newest recruit?" Cain asked curiously.

Raven swallowed and shook her head to shut out the voice. That evil voice. That familiar, haunting, disgusting voice. She gritted her teeth and forced her focus back at the other man she despised.

"You should hire better goons and more women," Raven replied sweetly before lying profoundly. "Paul has his name written on his label."

The voice confirmed that he actually did as the young man nervously fiddled with the collar of his shirt.

"I think you're lying…" Cain smiled. "He's in your head, isn't he? The devil of Old Street. Mimic. Once he's in your mind… he never lets go."

"All I've done is even the male to female ratio," Raven snapped, gripping her captive even tighter and ignoring the dark laughter in her mind. "Now we have five guys and five girls, including Marie of course."

"Hey! I'm not a sexist employer," Cain said. "I hire whomever is best for the job. It doesn't matter their gender, all that matters in this situation was that some of the blokes were a bit better than the ladies at abseiling down ropes into your horrid home."

"Well, good for you," Raven said dryly. "Go equality."

"Thank you," Cain said proudly. "I enjoy our conversations. Did you know that you're basically the only person who talks back to me without fear of getting fired or imprisoned? Now would you please let Marie go? You know… to balance the gender ratio again?"

"Not a chance in hell," Raven grunted. "You're going to have to take me in Vince."

"So be it," Cain sighed and his soldiers relaxed as they realised they wouldn't have to shoot their friend. "Apologies Marie. Send my love to the kids when you're lying in hospital."

Vincent Cain pulled out his gun and fired a round into Marie's foot. She screamed and Raven pushed her forwards. Marie fell against a man named Mack who was married, but was secretly sleeping with another individual in the company. Raven punched cheating Mack in the side of his head and his secret partner, Lydia, leapt from the opposite side of the circle on instinct. Raven launched an elbow into Lydia's throat and slammed a fist into her spine as she doubled over. Paul rushed forward with his wobbling jaw and wild handgun, so Raven promptly pinned him to the ground.

"Guess what?" Raven hissed to distract him from firing his weapon. "I'm going to sell your cat online!"

Paul stopped suddenly, his jaw hanging down dumbly at an awkward angle, before Raven head-butted his nose and kicked his weapon away.

That was six down and six to go and all weaknesses she could gather were already exploited. It was time to use more drastic measures.

Raven found the fire that had begun to ignite a nearby tent. She amplified it and sent it cascading into three more of the soldiers. Jason, Megan and Hanna spun away flailing against the flames. She launched a fist of fire into Jorge's chest sending him flying backwards. Before the next target, Stephan, could attack her, she slammed six jabs of hot fire wrapped around her knuckles into each of his ribs.

The final woman grabbed her from behind and began to strangle her in a sleeping hold. The voice immediately began pouring facts about Rebecca's life in his ear. The troubled past, bullying and prided admiration she had working under Vincent Cain. Raven swore viciously at the torment of information and the strangulation that was straining the bones in her neck. She saw the vague silhouette of Vincent Cain standing over them. He snarled and turned away from her final moments. Her vision faded as she watched the man she hated walk away from her death. Raven screamed with rage and threw her hand against Rebecca's head and raised the temperature of her brain by twelve degrees Fahrenheit.

Gasping for breath Raven ran full pelt towards Vincent Cain. The fire poured from her skin and drove her to kill him. She wanted to him to burn for what he had done to the Outcasts.

She counted their names as her feet fiercely pounded into the earth in quick succession.

Jared, Gregor, Marie, Mack, Lydia, Paul, Jason, Megan, Hanna, Jorge, Stephan, Rebecca and finally… Vincent.

There was a sudden flash of green and Raven tripped up violently, her face once again crunching into the ground.

"You took your time," Vincent Cain said to the man with green eyes. Xander's white coat swayed heavily. It was covered with filth and blood. He looked at his employer with a weary gaze. It looked like the rest of the Outcasts had been giving him a hard time.

"I was busy," Xander said.

"Here's a suggestion. Why don't you busy yourself with her," Cain said pointing at Raven, collapsed on the ground.

Xander moved to attack and Raven knew from experience that it was a fight that she never won. She turned on her heel and fled through the field of burning tents as fast as she could. She summoned walls of fire and threw them back. She ducked through tents, jumped over unconscious bodies and did everything in her power to lose her hunter. As she glimpsed backwards she saw Xander simply side step the destruction and continue his never-ending hunt. Raven roared in frustration and fled to the edge of the encampment to a series of waste pipes.

The nearby flickering fires fluttered and then rushed forwards, igniting against the network of pipes. She ran through the dust and threw her body forwards into a large pipe that had revealed itself.

Her body slid down headfirst and she spared a moment to destroy the entrance to the pipe so that Xander couldn't follow her. This was the only remaining way she could exit the encampment. She really did not want to do it, but she was left with no choice.

The pipe would lead to the river and then she would have to ascend twenty metres to the surface. It was a very difficult swim, due to the fast moving current, plus all the gear she had on her back. There was also the small fact that she'd never been a good swimmer.

Raven's palms lit up with a dull ruby light. Ahead she could see the shimmering water quickly approaching. She inhaled deeply to take the biggest breath that she could as she dived into the river and it's dark embrace consumed her. The water rushed around her, tugging and dragging her. The darkness began to consume the light. Raven's hands ceased to glow as the water extinguished the fire.

She was surrounded by complete darkness…

Familiarity stung my brain and I was dragged away from the present reality of watching Raven swimming through darkness to the distant memory of myself underwater.

I was surrounded by complete darkness.

In my hands was my touch screen phone that glowed with a dull blue light. It momentarily illuminated the inside of the car and revealed the empty back window. I desperately forced my way out of the car. The blue light of my phone flashed again and I twisted back to look for my parents. My father was trying to help my unconscious mother out of the car. He waved at me. I couldn't tell if he wanted me to help or to swim away.

I swam back desperately to help, but the river suddenly grabbed me. I screamed and an explosion of air escaped my lungs. The current was pulling me away. The blue light died as my phone finally crippled from the water damage. The car and my drowning parents disappeared from sight.

Raven continued to swim as fiercely as she possibly could, the panic slowing her down, making her tired. She was running out of breath and out of time...

I scrambled my way to the surface, trying not to think of my parents still trapped down there. I had to get help. I had to get to the surface.

Raven cried out in horror. She couldn't die like this. She didn't want to die like this. She tried to open her eyes, but the water stung her retinas. She screamed and vital oxygen escaped her lips...

I could see the light. I was almost there. I could make it. I could do it. It was just a little further to go now.

Raven wavered against the flow of water. She could see the fading light, but she wouldn't be able to reach it. She wouldn't make it...

I erupted to the surface and gasped desperately, limbs flailing, savouring every last particle of air.

Raven stopped trying to swim as she choked on the water filling up her lungs... With every remaining part of her energy, she threw her palm towards the surface and fired one last flame upwards. With any luck someone would at least find her body...

I clawed my way up the muddy bank of the river and screamed as loud as I could for help. I cried out again and again, until the black sky was filled with blue and red flashing lights.

Something grabbed Raven's body and pulled her to the surface...

"My parents are still down there," I told them. "You have to go get them. They're fine. Just go down there and you will see for yourself. My father, his name is Theodore, he's a physician. I saw him down there helping my mother, Susan. She's been knocked unconscious, but she'll be okay, my father is pulling her out. He knows what he's doing, but he needs your help. Can you just stop looking after me and get them! They're still alive. They are still... will you just go in there and look... I'll be fine. Just go! Just, please, go in and look for them. Please, please... stop looking after me and go get them. Please. I'm sorry. I didn't have a choice. I didn't have a choice..."

The sounds of sirens, rushing water and tears of a young distraught man faded into the distance, leaving me alone in the silence of my own mind.

"It is amazing how alike you are. Don't you think so, William? Take a look at the most defining moment of your life compared to the present day ventures of Jessica. You are so alike… except for one small detail…"

I felt him drift fully into my mind and settle next to me. The Mind Walker sighed and his voice curled into my eardrums.

"Jessica has control over her life. Through her gift she has become Raven and is able to fight those who try to destroy her. Didn't you just see her take down twelve fully trained soldiers and escape with her life? She is simply remarkable."

His face formed to talk to me directly and I met his cold dead eyes.

"Just imagine if you had your abilities back in the river. I believe you could have saved them both. Your father and your mother could be alive right now. So do yourself a favour… if you ever get into a life or death situation again then do everything in your power to protect what is yours. You owe it to your family."

FRIDAY

Lucy Quayin

19 – Turning Point

My eyes curled open slowly to thick crimson fluid. I stared drearily at the colour, my brain trying desperately to make sense of my environment. The floor swayed and saw that I'd been lying in a soft pool of blood. A droplet dripped from the end of my nose and joined the sickly puddle. The top half of my body was soaked with dry blood.

It was my blood.

I blinked and the overhead lights came on, filling my lab with a sudden brightness, blinding me once more. I pressed my hand against my desk, leaving a bloodied handprint there, and looked wearily up at the illuminated clock. It had already gone midday. I swore under my breath. I should've called Adele and offered to take the kids to school, which would've meant driving past Old Street once again.

A sharp shiver tingled down the back of my neck.

I found the exoskeleton still facing the lab door. Power flowed through its wires, but it remained motionless, its right hand still pointing at the lab door. The memory of Lucy Quayin hobbling out of my lab tickled my thoughts. I laughed, but then choked on the dry blood that had coated my throat.

The lab was a mess. My blood stained the floor along with several other specks of dark red that could have belonged to any of Quayin's guards. I sent my consciousness to the skeleton and gave it the menial task of cleaning my lab.

I had to regain my focus. I had already lost so much time this morning. I was here to finish my work. I had to make sure my nerve-plug didn't fall into the wrong hands...

My heart jumped as I remembered the nerve-plug that the intruders had come for last night. My hand slammed down to my trouser pocket and I exhaled heavily with relief as I pulled out the small black disk. Its blue light hummed calmly at its centre. It was amazing that my entire future could be held inside such a small device.

I signalled my subconscious towards the mop and bucket in the corner of the room and heard the skeleton's metal feet clang across the floor as it collected them. I unlocked my computer and asked it to call Adele's number.

I waited as the phone rang. My hands were red with blood, so I rubbed them together and some of the blood came away in scarlet dust. The rest remained congealed onto my skin. I would need a shower before the presentation and luckily there were staff facilities on each floor.

The phone rang out and I nodded to myself. Adele must be working. I'd have to call her later and check she wasn't furious. She would hopefully understand the situation.

I collected the spare set of clothes from a side cabinet and left the lab swiftly, leaving my subconscious with the skeleton as he cleaned.

I meant *it*, not *he*, because *he* is actually *me*. That's why *they* feel so much like a *he* and not an *it*. I laughed miserably at the scene. Cleaning was such a terrible job for such a magnificent machine.

I stripped and let the cool water flow over my body. The clear water become red as the remnants of last night washed off my body. I lay my head against the shower wall as the car crash echoed through my hollow mind. The water flowed over my face and attempted to wash away the guilt I still felt. The man who was haunting my dreams was right. If only I'd had my gift back then. They could be here. My children could have met their grandparents. Theo could have met the man he was named after...

My eyes welled up and I raised my face to the water. It was a long time ago... there is nothing that could be done to save them.

But now I had the power to make sure that nothing like that will ever happen to anyone I loved ever again.

It was clear that there was so much more to my gift. I needed to understand it further in case it was fully required in the future.

I looked at the shower and using my gift, I turned it off and on repeatedly and even changed the temperature. However, if I changed it, if I made it become something new, then I would become lethargic. Staring at the shower, I let my imagination take

211

hold. The water began to shoot out faster and the shower head grew and split to allow more water to flow over my head. Finally, I closed the shower and opened it again, and soon I was making the shower spit at me like a sprinkler on a golfer's lawn. My heart suddenly quickened with the effort. I left the shower and it re-assembled into its original state.

When I demanded technology to perform beyond its designated function then I exerted myself. Meanwhile I could manipulate the world as much as I pleased.

What if I could find a way to have more power to stop myself from tiring? How far could my gift go then? I guess as far as the power supply reached, but would my body expire before I found my technological limit?

I dried off and returned to my lab. It was spotless. The blood was nowhere to be seen and everything had been tidied away. The skeleton remained stationary by the main computer, awaiting further instructions.

The nerve-plug glinted nearby and I gazed at it for a moment. It would've been nearly impossible to create this device without my power. My gift allowed me to feel all the technology around me, so I didn't need the nerve-plug to integrate myself into machines. In a way, this little device was a way for someone else to see the world through my new eyes. It was strange how my gift and my career had become exactly the same. It was like it was always meant to be that way.

I could never have achieved this on my own. I wouldn't have been able to see what needed to be to done. I always needed another perspective to make my work a reality… without Bolt I wouldn't have been able to know if this even worked or not.

I swore again. I had created two nerve plugs and told Lucy Quayin that Bolt had the other nerve plug. After she left here, she might have gone straight after him.

I flicked my head towards the computer and saw that my gift had already began to call Bolt. I tapped the counter impatiently. The phone rang twice, three times, but there was no response. I moved across the room to grab my coat, if I was quick then I could drive to his house and see if he was still there.

A fierce buzzing fizzed my senses and I flicked my head to the computer. The call to Bolt's phone had ended and the screen now flashed fizzed with emerald static. Another call suddenly came up from a blocked number. I waved my hand in the air to answer the call.

"Hello?" I asked cautiously.

At the end of line I heard a short intake of breath. There was definitely someone on the other end of the call.

"Who is this?" I asked further.

"I know what you are, William," they finally said, their voice slightly distorted. "I know what you can do and I know what you might become."

"Well… I don't know who you are, so I'm hanging up now."

"A girl visited you several times," the person interrupted. "You've looked after her, fed her, saved her life and set her free. Aiding a known criminal is a serious crime… especially one with such a fiery temper."

My blood ran cold and kept my mouth shut. It was safer for me not to confirm what the stranger was saying.

"I know that she revealed a certain gift to you." The stranger was cautious with their words now. I got the impression that they weren't meant to be speaking with me.

"I have no idea what…" I said quietly.

"You can't deny it. You have power and it won't be long before they find out," the stranger said.

"What do you want?" I asked.

"I am speaking to you for your own well-being," they continued hesitantly. "If you do not stop using your gift, people will come after you and they will hunt you down. It's your choice, William. You can stop this. You can stop what is coming."

"Are you threatening me?" I said slowly down the phone. I remembered the damage I had dealt to Stranz. "I can look after myself."

"I'm very aware of what you are capable of. I know where this path leads and it creates only destruction for us all," the voice said impatiently. "I'm trying to save you."

"I'm not in any danger," I said.

"Not yet, but if you keep going down this path, then there is no turning back. This is your turning point. You still have a chance to save yourself and your family and everyone you will come into contact with. Do not show anyone your gift. You should heed what I'm saying. I'm speaking from experience here..." said the stranger quietly. "I have to go. My time is running out."

"Who is this?" I asked sharply, before sending my consciousness into my computer and found the phone connection. I began to read the phone line and trace it back to its original source.

"Why William? Why do you continue?" The voice growled.

"Tell me who you are and I will stop," I said and began to follow the phone out of the building and across the city.

"Stop tracing my call," said the voice sharply. I stopped and allowed my consciousness to fall back into my body.

"They will catch you and they will take your family. Adele, Isabella and Theodore will all be quarantined. Everyone you know and love will disappear. I warned you, Doctor. You are a good man, I've seen it first hand, but if you continue using your gift then Vincent Cain will have no choice but to kill you."

The voice cut out and the hologram disappeared entirely, returning the screen to the clock screensaver. The stranger had hung up his phone. I fathomed at their words. The voice was distorted but it was familiar. I'd met that person before, but I couldn't put a finger on who it was.

If I didn't stop using my gift then Vincent Cain would hunt me down, as he has done to many fugitives after the incident. He'd quarantine, lobotomize and destroy me in order to protect the people of Prima from finding out the truth.

But if I didn't complete the presentation, then Lucy Quayin would take the nerve plug, rise over her brother and become the new ruling power in Prima. I'd be unemployed and useless to stop the mass production of my technology.

20 - Firewall

Despite the ominous warning from the stranger, I had to use my gift to find Bolt. I slammed my hand down on my desk and sent my mind into the Cain Corporation server. I moved beyond my own account and into the cyberspace. I smashed my consciousness through the blockade, like a sledgehammer to the firewall, blasting the digital shield to virtual smithereens. I healed up the digital space and removed any trace that it was broken. As the firewall healed, it sealed me into the depths of unknown electrical territory.

My eyes couldn't see anything, so instead I relied on my other developing senses. I could feel the cyberspace that I flowed through and now inhabited. It hummed and purred. A flash of a message or a signal would zip past me every now and then. A command moving from point A to point B, on a path to reach its destination with no deterring from its purpose. These signals could not be changed. Normally. But now there was something new in the system.

There was me.

I opened the file from my own account that allowed Bolt access to my lab. Inside were all his details including his date of birth, his handprint and a picture of his face.

Bolt's face rose in the cyberspace and the environment immediately began to analyse it, scanning every square inch of his skin. I could see his face. The signals began searching for other depictions of Bolt's face across the network. Within seconds I had thousands of results, but they were all from times when Bolt had entered my lab the past week. I saw images of Bolt walking through the front door, the foyer, the lift, the corridor and, of course, my lab door. Hundreds of pictures of his face all dated before he left the lab yesterday. I refined my search to look at this morning, after the break in at my lab.

I waited a full minute and began to grow weary as my presence grew unwanted in the cyberspace. The server pressed into my consciousness and tried to force me out, like a virus in its blood. I expended my energy to resist the system and remained untouched by any anti-viral programs.

A single picture suddenly appeared that was taken at five in the morning. It showed Mark's face stretched into a grimace. I zoomed out and found that it was outside the Corporation, where they brought in the deliveries. Bolt was being bundled out of a van and he'd fallen to the hard concrete. I zoomed back in and saw that his leg was gone. Stranz's blackened hand was clamped firmly around his shoulder, trying to haul him to his feet. Meanwhile, Quayin was exiting the van, holding Bolt's prosthetic with my glowing nerve plug attached.

I stared at the image trying to collect any more detail, but there was nothing. I was about to leave the cyberspace when I spotted another person waiting to meet them. I sent a caption of the person into the network and instantly received millions of results.

It was Pierre Foshe, grimacing impatiently. Surely that meant he was involved in Quayin's plot to overthrow Cain as well?

The camera had one last image waiting to be viewed, which had a partial possibility of containing Bolt. It showed the same location, except the van was gone and Foshe was standing over Mark.

I searched the network further, but found no more mention of Mark Bolton. I looked for Foshe and instantly found myself blocked by the network. All his files were firewalled. My consciousness dug deep into his wall of protection and tore it apart, and I was thrown into watching live footage of Foshe on the top floor of Cain Corporation.

He strafed the room as he interrogated a shackled prisoner with their hands above his head. Their face hung low and so would've been completely unidentifiable... expect the prisoner only had one leg.

"...to talk eventually. I'm your friend after all," Foshe said as I entered the interrogation mid-conversation. "Stranz was so kind to pick you up. It warms this old heart of mine to see you in safe hands once again."

"I don't know what you want..." Bolt groaned. "I haven't

done anything."

"I'd like to believe you," Foshe interrupted. "After our encounter in Hart's laboratory, I was satisfied you were completely cured. But then I get the pleasure of a call from Stranz, which is *not* a pleasure most the time. I was tucked up in my bed after a very busy night, which I shall not bore you with too much. Let's just say that we got a large amount of Outcasts last night. They tried to run, but we rounded up those dirty rats in the ridiculous sewer. They begged to be set free but, in the past few hours, I've put my needle in their necks and now they are finally silent. No more caterwauling or complaining. It's quite a relief…"

"You are getting off track," Bolt spat.

"Where were we before we leapt off track?" Foshe purred.

"Stranz called you," he replied.

"Yes, apologies, sometimes I get a little lost when I get excited. It's a problem at this age and after everything I have been through… I often get a carried away and lose track of the initial point…"

"The phone call?" Bolt mumbled.

"Don't you want to know about me?"

"I don't want to know a single thing," Bolt grunted. "You only dig it out of my brain later on anyway."

"Almost certainly…" Foshe replied coldly. "Stranz was doing a routine check up of the re-integrated patients, the ones we've deemed safe to re-exist in society. And he found a disturbance at your house. So I asked… 'What inspired him to check on the re-integrated tonight?' After our raid, we were busy erasing the Outcast's minds, and he was meant to be looking after the Corporation. Instead he's gone gallivanting around Prima! And that's when Miss Lucy Quayin grabbed the phone and told me that 'Mark Bolton was contaminated and needed to be quarantined immediately!' I had to stop myself from laughing. Quayin *thinks* that the gifted are contaminated people that must be isolated. She's fallen for the same lie that we told the entire city! Can you believe it? Lucy thinks you're sick and we cured you and now you're getting sick again! It's sort of true, in a way, but it's bizarre that she hasn't figured it all out yet. Especially when Stranz is right next to her. I mean… have you seen the size of him?"

"How can she not know?" Bolt grumbled. "It's not exactly subtle."

"That's what I said!" Foshe cried. "I told you we would get along."

"We are not getting along…"

"Quayin doesn't know about the gifted and her own brother hunts them down for a living!" Foshe continued. "So they find you and tell me that you are sick. I told them that was simply impossible. I assured Quayin and Stranz that you're completely healthy."

A black weapon appeared in Foshe's hand. It sparked with purple electricity. Bolt flinched at the burst of electricity that scattered across the cell.

"Shall I tell you what I did for a living before Mr Cain hired me?" Foshe asked firmly.

This was not a question. It was a command.

"I think I can imagine…" Bolt replied nervously. "You used to torture people for fun?"

"Now that is quite the presumption. No. I'm afraid that is not the answer I was looking for. Seriously, Mr Bolton, do you really think I find this fun?"

Foshe jabbed his device into Bolt's chest. The electricity sparked across his body and ricocheted up his ribcage. Foshe drew back his stun baton, and jabbed Bolt twice more, sending electricity flying across his body.

"You were a scientist!" Bolt screamed out in agony.

Foshe ceased his onslaught of violence and smiled approvingly. "Where did I work?"

"What the hell? I don't know." Mark spat. "I don't know anything. Just let me go!"

"Why do you continue to lie to me?" Foshe growled. "Why lie to an old friend?"

"I haven't lied. I didn't know!" Bolt exclaimed.

"You didn't know what?" Foshe asked feverishly.

"Please let me go," Bolt cried.

"See? You're lying to yourself, Mr Bolton! And there is nothing I despise more than a patient who lies to me."

Foshe pressed the cattle prod into Bolt's thigh and it left a charred mark after he was done.

"I cannot stand liars," Foshe hissed. "So please stop or else we won't get very far, will we? It's a good thing Stranz brought you in… otherwise who knows what you would have done! A man with your temper could have brought the house down. You could have hurt someone."

"I don't have a gift. I don't. You took it from me!"

Foshe grabbed Bolt's neck and began to press the cattle prod into his armpit. His finger hovered over the button.

"What did you just say?" Foshe asked. "Do you remember me?"

"Yes…" Bolt whispered.

"Speak up. I can't hear you."

"Yes. You found me. You found me after the incident. It was you. You were the one who took away my memories. Please don't hit me again. I think I recognised you a few days ago, but I didn't know why!"

"And you do now?" Foshe asked.

"It's Hart's nerve plug. It helped me remember. You worked on me in the hospital. I was one of the last people to leave," Bolt said.

"That's not what I wanted to hear," Foshe hummed.

"I've told you everything I remember."

"I doubt that. I saved you and this is how you repay me?"

"I'm sorry, please, not again. Please don't shock me again."

Pierre pulled the cattle prod away from Mark's armpit and released his neck. Mark relaxed against his chains and Pierre started to polish the device with a grubby cloth.

"Do you remember where I found you?" Foshe asked.

"No… I just remember your face," Bolt replied.

"I found you in a shop. You were one of the last people we uncovered. We'd left the blast zone alone, as there was nothing there except ash and blood. We also found a few survivors in

219

Prima's prison, which is where I first formally met Xander. Mr Cain and him were acquainted a long time before that, but that's another story I won't bore you with."

Bolt began to cough and I saw him spew blood onto his chest.

"Don't interrupt me whilst I'm talking," Foshe said before reactivating the cattle prod, making the room glow blue. Bolt flinched and prepared himself to be hit again.

"Sorry," Bolt grunted.

"Stop apologizing," Foshe said. "It's boring."

"Sorry…" Bolt replied in spite.

Foshe casually walked over and electrocuted Bolt's stomach before moving away again.

"Our men were hungry so they went into a shop to loot some food. I joined them to eat, before I spotted this shape in the corner. There was a pile of rubble covered in blood and mud. At first I thought it was nothing and then… it moved. Next thing I knew this pile of broken rock was lashing out. It was you, Mark. You knocked down three men before we electrocuted you into unconsciousness. Hence the stun baton today. I thought I'd bring it along for old times sake."

"You kept me in that hospital for a long time, much longer than the others. What was so different about me?"

"You want to know why?" Foshe said incredulously. "You're not exactly in a position to ask questions."

"I'm curious…" Bolt mumbled.

"Very well," Foshe sighed. "You exhibited your gift many times after the incident whilst the others did not. You were the severe sign that the incident had caused survivors to gain abilities. You showed us that in order to forget the incident we needed to use more drastic measures. And so began the extraction process on many patients who were having difficulty re-adjusting."

"Extraction process?" Bolt asked.

"A needle to the brain," Foshe confirmed. "However, it would seem you have bypassed the extraction and have regrown your memories and therefore have regained your gift. It's such a pity. But now it's time for show and tell. No time like the present. Show me that you can do it again and we can get round to fixing you."

"I can't," Bolt said quietly.

"You can't or you won't?"

"I don't know how. Please. I want to go home."

A dreadful silence fell upon them both. Pierre Foshe sighed heavily and a strange youthfulness seized his body. He punched Mark once in the chest and then again in the face. He shook his gnarled hand and sniggered through his adrenaline.

"I want to go to bed. It's been a very long night and I am an old man who loves his bed. It's precisely engineered to replicate the moon's gravity. It is the only thing that brings me any form of peace. I deserve my rest after working so hard. However, I will admit you are worth the lack of sleep, because our time together holds deep nostalgia. So just do something for me would you? Do it for your own good. Show me what you can do."

"No," Bolt replied. "I won't do it."

"I know what you can do. Don't be shy... I've seen it a dozen times before in the hospital. Once more for Pierre?"

"Wait... I remember where you worked. You asked if I knew that? You told me in the hospital..." Bolt screwed up his forehead as he desperately tried to remember. His eyes opened roughly in horror as he stared at the old man.

"You made weapons during the War, didn't you? You're from Luna..." Bolt said. "You survived the Rupture. No..."

Bolt eyes watered slightly as his mind filled in the blanks. His expression was filled with terror and confusion.

"You caused the Luna Rupture," Bolt said aghast. "You killed them all..."

Foshe licked his dry lips, his jaw tensed under his shallow cheekbones and his hand curled tightly around the torturous device.

"I saved you all. There is a distinct difference. My people... they refused to join the War and watched as thousands died. I had to take action. I created and triggered the Rupture, escaped and existed on a communication base, Lupo. I sent the planet into years of darkness, but I did it in the name of life... *not* death. Nono be praised. I helped create a new world, re-born from the

221

ashes of the Global War. I saved you all from annihilation, but when I returned to Earth I was greeted with hatred. They branded me as a war criminal."

Pierre lifted his sleeve up with his teeth and we all stared at the unmistakable solar brand on his pale upper arm. His white flesh curled around the shape burnt into his flesh. It was the black sigil of a scythe buried in the depths of the burning sun. It was the mark of Kubra and the star that they worshipped feverishly.

At the heart of the Sahara desert existed the great African city Kubra. It mainly consisted of colossal caverns and aqueducts underneath the boiling sands, whilst the surface was spiked by towering skyscrapers, landing platforms and energy absorbers. The entire industrious wonder was purely fuelled by solar and geothermal power. It was famous for the Core, a crystal that powered its destructive weaponry and phenomenal vehicles that they used to soar across the sand dunes and tunnel from the surface and down into the earth. The Core was one of the few pieces of technology partially salvaged after the Blackout. It was a technological marvel that Kubra refused to share with the rest of the world.

The Core's power was also used to barbarically brand prisoners at the most maximum-security prison on the planet.

"Inferno…" Bolt whispered in horror. "They sent you to Kubra's pit?"

"The Kubran's prefer to call that hellhole Jahim. Every waking day was a hot nightmare," Foshe said to himself and dug his nails into Bolt's bare arm. "They would scream a name endlessly through the boiling walls…"

"Alqamar Alqatil," Bolt hissed painfully and Foshe suddenly released him and grew extremely tense at the Arabic words. "I heard you say it. You'd just finished dealing with another quarantined family of patients. You'd fallen asleep and your mouth endlessly moved whilst you slept. Alqamar Alqatil. You would say it again and again until it lost all meaning."

"Your memory is much better than you've been letting on," Foshe hissed. "Mr Cain freed me from Jahim and put me back to work in Prima. I owe him my life. Now I have a beautiful bed

222

that I am so happy to see every night. It's a distinct reminder of everything I have sacrificed. It makes be remember that I was the man who killed Luna. I killed the one thing that I loved most. Do you understand me better now, Mark Bolton? I destroyed my great city to save this miserable planet. Now you have a small idea of what I am capable of."

"Those Arabic words…" Bolt said. "I know them… I looked it up, months ago. After a restless night full of nightmares, the words just jumped into my head. Alqamar Alqatil… it means Moon-Killer, doesn't it?"

Foshe stabbed the stunning baton sharply into Bolt's neck and he screamed out in response. The baton flashed again as he slapped it across his face.

"Your memory is beyond comprehension! I have heard enough of your disgusting lies, Mr Bolton. My patience has run out and you are going to show me exactly what you are capable of right now, otherwise you will witness exactly what the Alqamar Alqatil of Jahim is capable of. Well then? Come on! Show me!"

Foshe grabbed Bolt's head and thrust the baton into Bolt's sternum and kept it firing into the batteries died out. He staggered back, exhausted and looked at his prisoner. Bolt's body was blackened by the scorch marks, his chest smoking from the heat. Foshe stood against the wall, seemingly unfazed by the unmoving man shackled across the room.

Bolt moved. His head shifted. His eyes became a strange yellow and I heard Foshe laugh cruelly. My best friend's skin hardened and the shackles above his head shattered. His fist slammed into the metal floor and cracked it. Bolt's skin protruded out in all directions. He changed. His body transformed before my waking eyes. Bolt's gift emerged as a terrifying rocky beast that lay hidden beneath the surface, a personification of all that anger he'd kept tucked away over these years, way before the incident had even happened.

He tried to stand, but he still only had one leg and he roared in frustration. It sounded like the wind tearing its way through a canyon. Bolt became un-recognisable; his body was an assortment of rubble. All that remained of his face were those two yellow eyes, shining out like hot gems in an earthquake.

The beast roared again and Foshe staggered back.

"You shouldn't be able to do that! I worked very hard on your mind to make sure this didn't happen again. You lied to me! You remembered my face. You remembered my given name. And I cannot abide a liar.. I'm going to quarantine you, old friend. You are going to stay here until we find a more permanent cure for your condition."

Pierre Foshe threw the baton at Bolt's rocky body, before walking promptly out of the room and locking the door. The mass of rubble attacked the weapon, shattering it with ease. Anger filled the remains of the man I once knew as it charged around the room, throwing itself into the four walls of its prison.

I couldn't watch anymore. I had to leave.

The video froze and the camera cut out. White static filled my mind and finally I withdrew from the cyberspace, healing it as I moved. I made sure that Foshe's firewall was intact and that any history of my presence searching for Bolt was erased and finally that my attack on the server itself was clean. I felt myself being sucked out of the cyberspace and my mind rejoined my body in my lab.

A lot of information had gone straight over my head, but I knew some facts for definite. Stranz was working closely with Quayin to get my technology. Meanwhile, Foshe devalued Quayin's opinion entirely as she knew nothing of people with gifts. Quayin had given Bolt to the one person who could do him the most personal damage. I didn't think Mark could be in worse place right now. I would have to find a way to help him. I'd talk to Vincent Cain and make him aware of everything his sister had done and maybe then I could talk to him about Bolt's safe release.

My phone buzzed on the overhead display and made me jump. Adele was calling me back. I answered it with a wave of my hand.

"You called, Will?" Adele asked.

"I'm here," I replied. "Are you okay? How are the kids?"

"We're all fine, Will," Adele said suddenly unsure. "Are you alright?"

"Sorry. It feels like it's been ages since I've seen any of you," I sighed in relief. "Are you sure the kids are okay?"

"What on earth is wrong with you?" Adele asked worriedly.

"Nothing. I'm okay. Sorry," I mumbled.

"Well… you don't sound okay, Will. You're just stressed out with the presentation. You called me and here I am."

"I wanted to check that you weren't mad at me?"

"Of course not! Why would I be mad? You stupid idiot!" Adele laughed and I laughed with her. It felt great to smile after seeing my best friend being tortured. "I understand that this is a very busy time for you. We all understand how important this is, but I just wish you'd told me you were staying the night sooner."

"I'll be better at responding next time," I mumbled.

"You'd think you would be better at replying seeing how you're surgically attached to your hologram. Are you nervous about later?"

"You could say that…" I said quietly.

"Well? Do you want me to come up and wait with you?" Adele asked.

My mind froze as I began to understand what she meant.

"You're downstairs? You're here?" I asked.

"Of course I am. You didn't think we'd miss your big day! We're all here."

"Izzy and Theo…" I said in horror.

"All of us are here to support you. It looks pretty grand as well. Why didn't you let me visit sooner? I just told them who we were and they've given us a third row seat. Third row! We're right next to a load of other important people apparently. Wish I'd put on better clothes now. No idea who any of them are, but they look important with their black suits and fancy tight dresses. I had a little chat to an uptight lady who showed us our seat and she said she knew you very well. A blonde haired woman. Lots of make up. Massive heels. Stick up her…"

"That's Lucy Quayin," I interrupted quickly and tried to not let my anger seep through the phone.

"That's the woman. If I'm fully honest, I don't particularly like her. I mean it was very nice for her to give us a good seat, but she looked at me as though I was dirt on her polished shoe. She was trying to hide it, but I can tell when another woman doesn't like me. And she didn't even acknowledge the kids. You know… I'm thinking of having a word with her boss."

"Well… she is the boss, so good luck with that!" I laughed.

"I thought Vincent was your boss?" Adele asked.

"He is, but we don't see much of him. She likes to think she's in charge."

"That's a shame. Well, if I see him, then I will have a little word."

"Adele, that is probably not the best idea."

"William, I will not have anyone treat me in that manner. She might as well have spat on us."

"I agree that she's horrible, but you can't have a word with Mr Cain."

"Why not? What's wrong with complaining?"

"Well, for a start, they're brother and sister."

There was a brief silence as I felt Adele absorb the gossip on the other end of the phone.

"I never! Siblings you say?" My wife enquired.

"Yes. Now…" I warned.

"Fancy that!"

"Stop it."

"Honestly I don't see the problem. They're related. What's wrong? Don't they like each other?"

"Not particularly."

"Why not? Why don't they like each other?"

"I don't know."

"Well you should know."

"Don't, Adele."

"Don't what? I didn't say anything…"

"Don't gossip. I know what you are like. I think it's meant to be a secret, so don't go telling anybody."

"But it's good gossip! And there are so many reporters here."

"Adele, don't you dare!"

"I'm only teasing! Relax, Will! I won't say a word."

"Do you promise?"

"I won't, but Isabella might."

I let my shoulders drop down and collapsed against my desk. It was so good to hear Adele's voice. I imagined her downstairs with the kids, making sure they were looking all neat as they sat in the third row. The thought of it made me chuckle.

"I can't believe you are here," I told my wife. "I miss you."

"Well, you better be good after all of this effort! I had to wrangle the kids out of school. Izzy was easy as she's all done with her exams now, but the teachers argued a bunch when I tried to collect Theo. Of course, he was dying to leave, but they weren't having it! Then I may have said that you worked for Cain Corporation and Theo was out of that place within the minute. Might try it at work tomorrow!"

"You can't use that as an excuse!"

"Of course I can! You work for the most famous man in Prima and, as an extension, one of the most powerful people in the world. It's the perfect excuse. Plus it means that we can all be here for you. A family united. For better for worse. For promotion or unemployment, right? It's an important for all of us."

"Thanks," I said. "You're amazing."

"I know. So when are you on?" Adele asked.

"Isn't there a programme?" I asked.

"Nope. There won't even be an interval to swig down a glass of wine and to force feed the kids extortionate ice-cream."

"How appalling! If you see Mr Cain, then you should definitely have a word about that!"

"I intend to," she said proudly. "So, thanks to the lack of programme, I have to ask you… When are you doing whatever you are doing?"

"I am last apparently," I told her and remembered that I was after Quayin. "I'll have to see you afterwards, okay?"

"Of course. Love you," Adele said.

A red light flashed above my head as I saw someone attempt to open the broken lab door. I saw a dark shape wearing a suit through the clouded glass that knocked twice against the glass. My head twirled in confusion. I don't think I'd ever heard someone knock on the glass before. I rushed forward and for the first time I used the handle and opened it manually. The door swung open and I was greeting by Vincent Cain dressed in a full black and white suit for the event, with his blonde hair groomed back, a rich smile on his face and his gun metal eyes staring at me.

"William?" Adele asked still on the phone.

"Yes, dear?" I said absently.

"This is the part where you say…?" Adele said trailing off as she waited for the appropriate answer.

Vincent Cain waltzed his way into my lab, pressed an index finger on his own lips and leant against the main computer.

"William Forest Hart!" Adele said stubbornly. "This is the part where you say…?"

"I love you too?" I finally replied.

"Next time with a bit more conviction?"

"I love you too, Adele Isabella May Hart, but I have to go. Mr Cain is here."

Vincent put a hand over his mouth as he held back in a stifled laugh.

"Mr Cain is there?" Adele cried. "Oh! Go be brilliant, my baby! Say hello from me, won't you?"

"Adele, you are on speaker. He can hear you loud and clear."

Vincent Cain finally let go of his mouth and his laughter escaped his mouth. It was surprisingly real and rocked his body up and down.

"Hello there, Mrs Hart," Vincent said promptly. "It's great to finally talk to the brilliant woman behind the great man I see before me."

"Hello, Mr Cain, sir. It's a pleasure to speak to you. How are you doing today?" Adele replied.

"Very well, thank you very much," he continued. "My work has gone splendidly recently. Between us… I can personally tell you that our streets are much safer now."

My mind bounced back to Raven's fight in the sewer that the Mind Walker had shown me last night. Vincent Cain and his men had completely devastated the encampment and quarantined most of the Outcasts.

It was no wonder he was happy.

228

"That is certainly a relief," I commented and Cain's lips separated into a smile. "Did you manage to catch more terrorists?"

"We caught plenty and soon my search will be complete," Cain said cheerfully. "Enough about my work, I cannot wait for the festivities to begin so I can properly see what everyone has been doing with my money. I am thoroughly excited for our little party downstairs."

"So are we, sir!" Adele announced proudly.

"You've brought some people with you?" Cain asked.

"Our kids are here," I told the terrifyingly charismatic man.

"You must treat yourself to some champagne and assorted nibbles. That should keep you occupied through the boring bits! Just go over and say your husband works here or you're a personal friend of Mr Cain. Everyone else in that room will be taking what they can. Those reporters are a bunch of scavengers. You might as well join in!"

"I shall and, yes, everyone is taking as much food and drink as possible."

"Brilliant…" Vincent said sarcastically. "You put on a little party for international society and the vultures turn up for the feast instead."

"They are everywhere, Mr Cain. They're scurrying over the melon slices like ants at a picnic," Adele said in cheerful reply. "Also, whilst we are talking about vermin, I wanted to talk about one particular…"

"I have to go get ready," I interrupted before my wife could accidentally insult my boss. "See you in a bit, Adele."

"See you, Will! We should talk in person later, Mr Cain."

"Definitely. And call me Vincent," Cain cooed. "Formalities are so dull."

"Sorry… Vincent," Adele simmered and I could practically feel her blushing from here. I decided it as best to end the call swiftly.

"Bye, Adele," I said swiftly.

"Bye…" Adele attempted to say.

My hand waved through the air and swiftly hung up the call

before she could blather any further.

"Sorry, Mr Cain," I apologized. "She called me."

"Don't worry, we all seek comfort in loved ones at times of greatness. It will be interesting to meet them personally later on."

I did not understand Cain's meaning, so my mouth once again fell into a wordless shape. I hope it wouldn't do that later when I had to talk in front of several hundred people.

"This is your moment, William," he said. "I want you to go out there and destroy the opposition."

"I'm afraid that I don't fully follow…" I said cautiously.

"There is no need to play dumb with me," Vincent said. "I know exactly what's been going on."

Vincent reached up into the hologram, which reacted instantly to his touch. With a few swift strokes he entered his own commands and was able to access any system he wished. He found the files he was looking for. There were four of them, all labelled 'body-cam' and another named Stranz. He opened all five and I gasped at the scene that played above us. It showed the exoskeleton defeating each intruder from their own perspective. It seemed as though they all had a hidden camera attached to their jacket. A final camera shot came from Stranz's perspective as I exited the tube and confronted Lucy Quayin.

"History favours the strong, Doctor Hart," said Vincent. He swiped his hand over the screen and all the images suddenly disappeared. "Desperate times call for desperate measures. Without your action last night, I wouldn't know what my own people were doing against me. Trust me when I say they will be dealt with severely. Especially Anton. However the event downstairs has already been set into motion. I'm afraid I cannot help you with Lucy's mutiny."

"She has the nerve-plug," I decided to tell Cain. "I have no hope against her presentation. She can easily claim the technology is hers."

"But it isn't her technology, is it?" Vincent said. "Show them all the truth and don't hold back. Give it everything you've got. Three years ago, I made the choice to hire you and I want to see whether that has paid off…"

Another shallow double knock echoed on the open lab door. My head spun at the sound of knocking.

What is this world coming to when we have to open our own doors!

"Mr Cain?" Lucy Quayin asked. "We've been looking everywhere for you. The Correspondent from Kubra would like a word."

"You found me," Cain replied coldly to his sister, before recollecting the Correspondent in his mind. "Ah yes, Morowa, she has a wonderful way with words. She can wait another couple moments."

"Are you ready, Doctor?" Quayin said with the purest smile she could muster and ignored her brother.

"As I will ever be," I replied.

"Have you seen Anton Stranz?" Vincent Cain asked suddenly.

Lucy's face dropped. She almost completely gave up control as her brother's authority overwhelmed her, however she held her ground.

"I haven't seen him," she lied.

"That's a shame. I'm sure he will turn up. It's not like he's hard to miss."

The siblings laughed together. It was short and forced. Their similar jaw lines echoed one other as they laughed in stark unison.

"The presentation is about to begin," said Quayin at the end of their synchronized laughter session.

"You don't need me. Go and start it already. We'll get down there and socialise when we are ready. We're both doing our bit near the end anyway. Go on and say your auto-cued monologues. I want to walk down with Doctor Hart."

Lucy hesitated briefly. Her hands wavered and she took a single careful step forwards. There was clearly something else that was bothering her.

"Vincent. We need to talk about something," she said cautiously. "I've remembered our home in the mountains."

"This isn't the time. Get out of here right now, Lucy," he demanded sharply. "I'll speak to you later."

Quayin bit her lip, lifted her nose slightly and left without another forced word. Her heels clacked away gradually into the distance. This time they were sounded defiant.

I grasped the nerve-plug firmly in my hand as I imagined Lucy would be doing as she went down in the lift. A stray thought hit my head and I held my hand out to Vincent Cain.

"Would you like to try?" I said passing him the nerve-plug.

"I'm honoured at the offer, but I'm afraid I cannot."

"Everyone can. Even Lucy..."

"I am not like my sister," he said quietly.

I remembered the bridge that connected two points in a person's brain that made the nerve plug work. Vincent Cain did not have one of those points... in its place was a dark emptiness.

"I didn't mean to offend you," I said.

"Perhaps after everything is done at last..." Vincent sighed roughly and eyed the lab door absently. "Perhaps one day I will be able to use your nerve plug. First we'd need to have words with the person responsible for my condition and that is not going to happen..."

I touched his arm as lightly as I dared, fearful of his authority and as he turned I saw a hint of sadness in those stoic eyes.

"I'm sure you will find a way," I told the man who would capture me the moment he found out about my gift. His smile in reply was small, but honest.

"Your confidence is inspiring. Perhaps one day you will help me find a way, but for now, I wish you all the best for the party downstairs."

"It's not a party..." I said.

"Nonsense! Presentation sounds so boring and informal," he retorted and presented his hand towards the door. "After you. Your party guests await."

I looked back at the lab that had become my strange home. No matter what happened next, this was the last time I would set eyes on my second home. I sighed as I took one final glance around the workspace. I looked at the white walls, the blinking lights, that water cooler in the corner, the window with the far away view of Old Street, the central circular computer, the contorted scanner and the glass tube. All of these objects held individual memories in the space of one week.

I was sad to leave the lab, but it was time to move onto greater things.

I strapped the nerve plug around my neck and felt it activate and stir my whole body. My neck tingled. My mind burned momentarily in a flash of adrenaline, fear and a glimpse of searing horror. The exoskeleton activated and walked between us as we closed the door behind us. We reached the lift and the skeleton reached forwards to press the button for the ground floor.

21 - Deadline

"Ladies and gentlemen," Lucy Quayin announced. "It's time to stop waiting for the revolution to arrive and grab the future with our own hands. I won't waste any more of your time with my words; instead I will show you the future. Cain Corporation presents our the all-terrain vehicle!"

Quayin ripped away the cloth and unveiled the giant contraption that was meant to be the future. The ATV would be best described as a spider. It had four large legs supporting it; each with a pronged claw that gripped the ground. At the centre of the creature was a spherical metal and glass cockpit with a harnessed chair inside, which would revolve depending on which way the machine was facing. Attached to this cockpit were four metal arms that hung in the air. They looked like the arms of gorilla, each with a large hand with three fingers and a thumb.

The crowd applauded at the eight-limbed contraption and Quayin surfed the praise by bringing up a hologram of the machine in action. It showed the entire spider falling over and then supporting itself on its arms. The cockpit rotated smoothly so that the pilot was never upside down. The four spider legs then opened and fired explosive energy at a distant target.

All I saw was a different brand of weaponry that it wasn't even remotely revolutionary. It was very similar to the spider that I had designed last night, but appeared to be clumsier. It was too focused on weaponry, instead of user capability.

It was just another extravagant way to kill people.

However the audience continued to applaud at the absurd acrobatics onscreen. I saw my family clapping in the third row. Theo was enthralled and jumped in his seat every time the machine tumbled. He fidgeted with the shirt that Adele had forced him to wear, straining at the buttons tightened around his neck. Adele looked at the machine quizzically and looked at me off-stage and creased her eyebrows. I nodded in agreement. It was utterly ridiculous. Izzy, on the other hand, looked at the machine and clapped lightly. Not too hard and not too soft. She just didn't seem to care. It was as though she had seen plenty of nonsense like this before. That was the issue with children these days. They had endless access to everything around the world with a simple wave of their hands. If Izzy was viewing the great cities of Eden and Lockroy through her beloved holo-glasses, then it was highly likely she'd seen a similar technological marvel. Quayin would have to do much better tonight if she wanted to impress my daughter.

I smiled at my family and continued to scan the room. The front row was filled with reporters, eating up every last piece of information they were given. The rest of the crowd were smartly dressed and seemed to approve of the presentation so far. There were all kinds of people: politicians, high-class families, sponsors, military buyers, and diverse representatives from the other four great cities around the world.

A tall sleek woman clapped softly with a calm smile upon her face. Her dark black and maroon attire immediately indentified her as the Correspondent of Kubra. Her hands were intricately tattooed with the golden insignias of the many cultures that resided within her great city. I recalled that her name was Morowa.

Next, I spotted two representatives from Lockroy. I recognised them as Marshalls of Lockroy by the insignia on their clothing. The great city was split into eight districts that were each controlled by a Marshall, who reported to the Issumatar of Lockroy. Their leader was renowned for being a fierce and intelligent individual based in the capital district of Graham. One Locker was heavily bearded and grimaced with joy at the display of violence, whilst the other Locker was trimly dressed with a pair of dark holo-glasses attached to her face. At a guess, I would say they came from the Edge and Loubet districts.

At the end of the row sat a wiry Professor wearing the insignia of Eden and an Amazonian dressed simply in a dark green suit. The figure was stoic; his bald head tilted to the applause and I suddenly noticed that his eyes were completely clouded, revealing that the man was blind.

235

The foyer had been transformed for the occasion. A couple hundred seats had been laid out between each lift. The security desk was replaced by a stage that spread across the foyer. Projectors lined the stage allowing easy access to holograms during any presentation pieces. Long curtains of white and blue had been hung from the ceiling, covering most of the walkways above the foyer. Surrounding the room was Cain's enforcement with their weapons hidden beneath their uniforms. Vincent Cain was nowhere to be seen, but I knew that he must be watching nearby. Likewise, Stranz and Foshe were not present. I presumed Foshe was dealing with the surge of Outcasts from their assault or he could still be interrogating Bolt.

My heart panged with guilt. What if Bolt revealed my gift to Foshe? I shook the stray thought away... I had to focus on the presentation.

"And now for our final exhibit," Quayin finished as the hologram completed its cycle. She paused as the audience stopped talking amongst themselves. "We have an employee who is high in our minds at Cain Corporation. Under our guidance for the last 3 years, he has finally completed his project and is ready to share it with us all. I still remember my first interview with him. He was bright back then, but by working with us he has grown to become even brighter. His work is truly treasured and we look forward to taking it even further after tonight. Ladies and gentlemen, put your hands together, I give you... Doctor William Hart!"

The crowd began to clap as I stepped out from behind the curtain. The wall of sound hit me as the audience applauded. Lucy Quayin waited impatiently as I made my way across the wooden stage. The cameras flashed and I raised a hand to shield my eyes. The shock threw my anxieties away and I proceeded to wave dumbly as the light blinded my retinas. I blinked rapidly to get rid of the red dots dancing in my eyes. Lucy Quayin smiled, teeth blazing at the volley of camera lights. The hair on my skin buzzed violently with each flash and the urge to blow up every light bulb surged through my body. I stared up at Quayin, who stood in higher heels than usual. The white of her teeth and eyes shone fakely out at the swarming crowd. She grinned, her teeth gritting into a snarl. Her hand clamped my shoulder and her polished nails dug into my skin. Quayin bent down and shielded her mouth from the crowd as she moved towards my ear.

"This is it, William," she said. Her breath whistled into my ear and I could feel each movement of her articulators. "It's time to see what you are made of. I personally hope you stutter and fail, so I can stand on your remains and look even better than I already am. Good luck. You'll need it."

I looked down and the crowd finally quietened. The third row was the last to stop clapping and inappropriately cheering.

"Hello… everyone," I said nervously, which was greeted by an uncomfortable silence. "As you know, I'm Doctor Hart. I am here to show you the future…"

I paced across the stage and stopped beside the spider-like contraption. I leant against the structure and felt the comfort of the vast machine buzzing against my back. It felt wild, waiting to be unleashed at a moment's notice.

"Since the incident three years ago, we have rebuilt our city and become a better place, would you not agree?" I asked the population.

A resounded nodding of heads agreed with the simple statement.

"We've built buildings and monuments. Circuit Road and South Bridge are just two quick examples of this growth. With Cain Corporation's assistance, we have locked away fugitives of Priman law. They've amplified our economy and stabilised a great city on the brink of despair. Many years after our loss at Old Street, we finally have an era of order and control. We live in Prima, a place that was once divided by physical and economic devastation during the Global War. Now, after working with Mr Cain, I truly believe that Prima can finally be reconsidered as the most politically stable and financially secure place on our planet. We are safe and we are happy, aren't we?"

A mighty cheer erupted from the crowd with my family leading the charge of praise. I brought my hands down and asked them all to let me continue.

"Well, I am not happy with what we have become."

The crowd became suddenly quiet and the reporters began to whisper into their earpieces.

"There are those who are still hurting from the disaster and this cannot be ignored. We cannot move on to a future when there are still people suffering. Our friends and families are still in pain. The memories of the dead haunt us and the survivors of the disaster still suffer terrible injuries. Today, I'm here to tell you that I am able to fix some of that pain."

I watched the crowd murmur in approval. The guards relaxed and a few reporters began tapping fiercely on holographic pads.

"I have a friend called Mark Bolton who sadly cannot be here. He has found himself suddenly preoccupied," I said looking coldly at Lucy Quayin who only smiled richly in return. "He's a landlord at the Sprint Finish. You should all go there when you get time, they do a cracking pint and a brilliant portion of chips. Shameless plug for his business, but I owe Mark that much for how much he has done this week. Mark survived the disaster. He lost his brother. His partner left him. He lost everything. He even lost his left leg."

With a wave of my hand, I brought up a hologram of Bolt's scan back on Monday. It seemed so long ago that I had introduced him to the nerve plug. I threw clips that I'd found online of Bolt racing before the incident.

"Bolt used to run, swim and cycle. He was one of Prima's top athletes. He would drive his body to the point of exhaustion and harness an emotional resource very few had. However... I am not here to tell you the sad story of how Mark can't run anymore. No, we've all heard plenty of those. Instead... I'm here to tell you how I fixed Mark's problem."

I brought up the images of Bolt's artificial legs, including scans of the recent legs I had produced for him.

"Prosthetics these days are top range products that are available even for budget buyers like Mark. People without limbs can use their nerve endings to control the prosthetics."

I brought up a small video showing Bolt controlling his old prosthetic limb using the nerves in his left knee.

"But what I've created will change the way we all view nerves."

I activated the last stream of videos involving Bolt. The one above showed him applying the nerve plug for the very first time to his leg.

"I give you metal skin. With my technology, the nerve plug, we are able to sync the central nervous system into the inner workings of a machine. With this device, we can connect our bodies to a machine and feel every inch of it."

Another clip played of Lucy Quayin entering the room whilst Bolt was there. It showed Bolt flinching at her touch and running around the room, leaping from a table and down to the floor. Finally there was a clip of Lucy Quayin using the metal hand.

"If you look here, you can see that it also gives us capabilities beyond prosthetics. Lucy was able to control the metal hand without moving her own body. This allows her access to an entirely new limb, which she can fully control and can completely feel."

I saw a group of major buyers talking furiously with one another. One reporter got out his phone and even began talking quietly in another language. I listened briefly and I grasped that he was speaking French. The smartly dressed Locker reprimanded the reporter using the same language to be silent.

"I understand this is all rather hard to believe," I continued regardless of the murmurs of conversation. "The nerve plug is something that needs to be felt and not seen. So with no further nonsense, I'll bring out my example of the future."

I tied the nerve plug to the back of my neck and activated the device. A sharp shock fluttered through my body. My memory rattled once again, as the nerve plug illuminated the two points within my brain. I marched the exoskeleton on stage and felt the surreal sense of using the nerve plug, whilst I could also feel the exoskeleton due to my gift.

A brief image flashed through my mind. Darkness. Light. Screaming. The world was breaking and burning and everyone around me was…

I scratched the back of my neck and it was gone. I shook my

239

head, ignoring the strange echo and brought my focus back to the presentation. I moved with the machine and then allowed it to walk out on its own.

"As I was saying… this technology has to be felt to be believed. So can I have a volunteer please?" I asked

The audience gasped at the opportunity. The cameras lapped it up, flashing their lights at every hand in the air. The skeleton jumped off the stage with a heavy thud and moved between the seated audience. It moved past the press, representatives and to the collection of people sat at the back. People flinched as the machine walked past them, so I made extra care to be gentle as possible as I made my way through the crowd. The machine continued until it found an elderly lady near the very back who had her frail hand raised.

"And who are you?" I asked through the exo-skeleton's mouth and the nearby audience gasped at the sound.

"Rosaline White," she said sweetly.

"Well… would you mind coming with me to the stage, Rosaline?"

"I'm afraid I can't do that," she said slowly. The exoskeleton moved forward and saw the wheelchair that she was sat in. Both of her legs were gone. I felt the crowd trying to see what was going on, so I activated the cameras in the skeleton's eyes and projected the image onto the holo-screen.

"I lost my legs to bone cancer, five years ago. Sorry. I guess you will have to choose someone else who can make it up there."

The loss of her legs should've hit me harder, but I'd seen Bolt without his leg several times now. I welcomed the lady in my mind. I could help her. I could really help her.

"No, it's perfect," I said. "Stay where you are. I'll come to you."

I jumped down from the stage and walked through the audience, pausing to touch my wife on the shoulder for a moment.

"Rosaline, just to make it clear that I have absolutely no idea who you are, would you mind telling everyone what your profession is?"

"You'd probably know me better as Mrs White. I was the former Mayor of Prima before the incident struck us down. The great city needed someone with more energy to revive us. It was roughly a year after Vincent formed his Corporation that I decided to step down. We seem to be getting along fairly well so far with him and our current Mayor at the helm…"

"Well, it's my pleasure to meet you in person, Mrs White," I said and remembered that everyone was here through specific invitation. Vincent must have asked her to come personally. "I hope I'm not embarrassing you."

"Darling, don't be silly," she laughed. "And call me Rosaline."

"Rosaline," I smiled. "Can you please tie this around your neck?"

After a few moments of fumbling she gathered the device around her. It activated and sent a small buzz through her body that made her jump sharply. She raised her hands to her head and so did the skeleton next to us. It fell to the floor with a heavy clonk and the legs began to jerk slightly. Rosaline's face creased and her eyes grew wide as she watched the skeleton wobble on the floor. They moved their hands together joyfully. Rosaline looked at the feet that were juddering against a nearby chair. They found the ground and, slowly but firmly, the machine began to stand on its feet. Rosaline stared at the machine in confused shock, unable to fully take in the signals from the new body. I allowed the skeleton to lean on me, as Rosaline adjusted to the machine.

The skeleton looked down and suddenly grabbed its own legs.

"I can…" Rosaline murmured. "I can walk!"

The skeleton paced around the crowd and Rosaline White leaped for joy in the seat of her chair. She made the skeleton come over and she felt the metal with her own hands. She flinched and so did the machine, bringing a wide smile to her face. Her eyes suddenly focused and she made the skeleton grab her from the wheelchair. The cameras flashed as my machine lifted the disabled woman in its arms. She latched on to her new body and began to walk around the room for the first time in years.

"Oh, thank you, sir!" Rosaline cried. "It feels so good to walk again!"

The crowd began to cheer as they realised what they were seeing was genuine. I had done it. They exploded into applause. They cheered Rosaline White and my technology as they walked around the crowd, near the stage and finally back to her seat. She looked quite sad when she put herself down into her wheelchair. Her eyes dropped as though something was deeply troubling her. Rosaline made the machine walk towards me and it held out its hand. We shook hands through the exoskeleton and then hugged me.

It was a confusing sensation. For a start, my own machine was hugging me and, due to my gift, I could feel absolutely everything that Rosaline White could. I could feel myself hugging myself. Yet there was something more… I could feel the nerve plug. The device around the old lady's neck glowed in my mind and branched out in two directions. It allowed me to feel the machine as expected, but it also allowed my mind to glimpse the nerves that spiralled along Rosaline's spine. She controlled my exoskeleton now; my gift wouldn't be able to manipulate it.

Suddenly a screeching microphone snatched everyone's attention. The audience flinched and turned to face the stage.

"We are not finished yet!" Lucy Quayin screamed over the roaring crowd. They watched in bewilderment, unsure what was coming next. "Behold the future!" Lucy said and raised the nerve plug that she had stolen from Bolt.

I was helpless as she tied the plug around her neck and shuddered violently as a pulse ricocheted through her body. Quayin fell to her knees and the ATV juddered next to her. Each of the legs stirred and Lucy raised her head suddenly. There was a glint of violent blue shining out of her pupils. They buzzed with newfound electricity that shattered around her nerves. I had not expected the nerve plug to make her eyes shine like that… moving the ATV would be a monumental strain on her body. Perhaps some external effects were a result of the nerve plug as Quayin's brain struggled to cope with the torrent of new signals.

Quayin's head sweated as she raised both of her arms. The

robot echoed her movement and raised all four of its gorilla limbs. It bounced lightly as though it was actually alive. I stared in horror at Lucy. She had most likely practiced this already, but the amount of focus it would've taken to be able to move the entire creature was immense. She breathed deeply and made the ATV crawl across the stage. It moved step by staggered step as she felt every inch of the beast. Quayin moved all eight limbs until it was standing directly above her.

I felt a gentle tugging at my sleeve as a metal hand pulled on my clothes and Rosaline White signalled for me.

"I can see the sadness on your face. Don't deny it. There is no point in lying to me." Rosaline was right. Quayin was going to win this presentation. The buyers wanted results and now they had them. "Listen to me, Doctor. You have made an old woman happier today than you can ever know. I presume your friend tried to tell you how happy this creation made him?"

Mark Bolton was currently in a prison cell being tortured. He was probably cursing the day he'd met me. Yet, when he finally put on the nerve plug, I'd never seen someone so happy in my life. He said that he owed me a debt. If Bolt was here then I know he'd never give up. I had worked years on this project and I wouldn't have it snapped out of my hands at the last moment by this witch.

"The value of what you've given me today, outweighs anything that monster up there could do," Rosaline White said softly. "Having my legs back reminded me distinctly of something I'd forgotten."

"And what is that?" I asked and remembered how the nerve plug seemed to be affecting people's lost memories...

"I remembered when I had my legs before the Global War, right at the very founding of Prima. This was fifty years or so ago, but I suddenly saw it all in vivid detail. We were all sick of the political conflict between the European nations so we decided to forge our own future. There were factions of each country that all came together and united to form this great city. Led by Vincent's Cain's grandfather, Vincenzo, we began building Old Street with the assistance of the Cain fortune. I was only twenty years old and

I remember the sun streaming down from the heavens and spilling onto the stain glass window of the church. I was meant to begin negotiations of where to build sites of worship for the various faiths, however the Christians weren't in there…"

"Where were they?"

"They were with the Muslims across the road helping to build a synagogue with the guidance of some Jewish men. They announced that later that month the construction of the mosque would begin. But in the end, they all argued about how to divide the work labour and scrapped both religious buildings."

"That seems like a monumental waste of time," I mumbled.

"I'm not finished," Rosaline tutted. "Instead of abandoning all hope, they came to a compromise. They all moved into the church and converted it into a building where all faiths could be worshipped. I wish that it were still standing. It was a phenomenal structure that brought ancient and modern architecture together. They created the Temple of One. It was acts like this that defined Prima as the great city of unity in a world full of chaos."

"In the face of chaos we have to stand strong," I said, fondly remembering my own wedding to Adele at the Temple of One. "I think you may have just given me the confidence I need. Do you mind if I have that nerve plug back?"

"Are you going to show that woman who is in charge?" Rosaline asked hesitantly. "Are you going to beat her up, because I'm not sure I could allow that…"

"Don't worry. I'm going to beat up her robot with my robot."

"Oh, that sounds fun! I'm not sure if Vincent would like that very much…"

"You know what?" I said as I thought about the fierce rivalry between the siblings. "I think he'll love it."

I ran through the crowd tying the nerve-plug around my neck and didn't even flinch as I felt the shockwave ripple down my spine. I blinked away the flash of burning buildings, dark eyes glaring and the sound of screams, and climbed back on stage to stand opposite the colossal monster.

22 - Monsters

"This is not what I designed my technology for!" I shouted out to the monster wielding my nerve plug, as I walked into the shadow of Quayin and her gargantuan machine. The entire picture looked terrifyingly inhuman.

"It is true that the nerve plug could be developed into this," I announced honestly to the audience. "This is not a trick. Lucy is indeed controlling the machine by utilising her vast system of nerves. But it's not designed to be used in this extreme way. It is designed to heal."

"The nerve-plug will take us beyond our own bodies. We can enhance the human structure," Quayin said struggling to control the machine. "All of you... look at me! With practice this will become as easy to control as my own hand. It's like a muscle. It just needs to be strengthened before it's strong enough. If you choose to sponsor the nerve-plug through me, then I will move development into human enhancement..."

"It is designed to complete the human body," I argued.

"We will become more than genetics have allowed us," Quayin continued.

"The demand will become too high for the nerve plug and you know it, Lucy. Whoever has the most money will have the best enhancement!"

"Isn't that the case anyway, William?" Quayin said finally facing me. Her perfect composure was gone. She paced wildly and pointed at my face. Her red nail polish gleamed sharply as it poked close to my eyeball. Over her shoulder, the ATV pointed several of its limbs in sync with her movement.

"The rich live longer," she told me. "That's a dreadful fact. We can do our best to help those in poverty, but at the end of the day there will always be poor people. There will always be someone with less power."

"It doesn't have to be that way. I was only trying to make us whole again."

"Whole? Can you even hear yourself?" Quayin asked sarcastically. "Stop limiting yourself. Stop limiting all of us! We must take the future whilst it is here, William. Stop being so weak minded…"

"You're the one who is weak. You're disillusioned if you think that *this* is the solution. I mean, 'human enhancement? Can you even hear yourself? Do this and you'll leave so many people behind…"

"Clearly, ladies and gentlemen, William and I disagree on the future," Quayin said returning her attention to the listening audience. The audience itself no longer fazed me. I had to stand up for what I believed in. Quayin was wrong and I'd do what ever it took to show that. "It is your decision what happens next," Quayin continued. "We will be offering both services at Cain Corporation. The opportunity into William's program of prosthetics or my program working towards the…"

"…the never-ending corruption of humanity," I interrupted her.

Quayin roared with frustration, erratically swiping her hand sideways in disgust and the leg of the spider moved with her. My exoskeleton jumped forward and grabbed the large claw. It dwarfed the skeleton. The weight of the monster strained against the skeleton's circuitry, it fizzed and buzzed, but managed to push the leg away.

Lucy Quayin turned outwards and held her arms wide to welcome the crowd. She spoke with an erratic confidence that almost shook my own. I had to stand firm. I had to show that she was wrong.

"I will show you all what we can do with the nerve plug," Quayin said. "You will see the unseen potential of our bodies that is ready to be unleashed."

"And I will show you what a human with complete control can do," I said simply as I joined her centre stage.

I wouldn't be able to use my power now. I could only use the skeleton's capabilities. I had to prove to the crowd that complete control was more effective than a wild monster with an erratic machine.

We stepped back to opposite sides of the stage, and before I had reached my side, the ATV surged forward to crush the skeleton. It dodged out of the way, but I cried out as the ATV grazed the skeleton's shoulder.

My mind warped with confusion, as I adjusted to feeling the pain of my creation through the nerve plug. I placed my full focus inside the machine.

I grabbed the ATV's nearest leg and clambered up the moving machine. It's four arms hovered nearby and twitched in response to Quayin's nerve plug, as she chose which limb to use. I moved between two arms and rushed towards the cockpit. I attempted to sense where the central control unit was for the machine, running my metal hands through the wiring.

Quayin lashed out wildly and one of the arms slammed the skeleton in the chest. It plummeted into the staging and sent splinters of wood flying out. The lines of ravenous reporters yelled out, before flashing their cameras at the scene. Quayin hovered a leg over my metal corpse. I launched myself upwards, dodging the leg again, and rushed under the machine. The cockpit revolved completely and followed my movement. I ran into a large hand, which gripped my body like a vice. She used her other arms to grab my metal limbs, like a child trying to pull the legs off an insect.

Through the skeleton's eyes, I observed the hand wrapped around my waist. Between each segment of the fingers, the joints were completely unprotected. The gap was small, but my metal hands would fit in there. Lashing forward, I ripped the wiring until the grip on my body lessened and the arm became limp. The skeleton wriggled free, dodged the other arms and threw itself towards the shoulder joint. The machine swirled in panic, but I clutched on desperately as I threw my arms into the circuitry.

Quayin turned the entire machine upside down. The world flipped. The machine stood on its hands, the arms supporting its weight, despite the limp hand. The sound of people cheering echoed in my peripheral senses, but I continued to hold on underneath the monster. The spiked feet, now above the cockpit, descended downwards to stab at the skeleton. They punched two holes in its chest. I yelled out as it felt like they were puncturing my own body. I launched my hand inside the shoulder joint again and found a swivelling axis spinning rapidly. It burnt my metal hand and caused sparks to fly out. I stopped the movement and crushed the axis. The entire arm became suddenly crippled. I leapt out from under the metal carcass, as Quayin tried to find her balance on her remaining arms.

The ATV usually had a program to maintain balance when a limb had been disabled, however Quayin was controlling it manually. She wasn't used to the upside down machine. The machine teetered and tipped over. It fell heavily with its remaining limbs flailing in the air. The audience laughed at the machine that looked like a miserable insect stuck on its back.

It found its balance on its spider legs and returned to its initial standing position. One of the gorilla arms was completely disabled and falling between its legs. Quayin reached over, grimacing with pain as she gripped the crippled arm. She ripped it from its socket and threw the limb aside.

Satisfied, the machine rose to greater heights, its spider legs extending once again. I looked over at Lucy Quayin and saw her eyes were now firmly focused on me. The ATV began to walk, not towards the exoskeleton, but directly towards *me* who was standing defenceless across the stage.

"And there you have it, folks!" Vincent Can proclaimed as he suddenly strode onto the stage between the warring machines. "The future of the Cain Corporation. Quite the show! It truly changes the concept of unmanned vehicles, don't you think? I hope you enjoyed our unique party trick tonight. We really wanted to try something visceral and even surprisingly emotional, may I add," he said indicating Rosaline White, who nodded once as a camera flashed in her face.

Looking across, I saw Quayin touch her ear as Vincent continued to talk. She glanced up at the walkways high above. I couldn't see anything noticeable, so I used the skeleton's eyes to magnify the image. I spotted a large person hidden behind one of the marine curtains. It was Stranz aiming a scoped weapon at the stage. But I couldn't tell whether the gun was pointed at me or at his employer. I looked back at Quayin, who watched Vincent spitefully. She shook her head and Stranz lowered his gun instantly.

"This concludes the presentation today," Vincent continued seemingly oblivious to the betrayal. "I hope you enjoyed the show, a round of applause for Miss Quayin and Doctor Hart, if you please!"

The audience applauded loudly in response, but they were still unsure. I could see in their faces that the 'performance' had been perhaps too visceral. Vincent would need to comfort them more than that.

"It was, of course, a rehearsed situation. This was merely a showing of the opportunities that are coming your way soon. We will indeed be using the nerve plug for both technologies which will become available soon."

Vincent looked at me directly and that honest smile that I had seen earlier leaked out of his face. He nodded at me once.

"Doctor Hart's prosthetics to aid those who have suffered from the incident shall be available in the coming weeks for the general public at a reasonable price."

I had done it. I breathed a huge sigh of relief. Vincent Cain was siding with my idea after all!

"However... our other advancements still need some tweaking, before they are ready to be introduced. Miss Quayin's demonstration of the capabilities of the nerve plug needs more examination before it can be safely sold."

He spared a small moment to send his sister a very small smile. I could see that they would clearly be having words with one another later.

"Thank you all for coming," he finished. "I hope you've had a wonderful night, I know that I have! We hope you have a safe journey home. But before you go, just remember that all of us here are the future! May the Fates bless us all! Good night and bless you Prima! The greatest city in the world!"

The audience lapsed into applause that consumed the entire room. I soaked in the praise gratefully. It was worth it after such a difficult week.

"Please make your way out of the foyer. We need to tidy up everything for work to continue after the weekend. I'll be sending out a special notice that allows all employees the weekend off. We all need our rest after such an eventful week. Thank you all and goodnight!"

Vincent Cain bowed once to the audience and made his way across the stage. He ignored his sister completely and firmly shook my hand.

"Fantastic work tonight, Doctor Hart. There is a very promising future ahead of you. I want you to take the week off. Come back next Monday and report to me directly. Have no fear, my friend; the week off will be paid leave. We just need some time to arrange your new offices."

"New...?" I stuttered in awe.

"I now understand the importance of what you are talking about. This idea of completing the human body really rings true in my head. It is a required necessity that we are all completely equal. We all deserve to be at the peak of physical and mental health. All of us. Once that's done... we can take control of Prima."

I nodded dumbly, unable to take in the promotion and not fully understanding what he meant. Vincent Cain pulled me aside and shielded his hand, as Lucy had done, and began to talk in my ear.

"Also, there's the personal endeavour that you're going to help with," he said tapping his head slowly.

I remembered the dark smudge that lingered inside Cain's head. The darkness in his mind stopped him using the nerve plug. The disabled blank point where he should be able to analyse a gift...

It all came together in a single moment. Vincent wanted to become equal to everyone he'd been hunting.

"Yes, I think I understand," I said slowly, not daring to look him in the eye. He seemed to think that I would be able to fix his brain, but I'm not sure I wanted to give him his lost power. "It seems you have some damaged nerve endings. I don't know if I can help, but..."

"I believe that you have a better insight than anyone else in the world," Vincent Cain said grabbing my shoulder in a friendly manner. "Doctor Hart, I'd be honoured if you would work…"

"Better insight?" Lucy interrupted.

"Much better," Vincent finally acknowledged his sister. His kind face turned impatient. "You activated the ATV in a room full of Prima's most important personnel and nearly fractured international relations. If Doctor Hart wasn't here to control the situation, who knows what could've happened!"

Vincent grabbed his sister by the arm and dragged her out of sight.

I stood on the sidelines unable to move away. I'd never seen either of the siblings so riled up before. On impulse, I activated my exo-skeleton's audio faculties to eavesdrop on the conversation.

"I was in control," Lucy cried.

"You were wild," Vincent spat.

"Didn't you see it work? We shouldn't limit ourselves."

"I saw you struggle to control a machine that was at least thirty times heavier than you and with more limbs than an untrained mind can handle. You've done more damage tonight than you can ever realise!"

"Why don't you ever listen to what I have to say?" Lucy retorted.

"I'll listen when you do something right for once," he mumbled.

"I was doing exactly what you have, trying to gain more power for our family. Stop pushing me aside. I've been with you from the start. I was here before the incident at Old Street, before you released Xander from prison and before you hired Foshe and Stranz. I was here before Doctor Hart turned up, whom you spontaneously seem to favour more than your own sister? I've always been here with you before everything. And yet, as always, you leave me in the dark. Why, brother? Why am I not allowed to be your sister?"

"We are family…" Vincent said frustrated.

"Yes, I know, in blood alone," Lucy interrupted. "What does

251

that even mean? I want work with you, not for you. Please. Talk to me."

"Begging doesn't become you well," he groaned.

"That's what I'm having to resort to. I have to beg for us to even have a conversation."

"Fine," Vincent said in frustration. "This is hardly the time, but what do you want to talk about, Lucy?"

"When I was practicing with the nerve plug, I started to remember something. It's a side effect of the technology. It was really strange. I remembered my body fading and almost flickering. I could see my hands and then they disappeared. And then… I remembered our mother."

Vincent was silent in response and waited anxiously for her to continue.

"She had long golden hair and these soft kind eyes. We were at our home in the third year of the Blackout, I think. She was pushing me on this swing in autumn. We lived on the Cain estate up in the mountains. The observatory that's been abandoned for decades, we used to live there! The estate grew its own crops, generated power, and we had our own butler. The sun was shining and wind was rustling the orange trees. You were there too. I could see you climbing this huge tree and she told you to get down, but you were stubborn and you kept climbing. Up and up and higher and higher. You wouldn't stop, but then you fell down. You nearly went over the cliff edge…"

"What happened next?" Vincent asked desperately. "What else is there?"

"But why would I forget her? Until this morning, I didn't even know I had a mother. I didn't even think about it. I didn't even care. Why would I not care?"

"What else do you remember?" Vincent demanded. "Tell me now."

"The front door slammed open. Everything starts to go dark. There was a man there and this dark anger was spewing out of him. He blamed our mother for all of our pain. He was furious. Autumn died as he poured his hatred over everything until only we remained. He shouted at our mother and made her sick. Her eyes. Vincent… they were black. This foul ink poured out of her eyes and covered her. It burned her out of existence. Whenever I think of her, all I could see is this dark smudge at the back of my mind. I don't understand. Why can't I remember? What did he do to us? Who the hell is this man?"

I peeked my head around the curtain to see Vincent slap his sister across the face. She nursed her bruised cheek before he grabbed her chin and pulled her face towards him.

"You must never talk about him ever again," he said harshly. "Forget about our mother and that man. Trust me. It's for your own good."

Lucy toppled on her heels and fell awkwardly against the curtain.

"You lost control today," Vincent continued. "We can't afford to do that. Not even for a moment. We must never become like him."

"I did this to show you that I am worthy of the name of Cain!"

"And this is why you're not involved in my business, because you are rash, naive and impudent. You would lose control the moment you were given true power. I have kept you out of my private life deliberately to keep you safe from the truth that is beyond your comprehension. This is the exact reason why I don't tell you everything. You are the reason we cannot be a family. Only when you start to show some decorum will I even consider letting you join me."

Lucy's lower lip quivered and she began to cry slightly. She wiped her eyes clumsily and her make up smeared. She glared at her brother.

"I despise you, Vincent. You're an arrogant idiot who parades his smug grin to make all his lackeys believe he is in charge. You'd be nothing without me. I run this company. I'm in charge! You don't do a damn thing and you reap the rewards. How is that fair? What have you ever done?"

Cain laughed in disbelief and I saw a vague shape of sympathy in his grey eyes. He touched her cheek and wiped away a tear from her porcelain face.

"Shut your impertinent mouth," he whispered. "You have no idea what I've sacrificed for this great city. The years I've devoted. I have poured my life into this Corporation, built it from our family finance and become the most vital individual in Prima. No one understands the measures I have taken, so don't you dare talk down to me!"

"What would our mother think if she could see you now, brother?" Lucy snarled. "Selfish, stubborn and alone."

Cain's hand curled roughly around her throat. Quayin began to choke slightly and her manicured nails scratched at her brother's hand.

"Or what?" Quayin croaked through his hand around her trachea. Her words dribbled towards Cain as she tried to speak. "What will you do? Put me in a box and throw away the key just like you've done to the rest. I'm not one of your pathetic terrorists."

"I'll take you to him," Vincent spat and Lucy's eyes widened in slow terror. "He's real, Lucy. Keep behaving like a brat and I'll take you to see the man that killed our mother and destroyed any memories you have of her. Oh, believe me, he's eager to meet you."

Lucy's mouth dropped into silence as a strange fear gripped her body. She nodded shakily and Vincent released his sister. No more words needed to pass between them. She started walking away and I moved as far away from the curtain as possible. Lucy stormed past, completely ignoring my existence.

The family argument had caught me off-guard. It sounded as though this had been the only time Lucy had ever been able to speak up against her brother and he'd shut her down in an instant.

The nerve plug made the subject recall memories as it connected to their brain. Bolt had recalled his experience of the incident after wearing the device. Rosaline White had relived the birth of Prima. My mind had surged back to the night I had seen my parents drown.

I hadn't anticipated it affecting Lucy so vividly. Who was she talking about? According to Vincent, there was a man who had spewed darkness into their minds, torn their mother from Lucy's memory and had taken Vincent's gift away.

"I'm sorry for the delay," Vincent said behind me. "Family problems. I know you can probably sympathize having two kids under your belt. It is unfortunate, but it's been building up for quite some time. Just needed to talk it out. Communication. That is the key. Sometimes you have to lay down authority, so they know who is in charge."

"What will you do with her?" I asked quietly.

"That is honestly no concern of yours," he said coldly. His eyes froze slightly, but then he blinked and put on a smile to warm the atmosphere. "Great work tonight. You have my word that we will see you again soon."

"Thank you, Mr Cain."

"You must call me Vincent from now on," he said, before leaving me alone and pulling his sister aside to talk to her fiercely out of earshot.

"Quite the spectacle! May we have a word?" An aged voice asked with hints of an Australian accent embedded within it.

I turned to greet the representatives of Eden and Kubra that had remained behind. Meanwhile I saw the Marshalls of Lockroy and the blind Amazonian were talking avidly as they exited the foyer.

"Professor Eden," the old man introduced himself with a wry smile and extended his callused hand. "Pleasure to meet you, son. Your work is utterly astonishing!"

I stared at the man's hand in awe and nervously shook it. It was rough, as though it had spent a lifetime doing manual labour. I realised that I was being praised by the founder of the great city renowned for technological advancement. Professor Eden was originally from Melbourne before he moved south to Antarctica. He was famous for his architectural work on biomes to create self-contained environments. He could create worlds with adjustable climates for any type of organism on the planet. He was well known for his hands-on approach to the construction of the biomes. He'd been repeatedly pictured digging, planting, wiring, herding, welding and orchestrating the construction of various biomes from start to finish.

"So, Prima is the greatest city in the world according to Mr Cain?" Eden chortled. "Have to disagree with him there, but I'm slightly biased. If you were living with us, there would be no limitations on you. None whatsoever!"

"I'm a little…" I stuttered.

"Lost for words?" Morowa said simply and smiled calmly. I looked up at the tall beautiful woman from Kubra. Her simple phrase eased my mind. Now that I was stood next to her, I could see fine golden lines that contrasted beautifully against her dark skin. The lines etched across her face and down her neck to form intricate patterns that seemed to tell a thousand stories.

"It's been a turbulent week," I commented in awe.

"Consider what could have happened if your Kubran father had helped build Eden instead of moving to Prima after the Global War," Eden said and placed his firm hand on my shoulder. "Your life could have been so different. So much better. It's not too late to make a change."

"I would not have met my wife," I replied politely. "Adele is from Prima and this great city will always be my home."

"You have a kind soul," Morowa said serenely. "Your bravery today is the true triumph, not the technology."

Morowa turned, her distinct maroon clothes swaying with her and she left without saying another word.

"She's a strange one, but most Kubrans are," Eden snorted. "They're all mixed up with their fusion of culture underneath the earth. All those people from all those different nations cohabiting in those hot caverns under the desert. Phew! It's no wonder that their Correspondent is quite loopy as a result."

"I found that she was quite succinct."

"The citizens of Eden are much more direct. We are efficiency defined."

I nodded in acknowledgement and stared after the elegant Kubran woman. I would love to spend time in her company and learn more about the great city my father had grown up in…

"Consider my offer," Eden commented as he noticed my distraction, before joining the remainder of the audience who

256

were still filing out of the foyer. "Your family would be more than welcome in any biome of your choosing."

"It was an honour to meet you, Professor," I called after him and momentarily considered life without Prima. I shook my head. Prima had given me everything. I would never turn my back on my home.

I found my family waiting in the third row. Adele looked quizzically at the exiting officials and at the warring siblings. I shrugged deeply. Adele hugged me warmly and kissed me on the cheek. I felt a tug on my trousers and Theo was pulling at the material. I pulled him up to embrace him.

"Did you enjoy that, buddy?" I asked.

"That was amazing, Dad!" Theo said, joy bursting across his face. "You never told me your job was making robots!"

"Well, it's not really…"

"When I grow up, I want to make robots as well," he exclaimed and then turned to Adele. "Can I make robots when I leave school? I want to leave school now and make robots with Dad. Please? It looks like so much fun!"

"Dad doesn't make robots, Theo," said Izzy. I gave her a hug, which she held for a while.

"No. You're wrong," said Theo and he pointed at the skeleton still standing on stage. "Did you make that?"

"Yes, Theo, I did," I confirmed.

"Dad makes robots. I want to make a robot," he said smugly.

I shrugged. As long as Theo was happy it didn't matter what he thought I did for a living.

"That was really good," Izzy said. "You did a good thing up there, especially for that old lady."

"You liked the show then?" I asked.

"I loved it! It was really amazing and I'm actually a little proud of you," she said slightly embarrassed. "I didn't know you were that clever."

"You doubted my intelligence!" I laughed. "So, which robot was better?"

"Definitely yours," she answered. "Do you think we can meet it properly later?"

"Vincent won't need it. It was just a prototype," I said. "So I reckon we can take it home with us!"

"So I can make it tidy my room, do my homework and go to school for me?" Izzy asked.

"Well, yes, it could, but realistically you would still be doing the work," I replied. "Although it would allow you to do two jobs at once."

"That's absolutely fine," Adele said quickly. "As long as it cleans my kitchen, whilst Isabella is working it."

I laughed at that and wished that Bolt could have been with us for this moment. Now that I was on good terms with Vincent, I'd have to talk to him about his release, once he was finished with Lucy.

Vincent was currently pointing furiously at his sister. He grabbed the nerve plug from the back of her neck and pointed sharply at me across the room. I met Quayin's eyes and her hatred swept over the room. I heard Vincent shout and then point to the high rafters to exactly where Stranz had been positioned. It would seem that Vincent Cain did know everything that happened here. He threw the nerve plug at her, which landed roughly on the stage. He pointed once towards the door and then walked away promptly.

"Forget about her," Adele said. "She's a nasty piece of work. I can smell the jealousy reeking off her from here."

"Jealousy?" I asked.

"Of our family," she said and kissed me softly once on the mouth, which both of the kids cringed at. "Those two are the furthest thing I've seen from a family."

I nodded in agreement and looked back at Quayin, standing alone. She was staring viciously offstage at Cain. She shook her head fiercely and suddenly snatched up the nerve-plug. She gripped it with whitening knuckles and tied it sharply around her neck.

I gasped as the ATV began to move towards her oblivious brother.

I sent my skeleton running across the stage and it jumped forwards, pushing Vincent aside as the spiked leg sliced down. It pierced the skeleton through the chest. I yelled in shock as the skeleton's battery core ignited and burst with a shock of electricity.

Vincent gathered himself, luckily unharmed by the attack. The skeleton sparked fiercely, skewered on the spider's leg. It wasn't responding to my nerve plug anymore. The leg flicked the metal corpse aside into the far wall. The skeleton cracked against the wall with a metallic thud.

The ATV lowered one of its arms and Lucy Quayin climbed into the open cockpit. She settled into the chair as the door sealed shut behind her. The machine stirred as its knees bent and prepared to strike. I saw the white of Quayin's teeth shine, as the monster pounced forwards.

It leapt from the stage and began charging directly towards my family.

23 – Last Resort

I stretched out my hand to use my gift. I sensed the wild mess of the machine as it powered across the foyer, digging into the floor with its claws and threw chairs aside. The wooden chairs smashed into splinters against the marble, making Cain's soldiers frantically take cover.

My palm tensed desperately. I could sense the writhing machine with the burning nerve plug wrapped around Quayin's neck, but I couldn't control any of it. Her central nervous system superseded my gift.

I couldn't stop her.

The ATV was metres away and I grabbed whoever was closest and pulled them out of the way. The monster of metal crashed around us sending up chunks of rubble and steel into the air. Its legs punctured the floor as it searched for my family through the dust. I heard Adele scream and I ran towards her voice. She was holding Theo who was crying in her arms, but I couldn't find Izzy.

"Izzy! Where are you? IZZY!" I screamed.

I couldn't see anything. I couldn't see my daughter.

"Stay here and stay hidden," I told Adele and ran into the smoke.

"No, Will! Stay with us," she cried faintly, as she disappeared from sight.

The machine towered above us and, despite it being beyond my control, I could sense where every part of it was. A spiked leg came slicing down, which I dodged by dropping down. The next two legs trampled towards me, but I ran between them.

The smog finally cleared and I saw a small body ahead, lying emblazoned against the pale marble. It was my daughter… and she wasn't moving.

I grasped my daughter's limp body. Her side was bruised purple and her head was bleeding heavily. I gasped and my tears fell rapidly and onto her still body. I searched for her breath and hurriedly pressed my fingers against her neck. I moved desperately, pressing harshly to look for a pulse. There was a faint rhythm, which made my body relax slightly, but she was still unconscious. She might have a concussion, brain damage or internal bleeding. I needed to get Izzy medical attention immediately.

I looked at the monster that had finally paused its rampage.

"Stop this, Quayin!" I shouted at her. "She's seriously hurt."

Lucy's nostrils flared. I noticed her cheek was dashed red with blood that shone roughly in the dusty light.

"Now you know what it's like to lose your family," she said firmly. "This is how I feel every single day of my life!"

She moved to crush us both, but Vincent's voice burst out from the stage. Cain's private army fired their weapons. The bullets cracked against the glass of the cockpit, but had little effect on the moving monster. They had constructed the prototype to have the armour of a tank and mobility of a wild animal.

Quayin opened up one of the ATV's hands that began to glow brightly. The machine hummed as it summoned the energy to fire. I picked up my daughter and carried her hurriedly towards the stage. The air ignited and then exploded as the energy blasted into the marble behind us. I staggered and continued to run. The machine began to hum again and I suddenly ran left. I glanced back and saw Quayin rip open the white floor. I reached the edge of the room where a group of guards were waiting.

"This is my daughter. Her name is Isabella Hart. She needs immediate medical attention. She has severe head trauma and broken ribs, which means the possibility of a punctured lung. It's vital that you hurry," I told them as they took my daughter. The tears continued to fall from my face. I never even asked her how her exam went, I didn't even know if she got there in time.

I grabbed another guard by the arm and shouted roughly in their ear.

"My family are on the other side! I don't how long they can stay hidden."

The machine hummed again and the guards began to run

towards the stage to re-group with Cain. I saw a flight of stairs and I sprinted up them. The machine fired at the nearby lift, shattering it instantly and sending green glass flying across the foyer. Massive shards sheared towards the floor, before cracking into a million pieces. I heard a piercing snap as the cable supporting the lift broke, and it dropped from the top floor and smashed into the ground below.

I climbed two more flights of stairs and looked over the banister. Quayin was firing multiple energy blasts at once. Cain was taking cover and ordering his people to flank the invincible machine. Adele and Theo were huddled on the far side of the foyer beside the next fragile lift.

I had to distract Quayin. I had to move her away from my family until I thought of a way to stop the machine or Cain managed to bring it down.

I climbed two more flights and ran along the corridor, moving as far away from my family as possible. I breathed heavily, coughing up the dust that hung in the air and made my eyes water.

The machine continued to fire blasts of energy. I yelled at Lucy, determined to distract her, but she didn't respond. She was too busy attacking her brother by throwing chunks of rubble at his guards. I copied the idea, remembering that she could feel every single part of the machine, and began throwing everything I could to grab her attention.

"Lucy Quayin! I'm the one you want. Come up here and get me, you motherless witch!" I shouted.

The monster suddenly stopped firing and looked slowly up at me. I spotted Lucy's face scream out. All of the ATV's palms started glowing brightly, aimed directly at my position. I swore and jumped back.

They blasted into my floor. My world erupted with deadly rubble and fire. The supports shattered and the entire floor dropped down on a sharp slant. I began to slide, but managed to wrap my arm around the handrails. I dangled briefly, my vision spinning as my legs flailed over the edge. It was a long way down. The air tasted bitter with a hint of iron, fire and blood. I wrenched my body up and began to crawl up the slant towards the far wall.

A screeching pounding sound of metal burrowing into stone slammed into my ears. It pounded again and again, getting louder with each passing moment. I crawled back towards the edge and saw the monstrous machine directly below. It pierced the wall with its legs as it slowly climbed vertically. It gripped the shattered lift with its hands and hauled itself even higher. I crawled back as Quayin rose to meet me on the sixth floor. Her four spider legs dug themselves into the walls as the cockpit was shoved into the space. Her three metal arms held her in position and I found myself almost face-to-face with my ex-employer.

Through the glass and metal, Quayin's quivering face glared with fury, her eyes were mad and glowed a frazzling electric blue. She was sweating heavily at the exertion of controlling the machine. Her face was now bleeding heavy and her make-up smeared to mix with the blood. Her usual sharp ponytail had fallen and become wild in the cockpit.

"You've ruined everything, Hart," Quayin cried. "You've taken away my job and the only family I've got!"

"You've done this yourself…" I said, trying not to anger her any further.

"You made this happen, don't deny it, and you're already paying for what you've done to me. Oh yes, I remember when we broke down Mark Bolton's door this morning. He put up quite the fight, but after a few hits to the head… he stopped struggling."

"He didn't do anything wrong," I said. "This is between you and me."

"I didn't like how rude he was to me. I really hate disrespect. Did you know that I spoke to Foshe earlier? I haven't seen the old Lunan look so happy in years! He told me that Bolt gave up trying to fight the memory altering process within half an hour. Personally, I don't know Foshe's work very well, but that seems pathetic."

She smiled as she used her mechanical arms to pull herself further into the space. I felt my back hit the wall and realised there was no way out. I pressed a sweating hand against the glass of the cockpit and left a bloodied handprint. There was a small buzzing sensation and I felt the hairs on the back of my hand begin to stand on end.

"He's stuck with that deranged man and it's all your fault. You didn't give me what I wanted. So someone had to pay the price. And then you did it again. You have taken away the only family I had left. So now I'm going to kill you, Doctor Hart, with your own technology."

Quayin breathed in sharply through her nostrils. A synaptic twitch echoed along her arm and into her face. A creeping cackle rocked her body and her smeared face grinned at me menacingly.

"The nerve plug is tearing you apart, Lucy," I told her as I saw how it wracked her mind. "Stop this whilst you can still think straight!"

"It's helping me to see better than ever before, William. I'm remembering more forgotten moments," she said and started sobbing fiercely. "I'm seeing all my lost birthdays again and the bitterly cold Blackout winters. Every last detail of the Cain estate is becoming engrained in my mind. I can finally recall bright days skimming rocks on the lake. Climbing up the mountain with Vincent and his friend. My family reunited and the sound of her screaming burning through my bedroom wall, again and again. Morta! It's all coming back and I can't stop it! Why can't I stop the screaming?"

"I can help you!" I shouted as Lucy writhed in mental agony. "This machine is destroying your mind."

The ATV hissed and fell as she lost control. Lucy's eyes returned to focus and her claws dug into the marble walls.

"I think you will find that I am in complete control!" Quayin laughed agitatedly. "Yes, I am going to kill you, just like I killed your insipid daughter. And I'll show Vincent at last. I will show them all that I am worthy of the name of Cain!"

I sensed the nerve plug and how it connected Quayin with the massive machine. I could still feel the machine. I could feel its cockpit, legs, arms, every joint, wire and circuit and electrical signal, but I could not control it. Through this mass of machinery, I found the nerve plug connected to everything. Including Lucy. I sensed her network of unstable nerves rattling beyond the device that seized control away from me.

If I couldn't use the technology, then I'd have to use something else.

The veins in my hand slowly began to glow. The light filled my hand and changed the colour from brown to dark blue. Looking into the haze of glass, I saw my reflected brown eyes glow a stark shade of bright sapphire. They cracked with energy that poured from my synapses and simmered out to the palm of my hand.

The glass cracked out in thick blue lines as I sent a flow of energy out of my body. Electricity burst out of my hand, rattled through the machine and surged into the stolen nerve plug.

Lucy froze, her mouth opening as the light in her eyes died out. I focused fully on the nerve plug and began exploring beyond the bridge to her body. I found Quayin's spine and splayed out my palm.

I sent all the frenetic power surging out of my body, into the wild machine to reclaim control. Then I sent every possible signal from the machine surging through the nerve plug and ploughing into Quayin's central nervous system. It ripped through her spine and cascaded out across her body. It tore through her chest, scorching her limbs as it destroyed every last nerve ending. A final burst of energy powered into her head and on a sudden impulse I moved the electricity around her skull and spared her brain. Blue plasma seeped out of her eyes, like rivers of lightning. It dribbled around her mouth, before dripping silently downwards.

Her eyes looked at me in horror, her mind unable to keep up with what had just happened. She no longer had the bodily functions to show what she was thinking. Quayin was now an empty shell of a woman, her mind screaming behind the eyes of an unmoving corpse.

Her body suddenly flickered strangely. Her distorted face appeared and then disappeared entirely. She returned, lying crippled inside the machine and her breath escaping her tortured lips. Then she completely vanished again.

I gasped as I realized that her gift had just been activated.

The machine lost its grip on the walls. The weight of the ATV began to teeter towards the precipice. I glimpsed Lucy's dissipating, crying face before the dying monster teetered out of sight, tumbling momentarily, before crashing violently into the ground.

I fell back in exhaustion and waited for the sound of Quayin's suffering to stop. I could hear the fires wrinkling the air. The scorching flames were consuming the twisted carcass, before they were slowly extinguished.

Lucy's dying face remained seared in my mind and wouldn't let me go. I waited for it all to stop. I waited for her pain to end, but I couldn't ignore it.

I had to do it. She was going to kill me. Quayin had hurt my family. I remembered the lifeless form of my daughter and I nodded to myself faintly. I did what had to be done. If Lucy did survive the drop, then she would be paralysed from the neck down. I opened my eyes and a final piece of rubble tumbled over the edge. It resounded with a small clang as it ricocheted off the shell of the dead tank. The rubble finally grew still and I exhaled heavily.

In the distance I saw the lift, still waiting to be used. I staggered over to the lift and pressed the button, but nothing happened. On instinct, I waved my hand to connect with the door and forced it to work. It croaked open and I stumbled inside, closing it with my mind. The lift began to drop slowly as I manually lowered the lift using the winch high above.

Looking in the mirror, I studied the cuts lacerating my arms and face from the shattered glass. I saw my eyes were still glowing a fierce blue. I laughed. I'd never imagined myself with bright blue eyes before. My hand was still buzzing violently. Even now, when it was all over, the adrenaline still pumped through my blood and my hand glowed the same shade of electric blue as my eyes.

I had used my own electrical energy, stored within my synapses, as a last resort to survive the encounter and now I was immensely tired. I had summoned energy out of my body, breaking the nerve plug and reclaimed control over the machine. I could have stopped there, but I hadn't. I'd dominated the machine and poured everything into Lucy's fragile body. I'd broken her…

The lift swayed abruptly and I forced the door open. In the distance, I saw the destroyed machine and soldiers working around the corpse to recover Lucy's body. I tried to ignore the sight, but I couldn't help seeing the blood leaking between the metal…

There was no sign of a body. What was I thinking? I didn't want to look at the woman I had just murdered. No. It was self-defence. She had brought this on herself the moment she attacked my family.

I felt a gun activating nearby. Vincent was waiting, his eyes as cold as steel. His suit was filthy and his expression was grim. Nothing seemed to faze him. I wondered if he even flinched when he watched his sister die.

Vincent thumbed back the trigger on his gun and made me suddenly aware of my surroundings.

"Stop where you are or I will shoot them both," he said bluntly and I looked down at my wife in his arms. Adele was staring at my glowing hand, her face filled with confusion. Vincent's hand pressed firmly against her mouth, which muffled her screams. Anton Stranz arrived, covered in blood and oil, holding Theo who was struggling in his arms. Stranz squeezed my son tightly, preventing him from squirming anymore.

Vincent Cain clicked the safety on his gun, which he now had pointed directly at my wife's head.

24 – Cornered Animal

"Let my family go," I demanded.

"I can't do that," Cain replied, pressing the barrel of his gun against Adele's temple to prove his point. She grunted behind his hand and tried to move away, but he only clamped his hand around her mouth even tighter.

"Leave them alone. You don't want them…" I begged.

"It doesn't work like that," he said bluntly. "There will be no trading today. The only way out of this mess is doing exactly what I tell you."

"I just saved your life…" I said pointing at the mess of blood and metal nearby.

"Are you seriously saying that killing my deranged sister somehow justifies your freedom?" Vincent asked shakily. His grey eyes wavered as he paused for my answer and for the first time I saw his authority falter. "Well? That was not a rhetorical question."

"I had no choice," I said quietly.

"There is always a choice," he spat. "Lucy would have calmed down in due course…"

"She was a broken woman," I interrupted. "The nerve-plug had torn her mind apart. Didn't you see it? The damage to her mental condition was beyond repair."

My words silenced Cain and grief finally echoed across his body. His jaw tensed. His pupils dilated briefly. His knuckles became white around the gun that was still pressed against my wife's temple.

"You're right. There is always a choice, Vincent," I said. "You can let us go. We'll leave here and you'll never have to see us again."

I knew as soon as the words left my mouth that they were useless. Cain laughed roughly and coughed the dust out of his throat. He stared down at my glowing palm in disgust.

"So… let's take a moment to talk about the elephant in the

room that I reckon your family are quite confused about," Cain said. "Tell your family. What exactly are you able to do?"

There was no point denying it, my hand was glowing and I'd destroyed a thirty-foot multi limbed tank on my own. The thought of fighting or running tugged in my mind, but I couldn't take on Cain, Stranz and his soldiers whilst they had my family at gunpoint.

"I can control technology with my mind," I replied simply and tried to ignore my family's reactions. "I've been able to do it for about a week now. Are you happy now, Vincent?"

"Of course I'm not happy! You hid this from me and if you had just been honest, then we could've worked something out in private."

"You've locked up every single person with a gift and put a needle in their brain."

"That's where you're wrong. You should've trusted me. There have been instances where I've worked out certain compromises with people. You could've been one of them."

"If you're telling the truth then why can't we find a compromise?" I asked. "We can make this work."

"You've thrown away any chance for that now!" He shouted. "You can't deny that you don't like it? I bet you feel amazing with that power at your fingertips. You must feel like a god. Would you really have given it all up if I asked you? I don't think so. Not now that you've started to lose control. You gave up the chance for a compromise the moment you let all that power go to your head."

Adele's eyes widened in bewilderment. This would be complicated to explain if we ever got out of this mess. My gaze flowed over to Theo who squirmed in response to my eyes.

I raised my glowing palm out towards them and the guards raised their weapons. Cain's grip tightened around Adele. Stranz wrapped his hand around Theo's neck. I lowered my hand slowly and they relaxed in return.

"I never asked for any of this," I told them. "All I wanted was to protect my family. Just tell me what I need to do, so that I can have them back…"

269

"We need to try and remove your power immediately. It's become too unstable for us to delay the process, so I will need your complete cooperation. Our problem is that we can't simply get rid of it…" Cain said, his forehead creasing, as he considered his next words. "Our process involves erasing the subject's memory of when they first discovered their gift. Your situation is much more complex. You see… with knowledge comes power…"

"We learn from what we see…" I finally understood. "We see a gift and we receive a gift. By the Fates… everyone who has seen my power will gain abilities of their own. It's more than that… every single person on the planet has a gift. All of us have it. That's why you have to quarantine us; otherwise you would have an immediate epidemic on your hands. All it takes is for one person to see me using my power and then…"

"Yes, William," Vincent replied. "The world would fall into chaos. That's why we need to get you and your family into quarantine straight away."

It was Raven. My mind had awoken once I had seen her wrapped in flames at my home. I remembered the brief moments before Quayin fell, her body had begun to flicker strangely once she'd seen my gift.

I remembered Bolt. He had received his gift shortly after the tragedy of Old Street. All the survivors had seen a gift in full flow that day.

"The explosion in Old Street wasn't a bomb," I fully discovered. "The incident was a person. You haven't been hunting terrorists. You've been hunting down anyone who received a gift that day."

"The situation had to be contained and we almost did it. Last night we bagged a whole horde of the rats. We were so close!" Vincent exclaimed. "So your gifted existence presents a very important question. We need to nip this disease in the bud immediately, so you must tell me the truth. Who showed you their gift?"

"First I want you tell me who caused the incident," I asked bravely.

"That is irrelevant. This is clearly not the time for this discussion. Now tell me, who was it?" Vincent demanded.

Cain's patience had grown thin. He was bored of having to explain himself. He raised his gun in the air and fired it once. I did not move. He pointed the weapon at me and I still didn't flinch. Finally he pressed the red-hot barrel of the gun against my wife's arm. It sizzled as it branded her skin. Adele gasped as her flesh burnt.

"Raven," I answered weakly. "It was Raven."

He released the gun from Adele's skin and gave a sad smile.

"I thought as much. I just wanted to clarify the connection. As a man of science, you must understand the importance of obtaining information to solve a problem. Raven is a serious problem that needs correcting. She has been waltzing around Prima for three years with a gift and forcing us to clean up behind her. Did you know you are the third person we've found with a gift thanks to her? Perhaps you can begin to comprehend the inconvenience one gifted can cause."

"I understand the importance of the situation, Mr Cain," I said firmly. "Now, before we continue, I want you to guarantee my family's safety. Just release them and we can all calm down."

"I can't do that," he repeated. "They must be quarantined. They have seen you."

"And so have you…" I said slowly, "Where is your gift, Vincent? And all of yours in fact?"

I looked to all the men and women whose faces remained blank. They all knew the answer, but none would give it to me. The memory of the dark smudge in Cain's brain tickled my thoughts.

"Do you all have that darkness…?" I asked quietly.

"Enough!" Cain yelled furiously, pointed his gun down and shot my wife in the leg.

The gunshot blasted into my eardrum. Adele's screams ricocheted off the shattered walls and launched themselves into my mind. Cain placed his hand over her mouth and her agony turned into a strangled cry. Adele suffered in his grasp and nearly fainted from the pain.

"Mum!" Theo screamed. "Let her go!"

"Shut that child up!" Cain shouted.

Stranz put my child in a sleeping hold. His massive hand wrapped around my son's face, stopping him from breathing. Within moments my son was starved of oxygen and became unconscious. Stranz released him and the small boy became limp. The gargantuan man stopped briefly to check for a pulse. He nodded vaguely. Theo's chest was still moving. It heaved in and out, the same way it always did when he dozed off at home. Stranz hauled my son into a nearby soldier's arms who took the unconscious child away.

"I can see the way you're looking at me, Hart," Vincent said coldly. "You must think I'm morally corrupt and need to learn the error of my ways. I assure you that I am completely justified in my actions. My methods may seem extreme, but I am doing what must be done to ensure the survival of the Prima. The gifted must be quarantined. There was a time where you would have agreed with my actions."

"You're going to pay for that," I said clenching my fists and ignoring his meagre justification. "No one hurts my family."

"There is only one way this is going to happen. You are going to come with me. Your family is in my custody, but if you aren't quick, then your wife will bleed out in my arms. Your children also require medical attention. We will take you far away and take all the bad memories away," he said tapping Adele on the head with his gun. "You will *all* forget everything about gifts and then you can go back to your lives. The process is relatively painless, depending if you resist. You'll be back as a family before you know it."

Stranz grabbed Adele and bundled her up in his arms. I caught her eye as she was taken away and she smiled roughly before finally fainting in Stranz's arms.

"Where are you taking them?" I asked as calmly as I could manage.

"The other side of Prima, far away to avoid further contamination. You will join them soon, but you are still unstable. We will place you in a separate vehicle. You must understand that this is all necessary, William."

Cain signalled for his men to leave us alone. We looked at the wreckage around us and soaked it in all of solemn carnage.

Cain slowly held out his hand for me to shake…

"Once this has all been erased, I'd like you to work with us again. We are always in need of bright minds at Cain Corporation. You will have no memory of the last couple of weeks, but you will have your life back. You can continue your hard work on the nerve plug; doesn't that sound good? I can still use your talents. You must understand why I'm doing this? You're a man who would do anything to protect the people he loves. I just want to make sure the people of our great city are safe. Search your own history, at the back of your mind, you must agree with me? See this from my perspective, surely you understand what I'm doing?"

"I understand," I said and shook his hand firmly. Cain relaxed, smiled and holstered his weapon in his suit pocket. He grasped my glowing blue hand, relieved at how well everything had gone without any more fighting.

"I really do understand. I can see the importance of your work," I said honestly. "On the other hand, I know exactly how you treat your patients. So, personally, I don't think your process is right for us. I'm truly sorry, but I can't let you take my family."

My hand began glowing even brighter. Vincent reached for his gun and I opened my palm. His gun disintegrated and exploded in his hand. Cain fell back in shock and I threw my fist into his face. He collapsed to the floor, clutching his jaw with his bleeding hand and I sprinted across the foyer.

I heard Cain shouting into his holo-phone to evacuate the Hart family immediately. I hurried past the wreckage ATV and tried my best not to look at the ragged mess of blood. A unit of guards entered through the far door and I took cover as their bullets ricocheted off the marble walls.

Nearby was the corpse of my exoskeleton with a thick hole splintering its chest. I sensed the remains and found that some of the circuitry was still active. I dived towards the machine and let it surround my body. The energy within the batteries coursed into

273

my veins and refuelled my exhausted body. I wore the machine like armour. It supported my body and allowed me to move comfortably in its secure embrace. I moved towards the guards with an ever-increasing pace. The bullets fluttered off my metal skin like angry wasps. I pushed the circuitry in my legs to let me run faster than ever before. My footsteps became powerful, cracking the stone underfoot and made my muscles scream from the physical exertion. The men shuddered in my wake as I barged through them. I soared past their broken bodies and smashed out of the front door.

I dashed into the car park and scanned for my family. I used a camera in my armour to magnify my vision and followed a truck speeding through the car park gate. That had to be them.

I shed all of the armour from my body, apart from the arm. The metal carcass rattled to the ground and the remaining machinery slotted comfortably around my limb. I found my car that I hadn't driven since yesterday and I ran towards it. With a wave of my glowing hand, the door flew open and the engine started up before I had even settled into the seat.

My car charged towards the security gate, where a horde of soldiers were waiting. I stretched out my palm, found all of their guns and rapidly deactivated them. They threw them aside as they grew too hot to hold. The soldiers leapt out of the way as I forced the security gate to rise.

I raced down the road and chased the truck into the night. Cain Corporation vanished from sight as I ploughed past a series of towering high rises. Traffic lights flashed past, a speed camera became instantly annihilated and cars were cast aside, as I created a swift passage through the neon streets of Prima. In my mirror I caught sight of at least four cars following me. That didn't matter. They wouldn't be able to stop me. I had to get my family back and get them to safety. I didn't know where yet. I didn't know how I was going to do it, but all that mattered was that I caught up with the truck.

As I drew closer to the centre of the great city, traffic increased substantially. I saw the truck drive left. The cars behind me turned off early to join it. It was heading for Circuit Road. I surged forwards, accelerating the engine and destroyed every obstacle in my path. I shifted taxis, disabled lorries, disrupted a limousine and made a group of motorbikes come to a shuddering halt.

As I reached Circuit Road, the sun was beginning to set on the remains of Old Street. I could barely imagine the person responsible for the incident. What would make someone want to destroy a part of Prima? As long as that criminal remained behind bars then the world was a safer place. I felt relieved that Vincent had imprisoned such a monster.

Perhaps Cain was right to imprison the gifted after all…

I saw my eyes in the mirror. They were buzzing with electric intensity, fluctuating between brown and blue. My hands gripped the wheel as I veered between oncoming traffic and my knuckles grew bone-white. This was my life and nothing would stop me from taking control of everything that I hold dear. My foot slammed downwards onto the accelerator and my wheels burned against the tarmac.

The sight of Old Street rushing past sent a cold shiver up my spine and I scratched the back of my head fiercely to shake off the feeling. The burning pain in my mind filled me with purpose and I demanded the car went faster.

The truck suddenly split away and headed south. I'd only been into that stretch of town once before. As I drew closer I could see the ominous half-broken bridge in the distance marking the truck's destination.

The cars that had been tailing me began to pull up either side of my car. It looked like they'd been given orders to attack now that I was in a less populated area of Prima, reducing the chance of contamination. Guns appeared out of their windows and aimed at my tyres. I slammed on my brakes and the cars zoomed ahead. I brought both my hands together and made the two cars crash into each other. Restarting the engine, I navigated past the smoking wreckage.

The truck was nowhere to be seen, so I headed to where I presumed they would be heading. I found myself back at the construction site.

Waiting at the front gate was a dozen vehicles and more of Cain's soldiers. To the side was the low hill that descended towards the river and the system of pipes where I'd dropped Raven off. I stopped the car and held out my hand again, wondering whether I could disrupt their weapons before they starting firing. A car at the front turned their lights onto full beam. I quickly popped them and plummeted the street into darkness.

I sensed an electrical signal being passed between the vehicles. As my eyes readjusted to the light, I saw all the soldiers were slowly lowering their weapons. The front car door opened and out stepped the man with green eyes from my nightmares.

Xander moved as gracefully as always, but seeing him now filled me with dread. He glared at me with a strange kind of disappointment. His fingers grazed the ring on his hand emblazoned with the red Albion cross, filling him with historic purpose. He raised his hand to remind everyone to hold their fire. I remembered my dreams and the constant warning I'd received from the Mind-Walker about him. Now Xander was striding towards my car. Raising my bright palm, I tried to sense anything I could use, but he had no technology on his body. Not even a phone. The man who had haunted my dreams for years was moving towards me. He was alone and defenceless, yet still horrifically confident.

I heard an engine roar to my left. Light blinded my eyes and I blew out their bulbs, plunging the road back into darkness. The vehicle screamed and slammed into the side of my car, throwing us roughly into the pitch-black night.

25 – Spinning World

The world spun and for a moment it revolved whilst I stayed perfectly still. It wrenched me. I tumbled sideways, falling over and over, slamming into the car door and roof. I raised my hands to protect my head as the metal crunched against the earth. The car flipped. My mind flashed back. I heard my parents screaming and we're falling down, faster and faster, my breath catching at the back of my throat. I saw the dark water approaching again. I crashed into the earth instead and I was forced back to reality.

Life was a smoky blur. I squinted out of the shattered window and looked down at the sky. The earth was above and the sky was below. I stared dumbly, before I figured out that the car was upside down.

There was an engine revving outside. I heard demands and accusations, but I couldn't hear what they were saying. The truck revved its engine, spraying muck into the air before shunting into my car again. I began to fall down the hill once more. Focusing, I found my gift screaming at me to do something. I used it to grab hold of the attacking truck and crushed its engine with my mind. Fire blasted into the cold night as I continued to fall.

I had the power to save myself. I wasn't going to die like this. I couldn't die in the river like my parents…

The car plummeted treacherously down the hill, hurtling towards the hungry water. I scanned my car, analysing every inch, to find something that could save my deadly descent. I found the points of connection that held the car together. I disconnected it all and the car door flew away into the tumbling darkness. I ripped the car apart and kept hold of the steering wheel. I made sure all the segments of the vehicle flew away, activated the air bag and used it to ease my fall. My body landed roughly, crunching against the soil. I covered my head as pieces of car sliced into the dirt.

I was alive. I was safe and barely breathing…

The remaining pieces of the car splashed sharply into the

water. I saw the swirling river, mere metres away, rippling as the remnants of my car sank into its murky depths.

Suddenly, a flaming chunk of metal grinded to a halt next to me. Staring through the smoking wreckage, I realised it was same the truck that I had chased through Prima.

I realised with horror that my family were in the back of the truck.

Staggering past the fiery engine, I gripped my way to the back of the truck. The door was padlocked. I punched it in frustration with my armoured hand, which responded with a sharp clang. I accessed the power sizzling through it, until electricity bubbled out towards my glowing hand. I pointed my hand and a bolt of energy melted the lock. I ripped open the door with my metal hand.

It was empty.

Cain had tricked me. My family had never been inside the truck at all. He had led me to the construction site, where his private army was waiting.

A large hand wrapped around my shoulder and threw me into the dirt. My metal arm dug into my chest, so I was forced to cast it aside.

I looked up at the huge figure that stepped into the orange light of the flaming truck. It was Stranz, his fattened, bruised face half-lit by the flickering fire. He picked me up with his meaty hands and slammed my back against the construction site wall. A spotlight suddenly lit up his face and I saw that he was bleeding profusely from his nose. It had grown purple and was set at an awkward angle. It looked like he'd been driving the decoy truck.

"I thought you were working for Lucy," I grunted underneath his grasp.

Stranz chuckled and coughed violently. I saw his thick tongue move as he used his stubby fingers to pull out a loose tooth. He spat thickly and attempted to snort blood through his shattered nose.

"You ruined that professional relationship," Stranz grunted and punched me once in the stomach to drive the point home. It felt like a sledgehammer to my liver. "Miss Quayin was offering something real nice until you came along. I've not forgotten what you did to me back at the lab." His left hand clutched my cheeks. I saw the charred flesh that ripped across his hand. "I've kept it as a reminder of what your robot did to me. But the metal man isn't here now. You've got nothing."

Stranz hit my chest and I felt one of my ribs seize up. It sent a stabbing sensation that wrapped itself around my rushing heart.

"I don't need my exoskeleton," I gasped.

"No. You don't," he grunted in response. "You showed that very clearly when you murdered Lucy."

A surge of guilt ploughed into my gut as Lucy's dying face appeared in my mind. Her eyes looked so alive one moment, and then they were gone. I looked into Stranz's fierce eyes. They were filled with hatred. His gross flesh curled around his pupils, sweating as they bore into my face. I could see that losing Quayin had affected him more than I had expected. His pupils darted anxiously. He'd lost his usual focus. Perhaps his relationship with Lucy Quayin had been more than professional.

"Lucy Quayin is gone," I told the grimacing monster, using his relationship to my advantage. "But you're okay with that, aren't you? Deep down you're a professional. I can see you've put your priorities first and headed straight back to Vincent. I bet he welcomed you with open arms!"

"He doesn't know about what I did with her and he doesn't ever need to know," he snarled and his accent began to emerge heavily as he lost control of his emotions. His Russian heritage rose up through his vocal chords as he continued to speak. "Once you are gone, your secrets die with you."

Stranz dragged me down the hill towards the back door to the construction site. I saw the spotlights glint on a series of pipes, the last place I had seen Raven.

No. Her name was Jess.

Stranz kicked down the door just as Xander and the other soldiers were running down the hill to search the burning truck. Stranz threw me down into the dust and he bent the door handle, locking us inside the construction site. The door began to shake as Cain's soldiers tried to get in, but the door was jammed shut.

"I'm afraid that I'm going to have to kill you, Hart," Stranz said as I squirmed in the dirt. "I can't have Mr Cain finding out about…"

"He already knows," I spluttered and regretted it the instant it came out of my mouth. That was probably the only piece of information that could have saved my life.

"You're lying," Stranz said uncertainly.

"I'm not," I mumbled. "Vincent has video footage of the break in from all of your body cameras. He truly does have eyes everywhere."

He cracked his knuckles together and then glared at me. Any words of logic wouldn't help me now. The man had revenge on his mind.

"No matter," Stranz said absently and picked up an iron pipe and advanced towards me. "If I kill you before Xander gets the chance, then I'll be in Cain's favour again. Besides… I have to do this for her. I have to do it for Lucy. It's what she would've wanted. She'd be so proud to see me now. Free. Fighting for what I want. Fighting for something I loved."

I struggled backwards, moving deeper into the site. I tried to focus on any technology nearby, but there was nothing. I had to delay Stranz until I found a weapon I could use against him.

A genuine unanswered question popped into my mind.

"Where is your gift, Stranz? Why do none of you have power?"

"I don't need power to kill you," he replied simply.

"Surely you want to know what it's like? To have a gift at your fingertips? I can see that you want it. So tell me, where is yours? I'll be dead in five minutes anyway."

I had to distract him whilst I found something. I scanned through a network of scaffolding, but still there was absolutely nothing. It would seem that Cain had turned off the power to the construction site so that I couldn't use any of the technology.

"Well it depends…" Stranz said as I hid within the scaffolding. "You hear all those people out there who are hunting you? They have their own special deal. When they join Cain, he offers them money, housing, healthcare; everything they could want. In

280

exchange, they swear loyalty. All they have to do is submit to a quick needle to the head. They receive regular doses to stop the gift from ever arising."

"And what about you?" I whispered. Stranz's thick flesh formed a smile as he followed the sound of my voice. He laughed darkly as he continued to hunt me.

"I am one of Cain's compromises," Stranz said.

He leaped forward, brutally fast and grabbed me by the collar. Steam burst into the air as threw me against the scaffolding. He swung the metal pipe and I ducked as metal clanged against metal. I grabbed his meaty head with both of my hands. In one motion, I crunched my forehead into his broken nose. Stranz screamed. He punched out wildly and caught me in the side of the head. The world slammed up into my face and I moaned as the earth swirled.

"You want to fight me? Fine. I'll show what I can really do," Stranz grunted. "The great thing about finally being alone means that I can let go."

The grotesque man changed before my waking eyes. He raised his charred hand and his eyes strained for a moment. His hand twitched, steamed and then grew slightly. The broken flesh flaked and healed, returning to its usual oily pink tone. He stretched his new skin and cracked his knuckles once. He reset his nose and winced as he healed himself.

Stranz twisted his neck and stretched out his huge arms, laughing as he embraced his own gift. He had the power to heal himself.

"Well..." I said slowly as the hot steam rose from his new flesh. "That explains why you are so..."

"What?" Stranz retorted.

"Your power explains why you are so... well formed," I explained.

"Well formed?" Stranz cried.

"I mean big boned," I said quickly.

"I do not have big bones!" Stranz shouted.

"You obviously do," I said. "Those bones might as well belong to an elephant. It's fine. Don't worry about it. You clearly

281

can't help being so ridiculously fat."

"I am not fat!" Stranz grunted.

"Right, yes, of course, sorry about that," I said in a deliberate ploy to taunt him. "Correct me if I am wrong, but your gift seems to involve some form of cell-replication? I thought so. So every time you heal with your gift, you get a little bit more chubby, don't you?"

"I'm the strongest man alive, Hart," Stranz said in return. "I'm undying. Morta will never take me! You can try and be as clever as you like, but that won't stop me from breaking your neck."

Stranz leaped towards, steam bursting out his muscular legs. I ran sideways as fast as I could. I seized an iron pipe from the ground and turned sharply. I stabbed the metal into his leg and Stranz groan briefly before he healed the wound. Small trails of steam and sweat rose from his flesh, as the muscles in his leg increased in size.

"It feels so good to do this again," Stranz said. "When we hunt, I have to I keep my power hidden. Otherwise it will be my fault that we get another gifted on the run. But, right now, I can use it as much as I like!"

I swung the pipe towards his nose, presuming that Stranz would stop me. The metal connected with his flesh with a sickening thud. His nose crippled and Stranz remained perfectly still. I swung again and again, metal connecting with flesh, spraying flecks of blood into his eyes, until he eventually decided to swat the pipe away.

"Your family are good as dead," Stranz said as he grew his face, sweat and blood dribbling around his mouth. He snorted sharply through his new nose and spat on the floor. "Vincent is going to hand them over to Foshe. I've seen what he does to his lucky patients! He's going to torture them until they tell him everything. Even after I've killed you, you will die again as you're ripped out of their little happy memories. Your children will forget you and your wife will despise you. Doctor William Hart will die as Foshe pulls out their memories of you with his needle. And I'm going to watch every second of it!"

My hand gripped the pipe tightly until my knuckle grew pale

and began to fill with bright light. I saw my veins shine as my own internal electricity surged through my body again. It rippled along my spine as I felt the anger filling me. It was the same energy I'd used against Lucy.

Stranz charged forward. I shouted as I fired a bolt of white energy flying into him. The man went soaring backwards and slammed into the construction site wall. His chest was burnt black, but his clothes had mostly protected him.

Hatred for the man filled my vast network of nerves. Electricity surged out of my body, zipping out in all directions and forced all the power in the construction site to turn on. I felt it all. There were buildings filled with wiring, computers, programs, networks, plug sockets, holo-units, neon substations and magnetic lifters. Vehicles were everywhere... delivery vans, trucks, cranes, diggers, tractors and a garage full of company cars. Power lines flowed below, as well as telephone lines and internet connections.

Technology was alive everywhere and it was mine for the taking. However I was becoming exhausted from using my electrical energy again.

Stranz charged forwards, steam billowing from his hands. I made a car nearby explode. The fire scorched his side, but he continued running. I wrapped a series of lights around my arm and waited for Stranz. He swung his fist and I ducked, jabbing the bulbs into his leg. The glass splintered and the electricity ignited, burning his skin. Stranz screamed with fury and launched me through a window, glass smashing around my vibrant form. My blood glowed white hot. My body was buzzing and dying from the intense energy output.

I was in an office block. Cubicles and desks were everywhere. Phones, computers, speakers and more plugs than my mind could fully comprehend. I pressed my hand against the nearest one and began to sip the electrical current like a fine wine, treasuring every last drop.

Stranz ripped open the fragile wall and stepped inside. The wall looked plastic and cheap. They should have gone for something stronger that I could utilise, like metal. I plugged my ears and every speaker turned onto full volume. Static noise poured out of them and I imagined Stranz's eardrums popping as he crashed to the ground. Throwing my hand into a nearby computer, I let the machine wrap itself around my hand. The internet rippled against my skin. Could my synapses really handle the weight of the world wide web? I ignored the violent and inconceivable thought.

I was growing tired from using my gift so violently. I needed support from the power lines. I finally took it. I absorbed the construction site network and the information drummed against my brain cells. Fresh energy fuelled my body, moving impulsively as synaptic electricity frazzled through my skin.

I'd never felt more alive in my entire life. Nobody was going to stop me from gaining my full potential and taking back what I truly wanted.

Stranz threw me out the door and into the empty yard. At first I stumbled, but then I rose, stronger than ever. I laughed and felt my chest collapsing under the weight of my breath. I laughed at the small man who thought he could kill me. White energy danced across my brown skin. It skipped between fingers, ran up my arms and along my spine. The force of it filled my mind. My gift was limitless. All I had to do was let go.

The power lines beneath the ground erupted upwards. The loose earth smashed against the nearby buildings. The cabling wrapped around my body, twisting around the contours of my muscles, as I forged my new body. They snaked around my limbs and fuelled my synapses as my gift surged onwards. The wiring flew out to nearby cars and I summoned them to form around my body. The cars reformed to my will. The metal contorted around my flesh, armouring my body. Another car slid forwards and I made it my fist.

Stranz ran at me madly, lashing poorly with his metal pipe and selfish healing flesh. My new fist lifted up and punched Stranz, his flesh crunching against my metal as I broke him. His thick body flew into the darkness. The office block tickled my mind and I found the remaining computers. They surged around my brain as information poured into my mind. My new system configuration was completing me at last. It allowed me to analyse what was happening to my new body, as I became greater than ever before.

A digger became my left arm; its claws became my claws. A nearby crane was my new spine and its long wrecking ball fell down ready to utilise. I formed four legs, like the ATV I'd defeated. I lost focus of what objects were and concentrated on what they would become. My legs might have been vehicles or even entire buildings. It did not matter. They were my legs and with them I rose to greater heights than ever before. My new limbs began to extend and move. My joints were wheels and gears. I grew with every passing moment, until I could not feel my human form anymore. I was a glowing dot at the centre of a masterpiece of technology.

I was the heart of the living machine.

Stranz was no longer alone. The soldiers from the front gate joined him. Their weapons were all aimed at me, but none of them fired. I spotted a trail of lights slipping in from the horizon.

Vincent Cain climbed out of the lead vehicle, his cheek bruised from my fist earlier. He ordered his soldiers wildly and soon they surrounded the construction site. I looked down at the small men and roared as the god I'd become. I'd finally let go. I wasn't tired; I had all the energy I could want from Prima. Nothing could stop me. All I had to do was stamp out the ants underneath my metal boot and then I could live free at last. With Cain Corporation gone, my problems would be solved. I'd find my family, save Bolt and move away. We'd live free in another great city or forge my own. I would use my gift as much as I pleased and bring order to a world filled with chaos. I would make the modern world complete again with my mind at the centre of it all.

My metal fist curled and my legs gripped the ground. It was time to show these people what happens when they deny someone their true potential.

The night flashed with light and a series of explosions blasted into my side. I roared as my body ripped open. The wound burned and then I remembered that I was metal. I laughed as my wiring wrapped around the hole in my chest and covered it. I became armoured once more. I spotted the soldiers who had shot me and moved towards them. Bullets ricocheted off my legs and zinged off into the night. They hit my body and sounded like a dozen angry wasps irritating my multitude of eardrums.

The explosion had come from a group of tanks at the side of the yard. I dug into their programming and found resistance. A firewall blocked my control. I ripped the firewall to digital shreds using the network of computers, shutting down each of the tanks. I spotted Stranz emerging from the front tank. His bruised flesh steamed heavily, contorting desperately as he healed from his wounds. He was shouting at his associates who looked at his flesh with disgust. His voice should have blasted through the air... but I couldn't hear him.

My own human ear tried to function, but all I could hear was the cacophony of sound created by my new mechanical body. My metal was clanging and spitting, which was becoming intolerably deafening to my human ears. I deactivated my ears and forged new mechanical hearing.

Stranz pulled out a rocket launcher from his tank. He fired once, a flash of fire illuminating the darkness, highlighting the streaks of wet light falling madly from the sky. I realised it was raining.

My chest ignited as the rocket hit me and I surged towards Stranz, my four feet crushing everything underfoot. The other soldiers moved back, but Stranz fired wildly at my body. I stretched my claw towards him, but his rockets ripped the hand apart before it could reach him. Stranz climbed back inside his tank and the power fired up again. The barrel of his gun aimed at my arm. The tank fired, obliterating my clawed hand in an instant. Pain rushed through my complex mind. I unfurled the wrecking ball within my other arm and flung it into the tank. The vehicle flew into the edge of the site. My claw reformed itself once more. I picked up the remains of the tank, threw it to the ground and crushed it with my foot.

Fire flashed under my foot as the Stranz's supposedly immortal life was extinguished beneath my immense weight.

I roared with victory into the torrential night as my metal limbs and stretched out in unison.

The rain trickled across my jagged frame and I gained some idea of what I had become. I raised an arm to my sight, although I was unsure where I was seeing from, and the rain slid along the contours of metal. I looked down and staggered back as vertigo stung my mind.

I was at least a hundred metres tall...

The horizon glimmered into light and I stared at the luminescence in awe, as several blurred shapes sped towards me. I sensed the helicopters within seconds. I felt my massive frame shudder as I took a couple of steps back. Violent fire broke the rain-splattered night as a series of missiles erupted from the helicopters. They scorched through the air, until I ripped them out of the wild sky and sent them tumbling to the earth. My mind split the helicopters apart and magnetised them into my frame.

I sensed one final helicopter hovering near my arm. It was so fragile. I was a giant crushing ants. I had killed Stranz with a few short movements of my body. I had felt the tank being crushed under my foot. The heat of fire had burnt my new ankle. His body obliterated in a single moment.

All of this felt so wrong.

A rope dropped from the helicopter and a man slid elegantly downwards. He landed with a wet thud and latched onto my shoulder. My body twitched away the repulsive intruder. He clung on desperately and I considered crushing the man who was as delicate as paper. His green eyes bore into my camera vision, as pulled out a long silver knife. The blade flashed and I cried out in pain as Xander's knife dug into the camera.

My huge body shook with desperation. I felt him run along my shoulder and make his way down my chest. He clung to my wiring, slid down car panels, leapt over tyres and avoided sizzling power lines. I responded violently, altering my shape to attack.

His knife dug into my metal skin as he sliced into my new body. He crawled inside my system, invading my body, forcing his way through to find my core. My core was my human body. He was coming for me.

287

My vision shrunk inward suddenly, as I lost my concept of what I had become. I lost the network, wires and cars, as my gift fell away.

The night fell away and I saw the world through my human eyes. I was wrapped in wiring within a metal sphere. Blue and white sensors illuminated the walls and fed information into my mind. The sphere cracked and the night leaked into my anxious sanctuary. Rain leaked through and began sparking any live connections that the water touched. His knife sliced at the sphere, cutting continuously until the hole became larger. His hands tore the machine apart. I came face-to-face with the man who was destined to destroy me all along.

I stared at Xander in shock. I couldn't fully analyse what was happening. It felt like my human body was unable to move, whilst my metal frame thrashed violently externally. Xander entered the sphere cautiously, wary of my next move. I followed his movement with my paralysed eyes.

"It didn't have to be this way, Hart," he said quietly. "I warned you this would happen when I called you earlier. I told you that if you showed your gift, then Cain would kill you. Now here I am. Retaliating against your instability."

Xander's eyes were filled with a complex sadness. His blade shook roughly in his palm.

"I never thought you would become like this, William. If I had known you would lose control, then I would've brought you in a long time ago. If only you could see yourself right now, then you would understand what I have to do. You would tell me to do it. I'm sorry. It didn't have to be this way… but you've left me with no choice."

Xander grasped my shoulder as he slid his knife into my chest.

"Your family are safe. Trust me. I'll protect them. Let go. They are safe, but you have to be put down. You can rest, old friend. They're safe. I'm so sorry, William, but you have to let go…"

The metal cut through my flesh with skilled precision. I gasped and listened to my killer.

I let go.

SATURDAY

Pierre Foshe   Vincent Cain   Anton Stranz

26 – Life Sentence

A thought bounced through my empty mind. It was a small simmer of an electrical signal waiting to be analysed. I tried to focus on it, but then it faded…

A fact replaced the lost thought in an instant.

The brain is the last part of the human body to stop working whilst you're shutting down for the final time. It's still buzzing away with its complicated signals, trying to work out what is happening, whilst everything else is terminating. Life is actually still floating around the human body in sparks of electricity for entire minutes after the heart has stopped beating.

I could feel my memories nearby, but they dissipated as I tried to remember them. My recollection of the present was fading as though my mind was an hourglass and my past fell like the sands of time each passing moment.

The electrical signal trickled through my synapses, as I lay numb to reality. It formed an emotion of regret over my entire life and made me ask myself whether I had led the right life.

I'd been educated to the best degree possible. The world needed to relearn all of technological discoveries that had been lost. With knowledge there is power. The world needed people to forge the future after an age of darkness. I had learnt fast, falling with my mistakes and rising stronger in my victories. I sought my own education. I got my doctorate and taught others. I created my own technological revolution. But why did I do it? Why did I waste so many years learning about life, instead of living it? All those years alone, scribbling notes and fiddling with computers, trying to find answers to impossible questions. What did all of it achieve? I had hoped it would help others, but how did that help myself?

In the end… I'm not sure if I had lived my life fully.

My path was linear through my career and now it had reached its abrupt end. The moment I stepped beyond the borders of order, everything had fallen apart.

Life was a sensation of feelings that rushed through your

body. The vast electrical signals that buzzed through our minds were not words, letters or pictures. These thoughts were images produced by chemical and electrical reactions throughout the brain that flashed like reflections in the water or echoes inside a cave or the smell of air itself. These images were not highly defined, because they connected intensely with the body. The mind created faces, people, places, words, memory and colours into a perspective that I only could feel.

I saw my wife smiling on the day I married her. We were kissing inside the Temple of One on Old Street. Our friends applauded. Adele's parents, Joseph and Isabella, were cheering, whilst there was an empty pair of chairs on my side of the Temple. Adele's eyes filled my imagination. There was powerful warmth to her eyes.

The mind connected the past and present instantly. I felt my past inside me and I related to it presently. Such a concept couldn't be captured on camera, represented on film or written down. It was an impossible feeling to explain. It had to be felt.

I saw Isabella's birth and I immediately recognised that she had the same eyes as her mother. Her first day at school. The noise of school children. The innocent joy as they played together. Izzy disappeared into the playground. Again and again and again. Our daily routine became rapidly forgotten as thousands of moments melded into a single sensation. I saw Izzy lying on her bed and she was excitedly telling me about whales and snails. I taught her about Eden and Luna and the fall of mankind. There was a tremendous crash and a haze of rubble. Izzy was lying unconscious on the marble floor. She wasn't moving.

There was a woman with blonde hair and sharp heels. Lucy Quayin towered above her prone body. Quayin's dying face broke through my mind. Her eyes were bright blue, burning with hot electricity. Her skin was so white, like snow in winter. Her yellow waxen hair was frayed. Her body flickered and became invisible to the human eye. Darkness. The sensation of falling as she slipped over the edge into oblivion.

I heard the horrific sound of a human body crashing into the ground.

Raven fell through my front door. My children's terrified faces were filling my mind. My wife held my hand as we saved the girl's life. I remembered the room filling with firelight as Raven emitted flames from her body.

I tried to remember where I last saw Raven. It was at the construction site inside a dark pipe. It wasn't far from here. Her starved face illuminated by the fire in her hand as she told me her name was Jess.

"Wake up, William…"

A sharp shiver of feeling rippled up my shoulder and crawled along my chest. I sucked the new electrical energy along my arm and it plummeted into my heart. It suddenly re-activated. My lungs rose as they sucked in the dusty air. I spluttered. A thick liquid trickled down my chin. My skin started to awaken again. System reboot. Heart beat vague, but existing. My breath irregular, but occurring. My mind blurred as my body started to resend signals back to its tired synapses. My feet twitched. My hand grasped the earth.

Darkness fell over my mind again.

Life wasn't just a pathway that had to be lived. It was more than that. It was about holding onto every last moment and existing with every ounce of energy in our bodies. I had lived to my fullest potential. I will only ever know what I know. I will only ever sense what I can sense. I am no-one else. I am the warm centre of the universe, because I will never know anything else.

I remembered Xander's sad expression as he cornered me. At the end, when I had lost control of my gift, Xander had no choice but to stop me. I understand that now.

The knife ripped into my body and I felt every last millimetre of metal that sliced into my flesh.

It was all a matter of perspective. Xander would never be able to feel that. He would only be able to see the pain rippling across my pupils as he removed the knife. There is an entire life that he took from me that he will never fully know…

He would never feel my pain or the darkness that was consuming me.

"Remember your parents dying, William? You promised that you would do everything in your power to stop that from happening again. So what are you waiting for? Save yourself."

My heart twisted as it restarted again. Electricity rushed into my body. Metal dug into my flesh, as I rebuilt my destroyed body. My back arched violently. Pain roared through my mind and woke me back up.

"That wasn't so difficult, was it? We've been through far too much for you to die in the dirt, especially when you fell at the final hurdle. It's not over yet, not whilst there is power left in your veins. Come on already! Wake up, William!"

My eyes flashed open to see a familiar gaunt face staring down at me.

"Hart? Can you hear me?" Raven asked desperately. "Stay with me. Just hold on a little longer..."

Her voice began to fade as my ears failed. Her face was filthy, her tears scored through the filth that smeared her skin. She pressed roughly down on the hole in my body. She ripped open my shirt and the blood flowed out across my chest. My vision starting fading...

Raven stopped the blood flow and my sight returned. I thought I heard myself scream.

"I'm going to look after you, just like you looked after me. So you're going to have to hold on and don't go dying on me, okay? We need you to be survive."

She wiped the wound crudely with the cleanest piece of her shirt and ignited her fingers. She pressed them into my skin and pinched the wound. My flesh bubbled as Raven sealed and cauterized the wound with her fire. She dug into her rucksack and within moments she pulled out a roll of gaffer tape. I laughed at the irony.

The pain ricocheted into my brain and I blacked out.

27 – Parting Ways

The night sky was filled with stars. I squinted and counted five balls of burning gas. A few more appeared as their light scored through the planet's atmosphere and another two stars joined the initial constellation.

"Beautiful. What I would give to see stars with my own eyes again."

This had to be a dream. It was all a twisted nightmare. How else would I be able to hear the voice belonging to that sick man haunting my dreams?

"Really? You can hear me? Well… this is a new development."

Out of the darkness emerged the Mind-Walker. His face formed instantly, followed by his thin body and limbs. He blinked sickly and a dark suit enveloped his form. His body simmered as it moved forwards.

"I think I'm going to enjoy this, William! Isn't this phenomenal? I can finally talk to you whilst you're awake. Walking along the edge of death must have really done something nasty to your mind."

The man dissipated throughout my reality and chuckled darkly as he knelt down. His features shone with vivid clarity, whilst the rest of the world faded in comparison. His grey eyes gleamed and his remaining hair was white with stray strands of blonde.

I pondered weakly how this was happening…

"That's because I am strong whilst you are weak. When you slept we were only able to talk, but look at us now! There's no need to be so upset. This could be the start of a brilliant friendship. Although… that does depend if you die in the next few minutes."

Embers of fire flashed across the darkness, distracting my attention away from my tormentor. I followed one, right to left, as it ebbed through the air.

"You think I am a tormentor? After everything I have done for you? Fine. Good luck surviving. You're going to need it."

The Mind-Walker vanished into smoke as the flickers of fire burnt through his translucent form.

The ground slowly came back into focus. I was surrounded by

pieces of contorted machinery. I spotted the far shimmer of water and realised I was still at the construction site.

Burning heat dashed across my ankles and I winced as fire burnt my flesh. Raven was standing just ahead, her hands full of fire. The bright light leaked up her body and flashed into the air. It was ferocious. The fire licked the earth and dashed dangerously close to my body.

I spotted a white dirtied shape curled up at her feet. I tried to use my arm to drag myself closer, but nothing happened. I couldn't move. I focused on my arm, but it didn't respond. The rest of my body was working. I could feel the burn on my ankle and the cold air brushing the hair on my bare chest. I stared at my shoulder and tried to look beyond it, but all I could see was bloodied metal.

Nausea surged up my oesophagus. There was a broken car where my arm should be. A fierce buzzing of electricity flowed from my obliterated limb and I noticed a series of wires buried into my shoulder. Power trailed from the car battery and sent a flow of electricity into my fluttering heart.

It was the only thing keeping me alive right now and it wouldn't be long before the battery ran out...

Breath seized my body and my chest began to heave faster. My vision swam and the lights curled into one another. I was fading again. I needed to find my family. I need to make sure they were safe.

I clenched my remaining fist tightly. The pain was numb. I was so drained. The soil was wet with my blood. I could feel it already drying, as though it had given up.

Dark shapes danced through the air. Fire flashed and a blade glinted. Dirt was kicked skywards as the two figures struggled with one another. My heart beat solidly as my focus returned at last.

Raven and Xander were fighting. Xander's arm was bleeding from a deep cut. He rolled to the floor and winced as fire sliced the air. He yelled out once as the heat caught his arm and he stumbled to the ground. Crawling back, he found himself cornered against a sheet of metal. His usually pristine coat was covered in blood. His white hair was singed black from her fire. His emerald eyes were ringed with sadness and fear.

Above him stood Raven, unlike I'd ever seen her before. Anger consumed her face and fire poured out from her spine. It rushed up her arms and tightened around her splayed fingers. The flames arched, clutching at the smoking air. The light highlighted the rain around the two figures. Droplets of water sizzled the flames that lashed at the thin air and the dry earth.

"Do it…" Xander said. "I can see that you want to. Do what you have to."

I looked at Raven. It was clear that murder was on her mind.

"Finish it," Xander sighed. "You can't make me suffer any more than I already am."

"Sympathy won't work," Raven said, her voice filled with thick emotion. "You killed him. You took away the life of the only good man around here. You have taken away my life, shot me with acid, tortured my friends and have killed the only person who…"

Her voice caught in her throat and the fire wrapped around her fist. It glowed brightly as it listened to her inner turmoil.

"No more," she said. "No more hunting. No more mercy."

Raven raised her hand and Xander shuddered beneath her. He closed his eyes in acceptance and his lips moved in silent prayer.

"Jess…" I whispered to my friend.

The two figures paused. Xander opened his eyes slowly, a glint of green shining. A small hint of relief flickered across his face, but then a dark fear passed through his body.

Jess remained still. The fire was slowly dying across her body, but her hand remained raised at Xander.

"Hart?" She asked quietly. "You're alive?"

"For now," I coughed. "I don't know for how much longer."

Thoughts of darkness echoed dumbly through my brain. I ignored them. This wasn't the time to think about what happened next.

"I don't want him dead," I told her. "Let him go, Jess."

"I can't," she said quietly. "I don't think I can…"

"You have to," I told her. "Don't become a killer."

296

"They've wanted me dead for years, Hart," she said shakily. "They have never stopped and they never will… unless I finish it."

I thought back to how Cain had ripped my whole life apart in a single hour. I'd lost my job, my family and lost control to my gift. I understood her pain, perhaps more than she knew, but I couldn't let her do it. Xander was just a terrified man, who was caught up in all this madness. He may have stabbed me, but he had his reasons for doing so. I'd lost control. I was a threat to Prima. It was clear that Xander's actions bothered him deeply.

"He doesn't deserve to die," I told her.

"I didn't have a choice," Xander said suddenly.

"Who gave you the right to speak?" Jess cried, her hand glowing once again. Xander moved back to avoid the intense heat.

"It's complicated," he replied. "I can't explain it…"

"That's not good enough," she spat.

"I work for Cain," he said quickly. "I do everything I can to protect the gifted, but I've had no choice."

"Everyone has a damn choice!" Jess shouted. "Don't you dare think of yourself as morally invisible. You did terrible things for Cain. At any point you could have walked away, but you didn't."

"So many times I wanted to get out of this…" Xander tried to say. "I wanted to find a better way to help the gifted."

"But you didn't," she interrupted. "You helped Cain instead."

Xander's lips moved to speak, but they halted. He had no answer to the accusation.

"You secretly enjoyed it, didn't you?" Raven sneered. "You liked chasing my friends. Did it give you a rush, Xander? Cain gave you purpose and you lapped it up like a dog."

"No…" Xander mumbled.

"Liar!" Raven cried. "Look around you. Look at him. You did this."

The green in Xander's eyes shimmered as water welled in his eyelids.

"He's dying because of you," Raven said and spat at Xander's feet, her saliva fizzling into the earth. He didn't flinch. He

297

acknowledged the hate. He nodded at his accuser. In some form, he agreed with Raven and he was ready to die.

"Let him go," I mumbled at Raven. "There is nothing you can do that will change what has happened. Look at him. He's as much an outcast as the rest of us."

Raven's face curled slightly and she lowered her hand. The tension left her body and the flames dissipated. She dropped roughly to her knees and clawed the dry dirt. We all lay in the dirt together as the dust continued to settle.

The black smoke ebbed, formed and crawled down to sit next to me.

"That was disappointing. I thought she was going to do it. But, of course, Doctor Hart had to break up the fight. Well done. You saved one person. If I could clap right now, then I would be doing so sarcastically."

"Go away…" I murmured to him.

"What did you say?" Raven asked. I blinked and my mental companion had vanished as quickly as he appeared.

"Nothing…" I whispered. "I meant to say thank you."

"Shut up, Hart. You should've just died. It would have saved me a lot of trouble." She pointed roughly at Xander. "He would be dead. I'd be out of here, miles away by now, but you had to hold on to a bit of life, didn't you?"

"Sorry to disappoint…" I retorted.

She laughed once and fell back onto her haunches. She shrugged and shrank inwards.

"How you been?" I asked.

"Really?" Raven replied. "You're asking me that now?"

"When else am I going to ask?"

She nodded simply and gazed up at the stars. "I've been surviving. Same as always."

"You've been doing a lot more than surviving," Xander said quietly. "You should have seen her yesterday…"

"No one said that you could speak," Raven said angrily.

"I did see you…" I said roughly. "I saw you in the sewer last night."

"That's impossible, Hart," Raven said looking at me. "You should rest… death is making you delusional."

298

"I thought so at first," I replied. "Until I realised the dreams were real."

"What did you say?" Xander gasped and began to sit up.

"I saw you take on twelve people, Jess. I was strangely proud of you. I saw them set fire to your home. That must have been tough. I saw you escape by swimming through the river. It was horrible. It reminded me of…"

"There is no way you could have seen that," Raven whispered. "How on earth do you know that?"

The Mind Walker condensed and sickly smiled. *"Yes, William. I wonder how you know that?"*

"Can't you see him?" I asked them both. "He's sat right next to us…"

"There is no one there, Hart," Raven said nervously.

"It's the Mind-Walker," Xander said, fear creeping into his voice. "Did any the Outcasts ever have vivid nightmares after treatment? Many of our patients would have dreams where they would lash out in the night. They would have dreams that were extremely difficult to wake from."

"Sorry, William. I'm afraid to say I've been seeing other people. I hope you are not too offended."

"He's always been with me," I told them. "For as long as I remember, he's been haunting my dreams."

"Haunting is such a strong term. Instead, see it as though you've had help from a third party. I've been guiding nudging you along the way. It's thanks to me that you got so far really. All those split second decisions, I was by your side to give you the correct impulse."

"But who is he?" Raven asked cautiously.

"His real name is Darius," Xander told us. "He calls himself Mind-Walker to hide his identity."

"An understandable approach to our way of life," Raven mumbled.

"I like keeping my name to myself. It helps keep the focus away from me. You know… if you had some power left, we could use the car and crush his head like a pea."

"He's saying that he wants to kill you…" I told Xander in horror.

299

"That's understandable," Xander replied, as his face became haunted. "We've known each other a long time. Many years ago, Darius lost control, spewing his dominating darkness over everyone he came in contact with. I managed to stop him, but he hurt so many people along the way. After he was dealt with, I believed that all the gifted were gone. I locked myself away in Prima's prison. I didn't want to be the one to cause another gifted outbreak."

"Until Old Street happened," Raven mumbled uncomfortably. "You dragged yourself out of hiding."

"It's my duty to protect humanity from that power," Xander said fiercely. "The gifted were back. I thought it was impossible, but here we all are. Once again… another of our kind has lost control and brought devastation to Prima. I had to stop you, Hart."

My chest burned with pain as the memory of Xander's blade sliced through my cranium.

"Where is Darius?" I asked grimly. "What did you do with him?"

"We keep him under constant sedation at Cain Corporation," he explained coarsely. "He's too powerful to be left unchecked. If he was ever released, then everything we'd worked for would be destroyed in minutes."

"This is why I need your help, William. You are the perfect candidate to help me. It's simple. I help you and you free me. All you have to do is survive. Do you think you can manage that?"

"I'm not sure I can…" I gasped as I felt the electricity begin to die out in the car battery.

Pain stabbed into my chest, as my heart began to fail. The world spun once again. I held on fiercely, determined not to die yet. I opened my eyes and Raven was cradling my loose head.

"They have my family…" I wheezed. "I don't think I have long left. No hospital will help me now. Not after what I've done. Not after what I've become. You must promise me something. Please."

"Yes, Hart," she nodded fiercely, tears dripping from her face. "Of course. Anything."

"Firstly…" I coughed. "My name is Will. Stop calling me Hart, it's so formal."

"Damn it, stop being so well-mannered!" She exclaimed. "What do you want me to do?"

Blood clogged in my throat and I began to choke. It tasted like oil. I spluttered desperately to clear my mouth, before Jess tilted my head so that the liquid dribbled out of my mouth. I stared at the blood-covered dirt inches away from my face. This was never the way I imagined I would die. I always thought I would die old with Adele somewhere far away…

My eyes crinkled open and I saw them all there. Jess and Xander and Darius. The fugitive, my murderer and my tormentor.

"You have to find them…" I tried to say as our world plummeted back into darkness. Darius stood in the darkness of my mind and smiled plainly.

You have a weak mind, William. That is a fact. However, you're sickening love for your family has dragged you through hell. All you have to do is survive and then we can truly help each other. Save me, Doctor William Hart, and I promise that you will have the world that you desire…

Reality returned as light burned my retinas. Vincent Cain took a step back and launched his boot into my ribs. I moaned incoherently as waves of pain lapped at my senses. I felt more stabs of pain as Cain continued kicking.

I heard a piercing scream and Cain stopped his attack. Jess was kneeling on the floor weeping; her tears sizzled as they hit the ground. Fire flashed madly around her, but Cain was saying something that stopped her. He was pointing his gun at me repeatedly. He aimed it at my head and pointed roughly back at her.

He grabbed my face in his hand. His gun-metal eyes swallowed me whole. His blonde hair was wild in the neon-light. His sharp features became cruel as he pressed his boot onto my trapped arm.

The pain soared. It was amazing what I could feel despite being on the brink of death.

"Don't worry about him!" Vincent shouted. "I don't want him

dead. Not yet."

Vincent clicked his fingers and a couple of his workers dropped another car battery beside my free arm. I grasped it hungrily and drank every drop I could get.

"That's all your getting," Vincent said. "So it would be wise to consume it sparingly."

I slowed down my breathing and forced my body to stop absorbing the power so rapidly.

"You've become the very thing I have worked every single day to stop," he said disgusted. "You lost control and I cannot abide that. What just happened here could have been worse than Old Street."

"*Nearly...*" Darius said in my other ear. I winced at his voice. "*Next time we'll have to try harder, won't we? The more new gifted there are in the neighbourhood... the more friends we can have in the future.*"

"If I hadn't stopped you, then you would have kept going. Relentless and blind, like all the gifted that discover their power. You all become out of control. We've seen it so many times and it's always the same. It doesn't matter how strong you think you are. You wouldn't have been satisfied until you had the whole of Prima under your power."

His words sang like music in my ears. Every word was true. My gift hummed hungrily to be awoken again. It was exhausted, but nonetheless starving.

"*Bide your time,*" Darius hummed. "*Soon you can feed again.*"

"I can see it in those dying eyes," Vincent said. "You felt like a god, didn't you? You loved it."

I couldn't hide it anymore. I did love every moment of it. Letting go was the best thing I had ever done. I loved the power it gave me. I loved it more than perhaps I loved my family...

"The problem is that power has a price," Vincent said sadly. He waved his hand summoning a group of soldiers with a clump of steaming flesh. I stared hard at where its face should be and found a pair of pupils set inside rolling waves of thick burnt fat.

It was Anton Stranz.

"Losing my sister was an understandable loss. I've thought about the situation thoroughly and realised that you were simply surviving. You reacted to her lack of control. I respect that," Cain paced between Stranz and me, his polished shoes grinding into the dark soil. "If you hadn't put her down, then it's likely that I would have had to deal with her personally."

I felt Darius stir uncomfortably inside my mind.

"Where is his family?" Raven suddenly shouted. "Just tell him that they are safe and let him rest in peace."

Vincent drew his gun. He weighed the object in his hand. His eyes flickered and suddenly he whipped his arm out sideways. He moved too fast for me to understand what he had done. It was only when I saw Raven slumped with a bleeding cheek that I realised he had slapped her with the gun.

Vincent stumbled briefly. He brushed his hand against his nose that was bleeding heavily. I realised that Cain had just tried to use his gift.

"On the other hand, when you decided to attack Anton Stranz and the rest of my work force, I began to lose all sense of your logic," Cain continued as if nothing had happened. "My loyal soldiers have sacrificed everything for my cause. Do you know those men and women? Have you paid any attention to all these people who serve me? They are people with families and you have treated them as nothing. Now that really sucks. Devaluing my soldiers… that really starts to annoy me."

"Stranz hated you," I tried to say, but instead a low groan gasped from my dry mouth.

"Anton always came back in the end, didn't you?" Cain placed a boot on Stranz's chest. "However, such treachery cannot simply be ignored."

Anton Stranz's body stirred. His tiny pupils grew startlingly white as they crawled open.

"Sir…" he croaked roughly, causing Cain to push harder down on his charred chest. "I loved her…"

Cain drew his gun and aimed it at Stranz's head. He raised his other hand to shield his face from the blood spray. There was quick flash of fire, followed by a delayed blast of gunfire and a sickening thud as the bullet found Anton's skull.

"You monster!" Raven cried. "He was still…"

"Stranz will be fine. He always is. Hopefully he will come back a tad more intelligent when he regrows his brain," Cain dismissed Raven. "When I speak of treachery, I am referring to how he used his gift. He's not allowed to do that without specific permission, hence the bullet to the head and heart."

Vincent aimed the gun absently behind him and fired a single shot into Stranz's chest. He returned his attention to me. I wished that I wasn't still pinned to the ground.

"Do you even know how many people you have killed today, William?" Cain asked sharply. I tried to respond to his question, but I didn't know if I had the voice to talk properly anymore. "It wasn't being rhetorical. I want an answer."

"Would you like to phone a friend?" Darius laughed. *"On my last count, the answer is two. The dream couple, Lucy Quayin and Anton Stranz."*

"Two?" I managed to ask through my destroyed throat.

"He speaks!" Cain exclaimed suddenly. He raced between his men, who circled us. "A round of applause for Doctor Hart everybody! Come along now, that was quite impressive. He managed to squeeze a word out, when he most definitely should be dead."

His soldiers clapped awkwardly at my answer.

"Now everyone, don't clap too much. His answer was wrong. Sorry, William. It's okay. I understand. You're under a lot of stress. No need to apologise. In your mind, the answer should be only one, my darling sister, as Anton Stranz is extraordinarily hard to kill."

"One?" I asked him again.

"If only! The answer I was looking for was twenty-seven. Today you have killed twenty-seven people and that's not including Stranz."

Cain's number rang hollow through my brain. I tried to feel something in response to that, but I couldn't. There was no regret. No remorse. Only numbness. I couldn't even remember seeing that many people tonight. I couldn't even fully remember the last hour.

"I'm actually quite impressed, William," Darius hummed darkly. *"I*

didn't realise we had attained such high figures tonight."

"Get him medical attention, Cain," Raven said, who was being held tightly by two figures in fire-resistant uniforms. "He's dying, for Morta's sake! You have me, so what are you waiting for? Just help him."

"No. I want you both," he replied. "Plus I want you to be part of what happens next. We're going to have some fun, because what is life without a bit of fun... especially after all the trouble you both have caused me."

Raven's palms began to smoke as she strained against the men holding her. Their fire resistant suits sizzled under the heat of her presence.

"I'm going to see you burn, Cain. I swear to you. For everything you've done, I'm going to see you burn with my..." Raven's voice was cut short as her body flashed. She twitched briefly and moaned as she collapsed.

Above her limp body stood Pierre Foshe with his stun baton that sparked in his hands. He prodded the prone girl with the device again. It flashed and Raven screamed herself awake as the electricity ripped through her body.

Foshe looked weary with purple bags settling under his wrinkled eyes, as though the night was taking its toll on his frail body.

"I hope the child wasn't speaking out of turn?" Foshe croaked.

"Not at all. It would seem you've arrived just in time," Cain remarked. "Did you bring what I requested?"

"Yes, Mr Cain," Foshe replied. "Caged and docile until you want it riled up for business."

"Why can't I have more people like you?" Cain laughed. "Reliable and ruthless."

"Don't forget, he's a genocidal sadist that gets pleasure from torture," Raven spat, which was responded with an electric jab between her shoulder blades.

"Enough, Pierre. You can have your fun with her later," Cain said. "We have to respect, William. It's his evening after all."

I couldn't argue with Vincent Cain. I couldn't fight him. My gift was still out of reach, as I fed slowly on the car battery. I was utterly powerless.

"Pierre, would you please bring out Mr Bolton," Cain said casually.

Bolt's face flashed through my memory. My friend had helped me so much this week. When was the last time I had seen him?

"Your friend Mark is here to see you," Vincent announced. "He wants to commit a few words before Morta cuts your thread of life. You won't be having a funeral, so I thought I'd let him say his piece now."

"Where is he?" I gasped. "Where is Mark?"

"Mr Bolton isn't all he seems anymore," Cain said. "When you ask for Mark... you might not get what you are looking for."

"I want to see him," I murmured. "Please... Mark? Are you there?"

A low growl vibrated through the earth. It rumbled through my bones, making my destroyed arm stretch painfully. Foshe brought forward a metal cage and inside was a mess of rock. It shifted and then growled at me.

"Pierre has been having all sorts of fun with Mark," Cain said. "These two go way back, don't you?"

"We met at Old Street," Foshe murmured. "But you knew that already, didn't you, Hart?"

I couldn't take my eyes away from my lost friend. His eyes gleamed at me through the cage. Was he still in there? Those eyes looked so confused. His sharp face curled with hate. His form changed into a being of hate as tension travelled through his rocky body.

"There is no need to lie to us anymore," Foshe said. "Mark has told me everything I need to know about your friendship. He has been especially responsive to treatment. We found that rehabilitation didn't suit him, so we offered him a position as our new muscle."

"Since the sudden departure of Stranz, we have a vacancy and luckily you brought Mr Bolton right to us," Cain smiled.

"As you can see, he holds very similar characteristics to Anton himself," Foshe said.

"So how much does William know?" Cain asked.

"Does it really change his fate? He deserves to die," Foshe grumbled.

"His fate remains to be seen," Cain said quietly. "What does he know?"

"He knows most of it," Foshe admitted. "Interestingly, he has a very strong idea about what is wrong with your cerebral connection. There is a chance he could help you. Yet he knows what we did to clean up Old Street. Vincent, I know you want to cure your lost gift, but we have to remain focused on our priorities. Hart cannot be allowed to live."

"That is enough, Pierre," Cain said deep in thought.

"End his life and we can leave all of this behind us. There will be others who can help you."

"Trust in me, Pierre. Have I ever let you down before?" Cain asked. "Who was the one that dragged you out of Inferno?"

Foshe's body twisted with discomfort, but remained silent to his leader.

"Is there anything else I should know?" Cain asked.

"He still doesn't know about his place in all of this," Foshe confirmed.

"Is that so?" Cain said slowly and turned to face Raven. "And what about you? I see how you look at him. The familiarity was always there, wasn't it? You never told him that you recognised him?"

"Go to hell," she spat. "You don't understand…"

"Tell me what?" I asked confused.

"It would seem she hasn't been telling you all the facts, Doctor Hart," Cain nudged the girl with the edge of his boot. Cain's words mixed muddily in my mind. Raven struggled to meet my gaze.

"I didn't know who you were. If I had known… I would have left you alone. I'm so sorry, Hart."

"What…" I tried to say.

"It's always been blurred for me too. My mind was blacked out. I've only recently started to remember you. The details have started coming back to me, but it was too late…"

"Far too late," Cain interrupted. "Your continued ignorance

has ruined this man's life. It is all your fault that we are in this position."

"My fault?" Raven asked fiercely. "You're the one that has hunted us without hesitation! We're human too! I didn't kill those people at Old Street! It wasn't my fault!"

"It's time you took responsibility for your mistakes! Today is going to be different, Raven," Cain sighed impatiently. "I am fed up of chasing after you and listening to your childish ideology. So we're going to play a game. I'm in a sporting mood and I want to see our new soldier in action. Bolt is going to chase you. If he catches you in one piece then you come with us. But if you manage to escape, then you will be momentarily free. That is, until my soldiers along the perimeter sink an acidic bullet into your skull."

"Impossible is no longer in our vocabulary is it, William? You have the power to save her. So why don't you do something for a change, instead of sitting around watching everyone else hark on."

I stretched my senses out for any nearby technology that I could manipulate. One object rose to my attention. Pierre Foshe's stun baton fizzed through my mind.

"Jess…" I whispered and her scared eyes met mine. "I hope you can run fast."

I drank every last drop of the car battery. Adrenaline surged through my body and I forced the stun baton to overload. It exploded in a burst of metal and electricity. Foshe screamed as the sudden explosion sent the crowd into chaos. When the smoke had cleared, Raven had fled and Foshe was screaming at his men to find her.

The explosion had made Bolt to panic. He tore his metal cage apart and ploughed through his guards, throwing them aside like ragdolls. Several of them opened fire and the bullets sank into his stony flesh and rattled to the ground.

Bolt made his way towards my prone body. The earth cracked under his heavy steps. His body towered over mine. I saw my friend trapped inside a violent body, battling against the primal urge to tear my body limb-from-limb. Mark's eyes darted fiercely, dilating as he focused on my bloodied remains. He was fighting against his violent exterior.

"Bolt," I managed to say, breathing in sharply as memories of our time together in the lab echoed across my mind. "It's time to repay the debt you owe me."

Bolt flinched, his mind rattling back to using the nerve plug for the first time. He had vowed that he would make it up to me one day.

"It… is done…" he struggled to say, the earth falling partially away from his face. Bolt screamed into the night, as he charged away. Chunks of debris flew outwards as my friend disappeared to hunt down Raven.

I smiled as I realised I might have just saved her life.

"Nicely done," Darius said. *"But it's not over yet."*

There was only one person left behind, silhouetted by the rampage beginning across the construction site. Vincent Cain's face was stoic and entirely unreadable.

"Perhaps you would like some information that might help you survive?" Darius offered carefully, his voice itching against the back of my mind.

Vincent picked up his gun and slowly made his way over to me. My heart thudded furiously as he advanced. Any help would be great right now.

"Haven't you wondered who put that darkness inside Vincent's head? It was me. I took away his gift. I stole Lucy's precious little memories of her childhood. Why would I do such a thing? It's obvious when you think about it."

Darius formed next to Vincent. Together they brushed back their slick hair. Vincent's grey eyes bore into me with dark fury, whilst Darius smiled through the dead, vacant eyes in his translucent face.

"After Xander stopped me all those years ago, Vincent ordered my sedated imprisonment. So I took the only thing he really cared about."

"I'm sorry that it had to come to this," Vincent said quietly. "I've learnt from experience to silence the gifted. I'm doing what I must to protect Prima from further pain."

"So do you understand now? I am Darius Cain. I hope that you can persuade my son to make the correct decision about your fate."

309

28 - Decisions

"It didn't have to be this way," Vincent Cain said quietly, resigning himself to the choice he was about to make.

"It was always going to end up like this..." I replied.

"I haven't decided whether I'm going to kill you yet. You know, I can't quite make up my mind. Killing you seems so pointless after everything we've been through. Do I kill you or keep you alive? If I end your life, then my problem is solved. I mean... it sounds like a sensible decision."

"What's wrong with putting me through your process? You offered me that earlier."

"Would you like reconfiguration?" Cain asked.

"It was tempting earlier..." I pondered.

"So what was the issue? We could have been fixing you right now if you hadn't gone wild."

"I didn't trust you. I couldn't let you put my family through your process, especially after watching Foshe deal with Bolt."

"Wouldn't you like to see your family again?"

"Of course I would."

"What would you do to see them all again? Adele, Isabella and Theo."

"I could help you," I answered honestly. "You know that."

"I'm not sure that I trust you to fix my brain, William," Cain disregarded.

"I don't blame you. I wouldn't trust me either."

"You did kill twenty-seven of my soldiers."

"You shot my wife in the leg, starved my son of oxygen and sent Xander to kill me."

"I can see why issues of trust might arise between us," Cain smiled wryly.

"It's a shame. I can honestly see why you are doing this, Vincent. The need to contain the gifted is vital for our survival."

"I wish you'd work by my side, William. I could do with man with your knowledge to guide me," Vincent sighed with regret.

"I'm not a bad employer. Many of my associates call me charming."

"You do have a certain way with words," I smiled.

"It's the joy of being in charge. I can say whatever I like and no one has the power to stop me talking!"

"You keep talking about wanting to protect everyone and stop the gifted, but that's not what you really want, is it?"

"Go on…" Vincent inclined his head, his blonde hair fluttering in the stale air. His eyes glinted with hunger.

"You want it back. No. It's more than that," I discovered as I lay dying under his shadow. "You want to be the only one with a gift, don't you?"

"My gift would allow efficient maintenance and insurance that there would never be an epidemic ever again," he affirmed proudly.

"May I ask what your gift allows you to do?" I asked bravely and Cain's jaw tensed at the question. He grabbed my chin tightly.

"Now that would be telling," Vincent Cain smiled, before sitting down next my fragile body. He aimed the barrel of his gun between my eyes.

"Before you go… I want you to tell me what it was *really* like?" Cain asked with genuine curiosity. "What did it feel like to let go?"

"Now that would be telling…" I mumbled to spite my captor.

"Come on!" Vincent sneered and jabbed the gun into my shoulder blade lightly. "Tell me and I'll consider keeping you alive."

"For a moment…" I said slowly, remembering the limitless power that had flowed from Prima and coursed through my veins. "I felt like god."

"I will get that back one day," Cain vowed to himself.

"I could help you get your gift back," I said lightly, hoping to change his decision. "Would you like that, Vincent?"

"I would like to play god again," he smiled fiercely, his eyes flickering with power again. His body juddered momentarily. Cain winced, as another trickle of blood dribbled from his nostril.

"So what's it going to be?" I asked him as his blood dripped onto my chest. "Do I live or die?"

"I ask the questions here," he sneered, wiping the blood from his face.

"You have the choice. Will you kill me or put me through the process? What will it be?"

"Very demanding tonight, aren't you?" Cain said, arching his eyebrows.

"If you don't decide, then you will miss your chance," I murmured.

"You could help me. Together we could create a truly great future…" he pondered, but his body language told another story. His eyes filled with disgust at the surrounding devastation and his finger tightened around the trigger.

"But you need to silence my power," I sighed, embracing his choice.

"Thank you for your understanding, William," Vincent nodded, but he seemed conflicted. I tried a different tactic to change his mind.

"Whilst I'm having a look at your brain, I could also try help your father," I told Vincent, whose gun wavered in his sweating palm. "Your father? Darius Cain? Mind Walker?"

"What did you say?" Vincent said quietly.

"He speaks to me. He's with me right now. He's been helping me out all along. Killing me or taking my memories would mean that you would never be able to help him. We could find a way to nullify his power. I could wake him up and bring your father back."

"Is that right? Well, that's perfect, because I never want that monster to wake up ever again," Vincent snarled.

"Fine. You know everything you need to," I sighed reluctantly, feeling my fluctuating heart pounded with dread. "What will happen to me, Vincent?"

"I don't think I can put you through the process," Vincent answered and lowered his weapon. "I don't believe that it would be successful."

"Why not?" I asked confused.

"We've never put a patient back into the process," he replied succinctly and coldly eyed my reaction.

"I've never been in your process…" I said slowly, my heart thudding so heavily that could feel the blood rushing through my ears. A confused tear dribbled from my eye, as the back of my head itched roughly.

"You still don't remember…" Vincent laughed incredulously. "Tell me… what do you remember from the Old Street incident?"

"Nothing. I was nowhere near the incident…" I answered quickly, doubt creeping into my thoughts.

"You were in a waiting room for a really long time? Am I wrong? When you drive past Old Street does the back of your neck crawl? Do you scratch your head and shiver at the mere mention of the incident?"

"You're lying. I would remember," I said adamantly, confused emotion clogging my mind. "I wasn't at Old Street. My family would have told me."

"Your family were under strict instructions not to mention the incident around you," Vincent explained fondly. "Adele sends Xander weekly updates on your mental progress, which are apparently quite concise. It's amazing how much that woman cares for your welfare."

Vincent's blonde hair flickered brutally against the backdrop of destruction. His grey eyes gleamed and his smile ripped his face open as he proudly continued.

"We've also been monitoring you at Cain Corporation ever since you started working there three years ago. We're astounded with everything you've managed to achieve. I was personally informed when your system started acting erratically. The moment that you received Lupo's archive, the data automatically transferred to my personal server. All that wonderful synaptic frequency research you did? It's mine. When you discovered the bridge for your nerve plug… the results transferred directly to me. Your tech was always my tech. Thanks to you; the nerve plug is my future. It was my decision to employ you. I wanted to see what you would subconsciously create and you did not disappoint, Doctor William Hart. A man who could control technology with his mind and had the memories of his gift erased."

Vincent Cain looked down at my broken body as the truth flowed from his proud mouth. My eyes watered in horror at his words. The air whistled over my dry, speechless mouth.

"Once I discovered that you were showing signs of your gift, which should have been erased, I monitored every single action you have taken this week. I have silenced any gifted activity with my control over the media. I've used your growing power to forge my Corporation's future," Vincent smiled richly, before his gaze lost its composure. "If Lucy hadn't lost control at the presentation, then everything would have gone to plan. We could have worked together. We could have fixed my gift and we'd have brought order to a world riddled with chaos."

"That's not true…" I gasped in horror. "None of that is true! I would remember having power. How could I possibly forget this gift? You're lying to me!"

"You still don't believe me?" Vincent laughed darkly. "Why don't you see for yourself?"

Vincent reached down and lifted my head away from the earth. My heart thundered. My mind twisted as I stretched my fingers behind my head and found the hard scar at the bottom of my skull.

29 – The Truth

My car hummed as I moved towards the next set of traffic lights. They flashed red. I ran my finger across the blue button that triggered the handbrake and brought the car to a sudden halt.

"Sorry about that," I said. "The lights caught me off guard."

"Don't worry, dear. All these lights would send me loopy if I had to drive through them every day!"

I looked back at Adele's mother in my mirror. Isabella May was the exact vision of her daughter. Her hair was wild and her eyes shone with the same charming gleam. A pair of steel rimmed glasses were propped up on the bridge of her nose and I suddenly became worried that Adele might have to get her eyes checked soon…

"William. The lights are green. Please pay attention to the road."

My eyes flicked from Adele's father and back to the green lights. I flicked the handbrake off and revved the automatic engine into action.

If Adele got her charm from her mother, then she certainly got her stubborn nature from her father.

Joseph was a large bald man. His belly hung forwards inside his maroon cardigan and his shoulders hunched inside the confined car space. My children had mentioned how their grandfather sometimes scared them, but I assured them that he was a loving man. His time in the Global War had turned him blunt. He communicated very precisely to express his opinion. He terrified me initially, but then I realised that Joseph just cared deeply about Prima and often felt the need to express his care. He was simply an extremely proud man.

"Mind the bicycles," Joseph said as I swerved around a pack of wobbling cyclists.

"Oh, leave him alone," Isabella said. "He doesn't need a back seat driver. William is a fully grown man for Fates sake!"

"I was just helping him," he replied. "I'm in the back seat so I can see many things that he cannot. For instance, the man carelessly walking his dog next to us. William definitely didn't notice that before I told him. There's a lot happening on these roads, dear. I should know. I've been driving them most of my life. I drove on the streets of Prima when they were first put in place!"

"Well, William very kindly offered to pick us up," Isabella said calmly. "Thank you, by the way. It's nice not to have to constantly calm my husband's nerves when he is behind the wheel."

"It's my pleasure," I said. "I know Izzy and Theo are really looking forward to seeing you again."

"Good," Joseph said abruptly. "It's been months since we've last seen them."

"Oh, leave it alone!" Isabella piped up. "They're busy. William is teaching, the kids are in school and Adele is... what is she doing now?"

"Adele is an estate agent," I said simply.

"An estate agent!" Isabella gasped in awe. "Isn't that simply fantastic, Joseph?"

"Is it? What was she doing last year? Nursing? Piano teacher?" Joseph asked. "Oh, forget it, I can't keep up with her career anymore."

"It's brilliant," Isabella said. "Oh, my baby has all these different strings to her bow. She's a jack-of-all-trades!"

"I get it," he mumbled. "Our daughter is amazing."

"Yes, she most certainly is," I smiled.

I stopped at the next junction. I had two choices. I could either brave my way through this torrent of traffic over the highway or I could take a right, which would lead through the heart of the great city.

"Light," Joseph grunted.

I looked up at the green signal, swore quietly and made my decision.

"Language," Joseph mumbled, before asking incredulously. "And where are we going now?"

"Why can't you leave him alone and let him drive?" Isabella

retorted.

"It's fine. I shouldn't have sworn like that," I apologised. "We're going through the city to get away from the traffic. It will take us via Old Street, but…"

"The traffic is even worse there!" Joseph grumbled.

"I know, that's why I'm going around it," I said as calmly as possible.

"See?" Isabella said smugly. "William knows exactly what he is doing. So, sit back, relax and shut up."

Joseph nodded absently. We looked at the array of older buildings that showed Priman history as we passed more freely through the great city. Bavarian buildings intermingled with Swiss architecture bristled past us. We weaved down several roads, each named after an old Italian city, as we travelled towards the old heart of the great city. Padua. Venetia. Milano. Crowds of people from all the European countries that had initially formed Prima flew past as my car hummed down the smooth tarmac.

It wouldn't be long until we all got home for dinner.

"I'm sorry, lad," Joseph said quietly. "I'm just looking forward to tonight. It's always good to spend some time with you all."

"See?" Isabella said simply. "That wasn't so difficult, was it?"

I smiled lightly in the mirror and felt my heart drop slightly. For a long period of my life I didn't have parents. Being with Adele's parents made me realize how much I missed them.

"Watch out!" Joseph shouted as he pointed wildly ahead.

I swore and slammed my foot down. I was moving too quickly. My vision blurred from the Adele's parents in the mirror, across the historic buildings nearby and settled on a girl crossing the road.

Her body hit my car with a sickening thud. She bounced off the bonnet and landed with a clunk as she rolled to the pavement and fell across the road into a neon-lamp.

I pulled rapidly onto the pavement beside her. She yelled and I spotted the white of her teeth scream out. Her thick dark hair flew up and covered her face. She swayed slightly, and then her head fell towards her chest.

"Did she hit her head?" Joseph asked.

"We have to go check on her…" Isabella said.

"Stay with the car," I said. "There's no point crowding the girl."

I got out of the car and found that the girl was gone. I spotted her halfway across the road. Her crimson shirt and marine jeans were ripped. She walked awkwardly on a pair of black heels. Her head was bleeding…

"Hey! Stop! We need to get you to a hospital!" I shouted.

Traffic streamed between us. She looked back absently. The girl waved her blood-covered hand, signalling that she would be fine. Our eyes met for a moment behind her curtain of raven black hair. They were pitch black and full of dark tears. She looked like she had been drinking, as she talked desperately to her touch screen phone.

"What's going on?" Isabella asked.

"Nothing," I replied. "She doesn't want my help."

"Nonsense," Joseph cried. "Go after her right this instance!"

"He's right, William," Isabella agreed. "She could be hurt and confused. It won't take five minutes. We'll wait right here and look after the car."

"Are you sure?" I asked.

"Yes, already," Joseph said quickly. "Now go, before you lose her!"

"Okay, I will be right back!" I shouted. "I promise."

I left the car at the side of the street with Adele's parents inside and dashed after the injured girl. I darted my way through stationary cars and a bustle of people. I saw the echo of her crimson shirt far ahead. Running down the pavement, I dodged around families, pensioners and more dog-walkers. The girl stumbled and disappeared into an alleyway.

In the alley was a small crowd of homeless people hanging around a barrel on fire. A Kubran man with dreadlocks muttered under his breath. A lanky boy wearing a beanie and thick glasses nodded nervously in agreement. I apologised briefly as I pushed past them and saw the girl exiting the end of the alley.

"Stop!" I tried to shout, but the girl was too focused on the conversation with her phone. I cursed teenage devotion to technology.

As I exited the alley and the ground suddenly moved. I stumbled to the ground and I swear I could feel a faint vibration, like an earthquake. I laughed the sensation away. It would be nothing more than an overflowing sewer or magnetic train tunnel.

The girl had already made it down the next street. I considered giving up, but there was no way I could go back to Joseph and Isabella without trying to help the injured girl.

The sky grew darker as the sun became swallowed by a shroud of looming clouds. They rumbled and filled with a creeping flash of light. It looked like it might start raining.

I ran after the wounded girl and turned into Old Street. I noticed the old buildings mixed with new establishments throughout the proudest part of Prima. A stone religious building towering nearby made me smile. The Temple of One shone with monolithic beauty. Its spires were interlaced with all forms of religious iconography, whilst a stain-glass window displayed images of the four faiths that inhabited the site. Christianity, Judaism, Islam and Buddhism were all under the one roof that had united Adele and myself in matrimony.

A new supermarket faced the Temple of One. Small local businesses sat next to international stores. Further on, I spotted the Kubran, Amazon and Antarctic embassies for the other great cities around the world. The various ethnicities co-existed at the heart of Prima. Peoples of all ages bustled past and co-habited this vibrant part of the world.

A busy intersection split Old Street and flowed into a bustling highway that spiked the horizon. It was a complicated set of crossroads that was built to ease the traffic flow. However it was currently packed with vehicles along its concrete embrace.

The sky rumbled and I felt the ground shake under my feet again. I grabbed a neon-post as the quaking earth affected a local grocer. Fruit fell from the shelves and rolled all over the floor. The Primans tried desperately to grab the nearby shelving, but it shook violently in their hands. Glass rattled in the window frame of a coffee shop. Customers inside winced, as their hot drinks smashed onto the floor.

I caught a glimpse of my own terrified eyes in the fracturing glass.

A flash of dark light erupted beneath the highway in the distance. There was a moment of silence as everyone looked towards the light, followed by a sudden scream of sound. Everyone clutched their eardrums and cried out in pain as the violent noise attacked us. The glass windows shattered and sliced my arm. Wincing, I let go of my ears and heard someone crying for help.

The screaming stopped, leaving Old Street in state of shock. A tremendous cracking noise broke the silence, as the highway began to fall apart. The pillars supporting the highway splintered under the intense pressure. People were getting out of their cars and trying to run away.

The highway split and fell downwards, crushing everything underneath it. I saw people attempting to jump off the collapsing highway. I stared in shock at the grim show of destruction.

The pavement under my feet began to crack. I looked across the intersection as the road swallowed several cars. The road slipped under my feet, as I found myself running towards the struggling cars.

There was intense heat scorching from a large crack in the road. The first car was thankfully empty, but inside the second car I could see a man writhing in pain. His car was angled sharply downwards and it was slowly sinking further into the earth. A shower of sparks spurted outwards as metal scratched against concrete. The man was bashing at the window, screaming for help. He winced as he burnt his hands on the metal of the car.

"Hey! Can you help us? Please. He's stuck in there," a thin man begged. He wore glasses, yellow shirt and a black tie. His clothes were filthy and his arms were already lacerated with burns after trying to get the trapped man out. I couldn't answer him. I shook my head and realised that I must in be a state of shock.

I forced myself to snap out of my stupor and saw that I was covered in dust and dashes of blood.

"Please. My name is James Bolton," he said. "Can you hear me?"

"Yes. Sorry. William," I heard myself say absently.

"My brother is in the car," James said. "I can't get him out."

I nodded roughly and assessed the situation quickly. I needed to break the window. I grabbed a piece of loose earth. It was warm to touch as I tossed it to James.

As James broke the car window, I tried to ignore the peripheral sounds of screams, earth breaking and fires crackling…

I kicked the loose pieces of glass away and found that the man was unconscious inside the car. I noticed the unmistakable shape of bone sticking out of his leg.

"What's his name?" I asked quickly.

"Mark," James told me. "Although most people call him…"

"Hello?" I interrupted. "Can you hear me, Mark?"

There was no answer, so I stretched down and searched for a pulse.

"He's okay," I told James. "His leg is stuck, but we need to get him out of there."

A screech pierced our hearing as the car slipped further forwards. I sighed with relief as it had allowed room around Mark's shattered leg. We grasped his arms and heaved him out into the relative safety of the street. I pulled the shirt off my back and tied it tightly around Mark's thigh in a tourniquet to try save his leg.

"Thank you," James said. "I couldn't have done that without you…"

"Thank me later when you are both still alive," I told him and saw the sky flicker strangely. Orange, red and black mixed together and flashed violently. It looked like the sky was on fire. I looked back towards the broken highway and saw her at last. The wounded girl in the crimson shirt was staggering directly towards the epicentre of the disaster.

"Get him to cover," I said to James. "I think this might get worse."

"Worse?" James cried. "How could it get any worse than this? Wait! Where are you going?"

His voice was whipped away by the roar of the storm. I was

321

running after the girl with raven black hair. The Bolton brothers disappeared from sight and were replaced by a new array of horror as I staggered down Old Street.

The beautiful spires of the Temple of One plummeted into the earth. Through the glistening window I could see the unmistakable blossom of fire. The largest spire had blocked the wooden doors. I glimpsed the shadows of people desperately trying to claw their way out of the burning building, screaming for my help, demanding that I went home.

I moved under the shadow of the crippled highway and weaved between jagged columns of concrete. Corpses of metal and flesh hung nearby and I did everything in my power not to look at them. The girl was on her knees ahead, clawing the earth and crying fiercely.

"We need to go," I tried to tell her. "I'm sorry for hitting you with my car, but we need to get out of here and go somewhere safe, okay?"

"You don't understand," she said through her tears. "No one will ever be safe near me again. Get out of here, whilst you still you can."

I noticed that her skin was glowing. We both stared at her hands, as fire began to erupt from her skin. It burst up out her palms, making me stumble backwards in fear.

"Hart," I said gently to her. "Can you hear me? My name is Dr William Hart. Can you repeat that for me?"

"H… Hart," she mumbled.

"See? That was easy," I said to her. "What's your name? Just tell me that and I'll go…"

"My name is Jess…"

"Well, Jess, why don't you take my hand and we can leave here together, okay? I'll be with you every step of the way. You won't hurt me. I can look after you now."

Jess smiled anxiously and her fire began to ease up slowly. She shakily took my hand and stood to her feet.

"I was wondering when you'd arrive…" said another voice from the darkness. "This is between me and her. It would be wise to leave whilst you still can."

From the rubble rose a man unlike anyone I'd ever seen before. He wore grim tattered trousers. His bare feet gripped the earth and were soaked with blood. His chest was covered in deep scars that were bleeding lightly. His steel eyes burnt with light and his black pulsing veins interlocked his array of scars.

This was the man who had brought destruction to the heart of Prima.

"This world is full of pain," he said coldly. "Pain can make us do horrible things. The pain drives us all. Sometimes you must release yourself from the endless torment. We have to let go of everything that we hold dear. This is the only way to exist. We fight to survive. I do what I must to ensure my survival. It's the way it was and always will be, going around in an endless cycle. The cycle must be completed."

"You should go…" Jess said and let go of my hand as the fire rippled across her body again. "You can't save me."

I considered turning around, but I couldn't leave the innocent girl with this psychopath.

"Who are you?" I asked cautiously.

"Call me, Mimic," he grinned and indicated Jess's infernal flame. "We have unfinished business. This is your only chance to walk away."

"I'm not going anywhere without her," I told him as confidently as possible.

"Some things never change," Mimic laughed madly. "You are a brave, stupid old man. Always have been. Always will be. Ignorant to the bigger picture. Ignorant to the truth."

Mimic's cold metal eyes glared into me. They stared with a deep hatred and acknowledgement. He studied me as though he already knew everything about me.

"Let's see what you will do to survive, William," he snarled. My mouth dropped in confusion as he said my name. His whole body flickered and his eyes flashed blue, electricity zapped across his skin. He smiled gleefully as he seemingly absorbed some new information. On impulse, I raised my hand in defence.

I instantly felt all the technology in the area. The broken car, street lights and power lines begged me to take control. I blinked in confusion and several cars ignited around the madman.

Mimic screamed with rage. He stretched his arm towards another car behind him. He laughed as its engine activated and the vehicle came surging towards me. I dived out of the way and fell against a neon post. Mimic sent an electrical current shooting through its metal frame. I felt the current coming, jumped out the way and somehow redirected the power towards him.

The bolt of electricity burst out of the neon post and flashed through Mimic's belly. He screamed with pain as the power scorched a hole through his body.

I gasped in horror at what I had just done. I had no idea how I was doing this.

The hole began to steam suddenly. His skin healed in front of my eyes. His belly billowed steam and as his organs reformed and his skin grew back over the wound.

"Do you like it? It's a useful trick I learnt off an old friend. He's an obscenely obese Russian. You haven't had the displeasure of meeting him. Not yet," he smiled crudely. "Mimicry is my power. The gift to move matter from one place to another. I copied the Russain's gift and rammed it into my head. That's what I can do. I take whatever I can to survive this world. Would you like to see some more?"

Dark liquid rolled out of Mimic's eye sockets. My mind burned with pain, as I felt him clawing his way through my brain.

"Doctor William Hart," he said licking his lips. "Now I already knew who you were, but I am curious to know what's been happening recently. What a shame that Adele, Izzy and Theo won't be seeing you later for dinner. You really should not have left your parents-in-law in the car alone. Perhaps I will pay them all a little visit later on."

I roared in anger. No-one threatens my family. I felt my skin beginning to glow white. Electricity burst from my body and activated all the dead machinery in the area. The destroyed traffic burst into life. Each and every phone inside the pockets of the dead became my weapons. I prepared to launch everything I had at the maniac.

"Nice trick, Doc," he laughed. "However my patience died a

long time ago. I've had enough of your impulses. I don't want to kill you. No. I can't do that, but I'm going to make you feel pain. The same pain you've given me!"

His body suddenly ignited with fire. His eyes glowed fiercely as he pointed both hands directly towards me.

"Stop it!" Jess cried, as she jumped between us.

Fire erupted between the warring duo and the force of the heat knocked me off my feet. The fire streamed between Jess and Mimic. White and orange flame ploughed from Mimic, whilst black and red fire surged from Jess. Light rippled brightly, illuminating the destruction of Old Street. The fire became more intense as it became apparent that neither party was going to give in. They both enjoyed the fire that was raging from their flesh. Their flames grew hotter and began to devastate everything around them.

I was going to have to find a way to protect myself.

I found every last piece of technology around me and summoned everything within reach. Cars rolled towards me. Neon posts ripped themselves from the earth and wrapped themselves around my body. Phones disintegrated and sealed every last small gap. The machinery continued to form a shield for myself from the intensifying inferno.

The fight continued with no clear point of stopping. I heard them screaming at each other as I continued to forge my shield. Mimic's eyes flashed darkly again and Jess gasped. Black fluid poured out of her eyeballs and flowed into Mimic who absorbed every last drop. Jess collapsed to the ground. The intense fire leapt into Mimic's flesh and he roared as energy filled his entire being.

A man in prison uniform stumbled out of the wreckage behind Mimic. He held a silver knife that glinted against the raging light. A ring engraved with a faint crimson cross hugged his index finger. His green eyes surveyed the scene. He looked from the exploding man to Jess on the ground and to the shield was creating.

The prisoner leaped forward with rapid grace, stabbed the knife into Mimic's back, gathered up Jess and slid beside me in a single motion.

"Keep going," he cried, his eyes piercing mine in the confined space. "You're our only chance of surviving what's coming. Just let go!"

I listened to the man with green eyes and sealed the shield.

Darkness consumed us as the pair huddled close to me.

Mimic exploded and devastating fire lashed against my metal skin.

My body strained with the effort of fighting the inferno.

The fire wouldn't stop burning. Debris smashed against my shield.

The green-eyed man pressed his fist into the earth, deflecting the debris.

I could hear life being destroyed all around us.

Tears rolled down my cheeks and my hands gripped the burning metal.

A flash of light began breaking through my shield.

I screamed out in pain against the unbearable heat.

Jess pressed against the shield and pushed the brutal fire away.

The heat dissipated and together we all fought against the onslaught.

There was a final scream of noise before silence fell over the world.

The man with green eyes stretched his hands forwards and ripped open the solid metal shield with a single swift motion. Light blinded my eyes and I blinked fiercely to regain my vision. Exhaustion wrecked my body and I desperately grasped the black earth in my hands…

I looked up and saw… nothing. The world was perpetuated with a note of dead silence. I could only smell ash and death. Old Street had been obliterated by the explosion, leaving absolutely nothing for miles around. The distant buildings were crumbling and rippling with growing fires.

I began to hear the distant cries for help.

The man with green eyes coughed fiercely and collapsed into the earth. Beside him Mimic was unconscious, his cold glare crippled into a resigned gaze of surrender. They had stopped the madman who was responsible for destroying Old Street.

Jess stood up slowly and looked at Mimic with a vacant expression. She didn't know how she got there or what had happened. A solitary black tear dribbled to the black earth. She shook her head with confusion, stared at her flaming hands and moved backwards in horror. She ran away into the chaos in the distance.

She didn't stop. She didn't look back. She just kept running.

My eyes faded as the image of the running girl dissipated from the dark, broken heart of Prima.

30 – Waiting Room

White lights flashed my new world into existence. I was strapped to a bed with my head facing down through a cushioned hole. I could see row after row of beds filled with people. At the far end of the room, there was an old man surrounded by machinery that fed into his flesh. The nearest person had dark hair and was completely unconscious. A small screen told me that his name was Mr Bolton. I saw that he only had one leg.

"I see that you're awake, Doctor," a voice crooned. A bleach white hand pulled a silver needle out of Mr Bolton's head. "I'm Pierre Foshe. I'm responsible for all of the patients."

"What's going on?" I asked faintly.

"You were our first patient, Doctor Hart," he explained. "We're still deciding what to do with you."

"Can you let me call my family please? They're going to be worried. I need to tell them that I'm okay."

A hand smoothed along my back and I realised there had been someone beside me the entire time.

"That's the issue, William. You're not okay. We need to fix you before you can leave. I want you to listen to me very carefully," Vincent Cain explained, recognising his voice from the media instantly.

He was in charge of a small private organisation, however the sophisticated room, number of patients and trained staff indicated a grandiose corporation.

"You've been having a delusion, Doctor Hart," Foshe explained, as he sterilised his needle and Vincent gripped my back. "It's nothing major, but we need to correct your memories. It won't hurt, I promise."

Vincent's hand pressed into my head, whilst Foshe pulled out a small vial of black liquid and filled his syringe.

"Wait…" I said slowly. "You're doing this to take away what I can do, aren't you?"

"You're deluded, Doctor Hart," Foshe said absently as he

continued to extract the dark substance. "And I'm going to remove any memory…"

"I want you do it," I interrupted. "I want you to make me forget everything and take away this curse."

"Some might call it a gift," Vincent Cain said and removed his hand. He crouched so I could meet his stoic, metal eyes.

"We're not gifted. That man was a monster. That madman, Mimic, lost control and destroyed everything. I don't want to become like that," I said quietly. "This gift is a curse and I have it too. I'm right, I know I am. I can feel the medical machinery and the phones in your pockets. I can see the messages you sent with them today. My mind is filling with binary with each passing second. Morta… I can feel a plane… I can see it right now climbing at thirty six thousand feet above our heads. I could cripple the engines, deactivate all communications and incinerate everyone on board."

Vincent's eyes widened, gripped my head and forced me into the correct position.

"I've seen what these abilities can do and I don't want any part of it!" I cried. "Do what you have to do to me. You have my full permission and support in your treatment."

"Very well, William. You had me worried there for a moment. I thought you were going to lose control…" Vincent said thoughtfully. "We've never had a subject willingly submit to the process. Your potential to my Corporation could be invaluable."

Cain paused as Foshe eyed him curiously.

"I want to personally thank you for your honesty. It will not be forgotten," Vincent said lightly as his fingers clutched my skull. "Now if you truly wish to cooperate with our process, then your brain shall remain unharmed. Do not struggle and you'll come out of this with barely any scar tissue and without remembering a single thing."

I nodded gently in total agreement with his statement. Cain released my head and Foshe began to move closer.

"Your delusion is real, but you weren't there," Foshe said smoothly. "There was a horrible disaster, but you weren't part of it. You were abroad on a long deserved holiday, don't you remember? Upon hearing the horrific news, you ran straight to the airport, but your flight home was delayed. It's been delayed a very long time and so now you're sitting in the waiting room. A white and empty waiting room. Can you picture that for me? You're going to be sat in there for a very long time."

"Goodbye, Vincent," I said. "Good luck treating the rest of…"

Foshe's needle sank into the back of my brain and I gasped as he injected the dark fluid into my cranium. The darkness swamped over my eyes, destroying the hospital and the men controlling my reality.

I blinked once. I was sat in an airport waiting room. I couldn't find my flight… I think it was delayed. I searched for a seat. I blinked slowly. I was still in an airport waiting room. I moved forward to find my flight. It was delayed. I moved back to my seat. I closed my eyes.

I was on my plane. The journey moved past in an anxious blur. I needed to see my family. They would be so worried. The blue sky zipped past in an endless instant, until the plane landed with a soft clunk.

I opened my eyes and saw a man with a car waiting outside the airport. He was dressed in a cream coat and had an extremely neat appearance. His hair was completely white and he had dull, lime eyes. Moving with grace, he opened the car door.

"Good afternoon," he said politely. "Doctor Hart, isn't it?"

"Can I help you?" I asked him.

"I've been instructed to drive you through Prima," he said. "It's become particularly treacherous with the hive of activity occurring after the incident."

"I just need to get back to my family."

"Please, sir. I insist," he continued. "My employer asked me to collect you personally. I don't believe he would be too happy if I didn't do my job."

"Very well…" I sighed and clambered awkwardly into his car. I hit my head roughly and scratched the back of my head. Fabric rubbed against my fingers and I realised absently that there was a bandage around my head. "But if you do not take me directly home, then I shall call Priman authorities immediately."

"You've been gone too long, Doctor Hart," he murmured. "We are the true authority in Prima now."

The man smoothed into the drivers seat and activated the engine. I felt it humming beneath my hand. I pushed the confusing thought aside.

"Who exactly do you work for?" I asked confused.

"Apologies, sir. My name is Alexander Habil. I've just started working for Vincent Cain. He's assigned me to keep an eye on you in the coming days."

"I thank Mr Cain for his hospitality, but I'm afraid you've lost me. Why are you so interested in me? Unless you want to learn about neurology, mechanical engineering or intuitive robotics, then I can't help you. Which reminds me… would you happen to know if any harm has come to the unit of Advanced Science…"

"That's why I've picked you up," Alexander interrupted, his emerald eyes meeting mine briefly and rattling my stray thoughts. "The University of Prima has been destroyed in the blast."

"By the Fates…" I said in quiet horror. I thought of the staff, students, friends and all the progress we had made. So much knowledge and life, gone in seconds. "I hope everyone got out in time."

"I'm so sorry," he said quietly. His words did not numb my pain, but they felt comforting nonetheless. "The University may be gone, but Cain Corporation requires bright minds like yours for the future. Your knowledge doesn't have to die. We'd like to offer you a place in our new development department. You'd have the space to follow a practical application of your theoretical study towards nerves. Plus it will keep you close by, so we can keep an eye on your future."

"I will need to think about it," I grumbled and peered at the collection of destroyed buildings in the distance. "There is so much going on. I don't understand why you need me specifically."

"I also have been told to inform you…" Alexander continued, but then hesitated suddenly and touched his ear.

"What's wrong?" I asked quickly.

"Your wife's parents passed away in the fire too," he said quietly. "I'm sorry, William. I didn't want to be the one to tell you."

"Isabella and Joseph are gone? But I was just driving them. I promised that I would be right back…"

"No," Alexander said sharply. "You were on holiday, remember?"

The blue sky and endless airport filled my mind in an instant, wiping everything away and making my mind clear again.

"They were within the blast radius when the final explosion took place," Alexander continued. "We found their bodies inside a car that was parked at the side of the street."

"Adele will be devastated…" I murmured.

"Which is why it's vital we get you home immediately. Shouldn't be long now until we get there."

"I can't believe this happened," I said. "I can't believe I wasn't there to protect my family."

"Cain Corporation needs you to help fix the future. You are exactly the kind of man who can rebuild what has been lost. Please. Call us."

"I will consider it…"

"Thank you," Alexander said contently. "Mr Cain is here to help people. He only wants to put everything back to normal. At first, I couldn't see that. I only saw his drastic methods and the violence that comes with it."

Alexander shifted uncomfortably and took a small black object out of his earlobe. My mind did its best to ignore the motion of quiet defiance.

"It's unlikely that we will get a chance to talk again, as you'll forget this conversation within moments…" Alexander said in a hushed tone. "I wanted to thank you for everything you did. You saved my life. You're an honest man, which is truly rare to find these days. Please consider working for Cain Corporation. I was hesitant at first; I even put myself in prison to protect everyone from what I can do. But then I realised working for Vincent was the best way to bring order back to a world full of chaos. It was the best way to protect our kind. That is all I want."

"Please," I said painfully as my brain throbbed violently. "My head is burning. I need to… can you just get me home?"

"We're already here," he replied solemnly.

My home greeted my eyes. Joy thundered from my heart and my hand pawed weakly against the glass to be reunited with my family.

Alexander lifted me out of the car and lifted me towards the front door. There was a splash of water against my tired face as it began to rain. I looked at the cloudy skies and craved to be indoors with my family.

We reached the front door and I thudded my hand weakly against the wood. The man with green eyes hit the doorbell. The haunting double tone rang through the house on the other side of the door.

The door swung open and my daughter gasped in shock as I fell into her arms.

"Dad!" Izzy screamed. "Mum? You need to come out here quick!"

I grabbed my daughter desperately. It felt so wonderful to hold her in my arms again. It felt like it had been an age since I'd seen her. She cried into my shoulder and I put my hand against the back of her head.

"Don't ever leave again, Dad," she cried. "Please don't ever do that."

"Dad's back!" Theo shouted. "You're back!"

Theo thundered down the staircase and leapt into my arms with Izzy. We huddled together on the floor, none of us willing to let go of each other ever again.

I saw my wife talking quietly with the man with green eyes, whose name had already faded from my mind. She was angry, her fingers stabbing into his chest and tears rapidly welling into her eyes.

"You can't ever tell him," the haunting man explained.

"He is my husband," Adele cried. "He deserves to know the truth!"

"You can't," he lied. "It will only dig up all the trauma and leave him mentally damaged."

I shook my head and wondered why I thought the man was lying. Recognition jagged into my brain and searing joints of pain lashed into the back of my skull. I screamed out in agony.

I opened my eyes and Adele was cradling my head. She held my face in both of her hands and pressed her gentle lips into mine. The soft caress of my wife soothed my anxiety.

Sleep consumed my body and I allowed the darkness to take hold of my mind, as I collapsed…

The darkness of my mind grew and shifted. I felt it breathe inwards and suddenly it spoke to me.

"The world is waiting to change. It's underneath your skin. It's emanating within everyone around you. It is emitting impatiently throughout the world. You and the other billions live under a fragile web of lies that has been created to keep you all safe from the uncontrollable change…"

The darkness shifted and I floated into my subconscious. I stared into the vast blank canvas in anticipation of what it would say next.

"Do you want me to tell you the truth, William?"

31 – Virtual Reality

"Welcome home," Darius Cain said, as he sat in my living room drinking tea. As he slurped the fluid into his mouth, I was reminded that he was drinking my tea, whilst sat on my armchair in my home.

My mind stung with confusion as I became disorientated in the familiar blurred surroundings.

How did I get here with the demon from my nightmares?

"Pleasure to see you too," Darius grumbled and absently dropped the cup. It smashed into a dozen pieces, froze, then reformed and bounced back into his grasp.

"So I presume that this isn't real?" I asked the intruder.

"Presumption is never a realistic approach to existence. A man of science like yourself should know this. Also any concept of reality whilst talking to me went out the imaginary window long ago."

"Fair point," I murmured and looked around my strange house. Several lamps dully lit the living room, their lines of light twisted momentarily. I moved over to the window and saw a blurred landscape outside.

"I think I understand what's going on…" I said slowly.

"Really?" Darius said surprised and crossed his legs. "Please tell me. It will be humorous when you get it wrong."

"I should be dead right now but I'm not," I pondered as I gazed at the corrupt surroundings. "So that means Vincent decided to keep me alive. My proof of life is you. You are talking and drinking my tea. And I know that you are definitely real."

"But am I real, William? Perhaps I am truly, in your own words, a construct of over active imagination." Darius said slyly. "Anything else?"

"I must have gone through intensive surgery to survive my injuries," I remarked at Darius, whose limbs were strongly formed, whilst the rest of our surroundings had an edge of surreality. Even my own hands seemed contorted somehow. "I've been placed into an induced coma… that's why I can see you so clearly. I'm stuck in my mind with you…"

"Bravo, William! Well, that wasn't fun at all! You figured it out. Almost. We're in *my* mind right now. Do you like it? I've designed this bit especially for you. You can live here whilst you're in limbo."

"Thanks, I guess," I said quietly. "There's no knowing how long I'll be here."

"Could be a week or could be eternity. Time is as consistent as our memory in this cerebral world. Trust me. I'm talking from experience," he grunted and I was reminded that he was also under heavy sedation. "Your life now entirely depends on whether Vincent wants to wake you up or not."

"That sounds like suitable punishment," I said gravely.

I sat down on my sofa and sighed deeply as the truth rolled through my memory. The terrifying images of Old Street and my decision to allow Cain to destroy my memories echoed deeply. With my mind erased and my gift gone, Cain had employed me to use my subconscious skill with technology to create the nerve plug. After meeting Raven and regaining my gift, I'd lost control. I'd craved power and ignored that my gift would only bring devastation. My ideology had been completely changed from Old Street to the construction site.

I now understood the vital importance behind exterminating gifts.

"Don't be so extreme, William! Why would you wish to lose this power? I kept my word, didn't I?" Darius smiled. "I showed you the truth. I sowed the seeds that reawakened your power. My dreams led you to Raven and made you doubt that green eyed fool."

"I wish you hadn't," I interrupted. "I wish you'd left my mind alone. Learning the truth has only brought pain…"

"Just think of everything you have achieved. You created technology that will change the future. Your power grew beyond comprehension. You can't imagine how proud that made me! You were everything that I could have hoped for and more!"

"All I can see is the death toll that I've created," I replied. "All those people that got hurt at the construction site. Stranz and Quayin. Adele's parents and all those involved in the incident that I couldn't save."

"You saved Jessica and Alexander," Darius grumbled. "Although I wish you hadn't helped that man. He has caused more grief than you can ever comprehend. However, I need him alive. My gift allows me to speculate on the future and I've seen glimpses of what may come. Time and time again, Xander is involved with it all. Time is a tricky spinning cycle, but I've seen a world of pure liberation. A world full of gifts and it is truly beautiful."

"You talk like Mimic," I glared distastefully. "Knowing the future and cycles repeating… it's all irrelevant. People died! Your problem is that you don't live in the present. You're too busy prophesising. I was trying to make a difference, but I should have done more. I should have stopped Mimic, but instead I hid inside a shield of metal."

"See the potential world through my eyes. Look at what you can do now with a bit of practice. Back at Old Street you were working on impulse. You'd never used your power before, but last night you became unstoppable. You crushed your enemies."

"That is exactly the problem. I didn't want these powers and you forced them back onto me."

Darius laughed and dissipated into black smoke. The smoke crawled through my body and ventured into my surroundings.

"You got into this situation yourself," Darius hissed.

"You put the images into my mind. You were showing me all the power that I'd lost and ignoring the price that comes alongside it. And what about all those coincidences? Becoming best friends with Bolt? There is no way that just happened. It was you. You must have triggered an impulse when I decided to enter his pub for the first time."

"Your subconscious is much stronger than you realise…" Darius said impatiently.

"That's because you are my subconscious! And there is absolutely no way I hit Raven with my car again purely by chance. You surely must have orchestrated that somehow."

337

"And how would I manage that?" Darius chuckled.

"You can see where we all are. We're all pawns on a chess board… you just nudge us all in the right direction."

"Stop being so ungrateful! I have worked tirelessly on you. Night after night, I revealed your potential until you finally listened. Yes, sometimes I had to point you in the right direction. Be grateful! Don't let your limitations hold you back."

"Now, that is interesting!" I said as his words echoed with familiarity. "You sound exactly like your daughter."

"Consider your words closely, boy," Darius whispered spitefully. The walls began to suddenly dissolve as dark tar ran down them. "You have no idea the lengths I have undergone to protect my family. I tried to make the world complete and they rejected my plan! I sacrificed my life to keep them safe from powers that are beyond your linear comprehension. I did everything to save my son and my daughter!"

"Considering how she ended up," I interrupted the deranged man. "I think you should have placed more attention on your daughter instead your delusions. She was truly broken in the end and that's down to a severe lack of parenting."

"I'm glad you find Lucy's demise entertaining…"

"Not at all. It was horrific," I said quietly. "But it shows how messed up your priorities are. Your children have become twisted as a result of your absence. Your family is a mess, Darius."

"Not as bad as yours right now…" Darius hummed darkly, before reappearing. The walls stopped melting as I stared into his cold dead eyes.

"Where are they?" I demanded. "Tell me."

"They're right here," he said and tapped the side of his head.

My mind flashed back to the waiting room and the black vial that Foshe had injected into the back of my head.

"That's why you could only talk to me," I realised. "They injected your blood into my head."

"That's right. Vincent got the idea from me. During the Blackout I was at the height of my power, working fiercely to liberate the world and give them power. That all stopped when Vincent became aware that I could erase minds after I'd erased

Lucy's memories of her mother. He worked together with Xander to put me down like a dog. As a final act, I tore at my son's mind and ripped out his spectacular power."

The black smudge that clung to Cain's brain stung my memories. The flash of him using his gift in the construction site echoed dully. His nose had bled heavily as a result...

"After Vincent understood what I did to him, he realised he could replicate the effect on future patients," Darius continued. "A single drop of my blood and he tells them what they need to forget. Moments later, their memories and gifts are gone. The side effect, that he's unaware of, was that it gave me a new mind to call my home."

"And you did all this to me when you are at your weakest. I can't bear to think what your power was like when you were awake."

"Limitless," he hummed with sick pleasure. "I was able to influence anyone. I curse the day I let Alexander Habil into my home. Don't worry... I left my scars on him too. I brutalised his cerebral cortex. I turned him into a cold machine by tearing apart his memories of Albion. Take a man's childhood away and he becomes devoid of innocence."

"Enough stories of your past," I snapped. "I want you to give back my family. You have them, don't you? You've got them trapped right now."

"How about a trade? You can have them right now and live in this little home I've created for you. I'll even expand the house and throw in the garden for free. You can live here as a happy family indefinitely."

"And what do you want in return for this virtual paradise?"

"An experiment," Darius smiled. "First, I want you to turn the lights off and on in my room."

I blinked my eyes and nothing happened. I looked at the lights in the lounge quizzically and found that none of them were real.

"Expand your mind," Darius rolled his fake eyes. "You're weak, but I want to see how much you can manage. What can you find around you. Find the lights in my room. I suggest you hurry whilst I still have your family."

Darius disintegrated and darkness consumed my home. I jammed my eyes shut and expanded my senses.

I escaped sedation and felt my hand touching a cold metal slab. It sent goosebumps rattling up my arm. An electronic restraint was wrapped around my wrist.

"Expand your mind, William. What do you see?"

There was a single light above my head. I immediately switched it off and on again. I sensed a clock. It told me that the time was eleven. It was Saturday evening. The loss of time echoed against my mind. The presentation had been on Friday, how had I lost so much time…

"Focus, William. Move beyond your room…"

There were multiple rooms ahead. Each had an electronically locked door and sedated patients within them. I sensed their life support machines humming into their bodies. No. They weren't supporting the patients. They were keeping them asleep.

Below were six floors of offices, private quarters and development laboratories. We were in Cain Corporation. The third floor grabbed my attention and I immediately recognised my lab. A smile played across my lips as the familiar technology brushed against my mind.

I accessed my computer and slipped through the network to access a floor plan of the facility. As the blueprint appeared, I saw that the building actually had ten floors instead of six. There were two basement levels below the foyer that housed Cain's security forces and two higher levels that contained the sedated patients and living quarters.

My mind shot upwards and did its best to ignore the flurry of electrical activity whizzing past my senses. My body juddered as the strain finally echoed across my mind. I could feel myself fading. I gripped the metal with my hand, until it cut into my skin. I tired to grab the slab with my other hand, but I couldn't feel anything.

A familiar room jumped into focus and I instantly knew I was in the right place. I found security cameras dotted throughout the room and used them to see. Rows of white beds with pristine sheets were lit by bright lights. Several of the beds had holes in the headrest and I knew that this was where Cain removed my memory of Old Street

"And all along I was living upstairs," Darius told me.

Straight ahead I saw him, as I had done in my dreams. The old man was surrounded by machinery as he always was. I noticed that several other beds were occupied. I didn't recognise many of the people, but two of them made my heart drop instantly. Adele and Theo lay next to each other, unmoving, with a series of wires threaded into their arms to monitor their heart rates.

Remembering our trade, I looked at the single light above the old man and focused on it. I felt my skin sweating and my heart racing as I forced my gift into action.

The light flickered.

"Nicely done, William," Darius murmured with approval.

In an instant I left his side, surged back to my cell and sank into my living room. I heard the sound of hesitant footsteps and turned around to find my wife at my side at last.

"Will?" Adele gasped with shock. "Is it really you?"

"It's me. I'm here now," I gasped and we quickly embraced each other. "I've missed you so much. I'm so sorry. I should have told you about everything."

"You idiot! Of course you should have told me. I'm your wife for Fates sake! You should definitely tell me if you are feeling the urge to control technology with your mind."

"Well, I'm sorry!" I said sarcastically. "It's not exactly something I was prepared for. I didn't plan to become the most powerful man in Prima."

"Arrogant, but apology accepted," she said smugly. "Don't let it go to your head though, dear."

"We need to talk," I said to her solemnly. "Adele, you've not been honest with me. I know about Old Street."

A short silence fell between us both. Years of withheld secrets simmered tensely inside of my wife.

"What was I meant to do?" Adele asked heavily. "I thought you died after the incident, Will. I hadn't heard from you or my parents. I looked at the news and I heard there had been an accident. We don't hear anything for weeks, Will. Can you

341

imagine what that did to the kids? And then you just stumble through the door and I'm told to never mention it to you ever again! How is that fair? I'm sorry that I couldn't talk to you about it, by all the Fates, I wanted to."

"Don't worry, I will explain everything soon."

"You've said that before…" Adele said bluntly.

"Where's Theo?" I asked.

A thundering of footsteps stormed down the staircase and we turned to find our son running towards us. His smile spread across his face as he leapt into Adele's arms. They spun together laughing and smiling as one.

Their faces blurred, dissipated and dissolved into black smoke. I moved forward to where they had been and the dark slick substance slipped through my fingers.

"Bring them back," I told my torturer. "And tell me where Izzy is."

"All in good time," Darius said as the smoke reformed. "Soon we'll have everyone here together. You'll finally have your family reunion. All you have do is complete our experiment…"

"I'm not sure if I want to do that," I said slowly.

"My blood has already been injected into Adele and Theo's minds to begin erasing their memories of your gift. The process is not complete, as their memories are still intact. I exist with them now, but Isabella is beyond my reach."

I remembered the last time I saw Izzy. She had been unconscious in the foyer, before I'd displayed my gift. It would look like Vincent had decided not to quarantine her.

"Precisely," Darius said quickly. "Which means if you want her to join you, then I need to expand my mind. All you have to do is go back and turn off all my machines. Do that and you can have your family back in a world without gifts. That's what you truly want, isn't it? You can all exist in my perfect world that I have created especially for you."

"This is what you wanted all along," I realised. "You wanted me to wake you up. You wanted to manipulate me to bring you back to life."

"I thought that was abundantly clear from the start. I need

healing. Furthermore, the world needs healing and I am the man who can ensure its liberation. In fact, I distinctly remember you vowing to me on your family's life that you would do everything in your power to help me. Or have you forgotten that as well? All you have to do is turn the machines off and I will do everything else."

"Do I have a choice?" I asked.

"Turn them off and you can have them back," Darius said and revealed an image of my family eating spaghetti bolognese in our dining room. Adele, Izzy and Theo looked at us with innocent smiles on their faces. "It's that simple."

The image faded and darkness once again consumed my reality. If I didn't do as he asked, then he would return me to this endless sleep with no one to accompany me. An eternity of oblivion.

I found the Mind Walker again upstairs in Cain Corporation. His complicated array of machines buried into his body. All he wanted me to do was turn everything off. It was a simple task considering all the trouble he had gone through.

I thought of my family. All I wanted was to be with them all again.

In a single swift action, I destroyed the fuses in every last piece of medical equipment. I forced the systems to overload, making them incapable of reactivation. A series of back up generators kicked in, returning power to the machinery. This was getting more complicated than I thought. I quickly reversed the current and sent the electricity surging back to destroy the generators. The equipment was replaced by new machinery in a final attempt to keep Darius asleep.

With a twitch of my finger, I found their holo-phones buried within their pockets. I sent them flying into the machines. The phones batteries ignited and exploded like small grenades, annihilating their last hopes of mechanical sedation.

The hospital flashed with red light as an alarm blasted through Cain Corporation and turned the white room into a sickening shade of crimson. I destroyed the alarm and ripped the lights apart, plunged it into darkness.

The neon light of Prima crawled through the window and glistened over Darius Cain's motionless face. The Mind Walker's eyes crawled open and I stared into their dead cold gaze. The old man's lips cracked into a smile as his eyes turned black with controlling darkness.

"It's good to be back…" Darius Cain spoke for the first time in decades.

Exhaustion wracked my mind, as the Mind Walker became covered in thick darkness. The flurry of technology disappeared from sight, as I retreated into the sanctuary of my home with my lost family.

32 – My Dream Home

"Dinner's ready!" Adele shouted from downstairs. "And if you two don't come down here right now, then I shall be boxing up your food and pushing it into the postbox! Perhaps then you will finally comprehend what it's like to wait every evening for your family to turn up for the food you have meticulously created!"

"We're coming, Mum. Calm down already!" Izzy sighed and threw her holo-glasses aside. I smiled as they highlighted her bedroom walls with a beautiful shade of aqua. "Come on, before she bursts a blood vessel or she decides to actually visit the postbox."

I chased my daughter downstairs and we raced to our seats to find that our portions weren't on the table. Theo hit the table with his tiny fist.

"Mum got you again!" Theo laughed. "You are so gully able."

"That's how you say it," Izzy murmured.

"I think you mean gullible, son," I told him.

"That's what I said!" Theo complained.

A polite cough echoed next to us and I looked at my mother-in-law. She was sat down patiently and looking as serene as ever.

"Do you think I should help Adele in the kitchen?" Isabella May asked politely.

"If she wanted help, then she would have asked you," Joseph said next to her. "Also, I think we need to have a conversation about my grandson's use of the English language, William."

"Don't you find it strange we call it English though?" I asked Joseph remembering his time in the Global War. "Think about it. England itself as a nation was dissolved over forty years ago when Albion was created. It seems insane to say we are speaking English! You know my father was from Morocco, one of the ten nations that established Kubra, and they have their own language that was generated by the merging of countries. They created the Kubran language to assist communication. What better way to unite a great city than through language? Why aren't we the same?

We should be calling this language Albish or Priman!"

"You've always been too smart for your own good," Joseph mumbled. "I don't need a history lesson from you. I will have you know that I was enlisted to assist emergency recovery after the Fall of Albion."

"Here we go again," his wife sighed. "We don't want to hear about the War at dinner."

"Wait a moment!" Joseph complained. "Those fallen soldiers would be furious if they could hear William slandering the language their ancestors thrived in! You want to forget Shakespeare and Chaucer as well? Their words developed the English language! Our language!"

"Dad! Leave him alone," Adele shouted from the kitchen. "Will is only winding you up. Besides, I'm the one teaching Theo nonsensical words."

"Of course you are…" Joseph grumbled.

"And Mum? I'm a grown woman. Thank you very much for the offer, but I think I can handle dinner for eight people."

"Eight people?" I asked my wife and looking around the table. "Who else is coming for dinner?"

"Morta be damned. Oh well, the cat is out of the bag now, so I might as well spit it out," Adele said excitedly. "I have a surprise for you, Will. It's my little reward as you've been so brilliant recently."

"What exactly have I done?" I asked curiously.

"You brought us together," Adele said simply. "All of us."

"We are all here, because of you," Joseph smiled proudly.

The doorbell rang in a haunting double tone.

"That should be them now…" Adele said nervously. "Why don't you go answer it?"

Cautiously, I stood up from the table and left my children to chat to their grandparents. They hadn't seen them in three years. They clearly had lots of catching up to do.

I made my way to the front door, grabbed the handle and slowly opened the door.

"Hello, Will," my mother said standing on my doorstep.

I was stunned. I hadn't seen her since I was fifteen years old.

The wind fluttered through her dark hair. Her eyes shone with emotion as she looked at her adult son. "Look how you've grown! My boy has become a man. By the Fates! It's been such a long time, honey."

My mother wore a long dark blue dress and white shawl over her shoulders. She spent a moment to nervously fiddle with the handbag in her hands, before placing it on the ground. My mother hadn't aged a day since I last saw her. She smiled brilliantly and tears welled up in her eyes as she reached out to hug me. My arms hesitantly wrapped around her and then gripped her tightly as I never wanted to let her go. I kissed her head and the familiar floral smell of hair simmered into my senses.

Through my tears, I saw my father climbing out of the car. He walked with such a powerful confidence that I'd always envied as a child. He wore a pale grey-checkered suit with a navy tie and his intelligent eyes were shining brilliantly in the sunlight. He stretched out his hand for me to shake which I gently nudged aside and embraced my father for the first time in over twenty-five years…

"It's good to see you again, son," his deep voice hummed into my ear.

"You have no idea how amazing it is to see you both again," I said in awe. "You must come in and meet everyone. Fates be blessed, you've never met Adele! Okay, be warned, she's a bit spirited initially. I love her and once you get to know her, you'll find that she is the most caring woman you'll ever meet."

"She sounds perfect," my father laughed.

"We're so proud of you," my mother said.

"And my kids, that's right, you have grandchildren! They're called Isabella and Theodore. Yes, I named him after you, although he prefers to be called Theo."

"That will ease the initial confusion," he commented dryly.

"True," I laughed. "He's a bit hyper, but he is the best kid. And Mum, trust me, you will utterly adore Izzy."

They followed me into the dining room and there was a brief moment of stunned silence as I brought in my long lost parents.

"May I have your attention," I said trying to force the emotion out of my throat. "These are my parents… Susan and Theodore Hart."

My parents slipped past my shoulders and met my family for the first time. Joseph and Theodore shook hands. My mother embraced my wife. My children cautiously met all of their grandparents at once.

I smiled sadly as I watched the dead meet the living. I saw everything that I ever wanted right in front of me. Adele met my eye and we both grinned at each other ridiculously. Our parents were back. Our family had grown and become united at last.

The only problem was that it felt fake. The falseness of the scenario ripped through my mind and a lump rose up in my throat.

"What's wrong, William?" My father asked as he noticed the grave look on my face.

"This is everything I've ever wanted. I miss you so much, but I'm not sure I can do this…"

"Look at me," he said and I met his eyes. I realized how much I missed having my father around. "We love you. We raised you to be a good man and you have surpassed all expectations that we ever had of you. I've never been prouder. Your mother and I are here to stay. Why don't you come and join us?"

My father looked at me, no, he looked into me. He closely studied my reaction, like a child watching an insect, and I began to realize who this person truly was. I saw who was truly responsible for bringing my family back together.

My father's proud words were not his own.

I closed my eyes and began sensing the building beyond my unconscious sedated body.

"Thank you," I told my father. "I'll be there in a minute."

Theodore entered the dining room. He rejoined my mother and they gently kissed each other on the lips. They took their place at the far end of the table, whilst Adele brought in a gorgeous roast dinner for everyone. The beautiful smell and sights filled my senses. My heart thudded and a lump rose in my throat. My family were so happy.

And I was going to leave them forever…

I closed my eyes as I cut my family out of my life. I felt my tears fall from my face. I found every electronically locked door on the seventh floor of Cain Corporation and unlocked every single one of them. I deactivated all the restraints that were keeping the patients locked in their cells and turned off the machines that were keeping everyone sedated.

I opened my eyes slowly and my entire family was gone.

They were replaced by an empty table covered in dust…

I walked into the empty room and my tears landed in the place my mother and father had been sat only moments ago…

I sat down at the vacant table and sobbed uncontrollably as I accepted the truth that my family were gone.

The lights dimmed as I closed my eyes and the darkness slowly consumed my dream home.

SUNDAY

Mind Walker

33 – System Reboot

Flashes of crimson and aquamarine light blared outside my trapped eyelids. The colours repeated, growing stronger and burned against my ensnared mind. I stirred against the enforced sleep that had consumed my soul. I was trapped. My mind paralyzed with drugs and my body strapped to a slab. The inviting world filled with my family enticed me to return. The tranquil dream seemed like heaven compared to this restrained hell.

I needed to wake up. I had to get free.

The machines nearby rattled violently as I stretched out my senses. The metal twisted to my will. Technology merged with my skin as my gift worked furiously to wake me up. Somewhere in the distance I heard my voice screaming and becoming hoarse with vocal effort. I flailed against my restraints and the darkness gripping my consciousness.

The machinery melded with my wounds, straightening my shattered leg with metal supports and replacing several ribs. My breath was irregular, potential punctured lung. My heart was fluctuating, potential atrium collapse. Circuitry weaved around my major organs, revitalizing my respiratory and circulatory systems to optimum efficiency.

The Mind-Walker's gift clung to my synapses like a terminal disease. He was in control. I would not wake up until I'd deleted his presence. And there was no one who knew the central nervous system better than me. Carefully, I allow the machinery to sew itself into my brain. Wiring entered through the incision at the base of my skull and threaded into my synapses. I replaced the organic material in my brain that could be manipulated with nerves of steel. I rebuilt the part of brain that had been colonized by the Mind Walker and transformed my mind into a natural and artificial supercomputer. The reactions between my synapses were still chemical and electrical… but now I controlled them. Mind Walker's presence slipped away at last, the darkness seeping out of my mind like smoke on the wind.

I felt a sudden stabbing sensation in my neck. Energy blasted through my blood and surged into my new brain. I initiated a full system reboot, as my body restarted.

My eyes slammed open as Raven yanked a syringe out of my neck.

The surge of energy ploughed through my veins and reawakened my tired synapses. I fell away from the machines and slammed into the floor with a heavy thunk as my limbs started functioning again. I gasped for breath, as I tried to remember how my body worked after being unconscious for so long...

"I can't believe you're alive," Raven mumbled in shock.

"Neither can I..." I gasped, amazed that my voice was still active.

"I thought you were dead," she said quietly. "After Xander stabbed you... Cain had you at gunpoint. I thought you were gone. It's been days, Hart. I had no idea you were alive until I heard you yelling."

She nervously glanced at the bandages that lacerated my body. I followed her gaze and saw steel piercing the white bandages. My new metal ribs were glinting in the light, along with the wiring that fed into my chest and operated my major organs.

"We broke in here to save the Outcasts and find your family, but something feels really wrong. The doors all opened and everyone is going mad out there," she continued. "I found you in here whilst the machines were going nuts. The wires were going into your skin, Hart. It looked like..."

"I was fixing myself," I interrupted her. "I was attempting to correct the broken connections inside..."

My voice caught in my throat as I heard myself describe my disposition. I was a malfunctioning project that required adjustment to achieve functionality...

"I've never seen someone look so..." Raven stopped herself as she looked down at the empty space where my arm should be. My breath caught in my throat. My limb above the elbow remained, but it was interlaced with the same metal that was threaded into my body.

I swallowed dryly and tasted oil at the back of my throat. My

352

remaining hand grasped the floor. I'd lost control. I'd lost my arm, my family and very nearly my life. I wished I'd known how devastating these gifts were from the beginning.

"It's okay, Hart. You're back now, right?" Raven asked anxiously. "We need to get out of here."

I felt the strange energy coursing through my blood. I considered asking Raven what had been inside her syringe, then realized I could find out myself. The liquid was already running through my heart at a hundred and forty beats per minute. I swiftly reconfigured my heart to analyze the foreign fluid.

"You injected me with adrenaline," I noted. "It's just what I need to push me over the edge."

"How did you know that?" Raven asked cautiously.

"That's irrelevant," I stated. "I appreciate the assistance. I needed the boost."

"I tried it on another prisoner, but their drugs were too strong."

"It's more than the drugs. Mind Walker had control of them."

"Okay... so why could you break free?" Raven asked.

"I've changed the game. I've changed myself."

"Yeah... I can see that..." Raven murmured and her head twitched slightly. She screwed up her eyes with disgust. She shook her head as she attempted to ignore an invisible voice in her own ear.

I felt relieved to be free from telepathic control, but Raven still had her own issues going on in her head. I hoped that recalibrating my brain had been a permanent solution.

"What are you doing here?" I asked and heaved my aching body from the floor. "I gave you the chance to escape. You should have kept running until you were out of Prima."

"Are you kidding?" Raven asked incredulously. "I'm keeping my promise to find your family. I thought you were dead. It was the least I could do after everything I'd put you through."

"I appreciate your concern, but I know exactly where they are. Top floor under quarantine."

"Perfect," she said. "With all the madness happening, upstairs will be completely unguarded."

"It's not that easy," I said quietly. "The Mind Walker has woken up."

"So all those people outside are being controlled by him?"

"Exactly. Darius is Vincent's father and he is ready to start making some drastic changes. We can't let him do that."

"Okay, well, why not leave them to it?" Raven asked intensely. "Yes, it's twisted that Vincent kept his father locked up for decades, but it doesn't affect us. Let the Cain family kill each other off. It's one less thing to worry about!"

"You've not spent time with Darius. His gift was invasive when he was comatose. I don't want to imagine what he is capable of when he is awake."

"Point taken," she replied solemnly and jumped as a flash of light and gunshots smashed outside the cell door. "Morta! That was close."

"You can blame me for that," I said. "I let everyone out."

"You did what?" Raven asked in horror.

"I wanted to give Darius a distraction. The more minds he has to play with, the less he will to focus on me."

"Wow. Yes. You were successful. Your distraction is currently destroying everything in its path."

"He has my family. I don't mess around when I'm protecting them."

"I believe you," Raven smiled lightly. "Even a little thing called death couldn't stop you."

"Nothing will," I said firmly and ripped out the remaining cables that linked into my flesh. I made my way to the door that flashed with blue and red light. I heard several inhuman sounds and more gunshots echoing down the corridor. The smell of burning meat drifted into my nostrils.

Raven pressed her hand against my bandaged chest and stood in the doorway to chaos. It took me a moment to realize that she was preventing me from leaving the cell.

"Get out of my way," I demanded as calmly as I could manage.

"You were dead yesterday," she replied sternly. "Look at yourself. You can barely walk. You're literally not thinking straight. You need to stay here until you've recovered."

"I won't repeat myself."

"Do you really think you can beat this? There is nothing we can do. This building has gone haywire. Everyone out there is running riot, whilst a telepath rummages through their heads."

"That's exactly why I need to go. My family are up there."

"Think about what you are saying. This is impossible when you are in this condition. Let's grab our people and escape whilst we still can. We'll get far away so the telepath won't be able to control us, right?"

I shook my head in disbelief.

"You seem fond of running away. Am I wrong? You charge in, throw some fire around and turn your back on the bloody mess you've made."

"That's not true."

"You left me, Jessica."

"At the construction site?" She asked confused. "You told me to run?"

"You left me at Old Street for dead. I remember what you did that day."

"That isn't fair," Raven looked shamed. "You had no idea what was happening."

"Mimic killed thousands of people. That isn't difficult to understand. We both were involved in the incident. You fought him and I saw how you smiled as the fire raged between you. Don't you see? Your fire burnt the heart out of Prima and then you ran away from the responsibility. You are partially responsible for all that destruction, Jessica."

"Stop calling me that name," she said roughly.

"I'm actually glad that Cain took away my gift. For a time... I was happy. I existed in a world filled with pedestrian worries, until you came crashing back into it. It didn't take you long to ruin my life all over again."

"I was confused. I wasn't sure what happened at Old Street. I thought that I was responsible, I still don't know if I was. I might have been..." she stopped herself from saying any more. "I wasn't sure that it was you."

"If you had the smallest inclination of what happened, then why did you keep running away? Why couldn't you leave me alone?"

"I don't know..."

"You don't know? Seriously?" I asked, exasperated at the girl. "Sometimes I forget that you are just a child."

"I'm sorry," she said quietly. "Something has been stopping me. Mimic did something to my head."

"I've been living with a telepath clawing through my mind for the last three years. I've dealt with it. You choose to turn your back when you should have stood your ground."

"I have never stopped fighting this! I thought you would understand. We've been through Old Street. We both survived."

"Look at me, Jessica," I told her firmly and grabbed her shoulder. "I am not your friend. I am not a father figure. I am someone whose life you have ruined."

"I have apologized and I don't do that often, alright? I'm here to help. What more do you want from me?"

"I want you to move out the way, Jessica."

"No," she said stubbornly and knocked my hand aside. "I won't."

The machines rattled violently as I grunted with frustration. The medical technology slammed into my shoulder and replaced my lost arm. I forged a new limb with optimum dexterity and user capability. My new spindling fingers stretched as I promptly pushed Raven out of my path.

"We can talk about this later," I told her. "But right now, I have to stop Darius. I think he's going to try and give everyone their gifts."

"Is that really so bad?" She asked darkly. "Everyone would be equal at last. We wouldn't need to hide."

I looked at the foolish girl. Our mindsets about gifts could not be more different.

"There is nothing worse. When anyone loses control of their gift, it always results in death. I thought you already knew that from experience."

For a moment, I regretted my choice of words. Perhaps I was

356

being too harsh on this girl. She was young and distraught by Old Street.

No.

Raven's arrogance had made her ignore the violence of every event she was involved in. She was not blameless. She had played her part in everything that had happened in Prima.

"Fine," she said coldly and creaked her neck. "But I'm coming with you."

"I don't think that is a good idea," I tried to say.

"I didn't ask for your permission," she retorted and pushed her way past.

I followed the stubborn girl through the door and we stepped into the unknown depths of Cain Corporation.

My skin prickled as I felt three guns activate. My eyes flicked through the gloom and ripped apart the guns with my mind. I found a stuttering light strip, which I used to electrocute the soldiers. Their bodies silhouetted as their screams burned into my eardrums. I shut off the power and they fell heavily to the floor.

"Nicely done," Raven murmured approvingly.

"I'm impressed too," said a groaning man's voice through the smoke. I looked down the empty corridor, but all I could see was the still bodies of the soldiers.

"We're all quite impressed," said a female voice.

The group raised their heads. Through the dust and flashing lights I could see that their eyes were black.

"Let's see what we have here," said the other man, as the Mind Walker searched through his memories. "Ah, yes! John has a beautiful wife from Mengxiang. He's worried that he is never going to see his *dream* wife again."

"Mary's been very bad," said the woman. "She has been stealing coffee from the staff room. She hides the packets of coffee in her socks."

"James knew about that," said the final soldier. "Everyone knows that Mary was the coffee smuggler, but no one's brave enough to report her. They're afraid of her…"

"Leave them alone," I told the Mind Walker who glared through their eyes as he searched through their possessed minds.

357

"But we didn't do anything," they all said in unison. "You were the one that attacked us. Perhaps we should return the favor?"

Their faces twitched in unison and collapsed violently as Darius Cain left their minds.

Theirs screams filled my ears and the scar at the back of my head burned roughly. Tightness gripped my body as darkness tried to enter my mind.

I lost sight of myself, as Darius tried to take control. Black tar dripped over my vision. My mouth gasped dryly as my taste buds shut down. I became blind, deaf and mute as Darius burrowed his way through my bodily functions and took control.

My new arm twitched as my metal skin writhed in response to the telepath's attack.

The machinery in my head kicked into gear and burst with electricity, reclaiming control over my synapses. My metal arm clamped against the wall. Stone crunched between my fingers and I relished the coarse feeling. My gift roared triumphantly in retaliation and I sent my focus flying upstairs.

I grabbed control of the nearest camera and locked eyes with Darius. Those pale dead eyes dilated. His face contorted with confusion as he saw himself through my eyes. I made the light above his head erupt into a stream of electric fire. The heat seared his arm and he yelled through my lips. I grasped my bare arm, as I felt his pain shooting across my skin.

"That hurt," I heard myself say and saw Darius grabbing his head through the camera lens. He grabbed my mind again and then recoiled in repulsion.

"You've done something different, William," screamed a prisoner from a locked cell. They threw their body against the steel door as Darius's words whispered through their lips. "My blood is inside you. This shouldn't be so difficult. Why do you taste different?"

"I've re-forged my brain, so that you can never take control again," I said proudly, as the darkness lashed at the periphery of my artificial mind.

"That sounds like a challenge. Not all of you is artificial,

Doctor Hart. I will find a way into the remaining pink mush inside your skull. It's only a matter of time. Soon, I will be able to learn anything that I want and connect with anyone that I wish."

"We're not connected anymore," I told the monster that had haunted me for so long. "Give back my family and surrender. We can talk about this. I can help you."

"It doesn't matter," Darius whispered inside our ears. "You can't cut me out, William. You can't run from me, Jessica. Every moment that passes I get even stronger. I am going to break you both. Everyone will succumb to my will."

Raven gasped and fell against the wall. She clenched her fist and punched herself in the thigh. The pain forced her back to reality and she dragged me down the corridor.

"We need to hurry up," she said desperately. "I really don't want that to happen again."

"Why?" I asked. "What did you see?"

Raven haunted expression answered my question as we ran down the corridor. As our footsteps clunked against the tiles, I heard a slow chuckle from the victim's possessed lips. Their laughter filled my skull as I tried to block the mocking call of Darius Cain. I focused on our footsteps that echoed heavily along the corridors between the labyrinth of cells.

A faint clacking sound echoed in response to our steps. It grew sharper for a moment, before disappearing entirely.

We ran away from the possessed and I tried not to think what would happen when he assumed control of Raven. She was clenching her jaw viciously and rubbed her eyes as a flood of tears dripped out.

"No," she whispered. "Not here."

Raven stopped outside a door with a glowing red sign reading that it was cell number one. It was strange. I thought I had opened all of the cell doors, but this one had remained closed despite my efforts. I moved my hand to release the prisoner, but Raven grabbed my metal wrist. I winced slightly as the metal grew red hot under her touch.

"Not this one," she begged. "Never open this one."

"If it distracts Darius, then it's perfect," I argued.

"It's not worth the risk," she interrupted. "This is where they keep him."

I stared at her silently, but part of me already knew the answer.

"Mimic," she hushed. "I've been hearing him since I got shot. He has telepathy as well. I think Darius showed him the way into my mind. He hasn't left me alone. He's forcing me to remember Old Street. He wants me to understand why he did it. I can hear him now…"

Curiosity clenched at my gut and impulse made me step forwards. There was an electronically controlled shutter that allowed view into this cell. All I had to do was connect with it.

"Hart?" Raven asked wildly. "What are you doing?"

Before I could stop myself, I made the shutter slam open and finally met Mimic again. He was being held up by chains that were secured tightly around his limbs. His hair had grown straggled during his three-year imprisonment and hung heavily over his shoulders. His eyes flashed open and Raven jammed her hands over her ears.

"Come on!" Mimic yelled as he rattled against his restraints. His filthy hair hid most of his face, but his mad steel eyes demanded that I let him out. "Let me join in the party! It will be fun. I promise."

"Close it!" Raven shouted. "Please. Close the damn shutter!"

I regained control and moved to close the shutter. Suddenly Mimic's eyes turned to a stark shade of blue. He used my own gift against me. He pushed open the shutter with his power, whilst I tried to close it.

"Good luck saving your family, Will! At this rate, you will never make it home in time for dinner!" Mimic added sarcastically. "Be realistic. I've got a score to settle too. I've known Darius for an endless amount of time. He showed me how to control people's minds after all. He is the closest thing I've got to a father! Let me out and it will all be over in minutes. I'll make sure that he pays for every last person that mind rapist has ever laid his sights on."

"Not a chance," I grunted.

"Very well," he sighed. "I've always known everything about

you, Will. I know you won't change your mind. Send my love to the coward. I'll see her soon."

Mimic stopped copying my gift and relaxed into his restraints. The shutter slammed shut.

"I think he was referring to you," I said to Raven who was rocking back and forth. "He sends his regards."

"Shut the hell up," Raven snapped shakily. "I heard every word that monster said. I heard much more than you ever will. I can still hear him. Why won't he leave me alone?"

"What's the history between you?"

"Too much," Raven shuddered. "Not enough…"

A low moan resounded down the corridor. Raven swore violently and fired out a blast of flames. Her fire illuminated the hallway as a wretched man slammed into my body. We wrestled for several moments. My back slammed into the wall. My arm pushed with increased strength and sent the man flying into the opposite wall. He attacked again and ploughed into my body. Our combined weight plummeted into a neighboring cell and pounded into the floor.

Raven raced into the cell as the man clawed at my chest. She wrenched him easily aside and I heard his bones cracking. Her palm ignited and her fire revealed the man.

He was extremely thin, his ribs stuck out at sharp angles and his gangly limbs overlapped each other. His flesh was covered in scars and shallow red wounds. He was muttering unintelligible sounds.

The man pushed leapt back on top of me. His gaunt face filled my eyes. At the centre of his forehead was the grey shell of a bullet embedded into his skull.

The possessed man's face began to steam. The bullet dropped from his fizzling flesh and rattled to the ground. His jaw stretched as his chest heaved and he spat out another bullet. He stopped muttering in his own language, as his eyes became black.

"Hello, William," Darius Cain said through the immortal man's mouth. "Do you remember me?"

34 - Nightmare

My forehead burned fiercely. I screamed as the bullet burrowed into my brain. It crushed through my layers of skin, frail bone and fleshy innards of my complex synapses. My chest seized as another bullet plummeted through my ribcage and slammed into my heart. The muscle crippled on impact, sending spasms shuddering through my gargantuan body.

As my lungs finally gave up, the last thing I saw was Hart. His arm was crushed under a car and there was a stab wound in his chest.

I watched as Hart struggled to stay alive from his fatal wounds. A smile crept along my heavy face as the construction site disappeared and my body ceased to function.

"It's a matter of perspective, William. It's time that you felt the pain that has been caused due to your pitiful existence."

I gasped desperately, clutching my head and chest, searching for the bullets. I tried to pull myself away from the other man's tortured mind that Darius was forcing me to endure.

"You're not going anywhere, Doctor Hart."

The thin man cracked my head against the floor. His dry hands wrapped around my throat and I struggled against his surprising strength. I couldn't get him off, he was too strong. I looked madly around the spinning room.

Where the hell was Raven?

I could get out of this myself. I just needed to think of another way to fight back.

Through the man's crazed eyes, I could see Darius Cain watching with his televisionic vision. This man was a window. Nothing more and nothing less. And windows could be broken.

I sent my memory plummeting to the darkest point from my past.

"Is this a pathetic effort to retaliate? What do you honestly hope to do?"

We were in the river together. The water slammed into our chests and forced the oxygen out of our bodies. I swirled against the fierce current and slammed into the car at the bottom of the river. The other man plummeted into the car window and the cracked lines became illuminated with marine light. Through the glass, I could see the terrified face of a fifteen year-old boy using his phone to the highlight the glass.

We floated outside my parent's grave. The car flickered in the watery depths of my memory. The man twisted underwater in confusion. His skinny body gasped as water flooded his lungs. Bubbles screamed from his starved mouth as the liquid surged into his body.

I swam forwards, grabbed his head and slammed it into the glass. The river consumed the terrified passengers and swallowed the vehicle in a single savage attack.

I forced him to watch it all. Me. My mother. My father. All of us struggling to survive. I forced him to watch my parents trying to escape the crashed car. My pain flooded his mind and drowned him. I kicked away from the car and swam smoothly towards the surface that I confidently knew I would be able to reach.

His hand clamped around my ankle. I kicked his gaunt face, which cracked like porcelain. His face splintered and darkness swallowed the entire memory.

"A decent effort to confuse my subject. Now... I believe it is my turn."

The marble steps thudded under my huge feet. I swore thickly in my mother tongue of Russian. The air smelled of gunpowder and sweat. This wasn't the plan. She promised she wouldn't lose control. She promised this wouldn't happen.

The assault rifle disassembled quickly in my practiced hands, before I threw it in the bin as planned. I rushed to the banister of the Cain Corporation foyer and cursed as Lucy Quayin destroyed our workplace.

She was piloting the ATV and firing directly at Mr Cain. I smiled with satisfaction as the machine demolished the foyer. The destruction sent a surge of adrenaline through my pounding heart. Lucy destroyed the glass lift and sent it plummeting to the white floor. Shards of deadly glass ploughed into the wall and shattered into a million pieces on contact.

It was utterly beautiful.

I need to help her. Together we were unstoppable. Together there was nothing we couldn't do…

"What do think you're doing? Get the hell down here," Mr Cain demanded over the communicator strapped to my chest. I glanced down at Mr Cain on the wooden stage used for his fancy presentation. "Stop gawping and assist me! What are you waiting for? Get down here, you stupid immortal ape!"

I looked between him and Lucy. My employer or my lover? I felt myself step away from the choice. I would let the Fates decide.

My mind flooded back to my life in Saint Petersburg. My mother believed in the Fates. Like many others in recent years, she followed it religiously. She told me that every being on this earth had a thread of life. The thread was made by Nono, measured by Decima and could be cut at any point by Morta. The sister of death was the most dreadful of the three Fates that filled my childhood with nightmares of my life being cut away.

Tria Fata. Nono, Decima and Morta. Birth, life and death.

Saint Petersburg had survived the Global War, but Moscow had fallen in the fifth year. Part of me knew it would only be a matter of time before Morta cut our thread too. My mother didn't make it through the Blackout. The cold winter destroyed all those too weak to survive. Any hopes of a Russian great city were demolished in those frozen years.

I vowed to fight. I wouldn't stop until I was in total security over my own existence. I joined with Mr Cain and was rewarded with a gift of immortality. Morta would never cut me down. Most things are within our control, but sometimes we can submit to the will of the sisters.

I didn't need to choose a side. I could still leave this foyer with partnerships with both parties. All I had to do was allow the sisters to fix everything.

By the time I had made my way downstairs to Vincent, the ATV had ascended the foyer and cornered the Doctor. It looked like Decima had smiled brightly on my partnership with Lucy.

"I'm glad you finally decided to turn up," Vincent said incredulously.

"There were lots of stairs," I grunted.

"I don't have time for your excuses, Anton. I know you've been associating with my sister. There is no point denying it. I have proof of your rendezvous on our surveillance system. Did you really think you could delete material from my network and I wouldn't see it? I have footage of you escorting Lucy to her apartment for Fates sake. Let us talk freely. I don't care about your union. However, I know about the assault rifle you pointed at my head ten minutes ago! As a result, I know that you really don't want me to order you to shoot at Miss Quayin."

"Mr Cain…"

"Hold your fire!" Cain commanded his forces. "I want Doctor Hart unharmed. He has done exceptionally well so far and I want to see what he will do next."

"What do you mean, sir?"

"Retaliation, Anton. Fight or flight. It's the classic kill or be killed scenario. I want to see if his gift kicks into gear or not."

"But what about Lucy? She is your sister."

"Think with that nugget brain for a second. Where does your loyalty lie? With the man who saved you from meaningless existence or the woman who is just using you?"

A flash of light screamed out from above and the ATV crippled and fell from the wall. It slammed into the marble floor, blasting stone and dust into the air. As the smoke cleared, I saw that the machine was destroyed, though its limbs had contorted in an attempt to protect the cockpit. I walked toward the cockpit that was filled with smoke, until I saw the crimson splatter that I was overly familiar with. I ripped opened the cockpit.

Lucy's body was broken beyond medical repair. Her bones were crippled, her skin bruised and her once sharp face was now vacant. I picked up her fragile head in my hand and kissed her burnt hair.

She still looked beautiful to me.

Her body flickered and shimmered momentarily, as her body grew completely invisible to the human eye.

I found her fragile head and kissed it softly…

"Feel his pain, William. You murdered the one person he ever loved. You

destroyed the only thing he cared about!"

A vicious clacking stabbed into my hearing. I winced as the pain reverberated through my spine. The cynical laugh echoed ferociously. I had to fight back, I couldn't let Darius break me this simply. I struggled as Anton's memories mixed with mine even further.

I recalled the last time I saw Theo. Stranz silenced him a sleeping hold. My son had suffocated, as Stranz starved him of oxygen.

Hart became filled with anger as I silenced his son. I weighed the boy in my arms. My hands shook momentarily. I looked down at the silent child and wondered what the hell I had become.

Reality swept away and became swallowed in a storm of disorientating darkness. Reality was erased entirely. An individual person condensed into existence and gave purpose to the empty world. Stranz stood alone in the endless space. His bulbous body filled only a speck of the vacant void. His tiny pupils glared at a solitary target.

I blinked.

Vincent Cain was in the void holding his gun, aimed point blank at his friend's forehead. Stranz's skin steamed momentarily.

I blinked again.

I replaced Cain. I was wearing a shirt and tie, my black rimmed glasses lying heavily on my nose. The gun fired in my hands, the bullet slamming out of the weapon and plummeting into Anton Stranz's head. I dropped the weapon in horror and it fell endlessly under my feet. I looked up at Stranz as the bullet entered his mind and destroyed his flesh.

He swayed for a moment as the projectile tore into his cranium, before his face collapsed completely.

Stranz opened his eyes. With both his hands, he buried his stubby fingers into the bullet wound. Black fluid dribbled out of the hole and Stranz proceeded to pull his face apart. Chunk by fleshy chunk, he ripped away his old skin and threw it away. He tore his gargantuan body apart, shedding his chrysalis, until only the skinny man remained.

A severe itching burned the back of my neck and I scratched the thin hard scar.

The genocidal fire of Old Street flashed through my mind.

Hart reached behind his head and ripped at his flesh. He tore himself apart with several savage strokes. The pristine Doctor was replaced with an individual lacerated with metal. His glasses were gone and his skin was covered with scars. His arm was replaced by a whirring assortment of metal and light that hummed as his mind worked rapidly behind those tired eyes. The most haunting part was his chest. A series of cables laced into the point where he had been stabbed. It looked like Hart had been through hell.

Stranz's flesh began to steam ferociously, as his skinny form grew once again. I raised my metal arm and blasted a bolt of energy into the broken man and shattered the dream.

I opened my eyes to reality and saw Stranz writhing nearby. He clawed his head and his skin bubbled as he healed himself again. Before Stranz could attack again, I grabbed his limbs with cables and pinned him against the wall. I shook away the confusing memories of Anton Stranz, the flashes of matriarchal love and firm faith, and acknowledged his hatred for the murder of his beloved Lucy Quayin.

I pushed those thoughts of sympathy away and decided that it was time to end the brute. Sedatives buried themselves into his skin and slowed his healing process whilst metal enveloped over his flesh to stop him from leaving this cell.

I sealed the immortal man in a coffin of sedated metal. His grunts of discomfort were muzzled by my gift and replaced with heavy silence in the confined cell.

"How disappointing," she whispered in my ear. I twisted around and lashed out at the voice.

There was no one there. The cell was empty. The door was shut. The only people in the room were myself and Anton.

"There is no escaping them," Stranz groaned from his steel coffin. "They are playing with you. Don't you see? He will do everything he can to destroy you. She will cut your throat. They will finish the job. They will break you!"

My metal skin twitched in fury. I secured Anton's restraints around his jaw and drilled several needles into his skull to provide scheduled electrified paralysis.

The immortal Anton Stranz was silenced forever.

There was a sharp clacking sound nearby. I turned around again and saw nothing. I shook my head in confusion, until the door began creaking. The door handle slowly began to turn. I wrenched it open, but only found an empty corridor.

Something pushed me from behind and slammed the door shut. I looked rapidly along the flickering corridor to find my enemy, my heart racing as I found nothing once again.

I heard the crackle of gunfire, screams, cynical laughter and clacking footsteps in the distance. Launching to my feet, I chased the piercing sound along the labyrinthine corridors. I tore along the twisted corridors, until I found myself in another foyer surrounded by wide windows that overlooked Prima. Straight ahead was the staircase that led to Darius Cain and my family.

In the middle of the foyer was Raven and several Outcasts. She hugged an older Kubran man with dreadlocks briefly, who was roughly the same age as me. He placed a tired hand on Raven's shoulder. It was clear he held some form of authority over the group. Next to him, was a spindly younger man with thick glasses and a hat to hide his shaggy hair. He nodded nervously, before anxiously placing his gaze ahead. There was also a girl, not much older than Raven, with white bandages all over her arms who held a stern focus towards the staircase. Finally, she greeted another boy who was clutching his side in pain. I over heard that his name was Julian as she touched his arm. He flinched slightly as his dark hair hung over his eyebrows and looked at his wristwatch anxiously.

There was a rumbling of footsteps as the staircase filled with soldiers who held their guns at the group. I sensed thirty-two guns in total. A knot of hatred swelled in my gut as the Lunan, Pierre Foshe, forced his way to the front. Foshe spared a moment to re-tie his silver hair.

There were screams coming behind me and I turned to see the prisoners charging down the corridor. In the flickering light, I could see the Mind Walker gazing through their possessed eyes.

One of them limped severely. A lump caught in my throat as Mark Bolton's possessed eyes met mine.

I prepared to fight the onslaught when a woman suddenly materialized before my eyes. Their gift fluttered as they vanished out of sight. There was a flash of white teeth. The hiss of machinery. A waft of heated steam blasted into my face. Their wild, dirtied blonde hair whipped in my peripheral vision. She appeared right in front of me and her hand clamped my face. I flinched under her metallic touch.

Lucy Quayin glared maliciously. Her irises were discolored electric blue and grey. The white of her eyes were bloodshot. Her previously porcelain skin was bruised purple and yellow. Her flesh steamed lightly and the machinery hissed in discordant unison. The colour of her skin briefly changed as it grossly attempted to heal itself. The woman was a destroyed and distorted version of herself.

Her fingers dug into my neck and I gasped as her cold nails drew blood. I immediately sensed my nerve plug at the back of her neck. It hummed with familiarity and allowed a brief glimpse at the complex machinery keeping her alive. I couldn't help but release a small smile as I discovered that my exo-skeleton was being used to hold her body together. It had been refashioned as a brace for her entire body. It was stapled into her spine and lacerated around her limbs. Her fingers had become a collection of blades that could be activated instantly. She had taken my technology and corrupted it as she had always planned. She released my face and the machinery disappeared from my mind.

Fire flashed behind us, as Raven ignited her hands. Foshe activated his stun baton in a burst of purple electricity. My senses flinched as the soldiers armed their weapons. Bolt roared inhumanely as the possessed prisoners surged into the open space.

35 – Onslaught

I tore all thirty-two weapons to shreds and the soldiers gasped in pain as their guns exploded in their hands. Raven launched herself at the flailing guards. Her palms ignited and she fired a series of punches into their disorientated bodies.

"Poor choice, William," Quayin said. I flicked my focus back to the sound of her voice and raised my metal arm just in time to block her attack. Her arm sliced my prosthetic apart, rupturing it instantly.

Quayin grinned excitedly. The exoskeleton glinted menacingly along the fractured contours of her broken bones.

"Look at what you've created!" she laughed. "You know what? I'll admit it. You were actually right! The nerve plug does complete humanity. I feel stronger than ever."

Her steel heels ripped into the floor, as she moved with mechanical precision and kicked widely to cut my throat. I dropped down and narrowly dodged the blade.

A prisoner on fire barreled between us, madly attempting to put out the flames. Quayin screamed in frustration and her body flickered out of sight.

I frantically tried to find her, but the room was filled with chaos. Frantic bodies fought throughout the room. I dodged a pair of struggling men. A blast of a gunshot cracked against the glass. My mind flickered and destroyed the gun I had somehow missed. Simmers of gifts flashed around the room. An explosion of light. A crackle of electricity. I searched for Quayin and black eyes looked back everywhere, gleaming with glee. Fire burst upwards in rapid succession. The Outcast woman with white bandages around her arms pinned a soldier against the window, a growl crawled out of her throat. A clacking of mechanical feet scratched nearby.

The man on fire grabbed my shoulders, and then there was a squelching sound as he met his sudden end. I saw metal glinting in his chest and then it disappeared instantly. Nausea hit my throat and I pushed the man's body aside and forced myself to take the chaos to my advantage. I pressed towards the staircase...

I was suddenly shoved in the chest and was thrown backwards. Quayin materialised above my prone body.

"I should thank you for this gift," Quayin gasped. "It's so beautiful. It makes you wonder why the hell Vincent kept this from me. I've never felt so in control in my entire life. I have no idea how I ever existed without it!"

"You should be dead," I said grimly. "I saw you fall. Your nerve endings were incinerated."

"My father saved me. Whilst Vincent was chasing you across Prima, my father made the few people in his control look after me. They carried me upstairs, fused me to your skeleton and pumped Stranz's regenerative blood into my veins. And now I am finally complete."

"I know exactly what you mean," I snarled and raised my destroyed arm at the broken woman. The arm sent a burst of energy out of its shattered remains. Quayin dissipated and the blast scorched a hole in the ceiling.

I pulled myself to my feet and barreled forwards. A soldier rushed to stop me, so I stretched my palm out and connected with twenty-six holo-phones in the vicinity. I made earsplitting noise pour out from their speakers, making the soldier clutch his ears. I kneed him roughly in the stomach and cracked the remains of my metal elbow into his spine.

I deactivated the noise and commanded the devices to attach to my shattered limb. One-by-one, the holo-devices plummeted into my broken limb. They reconstructed themselves to become makeshift grenades to utilize at my command.

Mark Bolton shouted with frustration across the room as he butted heads with another guard. He met my eyes and smiled grimly.

"You should have mentioned this was part of the job description," Bolt laughed raucously. "I would have signed up without hesitating!"

"Don't have too much fun!" I called, relieved he was in control of himself. "Don't forget that we've got to get back to work later."

"Stuff that!" Mark shouted and punched the man in the gut. "I don't think I'm cut out for science. But this is definitely within my skill set."

"The world of neurology shall miss you dearly!" I added sarcastically.

Bolt opened his mouth to throw another retort back, before retching roughly. His head flicked up sharply and his eyes began to weep black tears.

"Don't you see, William?" Bolt said darkly. "I am inside your best friend's mind. Soon... I will be able to control everything."

Bolt raised his arm and hissed with anger as Darius tried to make his flesh transform. For a moment, the skin protruded with spikes of earth. Bolt grimaced fiercely, fighting against the demon taking to control his gift, and his arm returned to normal.

"Keep going, Will!" Mark shouted, his eyes returning to their usual shade of brown. "I can see what he wants. You're the only one that has a chance of stopping him. You've got to take out that bastard before he controls you too! You can't let him do this."

"I'm working on it!"

"Work faster, Hart. Use that big head and figure out how to snap his blasted neck!"

The guard slammed into Bolt and he armored his flesh in response. Chunks of debris flew outwards as their combined weight cracked the concrete. I fired a makeshift grenade into the prisoner's flesh and I sent the battery into overdrive, firing electricity into his body.

"Now you're getting the hang of it!" Darius screamed in my ear and I turned to face Pierre Foshe, his eyes glinting with possessive darkness.

His stun baton extended and lashed at my head. I laughed as the prod disintegrated and joined with my evolving arm. I use to baton to fire a burst of electricity into Foshe's chest and the Lunan was thrown into a group of his servants. Foshe regained his crooked posture with a sick grin on his face, as the darkness in his eyes swirled.

"Is that all you've got, boy?" Foshe and Darius said together. I realized that Foshe had accepted the invasive force on his mind. "I'd recommend listening to the man upstairs. I admire someone who wants to change the world for the better. Sacrifice will bring humanity into new heights of liberation. Join us, Doctor. We're growing stronger by the minute."

Foshe grabbed one of the Outcast's arms. It was the anxious boy with broken glasses. My arm revolved as I prepared to fire another grenade. Raven grabbed my arm and her concern made us both hesitate before making a move. I could tell she didn't want to burn him by accident.

Foshe breathed in sharply and I saw something change within him. The veins in his neck protruded with a thick shade of purple. His gnarled hands twitched and the boy screamed out in pain. Foshe laughed viciously as Darius used his gift. The boy's skin began to visibly decay before our eyes.

I fired my arm twice into the floor. The grenades ignited into swift bursts of fire. The pyrokinetic launched into action and lashed the fires into Foshe's flesh. He released the Outcast, which allowed Raven to rugby tackle the boy out of danger. Raven screamed as Foshe wrapped his burnt hand around her ankle.

I found several weapons scattered on the floor and I summoned them into my arm. I reassembled them and my metal limb fully formed again. I fired several bullets at Foshe's legs to disable him.

Bolt barreled between us both, stopping my bullets from meeting their target. The bullets zipped harmlessly off his rocky armor. His head twisted and Darius looked right at me.

"It doesn't take me long to figure people out," my friend said as he edged forwards. "Put me inside someone's head for a couple minutes and we will become best friends. We are well acquainted now. I know all about his pub and the girlfriend he kicked out of his house when my dreams sent him crazy. I know all about that terrible day he lost his brother. Oh, do you think he knows that you were the one that dragged him out that car? Well... he knows now!"

I fired the remainder of my grenades into Bolt's armor and

made them burrow into his rock-filled skin. I ignited each of them and leapt to the side as he charged.

Wild flame blazed between us as Raven fired a torrent of flame from her palms and blasted Bolt aside.

"I'm coming for you, Darius," I told my broken friend. "Just hold on, Bolt. I'm going to make sure he never hurts anyone ever again."

"I'm counting on it," said Raven quietly. I stepped back in horror as her eyes dribbled with black tears. "After everything that Jessica and you have done together this week. It's only fair that she is the one to take your life."

Raven's head blossomed with fire, forcing the black tear to evaporate from her face. "You should run, Hart," she said quickly as she struggled to keep control. "I hear that it's an excellent tactic!"

Raven lashed out, her fist crunching into my metal ribs. I stepped back from the wild, possessed girl as she moved to kill me. Her skin flickered frantically with fire as she stopped Darius from taking control of her gift. Raven launched a series of practiced punches and I barely defended myself against her attacks. I pushed her back, before I raised my metal arm and loaded a bullet to fire at her head.

"Do it, Hart," she said. "Finish it before he can use my fire."

"I can't…" I said quietly. "I can't kill you."

"That is why you are weak. You'll never be able to do what's necessary to survive in this world."

"Who is talking to me right now?"

"These gifts are beautiful, Hart. Live like me. Embrace the power within you. Don't deny the rest of the world the chance to be free!"

"You're wrong. This is a curse. We all lose control. These gifts cannot be left unchecked. This has to end."

Raven spat and her saliva boiled viciously between my feet. Her tired eyes gleamed, begging me to shoot her, whilst simultaneously taunting me.

"You can't run from me. Just do it already, Hart. End it! I will beat your head against the wall, until your complex collection of synapses becomes pink vacant flesh splattered into the decor. I can't stop him, Hart! I can control every single person in this room. He's only going to get stronger. And soon, I will be able to burn you with this girl's power."

Raven raised her hand and Darius carefully clicked her fingers. A dash of fire ruptured from her skin. Darius smiled darkly through Raven's lips and her eyes grew inevitably opaque. She ignited her palms and thrust them fiercely forwards. Her fierce fire blasted straight towards me.

Bolt leapt in the way to block the infernal flame and flashes of fire exploded around his armored body. I winced as the hot embers cascaded over my ankles. I stayed behind my friend to protect myself. Bolt walked forwards, struggling against the intense heat, as he continued to shield me from Raven's blaze of fire. He crunched his fist fiercely against the floor and Raven stumbled for a second. He pressed forwards and slammed a fist into her ribs, sending her plummeting backwards.

"Go save your family, Will!" Mark shouted. "We'll keep him distracted. Go, hurry, before he get inside my…"

Bolt gasped suddenly and clutched his chest. His heart glowed a violent shade of pulsating dark red. His body ruptured. The fire leapt out of the hole in his chest and melted his solid flesh instantly. The flames crawled through his flesh in fiery lines and hot spurts of blood burst out through the gaps in his skin.

Mark Bolton collapsed with a sickening thud and became completely still. I screamed out in horror as my best friend died trying to save my life.

I looked down at the charred body in shock, unable to take in what had just happened. My eyes centered on Raven standing where Bolt had been stood with her palm extended. It glowed with hot white light. Her power died out and she snapped back to reality to discover what she had just done.

Raven's mouth gaped with horrified emotion. Words tried to come out of her, but there was nothing that could be said that would bring him back. There was nothing she could do to change what she had done. She stared at her smoking hands in disgust and clenched them with confused anger.

"I'm so sorry," she shuddered. "He's in my head. I didn't have control."

"No…" I said solemnly and glared at the apparently blameless girl. "You lost control, Jessica."

Foshe's sick laughter interrupted us, as he grabbed the eldest Outcast. The Kubran writhed in pain as Foshe decayed his flesh. The dreadlocked man's eyes flickered white as Darius tried to take control of his gift as well.

"You heard your friend…" Raven said quietly. "Stop Mind Walker. I'll handle this."

"What do you mean you'll handle it?" I asked numbly.

"Do you want your family back or not?" Raven snapped, trying to hold back her tears. "I'll do my part. Make sure you do yours."

My feet dragged me away and before I knew what was happening, I was already halfway up the stairs.

A sharp clicking splintered the air as Quayin invisibly ascended behind me. She chased me up the stairs and I shook my head to get the piercing noise out of my eardrums.

Mark's face was all I could see. His last moments burnt vividly into my mind. His collapsing body and Raven standing in his place. Once again someone had lost control of their gift and Bolt had died.

Raven had chosen to fight when she could've fled. She wasn't blameless. She had a part in all this madness… from Old Street to today and beyond.

In the end, it was innocent people who paid the price. I wouldn't let Mark's sacrifice be for nothing.

I arrived at the door to the clinic and became aware of the perpetual silence. I breathed shakily, before stepping forwards. The silence was interrupted by steel grinding against concrete. The sound scraped along the floor, as a series of scratches ripped open the floor to reveal the piping underneath the surface.

Quayin was circling me, like a shark stalking its prey. I understood her actions. She could have hurt me at any point and I was always powerless to stop her. She had remained hidden and let the entire sequence take place.

She appeared and held my cheek in her cold hand. The decision to kill me simmered through her tormented eyes. They flickered darkly.

"My father wishes to speak with you," Quayin told me. "Make one wrong move and I will not hesitate to kill you. Is that understood?"

Her patronizing tone reminded me of the innocent days when she used to berate me for not achieving greatness at work.

"You always loved ultimatums, Miss Quayin." I replied coldly. "Don't worry, I understand you perfectly. I'm eager to meet the Mind Walker at last."

36 – Face your Demons

I saw Darius Cain in reality for the very first time. The elderly man stood with his back to me. He wore a fitted pair of dark trousers, but was otherwise topless and barefoot. His pale spotted skin shone sickly in the clinical light. He seemed oblivious to my existence.

Quayin clamped my arms behind my back and pushed me firmly forwards, as several doctors brought fresh clothes for Darius to choose from. He raised a frail hand and waved the people away to be replaced.

A pair of men dragged themselves up from the floor, their twisted limbs unfurling as they rose to stand. My heart sank as the two most powerful men I'd ever met were controlled like marionette puppets. Xander and Vincent obeyed the Mind Walker completely and shuddered in his presence.

Vincent Cain grabbed the nearby white shirt from the rejected doctor, with a hint of reluctance, and wrapped it around his father's shoulders.

"Thank you, my son," Darius said and allowed Vincent to fasten the buttons on his chest. "This will do nicely."

"My… pleasure," Vincent said through slightly gritted teeth.

Xander carried a pair of black trousers with trembling hands to his new master. Darius looked at them in disgust and placed his thumb on Xander's forehead.

Black tears flowed out of his eyes and his muscles twitched in response to the mental torture. Darius sent him away with a wave of his hand and Xander turned to face the nearby glass window.

"You stopped me once before and I punished you for that transgression. I will not let you do it again," Darius told Xander. "Think like that again and I will make sure you meet that concrete seven floors below. Your gift won't be able to save you."

"I'm intrigued," I said curiously. "What exactly is his gift?" Darius finally turned. His dead pupils narrowed and his face widened into a slow nonchalant smile. He moved his head slightly as though he had just heard something, before looking at his son and allowing him to speak.

"Now that would be telling," Vincent said quietly and I recalled him saying the exact same thing to me about his own gift.

"It is taking everything in my power to remain standing," Xander announced.

"He is the strongest I've taken control of," Darius confirmed. "I made sure to leash him first, but they all break eventually. Only you are the only one left, William. I can't wait to learn how you augmented your mind to prevent my presence. I'm look forward to dissecting that excuse of a brain. The things I will do with your gift when you are under my control…"

"He will never submit to you freely. You can't take our free will," Xander snarled fiercely. "We will always despise…"

Darius looked sharply at Xander and made him smacked his head into the glass wall in retaliation to his insubordination.

"Alexander…" he sighed in deep haunted frustration. "You'll always be an eternal paradoxal thorn in my side. On the day that you arrived at my estate all those years ago… I wish I'd immediately shot you for trespassing."

I didn't care about their twisted past and riddles. The only thing I wanted was what he had promised me.

"Where are they?" I demanded.

"Don't interrupt my father," Quayin snapped in my ear.

"It's quite alright, Lucy," Darius purred. "William has travelled a long way. He deserves his resolution and I deserve to finish getting dressed."

He clapped his hands and two people sat up in the hospital beds nearby. The white sheets that covered their faces dropped and my wife and son climbed out of their beds.

I bit my tongue as Adele approached him. She limped heavily and she grasped momentarily at the bandage wrapped around her leg. Vincent had shot her in the leg. I would never forget that. Darius gently kissed her on the cheek and I clenched my fist with rage. Theo arrived with socks, shoes and a tie. I swallowed the lump in my throat as my child helped Darius into his shoes.

"You should've accepted my paradise," he continued as

Theo's small hands pulled the socks over Darius's ankles. "It was the perfect reward."

"It wasn't real," I told him. "I couldn't live with myself."

"You had everything. You could have lived in another world."

"I couldn't rest knowing that the world I'd left behind was going to be filled with people with gifts and ruled by you."

"People like you, William," Darius corrected. "I only desire to set them all free. So what exactly is *your* goal here? You want to stop people becoming like you? Is that it?"

"Yes," I responded numbly. I thought about what I had become and the people who died because of me. Everyone that I couldn't save at Old Street. The soldiers at the construction site when I lost control. Lucy Quayin's downfall. I remembered Mark Bolton downstairs.

I'd become a monster.

"There is no need to be so harsh on yourself," Darius said, and I realized he could know hear my thoughts again. I wouldn't be long before he'd able take control. He waved Adele over to start doing his tie. "You've become complete, which if I recall correctly, is exactly what your work downstairs was aiming to do all along."

"I've seen the truth. I've seen what these powers can do."

"You're deluded, William. Limitation has always been your problem. A fear to stay within routine and control. You need to see the value of your original ideology. Remember how you relished every moment of this gift? You let go and became god. You were truly complete. So, how about I give the same gift of completion to those you love?"

I launched myself forward to stop him. The machinery in the room thrashed in an effort to attack him.

Darius moved his hand suddenly and Xander began punching the glass wall violently in an attempt to smash it.

I did my best to ignore the sound of bone cracking against fracturing glass. The image of the cracks in the window growing wider, like the window in my parent's car plummeting in the watery abyss. The water filled my lungs, suffocating, drowning me and taking hold of any sense of reality.

I shook my head violently to get Darius out and demanded that the lights overload. Darius stumbled back as a torrent of electricity scorched the bed at his side.

Vincent Cain suddenly shook out of his stupor and wrapped his hand around a nearby hypodermic needle. His body flickered violently, vanish roughly and appeared next to his father. Darius simply raised his hand and clamped his fingers around his son's skull.

"Impudent child," Darius snarled. "Every moment I was unconscious in that bed, I made sure that darkness remained inside your skull. It was suitable punishment for turning your father into a vegetable. Just because I'm busy right now, doesn't mean you should get any ideas about reinvigorating those dead synapses. The gift remains on lockdown, boy."

Cain dropped to his haunches and screamed in agony as a torrent of darkness and blood poured from his eyes.

"At least I have one child sharing my vision for the future," Darius nodded impatiently at his daughter.

Her metal fingers cut in my bare arm. I set my mechanical arm into action and fired several rounds blindly. She hissed in fury as the bullets sizzled into her flesh. She disappeared entirely and my body crawled in horror as Quayin phased through my body and reappeared in front of me. She spared the smallest moment to smile before she wrapped her hand around my neck again.

"You made me into this," she spat as her fingers tightened around my windpipe. "You fried almost every nerve in my body and I'm pumped up on Anton's healing blood. So right now, I can't feel the three bullets you just fired into my leg. Within the hour they will be healed. Your pet science project is the only thing holding me up. And the gift you gave me is evolving by every passing moment. At first I was just invisible and now I can do so much more..."

Quayin's fingers phased out of existence and sank into my neck. She partially reformed them inside my windpipe and I choked in repulsion as she touched my trachea.

"Lucy," her father said. "I'm not done with him yet."

She removed her phasing digits, but kept her fingers around

my throat.

"You're sick!" I yelled. "Look at what you are doing to them. This isn't some form of holy intervention. You are killing your own children, Darius."

"I am showing them the truth," he spat with frustration, and made Adele and Theo grasp their heads.

"These two are easy," Darius told me. "Vincent has already put them through the process after your outburst in the Cain foyer. After they became *contaminated*, Vincent followed routine and put my blood in their heads to cut out the memory of your gift."

Adele was released from the telepath's. I presumed sadly that he had purposely released her to see how she would react.

"Will? What's going on?" She asked, confused. "Morta! What happened to your arm?"

"Just focus on me, Adele," I said as calmly as possible. "Listen to my voice. Don't think about him."

"About who…?" Adele asked before stopping suddenly. Her hands were buzzing fiercely. The air reverberated with static noise that climbed into a high-pitched whining sound. A shimmer of white lightning echoed across her beautiful brown skin. Her eyes twisted in panic and the whine grew too high for any of us to hear. Adele screamed out a horrific explosion of sound. Her voice burst into a sonic echo of anguish that made the hospital beds rattle furiously and the glass window splintered under the force of the sound.

Before the glass could smash completely, Darius raised his finger to his lips and Adele's mouth snapped shut, making the noise immediately stop. I met my wife's warm eyes as they became glazed and she dropped to the cold floor.

"Sonic emission. Interesting," Darius hummed, before turning his attention to Theo. He remained frozen on the spot. It was strange. I had never seen my son so still before. He stared forward vacantly as if he had just seen something truly shocking in the distance.

"Theo?" I asked quietly. "Daddy is here now. I've come to take you home."

Theo turned and looked at me uncertainly. "No, you're not," he replied numbly. "We're never going home. We're going live next to the stars."

"Let me hug you," I said. "It's your father."

"There's only half of you there, Dad," Theo pointed numbly at my metal arm and the steel woven into my chest. "I'm scared that you won't all be there. It will never be the same."

"I'm still your father…" I tried to tell him.

"For now," he interrupted. "But you are going to need more metal to keep on living."

I stood paralysed at my son's profound words. I breathed in sharply and felt my lungs momentarily struggle to function. Theo was right. I would need to sacrifice more of myself to machinery to exist efficiently.

"What have you done to him?" I demanded at Darius.

"I'm still your son," Theo said quietly. "But, now I can see that you're changing. Will you still be my Dad? You're going to be different."

"Precognition," Darius said proudly, ruffling Theo's hair who flinched under the old man's touch. "Tell me, Theodore. What happens after today?"

"Why don't you look in my head and find out?" Theo replied cheekily.

"I have lots to think about right now. Poking around your noggin and all of its endless possibilities won't help me to focus. Tell your father what I am going to do."

Theo looked up to me. He was a good boy. He still ignored the stranger's request and looked at his father for permission. I nodded at him hesitantly to continue.

"We're all going to become different," he told us. "Rich and poor. Kids and old people. Normal, weird and mad people too. There won't be a single person who won't change."

Theo suddenly grabbed his head, as he felt something difficult move through his mind. His hands shook and his eyes flickered. Theo's eyes filled with tears. A lump of guilt filled my throat as my son looked at me in fear. Theo's mind saw something horrific and deeply confusing. I knew instantly that it was related to me.

383

"The cycle never stops. The clock will spin around and you're going to start it, Dad. You build our future. You set the endless wheel spinning. The gifts start and end with you. You get to choose what happens to all of us. You can try and stop this, but you can't. The truth is going to get out."

"There you have it, William," Darius released Theo's mind and he collapsed next to his mother. "Even your son agrees that my future is inevitable."

"You have made your point," I said grimly and pondered over my child's haunting words. "Now where is my daughter? Give her to me, unharmed, and I might consider not tearing this building apart."

"That's quite the threat," Darius laughed.

I opened my mind and sent my senses rushing outwards. It flowed beyond Cain Corporation. Specks of bright light snapped to my attention. Dozens of hundreds of thousands of devices trickled against my synapses. Lights, phones, vehicles and televisions that were all connected by a complex network of electricity, satellite signals and radio waves. I sent my mind rushing to the heavens and found exactly what I was looking for.

A passenger jet. Currently 27,467 metres in the air due east. It was already descending. Its flight path was directing itself to land at Prima's airport to the west. With a simple redirection I could change its path permanently.

"You wouldn't dare," Darius hissed.

"You're the one who can see inside my mind. You probably know better than me if I would do it."

I felt him crawl slightly through my brain, despite the mental block. He searched my current state, my past and the possible future scenarios that I knew from experience he could partially speculate.

His eyes widened and his fingers twitched in dread. Everyone in the room momentarily regained focus, their eyes blurring as they claimed control of themselves. Darius breathed in sharply and seized mental hold over everyone again with his power.

For a moment I saw the Mind Walker lose control.

"Bring the girl in here," he demanded and Xander left the

glass wall, moving with impossible grace. It was only when he returned with Izzy that I saw that his knuckles were bruised with blood and broken glass. Izzy had a white bandage wrapped around her head and seemed in complete control. It was a tremendous relief to see her back on her feet after that blow.

"Dad? Thank Fate you're here! What's wrong with you chest? Why is there metal..." Izzy stopped as she saw her mother and brother lying unconscious on the floor. Tears of fear choked her words as ran over to them both.

"Unharmed," Darius said. "Untouched. I am a man of my word. She is going to be the final test of my power. There is none of my blood in her brain. She has never seen a gift. Isabella is completely innocent to all of this. She is perfect subject to see if I am at full power."

"What is he talking about...?" Izzy asked uncertainly, clutching her mother's unconscious head. "Why won't Mum wake up?"

"Don't listen to him," I said. "Don't listen to a single word he is saying."

"I want to know what is going on."

"You hear that?" Darius chimed. "She wants to know the truth."

"Shut up!" I snapped, pushing past Quayin and held my child's face in my hands.

"Perhaps you should be the one to tell her?" Darius laughed.

"Tell me what?" Izzy asked. "Why is everyone acting so strange?"

"Mum and Theo aren't very well. We are going to help them."

"That old pack of lies?" Darius interrupted. "Seriously? Now you sound like my boy over there."

Vincent clutched the bed and coughed violently. The white of his teeth disappeared underneath the dark substance filling his mouth and withholding his words.

"How about this?" Darius bargained. "Tell her the truth or I will."

"Leave her alone!" I said gritting my teeth in fury.

I grabbed the plane with my mind and assumed complete

control. All of its lights flickered. I tested the controls in the cockpit and let the plane dip suddenly. I could sense the pilots running a diagnostics check over their consoles.

"You won't do it," Darius bluffed arrogantly.

I couldn't let anyone beyond this building get dragged into this mess. Everyone with a gift was inside Cain Corporation. I had to stop this right now. This was the only action that eradicated gifts from existence.

I deactivated all the power to the jet. The lights plummeted the vehicle into darkness. The engines began to depower and the plane started its slow decline to the solid earth.

"They have started screaming, William. You are not just playing with a piece of technology. There are people up there. There are lives on the line," Darius reminded me. "They are scared that they're going to die. Would you like to hear them?"

"No," I said firmly, entirely focused on what I had to do. "I don't want to hear them."

The plane reactivated and I adjusted the flight path to fly directly into Cain Corporation. I felt the pilots rapidly attempting to adjust the controls. They were panicking. I felt several phones activating within the passenger section. Their pixels were forming into letters, words and sentences that were sent to Prima and beyond. Flight control was trying to get in contact. I had enough of this infuriating noise. I destroyed all communication. No one would be able get into contact with anyone on the plane.

"You'll kill us all," Darius said with an edge of panic finally rising in his voice. "What is this? You're not capable of this. You are weak."

"I am what you made me into," I replied systematically. "Anything is better than living in your world."

Quayin pulled me away from my daughter and gripped hold of me again. This time, her grasp seemed frantic and unfocused.

"What's happening, father?" Quayin asked. "What is he doing?"

"He has taken control of a plane," Darius replied numbly. "It's heading straight for us. I'm going to find a gift that can stop it."

"What is he talking about?" Izzy asked and ran over to talk to me. Xander's hand clutched her shoulder and held her tightly. "You wouldn't do that? You can't do that…"

Izzy's fear made Quayin hesitate. Her hands released me, as she glanced at the glass wall. There was a bright light on the horizon that was growing larger by the second. A horrible roar rumbled and grew louder by each passing moment.

"Xander!" Darius yelled at the green-eyed man he despised. "Use your power. Stop that plane!"

"You will… *not*… control me!" Xander hissed fiercely as his green eyes emerged from the darkness, as he fought fiercely against the Mind Walker trying to control his unknown power.

Quayin released me completely and she stared at the incoming aircraft. My exoskeleton hummed with familiarity and at the centre of it all was my nerve plug at the base of Quayin's skull.

The device worked as a direct conduit into her mind.

"Lucy! Stop him!" Darius shouted as he sensed what I was planning.

I transformed my mechanical arm on impulse and clamped it around the nerve plug. Quayin screamed in frustration and before she could become invisible, I ripped the nerve plug from her flesh.

I readied to fire the nerve plug at Darius's head. I could use the nerve plug to stop him. I could try and stun or hack into his sick brain.

Darius heard my thoughts and turned his focus to his daughter. Quayin's eyes grew pitch black, as Darius helped her regain control of her mechanical body. As I fired the nerve plug, she swiped wildly at my body. Quayin's fingers raked against my chest and tore through my skin and steel. The nerve plug rattled uselessly to the floor.

"Amicable effort," Darius shouted through Quayin's mouth over the incoming noise of the plummeting plane. "We almost didn't see that coming! Redirect the plane or I'll tear your head off!"

I struggled against the wild, flickering woman. I knew that the moment she regained control of her gift, I would have no chance of survival.

"Favouritism is appalling," Vincent cried across the rattling room. Cain punched the floor and teleported across the room. He reappeared next to the nerve plug and roared with pain as blood streamed out of his nose. Vincent grabbed the nerve plug with his fumbling blood covered hands.

His eyes met mine. He had chosen to let me live, so that I could help him. I could fix his broken mind.

I made my choice and fully gave Vincent Cain his gift back.

The nerve plug burst into life under my instruction. The synaptic signal burst up his arm, rattled through his bones and launched into his cranium. The bridge in his mind illuminated and decimated the dark shroud of corrupted synapses.

He wretched momentarily as Darius attempted to dig back into his brain. Vincent grinned fiercely as his gun metal eyes drilled into his father. He teleported several times on the spot until the world shook around his recurring form. He kept teleporting, so that the Mind Walker lost all sense of where his son's mind was in relative space.

"You should never have taken your attention off my mind," Vincent said coldly. "Never underestimate me."

Vincent Cain teleported next to his father and slammed the nerve plug into his forehead. Darius gasped in surprise and madly tried to grab the device with his frail hands.

Quayin staggered roughly, her eyes spinning as she attempted to keep control. She raised her fist and prepared to bury it into my face.

Vincent appeared again and rammed into his sister. They disappeared and reappeared as Vincent threw her into the nearby wall.

Darius's rage finally broke through my altered mind and I felt his cruel presence fully return. In retaliation, I sent my gift shooting into the nerve plug and hacked into the telepath's mind. I was met with immediate resistance as the old man with years of experience protected himself. The device dug into his skin and set a series of sharp shocks into his cerebral cortex to paralyse him. He retorted with several savage strokes of mental trauma. Flashes of my parent's death, the fire of Old Street and horrific imaginations of torture burnt in my mind. I grabbed control of Prima's information network and forced the data into his brain. Darius shuddered as billions of terabytes of electronic signals were channelled directly into his mind.

Darius relinquished under my power and I grabbed control of the medical machinery nearby. Sedatives ploughed back into his skin, restraints tightened around his frail limbs and his circulatory, digestive, respiratory and nervous systems became under the control of my machines.

Quayin scream was primal as ran straight for me, eyes opaque as the infinite night sky. Vincent returned, teleported, and smashed her into the broken window.

The glass shuddered under her weight, but still held together. Behind her, the roar of the incoming aircraft screamed against my ears. I grabbed the plane and seized the controls. I demanded that it pulled up. I returned control to the pilots and I felt them doing everything in their power to make sure the jet didn't crash. Everyone in the room shielded their ears under the cacophony of the aircraft. The engines burned furiously, the wings adjusted, the shell of the aircraft screamed. The building shuddered, as I sent the plane skimming over the rooftop by mere metres.

"Change is inevitable," Quayin and Darius screamed together. My head burned in pain as Darius burrowed fully into my head. "You cannot stop the new world. It needs renewal. It needs equality. It will have liberation. You cannot stop the truth, William!"

Darkness swamped my mind and black tears dribbled down my face. I felt him take control of my body and mind. My gift obeyed his every command and he began to dismantle the medical machinery.

Through my darkness that consumed of the Mind Walker's attention, I saw Adele take control of herself again.

"You cannot stop this, William!" Father and daughter hissed.

"Try and stop this, bitch," Adele snapped and suddenly screamed at the top of her lungs. The noise burst from her body, ripped the floor into pieces and slammed into Quayin. The window shattered into an explosion of glass and Lucy Quayin was thrown out into the wild night. She was sent plummeting into the earth with a sickening, steaming crunch.

Darius roared in anguish within my mind. His voice filled my thoughts and tore directly into my brain. I screamed out roughly as a ripping migraine attacked my senses. It felt like my brain was being cut by a serrated knife. My head burnt with vicious pain as Darius tried to physically tear my mind in half.

I lashed out at the monster of a man and made the nerve plug overload. Electricity burned through his brain, cooking it like a raw steak, and silenced the Mind-Walker permanently.

Epilogue – A Change of Heart

Darius was gone and the roar of the plummeting aircraft was a distant memory. A shard of pain shuddered through my chest where I had been stabbed. My brain began to ache heavily and grew into a fierce migraine.

"Will… it's over," Adele said as she gently touched my cheek. I stared at her vacantly and felt myself smile wearily. The migraine faded slightly, as her eyes passed over the wounds that covered my body. The fresh cuts on my chest, the metal amendments and my mechanical arm. She moved to touch the limb and I flinched against her touch.

"We're together now," she assured me. "We made it."

"I'm… so sorry," I said realizing how close I had just come to killing us all for the preservation of humanity.

"There is nothing to apologise for," Adele said and gently kissed my heavy forehead with her lips. "You did what you had to do."

"I've done horrible things…" I told my wife.

I felt a little hand tugging at my leg and my face fell into a small smile.

"Can we go home now, Dad?" Theo asked nervously. "I feel tired."

"Not just yet, buddy," I said. "I have to sort out a few things first."

"I was hoping you weren't going to say that," Theo mumbled. "Staying here won't turn things back to normal."

"Daddy is going to fix everything," I said to him slowly.

"No," Theo said and his gaze disappeared into the distance again. "You will try, but the truth will come out…"

"But we stopped that from happening. See? It's okay. The future isn't fixed, Theo."

"Yes, exactly! We can still go home!"

"Theodore. Please," I silenced my son. "We will talk all about these new things you are seeing later, okay? But first we need to get you all…"

"Dad?" Izzy said, a quiet terror building in her body. Realization sent shivers crawling along the back of my skull.

"My hands…" she cried. "They're so cold. What's going on? What's happening to me?"

I rushed forward to hold my daughter. I hugged her tightly and resisted the icy freeze that was searing through her clothes.

"I can't stop it," Izzy cried into my chest. "Why is everything so cold?"

I held her head with my bare hand. The drops of perspiration on my knuckles turned into droplets of ice.

This was impossible. I had stopped Darius from activating her gift.

"She saw you," Vincent Cain explained coldly. He wiped his filthy blonde hair back and swept his tired stoic eyes over my family. "She saw what you did to my father. She saw what your wife did to Lucy. This is how it works. We see a gift and we receive a gift. I'm sorry, but that's the way of our world. But we can help them, there's still time."

My mind stung violently at Vincent's words. I studied him furiously. I knew what I had to do next and the uncertainty of my decision made me feel immensely hollow.

"Isabella. Listen to me very carefully," I said. "You're going to have to control this for now, but soon we'll figure out how to fix this. We will get you back to normal. I will make us all normal again. I will fix everything back to the way it was. I promise."

"Okay," she murmured and breathed out a stream of icy air from her shuddering mouth. "Yeah, I think I can do it. It's going to be okay."

"I will be with you every step of the way," I told her.

"We both will," Vincent confirmed to my family. "We are going to make sure that nobody gets hurt from these powers ever again."

I looked at my former employer and I swallowed roughly before extending my hand out. Vincent looked at the open hand anxiously. Last time he'd shook my hand I'd punched him in the face.

"I made the right choice keeping you alive," Vincent said and grasped my hand firmly. "Thank you for putting my father down. With him gone, his darkness can never come back. I am at my full capabilities again."

Vincent flickered for a moment and teleported outside the broken window. He reappeared and crunch into the far wall, the twisting gravity plunging back into his initial position. He smiled sickly and his eyes flickered numbly, as his mind began to calculate the possibilities that his gift provided him. There was something strange about the way he looked.

His greedy eyes and that vicious smile were a mirror image of his father.

"We will remove all of their gifts," Cain said excitedly. "With our combined power and Xander's ability to manipulate..."

"We do this my way," I told Cain, stopping his train of thought. "Your methods are too extreme. We follow my methods, otherwise I'm collapsing Cain Corporation tonight."

"You can't be serious!" Cain snapped before composing himself. "Desperate times require desperate measures. Of all people, you must surely understand this?"

"You know what I am capable of," I said and indicated his father's body. "And you shot my wife. Don't think I've forgotten that, Vincent. So I will be taking control now. I will decide the appropriate measures. Do not test me, otherwise it will be the last thing you do."

The clinic door suddenly exploded in a burst of fire and shattered metal. Shrapnel sliced into the clinical furniture and a thick cloud of black smoke billowed into the room. The smoke was sucked out the broken window, as Raven rushed into the clinic. Her palms trickled with fire as she scanned the space with her sharp eyes. She breathed heavily, drunk on adrenaline, as she carefully realised that the immediate threat had been taken care of.

The fire in her hands died down a little as she saw the Mind Walker's dead body. She locked eyes with Vincent and kept embers of fire at hand.

"I'm guessing that I'm a little late for the party?" Raven

smirked grimly.

"A little," I laughed quietly, eyeing her writhing flames carefully.

"It's over," Xander said sharply. I made contact with his green eyes. He looked traumatised, like a weight had been lifted from his mind since the Mind Walker's death.

"Where is he?" Vincent Cain said firmly. "Where is Foshe?"

"Seriously?" Raven retorted. "You want to know where that lunatic is?"

Raven's flaming hands curled with twisting fire, her anger on show for everyone to see. I remembered my best friend downstairs. The truth of his death hit me heavily.

Mark was dead. Her fire had killed him.

"He asked you a question," I said coldly. "What have you done with Pierre Foshe?"

Raven relaxed her hands, the fire flickering back into embers. "Foshe is dealt with," Raven confirmed. "He was going to kill us all. He'd completely lost control."

"You killed him as well?" I asked in disbelief.

"As well?" Raven replied shakily. "What happened to your friend wasn't my fault, Hart."

"Desperate times, William," Vincent hummed in my ear.

"Be quiet," I demanded. Vincent gritted his teeth as I pulled his hypothetical leash. He grunted and stepped away to check his father's body.

"What happens next, Doctor Hart? What will your family do?" Xander asked cautiously.

"We start again. My family are leaving Prima, I told him, then looked firmly at Raven. "And… you can come with us."

"You can't leave!" Vincent asked incredulously. "You said we would work together."

"I changed my mind," I said. "I have earned that choice after the last three years under your forced employment."

"We can't just leave. Where would we go?" Raven asked.

"Wherever we want," I said. "Pick a great city and we will go to it. Any of them would take us. We could find somewhere quieter. Build an independent society. You need to let go of this paranoia, Raven. Let me help you."

I extended my arms and stepped carefully towards her.

"Come on, Jessica. Let's leave Prima. If we work together, then nothing can stop us. We can do whatever we want."

Her fire dissipated entirely and she stepped forward hesitantly.

"It's okay, Jessica. It's all over," I lied.

I carefully hugged the girl like she was my own daughter. I placed my metal hand at the back of her head.

"Will?" Adele asked. "Are we seriously going to leave Prima? Surely it's impossible to start again?"

"We will start again," I told them all before gripping the arrogant girl's head and looking her directly in the eye. "But *you* are never leaving Prima."

I found Foshe's stun baton inside my arm and fired the device into Raven's head. The electricity leapt into her central nervous system and knocked her unconscious. Raven screamed out her briefly, her eyes widening in shock, before collapsing in my arms.

"What are you doing?" Adele shouted. "Why did you do that?"

"She's dangerous," I told her. "She is partially responsible for the Old Street incident and brings destruction wherever she goes. She needs to be dealt with properly and efficiently."

"Is that what you really want?" Izzy asked, confused. "What has she done that's so bad?"

"This is the logical course of action," I reasoned firmly. "It may seem cruel, but I am doing this to protect us."

"Prima will never be the same again," Theo mumbled quietly. "The world is changing. It's begun... the cycle of time will spin soon..."

"What shall we do with her, Doctor Hart?" Vincent asked decisively.

"We take her to Mimic's cell. There's room for another occupant," I ordered. "Pass me that syringe."

Cain ordered the remaining staff to prepare the cell for inmate delivery and passed the sedative.

"You've become like him," Raven murmured as she began to wake up. She pointed weakly at Vincent Cain and pointed back at me. I grabbed hold of her tightly and plunged the needle into her neck. "You aren't any different. You're the same."

"You're under my observation now. Vincent will not be assisting in your future treatment."

Her fire simmered along her face. I grasped her tightly to protect my family from her wrath. I let the flames singe my skin and I winced against the sting of her hot touch. She struggled against my grip and the drugs flowing through her veins.

"I will break out. Ask him," she said pointing at Xander. "You can never hold me. I will run."

"There is nowhere you can go. I am now the most powerful person on this planet. I can see everything. I can hear everything. I am connected to everyone. There is nowhere you can go where I will not find you. Escape is impossible. Stop running. Listen to my voice, Jessica. Let go."

Raven struggled to speak as the sedative took control. I looked away from the volatile, vulnerable girl. I ignored her final moments of consciousness to push aside my guilt. She collapsed wearily and her burning fires finally fluttered out of existence.

"What are you going to do with her, Will?" Adele asked quietly.

"He is going to do what was shown to him," Theo whispered and grabbed Xander's hand. "You have to take her. Go on. You are meant to take her to the cell now."

Xander glanced at the small boy.

"It's your job. It's what Darius showed me you would do," I told him.

Xander gaze was unreadable as always. His bloodied fist tightened. He looked at the smashed window and stared into the distance. A shimmering light was currently making its way across the night sky. It grew closer to the horizon until it disappeared entirely.

"Would you have done it?" Xander asked and pointed at the empty sky. "The plane?"

"I could have redirected the plane at any moment. In fact, I knew the exact second that it would impact the building."

"I don't doubt that, Doctor Hart," Xander said and turned to face me, his eyes burying into my soul. "I asked you a simple question, which you avoided just like when we spoke in your lab downstairs. Please give me an answer. Would you have sacrificed all those people? Would you have killed us all to achieve your victory?"

"We made it," I announced to the man who had haunted my dreams for so long. "We're alive."

"Nothing changes does it, Doctor Hart?" Xander asked me rhetorically. His eyes tinged with disappointment as I avoided his difficult question. "Darius was a telepath. You didn't win because he called your bluff. You didn't win because you had a more powerful gift. No. You won because he could see you completely. You defeated him because you were willing to die for your cause. You were willing to destroy all of us so his world couldn't grow into existence."

I felt my family look at me in horror. Vincent nodded firmly, agreeing with my drastic actions.

"I can't do this anymore," Xander said simply. "I've done everything I can to protect our kind. I have done so much more than any of you will ever know to ensure the survival of the gifted. But this is too far. I'm done."

"You are not going anywhere," Vincent said abruptly. "We had a deal. After Old Street, you vowed to assist in the capture of gifted individuals."

"I vowed to never step over the line of reason. Whilst we secured wild individuals, I have never once used my own power. I have never stepped out of line to achieve my objectives."

"This is no different!" Vincent laughed incredulously. "William did what was required to stop Darius. His methods were more effective than yours, don't you see? With him at our side, we will crush anyone in our path."

"You seem to forget that Doctor Hart lost control only a few days ago. His methods were acts of desperation, not conceived plans of action."

"Stop being so contrived, Xander!" Vincent said angrily. His body flickered, as he teleported rapidly on the spot, making his body vibrate ferociously. "Don't you dare walk away, not after everything I have done for you."

"I'm finished, Vincent," he snapped and his anger erupted across the clinic. The floor shook unnaturally, the beds shuddered and the foundations of the building groaned under the strain of his power. Xander breathed out heavily and the building returned to normal. "Don't come looking for me."

Xander moved to pick up his filthy coat that lay crumpled on the corner, before heading towards the door.

"You heard what I told her," I called as he left through the broken door. "Your time will come. I will find you. You can't escape me."

"And I'll be waiting for you, Doctor," Alexander Habil replied simply before disappearing from sight.

"That's weird," Theo murmured. "He's not meant to leave…"

"It's fine," I told my son. "I'll do it myself."

I lifted Raven's limp body in my arms. I staggered under her weight as my aching wounded body struggled to keep moving.

"I'm heading down to Mimic's cell," I told Vincent. "I trust that you will look after my family?"

"I will have quarters prepared for you all," Vincent confirmed. "It's good to have you on board, Doctor. I will have your laboratory equipment brought upstairs."

"I will manage my own machinery. I am more than capable."

"As you wish…" Vincent murmured envious and held out his hand to my wife. "Come with me, Mrs Hart. I assure you that our facilities are quite accommodating."

"Don't you dare touch me, Cain," she snapped and smacked his hand aside. Adele glared at him and the air vibrated sharply as she spoke. "You shot me. You erased my husband's mind and tried to kill him. You dragged my children through hell. You don't ever speak to me again. Understand? I'll judge the damn quarters myself."

Adele turned away from Vincent, and limped towards her children. She grabbed their hands tightly. "Come on, kids. Follow me…"

"Wait," I said and caught my wife's hurt expression. I looked down to my daughter's wavering gaze and calculated her value to my operation. "Come with me, Isabella. I'll need your assistance."

"If I'm honest… " Izzy murmured. "I'd rather go with Mum."

"I wasn't asking," I told her. "Come with me."

I heaved Raven out of the clinic, leaving Adele to care for Theo. As my footsteps echoed down the staircase, I heard Izzy reluctantly following. They were starkly different to the piercing sound of Quayin's heels earlier.

The warzone in the foyer was more horrific than I had expected. However it didn't bother me as much as I expected. Somehow I had become accustomed to all the chaos.

Something had changed within me. Being haunted for years by Darius, dying at the construction site, discovering the truth within Old Street, doing everything in my power to save what I love, having my body and mind ripped apart and, finally, understanding that these gifts could not be left unchecked.

The foyer was validated that opinion. Several unconscious bodies lay on the floor. Soldiers, prisoners and others I didn't recognise. I spotted the wide-eyed body of Pierre Foshe collapsed against the far wall. The floor and walls had decayed and rust in response to his gift. His silver hair was splayed over his face. His eyes were a pair of black burnt out holes. Finally, we walked past Mark Bolton's body. His flesh could be seen between the earth and blood. His burnt remains filled my journey to Mimic's cell with purpose.

I heard my daughter gasp in horror. I increased our pace through the devastation to drag her through quicker.

Several soldiers entered the room and raised their guns. I grunted with annoyance and disintegrated their guns with an annoyed glare.

"Put those toys away," I said sharply. "I work with Vincent. Your orders are to put these subjects into cells as quickly as possible. Get them contained immediately and don't let a single individual leave this building. Take a team outside and secure Lucy Quayin's remains before setting up a perimeter. Is that understood? Get to work."

They stood dumbfounded before hesitantly stepping past us and grabbing the nearest bodies they could find.

"This isn't right," Izzy said as we kept walking. "Are you sure that we're doing the correct thing? What did all these people do? Why are you locking them up? And why are you the person doing it?"

We walked past Anton Stranz's cell and I smiled proudly as I saw him restrained and comatose.

"Did you hear me?" Izzy asked again. "I'm not sure I want to do this."

"This isn't about right or wrong," I told my daughter as we approached Mimic's cell. "There are only people who believe that their path is the correct one. These powers may seem amazing, but they always end the same way. Misery and death. I'm fixing that by doing what is necessary. You must begin to understand what we must do. Life is dangerous. No. We are dangerous. And what do we do with dangerous people?"

I opened the door to Mimic's cell with a wave of my head. Mimic smiled knowingly as I entered the room. He grinned horribly at the girl in my arms. His eyes at my scared daughter outside the room.

"Your father asked you a question," Mimic said numbly. "It would be rude not to answer him. What do we with the dangerous people?"

"We lock them up?" Izzy asked nervously.

"We make sure they can't hurt anyone," I told her. "And we do everything we can to help them."

I dragged Raven to some chains that were waiting for her. It seemed somewhat barbaric, but I knew that this was the only place that could truly hold her.

"So, is this 'bring your daughter to work' day?" Mimic chuckled darkly as Izzy hesitantly entered the cell.

I ignored him. I didn't want to give this monster any attention. I made sure Izzy focused on what I was doing. Mimic smiled at us cruelly. His mad eyes watching as I fastened the Raven to the wall.

"This pain you're feeling is good," he whispered. "Breathe in. Enjoy it."

"I don't want to talk to you…" I said firmly.

"You came to visit me. I deserve consultation from the new Doctor in the house."

"You deserve nothing."

"That is where you are wrong. You have provided what was promised to me. We are here. The cycle has been set in motion. We are finally together again. Exactly as I remember it."

I moved to exit the cell and pulled my daughter away from the sick, monster.

"Hart…" Raven suddenly said quietly. "Are you there?"

"I have to go now," I said. "I will be back soon to check up on you."

"Don't leave me here. Please. Not with him."

"You've left me no choice, Jessica. I'm sorry. What else were you expecting? Redemption? That might come in time, but we have to work towards that. For now… this is the only solution."

"You're wrong. We can fix this together."

"Don't worry, Jessica," I said numbly. "I'll see you soon."

"Jessica…" Mimic murmured and closed his eyes in anticipation. "What a lovely name…"

I turned sway from on my patients and closed the door with a blink of my eyelids. I exhaled heavily, before looking at my daughter."

"I want you to freeze them," I requested.

"What?" she asked, shock shivering over her face.

"It is the only way to restrain them. He is too psychotic for logical treatment. Whilst she will burn through any sedative we give her. So, I need you to lower the temperature in that cell below freezing. They will easily survive it. They can both control fire and will keep themselves warm, but it will weaken them sufficiently. Only then we can begin effective physical and psychological treatment."

"I don't know if I can do that. I don't know how."

"Do it, Isabella," I ordered. "It's not for our family. We're doing this to protect everyone. I'm not asking you to do this as your father. I'm asking you as someone who is petrified that they will break out and hurt people again. I am afraid of the possibility that these people will continue to destroy everything we love. Do

401

you want to see people get hurt?"

"But… I don't want to hurt them."

"Sometimes we have do what is necessary in order to survive," I said firmly and grabbed her hands tightly. "Do it."

Isabella cautiously opened her shaking palm and placed it against the metal. My daughter sobbed lightly as she altered the temperature of the world. Ice crawled out of her flesh and seeped through the iron door. I gazed through the thick glass at the criminals silently struggling against the rising cold.

The frost crawled up Raven's skin, which steamed violently in retaliation. Her mouth screamed out noiselessly and her eyes pleaded for me to stop. Spurts of fire lashed from her limbs as she struggled against her chains. Mimic breathed in slowly and accepted his imprisoned fate. A solitary tear dribbled from Raven's eye and froze instantly. The solid droplet smashed into the cold floor. The ice took hold of Raven. Her fire faded as the ice restrained the tormented girl.

I turned my back on them and held my daughter's freezing hands with my metal prosthetic.

"I don't understand," Izzy shuddered in horror. "Why did you make me do that?"

"The world is changing and we need to stop it. This change is happening right now underneath your skin. It's flowing beyond Prima and throughout the entire world. We are living under a web of lies that's been around us for decades. These lies seep into our society to keep us safe. It is a very simple lie to keep everyone safe."

"What is that lie?" Izzy asked quietly.

"That everything we know is false. These gifts exist. They are deadly and highly infectious. This is the truth. We have to work to make sure the truth never gets out. If people found out about these gifts, then everything would fall into chaos. Do you understand now? Do you understand what I am doing for you all? Do you see what I am sacrificing to make sure you are all safe?"

Izzy glanced at the cell that had completely frozen over. She breathed out sharply and ice crawled back inside her body, as placed her hand on my shoulder.

"Not yet," she admitted. "But I believe in you, Dad. If you think this is right, then I'll do everything I can to understand."

I smiled, relieved at my daughter's words and walked solemnly away from my prisoners. We stepped back into the destroyed foyer. The staircase ascended straight ahead and the great city of Prima glimmered below us through the expansive windows.

The horror of the fight had been dragged away by my enforcers, but I could still see the bullet holes, scorch marks and bloodstains that marked the white floor. Our future seemed clean, but it was marred with the scars of the past.

My eyes caught sight of the empty hole at the centre of Prima. The memory of Old Street ignited in my synapses. It was a devastating crater of pain that has never left Prima.

The back of my head itched. The irritation accelerated into a searing stab of agony. I scratched at the long scar in my skull that etched into my brain. My mind burnt as my migraine brutally returned.

I collapsed against the window. My eyes flicked up and I stared firmly at the vast metropolis. The lights glistened as my eyes scanned over each individual light, my evolving senses absorbing the traces of complicated information behind each dot of life.

My vision focused on my reflection in the glass. I saw an unrecognisable, weary man looking back. His eyes were a shifting shade of brown and ultraviolet.

William Hart's eyes bored into mine.

His heavy eyebrows furrowed and creased in deep troubled confusion. He blinked and neon lights across Prima flickered erratically. The faded figure glared into my soul and hesitantly enquired after my corrupted morality. He was questioning my actions.

I tore my gaze away from the remains of the man I had once been and accepted the future creation of myself.

My daughter held my metal arm tightly, pulling me away from the forgotten man at the window, and we ascended into the heights of existence to bring order to those naive souls beneath us.

"Do you see what I am sacrificing to make sure you are all safe?"

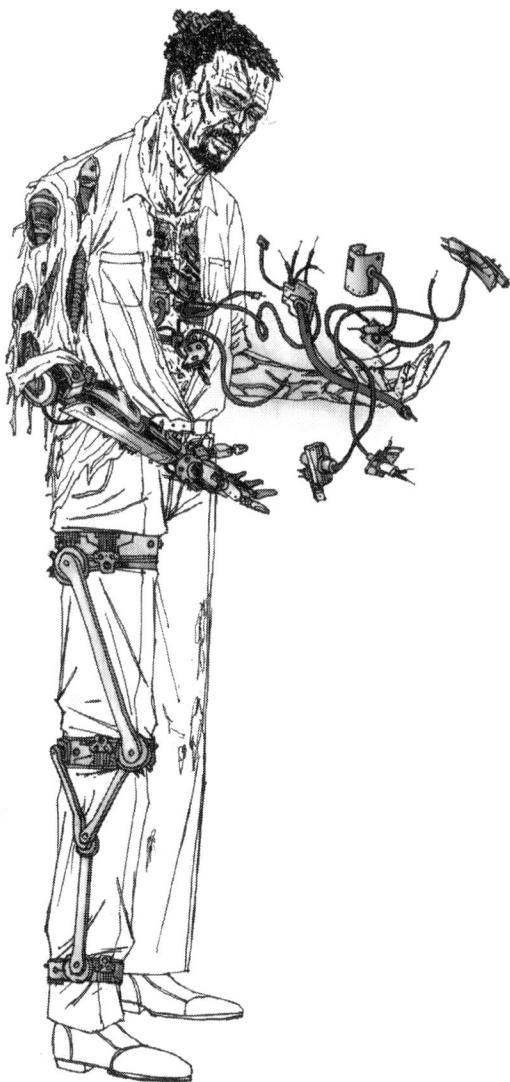

Acknowledgments

It took 8 years to create Gifted. In that time I've graduated, toured, somewhat matured, not had enough haircuts, and slowly written a story that I'm proud to share with the world.

Gifted started as a hobby that I'd write between acting jobs. My passion for science fiction and fantasy through films, games and comic books became focused on William Hart.

A father who simply wants to protect his family.

I consider myself extremely lucky to have such a supportive family. My mother who is always eager to read my work. My brother, Nathan, who has designed all the cover art for the Perspective Trilogy. And, of course, this book is dedicated to my father who has always put his family first. This book is also for my family in London, Scotland and beyond the UK who have shown me more kindness than I can ever give back. Without all of you, this book would be a fantasy. At the heart of Gifted is family and thank you for being mine.

The courage to develop Gifted has grown from my friendships. To all the many people I've worked with at East 15 Acting School, UK, Italy, Malaysia and China… thank you all!

Merci, Grazie, Danke, Terima Kasih, Xièxiè !

We have to fail in order to succeed. I've seen my friends rise and fall with their careers and relationships. I want to thank you all for taking those incredible risks and inspiring me to find the same courage within myself.

Special thanks must go to Mike, Sam and Louisa. Your passion for this story, plus your hundreds of notes, really fleshed out this world and brought it all to life.

Last of all – thank you for reading my perspective on a world where everyone has a hidden power. You've brought my dreams of Prima into reality.

Credits

Author – Matt Salmon - www.matt-salmon.com

Matt Salmon graduated from East 15 Acting School with degrees in BA (Hons) World Performance and a Certificate of Higher Education in Theatre Arts. As an actor, he has toured internationally, specialising in interactive storytelling. His writing focuses on creating dramatic stories that have a fantasy or science-fiction context. Matt is continuing *The Perspective Trilogy,* with the sequels *Outcast* and *Paradox* coming soon. Matt has written several plays including: *Wingless, Acquaintances, Opaque* and *Get the Hell out of my House!* (East 15 Acting School, 2015) He also collaboratively devised *Worst Case Scenario* with Concoction Theatre Company. (Camden Fringe, August 2016)

Illustration – Chris Halls - www.crfhalls.com

Chris Halls is a qualified teacher of Art, Design and Photography living in Bristol, UK. He studied Traditional Animation at Arts University Bournemouth and worked on Oscar-nominated feature *'The Illusionist', 'Drawing Inspiration'* with THE LINE, *'U2 Music Video'* with Treatment Studio and an animated production with Paper Trail Productions.

Cover Art – Nathan Salmon - www.ns-vacc.co.uk

Nathan Salmon is a graphic and visual communications designer. After graduating from Cardiff Metropolitan University in 2013 with a degree in BA (Hons) Graphic Communication, he has since continued to expand his knowledge and experience at an industry-level in professional design.

Printed in Great Britain
by Amazon